BLOOD AT SUNDOWN

BLOOD AT SUNDOWN

THE VIOLENT DAYS OF
LOU PROPHET, BOUNTY HUNTER

PETER BRANDVOLD

PINNACLE BOOKS
Kensington Publishing Corp.
www.kensingtonbooks.com

PINNACLE BOOKS are published by

Kensington Publishing Corp.
119 West 40th Street
New York, NY 10018

All Kensington titles, imprints, and distributed lines are available at special quantity discounts for bulk purchases for sales promotions, premiums, fund-raising, educational, or institutional use. Special book excerpts or customized printings can also be created to fit specific needs. For details, write or phone the office of the Kensington sales manager: Kensington Publishing Corp., 119 West 40th Street, New York, NY 10018, attn: Sales Department; phone 1-800-221-2647.

PINNACLE BOOKS and the Pinnacle logo are Reg. U.S. Pat. & TM Off.

ISBN-13: 978-0-7860-4348-4
ISBN-10: 0-7860-4348-2

First printing: January 2019

10 9 8 7 6 5 4 3 2 1

Printed in the United States of America

Electronic edition: January 2019

ISBN-13: 978-0-7860-4349-1
ISBN-10: 0-7860-4349-0

For the Badass Bowman Boys

Ray & Steve

from the Hills of West Virginny!

Chapter 1

Lou Prophet quietly pumped a fresh cartridge into the action of his Winchester '73, off-cocked the hammer, and turned to his partner. "How you wanna play this one?"

Louisa Bonaventure lay belly down on the face of the bluff beside him. She turned to him, one pretty hazel eye arched. "Are you all right, Lou?"

"No, I ain't all right. I'm in Dakota Territory. It's winter. It's colder'n a gravedigger's behind. There are sundry parts of myself I haven't felt since we left Deadwood early last week. In fact, I'm not sure everything's still where it's supposed to be and hasn't frozen off. I fear when I finally pull off my moccasins, my toes are going to come rollin' out of my socks like dice off a craps table. I need a hot toddy worse than I ever needed one before, worse than I ever hope to again. That said, why do you ask?"

"You asked me how I wanted to play this one. You usually like to call it yourself since no one—especially a woman—is as smart as you are."

"Oh, that. Well . . ." Prophet shrugged then, chuckling, turned his attention to the rambling, wood-frame roadhouse nestled in the snowy hollow down the bluff's far side. A skein of gray smoke curled from the building's large, stone chimney poking up from the pitched roof, behind the broad front veranda. "You called it right the last coupla times. You seem to have an eye for strategy . . . when your neck ain't in such a hump you can't see straight."

Prophet scowled over at her. "You don't got your neck in too big a hump to see straight, do you? I can usually tell—not by an actual hump but usually by how quiet you've been on the trail. Like a whiskey still about to blow from an overheated firebox. You can't hear nothin' until all of a sudden all hell breaks loose and your britches have caught fire an' your ears are ringin' to whistle 'Dixie'! I can also tell by the color in your cheeks. Usually, when your blood's in a boil and you're primed to go off half-cocked, to start shootin' at folks left an' right with those pretty Colts of yours, your cheeks are as red as the yams ole Ma Prophet used to grow in her garden patch."

Louisa gazed stone-faced down over the barrel of her Winchester carbine at the roadhouse below.

The trail of the thieving killers had led her and Prophet here, several days north of Bismarck. Judging by the tracks they'd been following along the old stage and army road north of Devil's Lake, all six killers were likely warming themselves with whiskey, women, and the fire popping in the stone hearth down yonder, while Prophet and his comely blond partner, Louisa Bonaventure—the infamous, notorious Vengeance Queen herself—lay belly flat against the frozen slab of this haystack butte lightly dusted with a recent Dakota snow.

The bones of Lou Prophet, born and bred in the warm and humid climes of north Georgia, were rattling from the cold. He couldn't feel his toes inside his high-topped, fur-lined moccasins. True, the Georgia mountain winters could be cold, but not like this. He thought he could feel the temperature plummeting like a bucket down an empty well. His breath frosted in the air before his face, freezing in the bristles of his nearly two weeks' worth of sandy beard.

Louisa turned to him slowly. Slowly, she blinked her long, catlike hazel eyes. "Two things we know for sure haven't frozen off of you, Lou."

"Oh? What two things are that, pray tell?" Prophet gave her a lusty smile. "Keep it clean, Miss Bonnyventure. This ain't the time nor the place for your farm talk."

"Your vocal cords."

Prophet shrugged with chagrin. "Well, shit, you know . . . I just know how you get when the devils we find ourselves on the trails of have killed women or children. And, you know, when these devils robbed that bank over Wyoming way, they . . . they . . . well, let's just not talk about it. I'm sorry I even brought it up, consarn my big mouth, anyway!"

"They kidnapped two young female tellers and held on to them, using them for their pleasure until they tired of them and tossed them away along the trail like used-up airtight tins but not without cutting their throats first."

Prophet ground his molars. "Damn my big mouth, anyway!"

"You go around back," Louisa said. "There must be a back door since there's a privy back there. I'll wait here until I see you're in position. Then I'll head on down the butte and go in the front."

"Like a proper lady."

Louisa sighed tolerantly as she continued staring down her carbine's barrel.

"That sounds all right to me, but don't you start thinkin' I'm a back-door sort of fella." Prophet grinned at her.

Louisa cast him a dull stare. He used to get that look from the schoolmarm back home, on the rare occasion he'd attended classes, that was. He was usually admonished with such a look after he'd slipped a snake into the girls' privy or had brought an old, dangerous blunderbuss to school to shoot squirrels during recess, or sundry other misdeeds his pa would later haul him out to the woodshed for.

Only, the schoolmarm hadn't been half or even a quarter as easy on the eyes as Louisa was, and she hadn't cut as fine a figure as Louisa did, either—though Prophet had to admit he'd never seen Mrs. Darryhemple in a snug pair of Levi's or a skintight pair of boy's-sized longhandles like the ones Louisa tended to wear in cooler climes, under her Levi's and tight wool shirts. Not that he would have wanted to see Mrs. Darryhemple in those clothes. Louisa, on the other hand, he could stare at all day . . . and all night . . . especially when she wasn't wearing anything at all.

Now he returned her flat, incriminating stare, trying not to imagine how she might look later standing before that popping hearth down there, the fire silhouetting her willowy, high-busted, round-hipped body, and shrugged.

"All right, I can see you're losing patience with this

old rebel, Miss Starchy Bloomers," Prophet said, "so I won't tarry any longer."

"Good."

Prophet leaned forward and planted a kiss on her peach-colored right cheek, enjoying the warmth, the smoothness, and the softness of her skin. "You just be careful, understand, Miss Starchy Bloomers? Without you, this old Confederate would be a drunkard and a fool, totally unmoored."

"We wouldn't want that to happen," Louisa said, rolling her eyes.

Prophet crabbed backward down the hill. When he was nearly to where Louisa's pinto and his own horse, the appropriately named Mean and Ugly, stood tied inside a fringe of bur oaks and cedars at the base of the butte, Louisa said just loudly enough for Prophet to hear:

"Lou?"

Prophet stopped crawling and looked up at her, brows raised.

Looking back at him over her left shoulder, Louisa held his gaze with a stern one of her own. "You be careful, too."

He gave her a wink then turned toward Mean and Ugly. He plucked his sawed-off, double-barreled, twelve-gauge Richards coach gun from his saddle, broke open the nasty-looking gut-shredder to make sure both tubes were wadded, then snapped it closed and slung its leather lanyard over his head and right shoulder, letting the shotgun hang down his back.

The gut-shredder cleaned up well at close range in tight quarters. He'd save it for inside the roadhouse, if he needed it.

He picked up his Winchester and felt hot breath on

his neck. He jerked his head away from his horse just in time to avoid a nasty nip to his earlobe, which protruded slightly from the muffler securing his hat to his head.

"Doggone it, Mean—you cussed cayuse!" Prophet wheezed, slamming his left, mittened fist against the horse's stout jaw. "You're plumb evil, you know that!"

The horse turned its head away, laying its ears back against its head, grinning and whickering softly in satisfaction with itself.

"Wicked hayburner," Prophet muttered, adjusting the muffler so that it covered his ear, then moved into the trees beyond both mounts. "The glue factory is too good for you. Oughta just put a bullet through your plug-ugly head!"

But then, he'd been saying that for years . . .

He jogged through the woods that encircled the hollow, keeping an eye on the rambling roadhouse through the tangled branches.

The building was flanked by a barn with a hole in its roof, a corral, a privy, a springhouse, and an old Halladay Standard windmill that sat askew on one broken leg. The roadhouse had fallen on hard times since a spur railroad line, completed only last year, now spoked north out of Bismarck for a hundred miles just east of here, rendering obsolete the mule and ox teams that had once pulled big Murphy freight wagons along the old stage and army road on which the roadhouse sat. Those teamsters had once stopped here overnight to indulge themselves in a hot meal, a glass or two of stiff busthead, and a warm bed.

Now, of course, the iron horse hauled the freight the stout-wheeled, high-sided Murphys had once carried, leaving the roadhouse sitting high and dry, so to speak, likely patronized by only the occasional cowpuncher off area ranches, woodcutters, and market hunters, maybe the rare cavalry patrol out of Fort Totten near Devil's Lake. Now and then a begging Indian—a Sisseton, Wahpeton, or Cut-Head Sioux— too proud or restless to be confined to the agency, probably hoofed it by here on a broom-tailed cayuse with painted rings around its eyes, pausing for a free cup of whiskey and a plate of beans.

Breathing hard from the jog, Prophet pulled up behind a stout oak and turned to the roadhouse. He was parallel now with the western rear corner. He could see a back door from his vantage atop a low rise, roughly sixty yards from the building itself. A half a dozen horses milled in the corral off the slumped log barn, munching hay from a crib, their collective breath rising like fog in the air that was darkening now as the winter sunlight, filtering through high steel-colored clouds, waned.

Prophet dropped to a knee, drawing the raw, cold air into his lungs. Holding his rifle in his right hand, clad in a deerskin mitten over a thin wool glove, he clenched his left hand into a tight fist, trying to work some blood into his numb fingertips, cursing the chill air at these northern prairie climes, berating his bad luck at having been lured this far north this late in the year, on the trail of lucrative bounties carried by a notorious gang of thieves, rapists, and cold-blooded killers, when he should be a good five hundred or so miles south of here, heading even farther south, toward Mexico, where he'd planned to winter along the sandy shores of the Sea of Cortez, sunning himself with a couple of supple señoritas.

He'd just taken his Winchester into his left hand

and was working blood into his right-hand fingers when a woman's shrill scream exploded inside the roadhouse. It was like a coyote's bereaved wail. Fast footsteps sounded on the heels of the cry—feet pounding raw wooden floorboards.

Prophet swung his gaze back toward the roadhouse in time to see the rear door fly open. A woman shot out of the door like a shell from a Napoleon cannon. Clad in a long buffalo robe and moccasins, she leaped off the small rear wooden stoop and into the backyard, running fast, loosing another shrill, horrified cry, and bolted straight back in the direction of the barn.

She was young and slender, with long brown hair, which flew back behind her in the wind as she tripped on something, nearly fell, then, regaining her balance, continued running straight out toward the barn. She looked profoundly delicate and nearly marble-white against the drab winter colors of the barnyard, even inside the bulky robe she wore.

"Oh no, oh no," Prophet said, his heart quickening.

Boots thundered inside the lodge behind the fleeing girl. A man burst out the door and onto the stoop, raising a rifle to his shoulder, bellowing, "Come back here, you little hussy!"

"No!" Prophet heard himself yell as he ran out from behind the tree.

The rifle of the man on the roadhouse stoop cracked twice, smoke and orange flames lapping from the barrel. The girl screamed and continued running toward a front corner of the barn.

The shooter ran off the stoop and into the yard, pumping another round into his rifle's action.

Running down the slope toward the roadhouse, Prophet shouted, "Stop!"

The man fired twice more. The girl jerked with both shots, bending forward as she continued running. Her knees buckled just as she gained the barn's front corner. She hit the ground and rolled wildly.

"Son of a *buck*!" Prophet dropped to a knee.

He thought he was within range now of accurate shooting. He chewed off his right-hand mitten, let it drop to the ground, then pumped a round into the Winchester and raised the rifle to his shoulder. As he did, the shooter swung toward him.

Prophet fired, the Winchester '73 kicking back against his shoulder. He was breathing too hard and his fingers were too cold for accurate shooting. That bullet and the next one he sent hurling toward the girl's shooter plumed snow-dusted dirt in the yard beyond the man.

Prophet quickly stuffed his mitten into his coat pocket, heaved himself to his cold feet, and resumed running down the slope. There was little cover between him and the yard—only a couple of widely scattered, small boulders and brush clumps.

"Hell!" the shooter cried as two more men came running out of the roadhouse to his right. "That's Lou Prophet!" he bellowed. "I knew I seen that ole rebel devil on our back trail! Ringo, saddle our hosses! I'll try to hold him off!"

The third man running out of the roadhouse glanced over his shoulder to yell through the open door, "It's Lou Prophet! Cut an' run, fellas! Cut an' run!"

The first man ran to the edge of the barnyard and dropped to a knee behind a boulder little bigger than a rain barrel. He poked his rifle over the top of the boulder and fired two quick rounds. The first bullet sliced a hot line across the outside of Prophet's right cheek while the second bullet nipped the sole of his left moccasin.

The bounty hunter cursed as he dropped and rolled up against a small, thick clump of shadbush growing up around a rock about the size and shape of a wheat shock.

From inside the roadhouse came the horrified cry of another young woman.

"Damnation!" Prophet spat out through gritted teeth. "They're gonna kill the girls, the blackhearted sons o' witches!"

Rising onto his right knee, he glanced over the shadbush thicket, toward the hill on which he'd left Louisa. His stomach fell.

Louisa was running down the hill toward the roadhouse. She was halfway between where Prophet had left her and the front of the roadhouse, running hard, her hat, secured to her neck by its horsehair thong, flapping behind her on the wind, her honey-blond hair bouncing on her shoulders, clad in a green and brown wool coat that dropped to halfway down her shapely thighs. The cuffs of her Levi's were stuffed down inside her high-topped, rabbit fur boots.

She clutched her Winchester carbine in her black-gloved right hand. She'd stuffed her heavy fur mitten into a pocket of her coat. Even from this distance, Prophet could see the gravely determined expression on her face, the menacing chill in her hazel eyes.

She'd turned her wolf loose, and the devil take the hindmost!

Chapter 2

"Louisa, hold on!" Prophet said. "Now ain't the right time to go in there, damnit!"

He pulled his head down as rifles thundered from straight ahead of him. Bullets plunked into the face of his covering rock.

They snapped branches off the shadbush thicket and threw them up over his head. Two tumbled onto his hat, which he'd tied to his head with his spruce-green muffler, covering his ears so they wouldn't freeze, turn black, and fall off.

Edging a look around the rock, he now saw five men—three in various states of dress. Four were spread out near the first man, triggering their rifles toward Prophet while another man, with long, bushy muttonchop whiskers and wearing a fawn-colored rabbit hat with earflaps, just then threw a saddle, saddlebags, and a rifle over the top corral slat, into the corral, then climbed in after them. His woolly chaps flapped around his legs.

Prophet snaked his rifle over the top of the rock and began returning fire, first planting a bead on the man who'd shot the girl, and squeezing the trigger, feeling a lurch of satisfaction as the girl-killer's right eye was turned to jelly as the .44 slug punched through his head.

Lou drew his head and rifle back down behind the rock as the other three men, on knees and spaced about ten feet apart outside the corral, threw lead at him. As they did, he heard glass breaking and peered around the rock's right side to see two more men busting out two of the roadhouse's side windows and poking their rifles through the sashed frames.

Those rifles, too, began barking, stitching the air around him with screaming lead.

Again, Prophet peered around the right side of his covering rock and the thicket. He briefly glimpsed Louisa running toward the roadhouse. Then she was gone from view. She was mounting the front veranda steps, heading for the front door.

"Damnit, Louisa!" Prophet grated out through gritted teeth as more bullets screamed off his covering rock and flipped broken thicket branches every which way.

He gave another bellowing curse and then heaved himself to his feet, racking another round into his Winchester's breech and slamming the butt against his shoulder. He aimed quickly at the three men firing at him from between the rear of the roadhouse and the corral.

He laid out one with his first shot. As the other one triggered a round toward Prophet, Prophet returned fire, his bullet sailing wide as the man flinched and lost his balance, throwing his left arm onto the ground to balance himself.

Prophet jogged toward him, grinding his teeth at

the lead punching into the ground around him, curling the air around his ears.

"Prophet, what the hell you doin' this far north, you Southern rebel sonofabuck?" shouted the man he was targeting just before the hammer of the man's rifle pinged benignly onto its firing pin.

The man heaved himself to his feet, pulled the two pistols jutting from the holsters thonged low on his thighs, and, raising them, clicked the hammers back.

Prophet strode toward him, yelling, "I come to kill you, you blackhearted Yankee devil!" Calmly aiming down the Winchester's barrel, he squeezed the trigger, and the rifle bucked against his shoulder.

He fired two more rounds, and then the two-gun pistoleer was rolling backward in the snow-speckled dust, throwing his six-guns high over his head.

Prophet's determined walk, resolutely flinging lead while seemingly mindless of the lead caroming around him, had so startled the other two rifle-wielding men that they'd taken off running toward the corral in which the other outlaw was saddling a horse. They fired as they ran, sort of half twisted around and bellowing curses.

Prophet dropped to a knee and emptied his nine-shot Winchester and whooped in satisfaction as the two went down, screaming and rolling up against the base of the corral.

The bounty hunter dropped the rifle and palmed his Colt Peacemaker, turning toward the two windows from which the other thieving killers had been slinging lead at him.

He'd just clicked the hammer back when another rifle began blasting away inside the roadhouse, evoking screams—this time not from women but from men.

One of the window shooters came hurling backward out his window in a rain of glass. He dropped his rifle and hit the ground outside the roadhouse and lay still as the man in the other window, left of the first one, shouted, "Oh no—it's that damn Vengeance Queen!"

He flew forward out the window, a long, tall hombre in nothing more than a union suit and pistol belt and with long, stringy hair. He dropped the pistol he'd been firing, turned a forward somersault in midair, and hit the ground on his back as the rifle continued blasting away inside the roadhouse, evoking more shrill curses and terrified screams from the remaining outlaws inside the place.

The long-haired drink of water outside the road-house lifted his head, shouted a string of blue epithets that would have set a nun's habit on fire, then rolled onto his hands and knees. He looked up to see Prophet walking toward him. The outlaw grabbed his pistol out of the dirt.

He looked up at Prophet again, his two silver front teeth winking in the wintry wan light.

"Kooch Ringo," Prophet snarled, and shot the man through his forehead. "Pleasure to put you down like the rabid dog you are!"

Ringo lay facedown in the dirt, quivering as though he'd been struck by lightning, blood from the hole in his forehead quickly pooling around him.

"*Hi-yahhhh!*" a man bellowed behind Prophet.

He turned as the man inside the corral, now astride a big Appaloosa, came bounding up from inside the corral to hurdle the fence facing Prophet. The Appy's eyes were wide and white-ringed, its ears laid back against its head. The rider's eyes, beneath the brim of his rabbit fur hat, were pinched and dark with rage, the hat's untied flaps bouncing around his red cheeks bristling with several days' worth of dark beard stubble.

"Prophet, you're done for, you fork-tailed devil!" shouted the outlaw whom Prophet, owning a keen memory for men with money on their heads, recognized as Wind River Bob Albright—a stonehearted gunfighter who'd once served in the frontier cavalry stationed at Fort Laramie until he'd been dishonorably discharged for running a prostitution ring involving young, orphaned Hunkpapa Sioux girls.

The Appy touched down ten feet beyond the fence, and Bob Albright, crouched low in the saddle, sort of hiding behind the Appy's head, batted his heels against its flanks, directing the galloping mount toward Prophet. The man's woolly chaps flapped about his legs and high-topped fur boots.

The bounty hunter raised his Peacemaker, aimed quickly, and fired twice.

Both slugs flew wide of Albright's head.

Prophet could have shot the horse. He *should* have, in fact. The trouble was, he liked horses better than he liked most men, so he always had to think twice or three times before performing what he considered a low-down dirty deed of last resort.

This time he'd waited a wink too late. The Appy was on him before he could get his Peacemaker cocked again, the horse bulling into him hard at almost a full run.

Prophet grunted as the horse punched the air from his lungs. The big bounty hunter flew a good ten feet straight back before hitting the ground hard, losing his hat as the knot in his muffler loosened beneath his chin. He lay dazed and grunting and cursing for three or four seconds before he rolled up onto his left shoulder and hip.

He'd dropped the Peacemaker. He just then realized that he'd lost the Richards twelve-gauge, as well. Both weapons lay too far away for a quick grab, especially in the bounty hunter's bruised and battered condition, his ribs barking like wild dogs.

Wind River Bob was swinging back toward Prophet from fifteen feet away, bringing his gun around, as well.

Bob aimed and fired, but the horse was moving, fouling Bob's aim. The shot spanged off a rock over Prophet's right shoulder. The cutthroat aimed his horse as well as his pistol at Prophet once more and, galloping forward, fired again.

Prophet threw himself to his left, avoiding another bullet.

Wind River Bob and the Appaloosa barreled on past Prophet once more, dust wafting in the chill air.

Shaking away the cobwebs from behind his eyes, Prophet hauled himself to his feet. The hip and shoulder that had taken the brunt of the Appy's weight were sore as hell, as were his ribs. As Wind River Bob checked the Appy down, turned it, and began galloping back in Prophet's direction, the bounty hunter sucked back his misery and dove for his Peacemaker.

Bob's next round plunked into the dirt just behind Prophet's right boot.

The bounty hunter hit the ground again, groaning against the agony in his cold, battered bones, and scooped the .45 off the ground. He hauled himself back to his feet and stepped sideways as Bob and the Appy thundered toward him. Prophet reached out with his left hand, grabbing the horse's bridle and jerking its head toward him.

The Appy gave a shrill, indignant whinny as its rear hooves plowed dirt beneath its belly, its barrel curveting sharply. As Prophet drew the horse's head toward him, he rammed his right shoulder hard against the horse's left side and against Wind River Bob's left leg. Bob aimed his cocked Schofield down toward Prophet, but the horse was falling sideways as Prophet continued ramming his shoulder against it, gritting his teeth.

Bob and the Appy fell over hard, and Bob's bullet sailed skyward.

"Oh . . . *ahhhh*!" Bob howled where he lay with his right leg pinned beneath the horse's writhing bulk. He lifted his now-hatless head, which was bald save for a band of brown hair above his ears, and hardened his jaws. "*Off!* Oh, get off me, you miserable cayuse!"

Prophet threw himself back off the horse and onto his butt, away from the horrified horse's flailing hooves. The Appaloosa gained its feet with effort, awkwardly, its saddle loose, bridle hanging askew from its head.

Bob gave another squeal as the weight left his crushed right leg. The Appy trotted off, shaking its head as though it had had its fill of such shenanigans. Bob lay inside the cloud of dust the horse had kicked up, writhing on his back while also stretching his left hand out toward the Schofield, which lay about three feet away from his outstretched fingers.

He stared toward Prophet, his eyes dark with pain and exasperation. He jerked his body back and forth against the ground, inching his left hand toward the pistol while holding his right hand against his right thigh.

Prophet heaved himself to his feet once more, wincing and spitting grit from his lips, a wing of his sandy, close-cropped hair hanging over his eyes. He held his left arm against his battered ribs. As Bob laid his hand on his Schofield, Prophet clamped his right boot down over Bob's hand as well as on the gun. He shifted all his weight—two hundred–plus pounds—to that foot, feeling the bones in Bob's hand grind against the unforgiving steel of the Schofield.

"Ayeeeeeee!" Bob cried, squeezing his eyes closed and tipping his head far back, so that the cords in his neck stood out like ropes in a ship's rigging. *"Ah! Ah! Ah! Ohhhhh—get off me, damn youuuuuuu!"*

Prophet grinned down at the man. Slowly, he removed his foot from the man's hand.

"There you go—feel better?" Prophet crouched down. Bob stared up at him, eyes growing bright in horror when he saw what was about to happen.

Prophet smashed the barrel of his Colt against Bob's left temple, laying him out cold.

Prophet swept his mussed hair back from his eye. He picked up his hat and scarf. He retrieved the Richards sawed-off and slung it behind his back and turned toward the roadhouse. He was breathing hard, sucking air through his teeth, gritted against his sundry aches and pains, and the cold wind nibbling his ears.

The roadhouse had suddenly fallen eerily silent. As silent as a church, the back door standing wide open, its inner depths as black as a mine. A fine, granular snow angled down. A chill breeze pelted the snow against the roadhouse's clapboard siding badly in need of fresh paint.

"Louisa . . . ?"

Prophet shoved his muffler into a coat pocket, pulled his hat down low on his head, and began stumbling toward the open back door.

He stopped suddenly when there sounded the shriek of breaking glass. Almost simultaneously came a young woman's agonized scream.

A man laughed raucously somewhere up in the roadhouse's second story.

"Louisa!" Prophet shouted, and lurched into a sprint.

Chapter 3

A little over five minutes before Prophet trimmed Wind River Bob's wick with his .45's barrel, Louisa kicked in the roadhouse's front door and stepped quickly to the door's right side, where the outdoor light, as fading as it was, wouldn't outline her.

As her eyes quickly adjusted to the dingy light inside the roadhouse's broad drinking hall, she saw a girl with a bruised, Indian-featured face lying across a table to Louisa's right, her molasses-dark eyes wide and staring straight up at the ceiling. The girl's throat had been cut. One arm hung down over the side of the table, as did both smooth, copper-brown legs.

Two men were crouched before two windows running along the wall to Louisa's left, beyond a crude wooden stairway. The men were shooting rifles through the broken-out windows, angling the barrels back toward the roadhouse's rear, toward Lou. They were firing quickly, pumping their cocking levers, empty cartridge casings arcing back over their shoulders to clatter onto the floor around their boots.

A bearded man stood behind the bar about halfway down the room, along its right wall. He was setting bottles onto the bar, as though preparing to load them into the large canvas war bag resting on the pine planks before him. His movements were quick and nervous.

Boots thumped and men shouted in the ceiling above Louisa's head. Another man just started down the broad wooden stairs to Louisa's left though she couldn't yet see him, for he was somewhere above the second-floor landing. She could hear only the fevered thundering of his boots growing quickly louder.

The gang, their hideout having been discovered, and not knowing how many had discovered it, was preparing to pull out.

The bearded man behind the bar had swung his head and his sharp, nervous eyes toward Louisa. He bellowed a curse as he reached behind him, pulling up a long-barreled, double-bore shotgun from where it had been resting atop the back bar.

"It's her!"

Louisa snapped up her Winchester and threw a round at him just as he stumbled backward and slightly sideways, so that the bullet merely shredded his right earlobe before shattering a bottle and the back bar mirror. The man bellowed another curse, hardening his jaws against the pain in his ear, and swung the gut-shredder in Louisa's direction.

As the big popper roared, flames lapping from one barrel, the report like the explosion of a keg of dynamite in the close confines, Louisa dove onto a table ahead and on her right. She hit the near end of it, and it sank beneath her to the floor, rising on its far side and becoming a shield—an inadequate one, she discovered a second later, when the man behind the bar tripped the shotgun's second trigger.

The buckshot blew a pumpkin-sized hole through the upper half of the table, maybe four inches above Louisa's now-hatless head. Scrambling onto a knee, Louisa poked the barrel of her Winchester through the big hole, aimed hastily, and sent two quick rounds hurling toward the man behind the bar.

He was just then tossing the shotgun onto the bar, knocking over several bottles he'd set there, and pulling up two long-barreled Smith & Wessons from holsters strapped around his broad waist.

Louisa's first bullet drilled a quarter-sized hole through his left cheek, just beneath that eye. His head jerked backward, nodding as though he were in firm agreement with something that she'd said.

Louisa's second bullet drilled another hole through the dead center of the man's forehead, jerking his head back once more and sending his whole body flying into the back bar. He blinked his eyes quickly as he rolled down the back bar's shelves, dislodging bottles left and right, and dropped to the floor with a resolute thud.

The man on the stairs was in full view now as he stopped four steps up from the bottom—a long-faced hombre with close-set eyes and long, lusterless blond hair. "We got trouble inside, boys!" he bellowed to the gang in general, bringing the Spencer repeater down off his shoulder and quickly aiming at Louisa, who swung her Winchester in his direction and shot him twice.

The slugs punched him backward, firing his own rifle into the ceiling. He fell onto the steps, howling and reaching again for the rifle. Louisa calmly aimed and punched another pill through his forehead, silencing his infernal caterwauling.

"Ah hell, it's that damn Vengeance Queen!" That had been shouted by one of the two men who'd been shooting out the windows just beyond the stairs, to each side of the large, fieldstone hearth in which a fire popped and crackled, tempering the smell of cordite in the air with the tang of burning pine.

The shooter who'd spoken swung his rifle from the window but before he could even get a fresh round racked into the breech, Louisa's slug punched a hole in his Adam's apple and sent him hurling back through the window, breaking out what glass had remained in the frame.

The other shooter, nearer Louisa, had already turned and was crouched over his Winchester, flinging lead at the Vengeance Queen. Bullets screeched through the air around Louisa's head, thudding into the front wall behind her and into the table, which she'd crouched behind once more, angling the table toward the shooter to act as a shield.

When she heard the shooter's rifle click empty, and the man say, "Crap!" she rose to her knees. Instinctively knowing that her own nine-shot carbine was also empty, she lifted her head from behind the table and snatched both her matching, pearl-gripped, nickel-washed pistols from their hand-tooled, brown leather holsters thonged on her thighs, beneath the flaps of her heavy wool coat.

The shooter flung his rifle away and reached for a pistol tucked into a shoulder holster between his quilted leather coat and his sheepskin vest. "Oh hell!"

he cried, his blue eyes sharp with terror, seeing that Louisa had the drop on him.

"That's where you're headed, all right." Louisa curled her ripe upper lip as her right-hand Colt bucked a quarter second before the one in her left hand bucked, both rounds thumping into the screaming man's chest and punching him straight back through the window out of which he'd been flinging lead at Lou.

A pistol cracked behind Louisa. The bullet was like a hot andiron laid against the right side of her neck, just above the collar of her wool coat. She flinched and swung around, raising both her fancy Colts to see a man standing on the second-floor balcony stretching across the saloon's far wall.

Louisa had started to squeeze both triggers, but now she eased the tension in her trigger fingers. The man—a big man with a black beard cleaved by a long, thick scar running crookedly down his left cheek— held a young girl clad in only pantaloons, a thin shift, and a string of colored feathers and faux pearls, one purple and one bright red ribbon poking up from the mess of light red hair wound and secured into several buns atop her head.

The girl was very young, Louisa judged. Maybe sixteen, maybe younger. She was missing an eyetooth. Louisa could see that because the girl's lips were stretched back from her lips in terror and agony, for the big man standing behind her had one beefy arm, clad in red calico, hooked around her neck, drawing her head back taut against his broad, lumpy chest.

He held a cocked, stag-butted Colt Lightning taut against her right temple. The fleshy hand gripping the gun was covered in small, light brown freckles. "Drop them Colts, woman!" the man bellowed through his beard, narrowing his dark brown eyes beneath the brim of a black, bullet-crowned hat to the front of which the moon-and-star badge of a deputy U.S. marshal was pinned.

That told Louisa which gang member he was— N. B. Stone. He'd killed a federal lawman several years ago in Montana, after murdering two doxies and a deputy sheriff in a whorehouse in Bannack. His way of thumbing his nose at anyone who would come after him for such crimes had been to pin the dead lawman's badge to his hat.

A badge of honor, so to speak.

"Hello, Mr. Stone," Louisa said, gazing up across the barrels of her aimed Colts at the man.

"Drop 'em, Bonaventure! Drop 'em now! I'll kill this girl—drill a hot one right through her purty little head. You know me, so you know I'll do it!"

Louisa swallowed down a tight knot of apprehension in her throat. As she moved forward across the room toward a second stairway ahead of her, sitting parallel to the saloon floor and angling up toward the second-story balcony, running parallel to the saloon, she kept the anxiety out of her voice as she said, "You'll do it even if I set down my guns."

"Stop there!" Stone bellowed, hardening his jaws inside his thick, black beard. "Stop there, or I'll shoot her!"

"No, you won't. You're not suicidal, are you, Norman?" Louisa kept moving toward the rickety-looking, unpainted plank board stairs ahead of her, kicking chairs out of her way. "You look like a man who enjoys life far too much to see it all end right here in this lonely saloon out here in the middle of nowhere."

Louisa put her right boot on the first step and,

keeping her eyes on Stone and the girl above her, near the top of the stairs, she said, "You have too much life left." She gritted her teeth but kept her voice calm, even. "Too much thieving . . . and raping . . . and killing to do . . ."

"That does it—I'm gonna shoot her!"

"No!" the girl cried, struggling against the man's chest.

Stone held her fast with his thick left arm, pressing his pistol firmly against her temple. "Please! Please, don't kill me!" Through tear-glazed eyes, she gazed beseechingly at Louisa moving slowly up the stairs. "Please . . . don't let him kill me! I . . . don't wanna . . . die!"

"He's not going to kill you," Louisa assured the girl, though she herself wasn't sure at all. "He's not going to kill you, because Mr. Norman Brian Stone doesn't want to die." Louisa gained the top of the stairs, stepped onto the second-story balcony, on the same plane now with Stone and the horrified girl, and kept walking ever so slowly, menacingly, toward them.

She shook her head. "You don't want to die here, Norman. Not now. Not like this . . . killed by a *woman*."

Louisa smiled coldly, jeeringly over the barrels of her nickel-washed pistols six-guns aimed straight out in front of her. "Do you, Norman? You don't want to be just another notch on the Vengeance Queen's belt, do you?"

Stone's cheeks turned red behind and above his beard at the notion of being killed by the notorious female bounty hunter.

"I'm gonna warn you for the last time!" Stone yelled, stepping back and jerking the bawling girl along with him, keeping her pulled taut against him, drawing her back through an open door, her bare feet entangling with his boots. "You put them hoglegs down, or I'm gonna blow her head off!"

"You do that," Louisa said, slowly following the man and the girl into the room, "and I'll blow yours off right after." She passed through the doorway and into the small bedroom crudely furnished with a dilapidated chest of drawers, a zinc-topped washstand, and a brass bed. The room smelled like man sweat and sex and tobacco smoke. A single lamp burned on the chest of drawers. "Think about it, Norman. Death. Annihilation. No past, no future. Worm food."

Louisa stopped just inside the doorway.

Stone stopped then, as well, near the foot of the bed, a window directly behind him. He held the girl as before, his beefy arm hooked around her neck, drawing her head back. Her face was red and soaked with tears that flowed steadily down from her horrified eyes.

"Please," she kept begging through her tears. "Please, please, please . . ."

"Think about it, Norman," Louisa said again. "You got your whole life ahead of you. What are you—thirty-five? Forty? You have thirty, forty years left. You don't want it all to end here today. All you've been. All you are. All you'll ever be. Killed in a remote Dakota watering hole"—Louisa curled her upper lip—"by a *woman!*"

Stone stared at her for a full ten seconds, thoughtful. He looked down at the girl writhing against him. He cursed as he turned back to Louisa. "If I turn her loose, you'll set your guns aside?"

"If you holster your pistol and turn her loose, I'll let you walk out of here. You can fetch your horse and ride clear. I'll inform Lou of our arrangement."

Stone turned his head sideways. His right eye twitched. "You're bluffin'!"

"My word is bond, Norman."

"Bullcrap—you're a kill-crazy bounty hunter! Everybody knows about you!"

"I'm that rare bounty hunter with honor, Norman. Empty your pistol, turn the girl loose, and live to eat another meal, to drink another glass of whiskey . . ." She glanced at the doxie's right, discolored eye and drew a deep, calming breath. "To beat another defenseless girl in some remote roadhouse . . ."

Stone's eye twitched again, skeptically. "You lower yours first. Shove it into your holster and secure the thong over the hammer."

"Not a chance. You're going to have to trust me. You holster that pistol and turn the girl free. I lower my Colts, and you walk out of here. I keep my guns. More importantly, you keep your life. Or . . ." Louisa hiked her right shoulder. "Kill her and die here today. Let this be your last day on earth." Louisa smiled. "The wolves will be dining well this evening."

"You're plum loco! I heard tell about you. Now I know it's true. You're crazier'n an owl in a lightin' storm!"

"Be that as it may . . ."

Stone's gaze was darkly pensive. Sweat dribbled down his cheeks and into his beard. He looked at the twin maws of Louisa's Colts aimed at his head. He shifted his gaze to her eyes. "All right. I'm gonna trust you. I'm gonna believe you're an honorable woman . . . despite all the men you've killed."

"Despite all the *bad* men I've killed."

"Let's not split hairs here. I'm gonna holster this pistol. Then I'm gonna turn her free. Then you're—"

"Then I'm going to step back out of your way and wish you a good rest of the day, Norman. Who knows—maybe we'll meet again someday."

Stone flared his nostrils and shook his head. "You better hope not."

Louisa smiled.

"All right," said Stone. "I'm gonna holster this hogleg."

"Get on with it," Louisa said. "Can't you see how frightened the poor girl is?"

"You're an honorable woman. Remember that."

"I'll remember."

"All right." Stone swallowed, lowered the pistol from the girl's head. He slid it into its holster, fastened the keeper thong over the hammer. Slowly, tentatively, he removed his left arm from around the girl's neck.

The girl gave a relieved cry and ran toward Louisa.

"Get behind me," the Vengeance Queen ordered.

The girl stepped behind Louisa.

Stone stared at her, anger sparking in his eyes. "Lower them Colts! Step aside!"

Louisa stretched her lips slightly back from her teeth in a shrewd, mocking smile.

The fear in Stone's eyes brightened. He jerked his arm up and pointed an accusing finger at Louisa. "You made a promise—you remember that! I held up my end of the bargain, you bitch!"

"Unlike my friend Prophet, Norman," Louisa said, sliding her lips farther back from her perfect white teeth, "I do not bargain with the devil."

Stone replaced his pointing finger with his palm turned outward. "Wait, now—hold on!"

Louisa's pistols bucked and roared. The girl behind her screamed as the bullets cut through Stone's chest and hurled him straight out the window behind him.

Chapter 4

Prophet shouted, "Louisa!" as he crossed the stoop and ran through the roadhouse's rear door.

He stopped ten feet inside the place and looked around. The two windows to his right were broken out, and a chill breeze blew through them, sawing against the few shards of glass remaining in the frames. A fire popped and snapped in the big stone hearth between the windows, lending welcoming warmth and tempering the rotten-egg smell of burnt powder with the perfume of pine.

A man lay on the stairs, limbs akimbo, blood oozing out of the twin holes in his chest and another in his forehead, pooling on the steps beneath him. A Spencer repeating rifle lay on the saloon floor at the base of the stairs.

No sign of Louisa.

Again, Prophet called her name, heard his own voice echo around the shadowy, cavernlike room. He also heard a girl's sobbing coming from somewhere behind the crude pine bar to his left. He moved slowly into the room, quickly emptying his Colt, spinning the

wheel and letting the spent cartridges clatter onto the
worn puncheons beneath his boots. He winced when
he saw a girl with distinctly Indian features lying across
a table before him, eyes staring upward in death.

Her face was badly bruised. Beaten. Blood oozed
from a broad gash across her neck.

As Prophet slid fresh ammo from his cartridge belt
and thumbed them into the Peacemaker's chambers,
through the open loading gate, he turned his head
to his left and saw Louisa standing on a second-floor
balcony.

The Vengeance Queen held a sobbing girl in her
arms—a young redhead several inches shorter than
Louisa and clad in only a thin shift, pantaloons, and a
necklace of some kind. Colored feathers hung askew
in the tangle of her thick, mussed hair. Rocking the
girl gently, holding the girl's head against her chest,
Louisa turned to gaze down over the balcony rail at
Prophet.

Lou stopped, loosed a relieved sigh at seeing his
partner still standing.

The girl in her arms slowly lifted her head to gaze
up at Louisa. Through her sobs, she said, "Why are
men so mean? Cruel? Why . . . why . . . do they have to
be so . . . *poison mean?*"

"They don't have to be," Louisa said, tonelessly.
"Some just choose to be. Maybe even most. There are
a few"—she turned to stare over the balcony rail again
at Prophet—"who don't. But even they have their faults."

Prophet turned his mouth corners down.

Louisa blinked as she turned back to the girl.
"There's no point in not facing facts." She pulled away
from the girl, glanced over the rail again, her eyes
finding the dead Indian girl sprawled across the table

near Prophet. Turning back to the redhead, she said, "You'd best go back to your room for a while. We'll try to get it cleaned up a little down there."

The redhead turned to gaze down into the saloon. She looked at the dead Indian girl, her eyes glazing with fresh tears. She turned to Prophet, and the skin above the bridge of her nose wrinkled with a vague incredulity, maybe even revulsion. Prophet thought he saw it, understandably, in her eyes.

She turned away and retreated through an open door, clicking the door closed behind her.

Louisa turned to Prophet.

"You all right?" Prophet asked her.

Louisa dug a lilac-colored hanky from her coat pocket, brushed it across the side of her neck, under her long hair, and looked at it. She winced.

"Bad?"

She looked at him. "No."

Prophet chuckled. It never ceased to amuse him that while Louisa had drained out maybe a hundred gallons of blood from well-deserving men throughout the West, the sight of her own blood made her queasy. Once upon a time, it had made her pass out. Over the years, she'd gotten more used to seeing it. Now it made her only pale up for a time, like a cloudy day.

She stuffed the hanky back into her coat pocket and began reloading her Colts.

Prophet twirled his own walnut-gripped Colt on his finger, dropped the pistol into its holster, beneath his coat. He secured the keeper thong over the hammer then walked around behind the bar. Two more men lay dead back there. The first one, sitting on the floor and leaning against the back bar, was an older, scrawny gent with long, grizzled gray hair.

His chin was tipped to one shoulder. Prophet might have thought him merely sleeping if it hadn't been for the bullet hole in the man's forehead. He wore a green apron, which marked him as the man—or one of the men—who likely ran the place. He'd apparently gotten crossways with the killers, most likely when the gang had first ridden up to the place last night. The apron-clad man was cold and pale and he was already stiff. The bullet wound in his forehead was crusted with dried blood.

He'd been dead nearly a full day.

Maybe he'd balked at pouring the gang free drinks, offering his doxies up for free, or at how the gang was treating the girls. Whatever the reason, he was dead. It never took much of a reason for Gritch Hatchley's men to kill. Judging by the amount of killing they'd done in the past, they enjoyed it.

The second dead man—a tall, fat, bearded man in a checked shirt and beaded, fringed elk hide vest—had been killed recently. Louisa must have killed him. He lay slumped to one side amidst the shards of broken bottles and spilled whiskey, blood oozing from the many glass cuts pocking his big, fleshy body.

Prophet crouched over him, pulled the man's head up by his hair. He recognized the round, crudely featured face from a wanted circular Prophet had out in his saddlebags. Brett Chaney, a killer from Utah who'd busted out of the Utah Territorial Pen some years ago and had somehow eluded being dragged back. His joining up with Gritch Hatchley and Hatchley's second cousin, Weed Brougham, who formed the leadership of the bunch, had made Chaney and the rest of the gang hard to run down.

Hatchley's bunch was a nasty pack of bloodthirsty wolves. They'd been running off their collective leash for a good three years, since they'd all thrown in together to rob banks, trains, and stagecoaches and generally rape, pillage, and plunder to the content of their black hearts, bouncing from one territory to the next, mostly northern territories, staying two steps ahead of the law, evading capture.

Until today, Prophet thought, letting Chaney's head flop back down against the floor littered with broken glass. He pulled an unbroken bottle of rye whiskey off a shelf beneath the bar, set it on the scarred oak, and grabbed a shot glass off a near pyramid.

"Drinks are on the house, I reckon," he said, casting a dubious glance at the dead, apron-clad gent. "Likely forever more."

The bounty hunter pried the cork out of the bottle with his teeth, spat it onto the floor, and splashed whiskey into the glass. He held the glass up in salute to the dead man and threw back the entire shot.

He smacked his lips then turned sadly to the dead apron. "Sorry, partner. Truly I am. You'll never again know the joy of a stiff shot of rotgut whiskey. Even cheap rye is bracing on a cold day that's gonna get even colder." He shook his head then glanced at the two broken-out windows flanking the big hearth in which the fire was dying. "It don't help we lost two windows." He turned to his partner, who was dropping slowly down the stairs, running one bare hand along the banister, staring at the dead Indian girl. "Hey, Vengeance Queen, was you born in a barn?"

Chuckling to himself, Prophet refilled his shot glass. He left it on the bar without drinking it. A vague apprehension touched him. He wasn't sure of its source.

Frowning, pensive, he walked out from behind the bar and tramped over to the hearth. Beside the fireplace was an ancient wooden feed bin filled with old newspapers, dry branches, and split pine and post oak. He fed several of the smaller branches to the fire, building it up gradually.

When the flames were dancing again, exhaling more pine tang into the room, he added a couple of split pine logs and then an oak knot that, if tended well, should burn half the night, holding at bay some of the chill pouring in on the breeze raking through the broken windows.

When he had the knot arranged to his satisfaction atop the grate, he swung away from the fire, eyes widening and lower jaw sagging as he realized what had been troubling him.

He turned to Louisa, who was striding slowly out from the bottom of the stairs. "Hey—we're a few owl-hoots short!"

Louisa gave him one of her incredulous, impatient looks from inside the tangle of honey-blond hair framing her cameo-perfect face with bee-stung lips. She wasn't wearing her hat, and her cream muffler hung from her shoulders. "What are you caterwauling about?"

Prophet counted silently on his fingers.

"We're a few wolves short of a pack," he said, looking around, frowning, fists on his hips. "More than a few. Several."

Lou walked over to the stairs climbing his side of the saloon hall and inspected the long-haired dead man there whom Louisa had drilled a third eye. Swinging toward where Louisa stood by the overturned table, near the dead Indian girl, brushing her gloved hands down her carbine's stock, Prophet said, "This is Joe Horton. So far I haven't seen Hatchley. Or the woman in the bunch—what's her name . . . ?"

"Sweets DuPree," Louisa said. "As deadly as Hatchley, but she's the half-breed's woman—Pima Quarrels."

"Where's Hatchley?" Prophet asked her. "I didn't see him outside."

"Are you sure?"

"No. I'll check again, but I'd recognize that varmint from a mile away. Probably smell him from that distance, too. He's almost as tall as I am. Nasty-lookin' devil with a big, thick head and a curly beard, and he wears a stinky buffalo coat. He's got a gold stud through his left ear. Resembles a mossy-horned bull buff, and he's got a temper to match."

"I haven't seen any ill-tempered bull buffaloes in here, Lou."

"I didn't see any out back. No woman, neither, save the dead girl. In here?"

"Only the redhead." Louisa jerked her chin toward the second-story balcony behind her and set her Stetson on her head, letting the horsehair chin thong dangle against her coat.

Prophet turned to stare up the stairs rising behind and above him, beyond the dead Joe Horton. "Anybody up there?"

"I haven't made it that far," Louisa said. "Pretty quiet, though. If Hatchley was up there, I think we might have heard from him by now."

"Just the same . . ."

Prophet palmed his Colt, clicked the hammer back, leaped up and over the dead man, and quickly but thoroughly checked out the second story. He found nothing but overfilled slop buckets, unmade beds, and the owlhoots' strewn gear.

"Nothing," Prophet said, dropping back down the steps, leaping the dead man again, and sliding the Peacemaker back into its holster.

Louisa had been waiting at the bottom of the stairs, holding her carbine in both hands at port arms across her chest, ready in case anyone besides Prophet came back down the stairs. Now as Prophet dropped into the saloon, Louisa turned to follow him as he walked along beside the bar and out through the rear door he'd left open.

He walked across the stoop and into the yard, stopping and looking around. Only one of the five men out here was moving. That was Wind River Bob. He was down on one knee, trying to rise onto the other knee but the leg that had been pinned under his horse wasn't having it. He was grunting and groaning and looking around—probably for a gun. Blood dribbled from the cut on his left temple, courtesy Prophet's gun barrel.

"Which one is that?" Louisa asked Prophet.

"Wind River Bob."

"Albright?"

"One an' the same."

"Are any of the others Hatchley?"

"Nope."

Prophet stepped over Kooch Ringo to inspect the other men he'd shot from a distance and hadn't gotten a good look at yet. He rattled off their names then turned to Louisa. "Hatchley an' the woman ain't here. Who're the fellas you hurled out the windows?"

"Let's have a look."

Prophet swung around and walked up the side of the roadhouse toward the front. Louisa, too, had a good eye for the men they were after. After all, they'd been on their trail for the past two weeks; she and Prophet had had plenty of time to study their likenesses and descriptions on wanted circulars, usually by the light of their nightly campfires and while coyotes yammered in the distance.

Louisa named both men she'd blown out the windows on either side of the fireplace as Charlie Seltzer and Billy "Hoe-Down" Scroggs.

She turned to Prophet, fists on her hips. "There's one more on the other side. N. B. Stone."

"No Hatchley," Prophet said, scraping a thumb along his jaw and looking around as though he thought the gang leader might appear out of the chill wind. "No Weed Brougham, either."

"And no Sweets DuPree nor Pima Quarrels."

Behind them, Wind River Bob groaned loudly as he sagged onto his butt, his injured leg protruding straight out in front of him. "I need help here! Say there—I need help! I'm afraid my leg is broken!"

Prophet and Louisa shared a glance.

The bounty hunters moseyed over to where Wind River Bob lay writhing and groaning. They stood over Bob, staring distastefully down at the vile brigand.

"Not feelin' too good this afternoon, Bob?" Prophet asked.

Bob looked up at him through pain-racked, dung-brown eyes. "I need a doctor. I think my hip is broke. Hurts god-awful bad!"

"Let me see."

Prophet dropped to a knee before Bob. He grabbed

the man's right ankle with one hand and laid his other hand over the man's knee.

"What are you, doin', Prophet?" Bob looked confused, fearful. He tried to scuttle back away from the bounty hunter. "Don't touch me, damnit. I need a sawbo . . . *ohhhh*! Jesus Christ! What are you *doin'*?"

"I'm just tryin' to see if your leg's broke." Prophet pressed his left hand down hard against Bob's knee. "How's that feel?"

"*Owwww!*" Bob howled, tipping his head back and trying to inch away again. "It hurts like hell. Leave me alone. I can tell it's broke. I don't need you to . . . *ohhh! Owwww!* What the hell are you *doin'*, you fork-tailed devil?"

"We're missing a few folks, Bob," Louisa said, standing over Prophet, staring down at Bob.

"*Wha . . . wha . . . what?*"

"We're a few wolves short of a whole pack," Prophet said.

"You really like that one—don't you, Lou?" Louisa said.

"Get your hands off me—damnit, Prophet! I'm an injured man!"

Prophet shoved down hard again on the man's knee. "Where'd they go, Bob?"

Wind River Bob threw his head back and howled like a gut-shot coyote. "*St . . . st . . . stawwwppp!*"

"Where's Hatchley, Bob?" Louisa asked the outlaw. "Where's his sidekick cousin, Brougham?"

"And where's the girl, Sweets Dupree?" Prophet added. "Oh, and the half-breed, Pima Quarrels. Where's Quarrels, Bob?"

"I don't know," Bob said, panting and staring at Prophet in horror. Even though the temperature was dropping fast now as dusky shadows filled the yard and more snow stitched the breeze, sweat beads dribbled down Bob's cheeks and into his beard. "How would I know where they are?"

"Bob," Prophet said, "let me check your hip."

"Nooooo!"

Prophet tugged on the man's right ankle.

Bob threw his head back and screamed. "Dam . . . dam . . . *damnit*!" he said, panting, when Prophet had eased up on the tension on Bob's wounded leg. "I think . . . I think it's separated."

"No," Prophet said. "It's your knee that's separated. It's swelling up on ya real bad. I think your hip is plum broken. Lordy, you're injured bad, Bob!"

The bounty hunter grinned devilishly and gave the man's right ankle another savage tug.

Chapter 5

Howling, Bob flopped back against the ground, slamming the backs of his fists into the finely churned dirt laced with hay, horse manure, and fresh snow.

Louisa stepped forward, placed her right boot over Bob's right knee. "Where'd they go, Bob?"

Bob sobbed, shook his head, then hardened his jaws and gritted his teeth. "You ain't new to this business—neither one of ya. You know I can't tell you that!"

Louisa rammed her boot down on Bob's knee.

Bob slammed his fist into the ground, wailing.

When Louisa had removed her boot from the man's knee, Prophet scuttled up to kneel beside the man's left shoulder, on the opposite side of Bob from Louisa. "Bob, I'm gonna turn my partner loose on you here in a minute. You are aware of what everyone calls her—aren't ya? The *Vengeance Queen?*"

"Yes, I'm very much aware of that," Bob said, dead sober.

Prophet poked his hat brim up on his forehead. "It ain't worth it, Bob. Let me tell ya straight. Look at her."

Bob looked up at Louisa smiling down at him, the

heel of her boot resting on the ground beside Bob's right leg, the bottom of the sole angling over the knee that was swelling up to the size of a wheel hub.

Bob whined deep in his chest.

Prophet said, "She'd love nothin' better than to put you through the worst kind of misery. A man like you? One that's known for sellin' poor li'l Injun orphan girls into slavery? That's been terrorizin'—not to mention *killin'*—the doxies here at the roadhouse? Why, Louisa's been *dreamin'* of this day!"

"I have, Bob." Louisa blinked her catlike hazel eyes slowly. "It's true."

"Besides," Prophet said. "What do you want Hatchley and the others getting away for? Why should they be allowed to ride free . . . free to drink and gamble and carouse to their hearts' content . . . while you're headed to a federal courthouse in Bismarck. Hell, your trial won't last ten minutes before they drag you out to the federal gallows down by the Big Misery. After the jury hears what all you've done—all the nefarious nasty deeds to them orphan girls and others—they'll hang you by the neck and watch you do the midair kick-step while the band plays, the dogs bark, and the doxies dance!"

"Think about it, Bob," Louisa prodded the man. "Do you really want Hatchley and the others running free, enjoying themselves, while you're feeding the angleworms?" She pressed her boot down on the outlaw's swollen knee.

Bob wailed. "All right, all right—stop that! Stop it—you hear? I see your point!"

Louisa removed her boot from the man's knee.

Wind River Bob stared up at her and Prophet, hardening his jaws in anger. "I see your point," he repeated, panting. "Hatchley and Weed Brougham headed east to Indian Butte. Sweets an' Pima Quarrels headed south to Sundown. We was all headed for Canada. No one expects outlaws to head north this time of the year instead of south, so we headed north. Leave it to you two crazy-assed bounty hunters to head north after us! Do you know what time of year it is? Prophet, ain't you a Southern boy?"

"Hear me when I say your point is well-taken, Bob."

Bob chuckled sourly, shook his head, brushed a tear of misery from his left cheek. "Hatchley an' Pima had a fallin'-out over Sweets. The half-breed thought he saw Sweets makin' candy eyes at Hatchley. Sweets always thought Pima should be headin' up the gang, and she's been tryin' to goad Pima into challenging Hatchley, but Pima didn't want no part of Gritch Hatchley. So Sweets—she started gettin' cozy with Hatchley."

Bob scowled up at Louisa. "What is it with you women? Sweet an' purty-lookin', but *savages*!"

Louisa smiled down at him.

"What are their plans in Indian Butte and Sundown, Bob?" Prophet asked.

"I don't know," Bob said. "Hatchley said somethin' about maybe goin' on to Canada after Christmas, then headin' south, when their trails had cooled. Brougham tagged along because Brougham wouldn't know what to do with himself without Hatchley by his side, makin' all the decisions. After the big fuss and them makin' up all sugar-like, Sweets an' Pima decided to forget about Canada. They decided to take their chances an' start makin' their way down to Mexico. We knew you was behind us three days ago, but we hadn't seen you on our back trail lately, so we got to thinkin' it was too cold for your old rebel ass, Prophet, an' you decided to head for Mexico your ownself. An' took her with you."

He wrinkled his nostrils at Louisa. "Pima's from Arizona. He don't care for this cold weather one bit."

Bob looked around, indicating the cold, snow-stitched breeze. "Can't say as I care for it, neither, by God!"

Louisa glanced at Prophet. "Think we can believe him?"

"Yeah, I think we can," Prophet said. "He knows what's gonna happen to him if I find out he's been lyin'—don't ya, Bob?"

Bob snarled, gave a little croaklike sob.

To Louisa, Prophet said, "Bob an' me will head over to Indian Butte for Hatchley and Brougham. Them's the two with the biggest bounties on their heads. Each is worth around five hundred more alive than dead, so I'll take them, *try* to take 'em alive. You'd just shoot 'em an' be done with it. Sweets an' Pima are worth more alive, too, so remember that. They're not worth as much alive as Gritch an' Weed are, but money's money."

Louisa didn't argue. "I'll head south to Sundown, pickup Sweets and Pima Quarrels. Both towns are on the spur railroad line. I'll wait for you to pull through on the train, then we'll continue on to Bismarck together."

She glanced at the dead men lying twisted around them. "We'll turn all this dead outlaw beef over to the U.S. marshal there and collect the bounties." She smiled sourly at Prophet. "Should make you a nice stake for Mexico."

Prophet grinned. "In the meantime, let's get inside

before I freeze somethin' else off . . . not that I probably have anything left that ain't already frozen. I'll gather up the dead later on, lay 'em out in the barn nice an' tidy, so the wolves don't get 'em. I want to thaw out and have another drink first."

"The girl?" Louisa stared toward where the girl in the buffalo robe lay near the barn.

"Don't worry, I'll bring her inside."

Louisa nodded, and they headed for the roadhouse.

"Hey!" bellowed Wind River Bob. "Aren't you forgetting something?"

Prophet and Louisa stopped, exchanged a look.

"What do you think?" Lou said.

"I think we should leave him to the wolves."

"I hear ya." Prophet looked at Wind River Bob staring over his shoulder at them in horror. "On the other hand, I think Bob's worth more alive than dead. So, practically speaking, I think I'm gonna haul his undeserving behind inside, thaw him out for the hangman."

"I'd call killing him good money well spent, but have it your way." Louisa continued on into the roadhouse.

"All right, Bob," Prophet said, dropping to his knees behind the killer. "Let's get you inside, shall we? Hangmen need to earn a living, too."

Prophet hauled the killer to his feet, Bob cussing and grunting and casting doubt on the purity of the bounty hunter's lineage. Prophet chuckled as he slung Bob's arm over his shoulder and began leading the injured brigand back toward the roadhouse.

Louisa came out the back door to stop on the rear stoop. In her arms she held the dead Indian girl who'd been lying across the table near the front of the place.

"Who cut this girl's throat?" Louisa asked Bob tightly.

Bob glanced at Prophet then cut his sheepish gaze back to Louisa. "Hatchley."

Louisa arched a skeptical brow. "Really?"

"It was Hatchley!" Bob insisted. "He called her scrawny and berated Burt Jiggs—he's the apron that ran the place—for not having no decent girls in his employ. He said they was all too skinny. Jiggs told him he had better girls before the railroad came through and wrecked his business. Hatchley, being drunk and smoking that nasty weed he likes to smoke, didn't like Jiggs's tone, so he shot Jiggs and cut the girl. Tossed her over the table. He spent the night with the red-head. She seemed to pacify him, likely got him drunk so he passed out. Slept till late this mornin' when he an' Brougham headed out, avoidin' a sure shootin' war with Sweets an' Quarrels."

"What got the other one shot?" Prophet asked, glancing over his shoulder toward where the dead girl lay by the barn.

"Ah hell."

"What was it?" Louisa prodded.

Bob sighed. "Don't hold it against me, now, but she overheard me an' Ringo talkin' about . . . about prob'ly havin' to kill her an' the other girl when we left tomorrow mornin'. You know—we couldn't be expected to leave anyone alive who seen our faces."

When Bob saw how Prophet and Louisa were looking at him, he added with no little exasperation, "That wouldn't have been professional!"

Louisa gritted her teeth as she came forward,

turned sideways, and chopped the side of her boot down against Bob's swollen knee.

Prophet helped Wind River Bob into the roadhouse and laid him down on a beat-up leather sofa angled before the fireplace. So Bob couldn't get his hands on any of the weapons strewn around the saloon in the wake of the shoot-out, Prophet tied Bob's hands behind his back.

"There you go, Bob," Prophet said, cutting the excess rope from around Bob's wrists with his barlow knife and shoving the injured owlhoot back against the sour, overstuffed sofa. "I hope you're comfortable. I didn't get those ropes too tight, now, did I?"

"Go to hell, you rancid grayback!" Bob pulled against the rope. "I need some whiskey to kill the pain. Fetch me a bottle!"

"I ain't here to feed liquor to girl-killers. You're so low you'd stick a rattlesnake in a man's pocket and ask him for a light!"

Prophet put a pot of hot water on the fire to boil and built himself a toddy of hot water, whiskey, and dark cane sugar he found in a crock behind the bar. He sipped two toddies while sitting in a chair before the fire. Bob snarled at him, like a leg-trapped wolf. Louisa, who abstained from alcoholic beverages, drank a couple cups of coffee. Louisa could turn men toe-down without batting one of her pretty, long-lashed eyes, but she never drank anything stronger than coffee, tea, milk, or sarsaparilla. Occasionally, she'd take a ginger beer.

When Prophet could feel his toes again, and before

the toddy could make him overly sleepy, he shrugged into his coat once more and dragged the two dead owlhoots—the one on the stairs and the one behind the bar—out to the barn. He retrieved his and Louisa's horses from the far side of the hill and stabled them in the barn with plenty of feed and water.

He dragged the other dead men from around the roadhouse into the barn, as well. In the morning, he'd tie them over their horses' backs. He and Louisa would split them up and each take half to Indian Butte and Sundown, respectively.

When he had all the dead killers lined up in the barn, where the wild animals couldn't get at them overnight, he carried the dead girl in the buffalo robe into the roadhouse and laid her out in a bed upstairs where Louisa had laid the Indian girl. He went back downstairs and fetched the body of the man who'd owned the place, Burton Jiggs, and laid him out on the floor beside the two dead girls. There was room on the bed for Jiggs, but it didn't seem right, somehow.

Prophet intended to send a sheriff for the bodies later. He'd summon one from Indian Butte. He thought the county seat was Devil's Lake. The roadhouse would be in the sheriff's jurisdiction. The county badge-toter could decide what to do with them, identify them, maybe wire any family they might have in the area.

Prophet had just gotten Jiggs arranged beside the whores, when he heard light footsteps behind him. He turned to see the third girl—the sole survivor of the Hatchley gang's depredations—walk into the room. She was small and pale and her thick red hair was like a tumbleweed around her delicate head. It hung in tangles down her back and over her shoulders.

She held a thick quilt around her small body, drawing it closed beneath her chin, which bore one small, dark mole. Her right eye was swollen, and there were a couple of nasty cuts on her lips, but they'd scabbed up all right.

She stood staring at the two girls on the bed. She didn't say anything. She just stared. A single tear gathered in the corner of her right eye and dribbled down her cheek.

Prophet sighed, pulled the bed covers up over the two dead young women. He pulled another sheet from over a chair and used it to shroud Jiggs. He walked over and placed his hands on the redhead's shoulders, drew her to him. She succumbed to the hug stiffly at first, likely repelled by his maleness, as was understandable, but finally she leaned forward and pressed her cheek to his chest.

"What's your name, darlin'?" Prophet asked her, holding her.

She took a moment to respond. It was almost as though she had to think about it.

"Antoinette Morganson," she said, finally. "Toni Morganson."

"I'm Lou Prophet, Toni. My lady friend is Louisa Bonaventure."

"I know," Toni said softly. He felt her nod her head against his chest. "I've read about you two before . . . in the newspapers." She paused. "They call her . . . the Vengeance Queen."

"They sure do."

Toni lifted her head and glanced up at him, her eyes vaguely ironic. "You sold your soul to the devil."

"Yeah, well, he was the only taker," Prophet said with a sigh, nudging the girl's chin with his thumb, playfully. "Come on, Toni. Let's get you back into bed. Gonna be a cold night. You got a fire in your room?"

Toni shook her head.

"Show me," Prophet said. "I'll build one."

Toni turned slowly away from the two lumps of the dead girls on the bed, and Prophet followed her out of the room and down the hall to an open door. Toni walked into a small room with walls papered in dark red with gilt wheat heads standing out in relief. The furniture was typically shabby. Snow ticked against the single, small window.

While the girl removed the quilt from her shoulders, appearing mindless of the fact that she wore nothing except frayed pantaloons and the thin shift, she crawled into the small bed.

Prophet got a fire going in the small, sheet-iron stove in the near corner.

"You hungry?" Prophet asked her, closing the stove door, the stove now creaking and wheezing to life as the fire grew. He turned to the girl who lay on the bed, staring up at the ceiling.

"I don't know," Toni said, frowning, as though that, too, had been a difficult question.

"I'll see what ole Diggs had downstairs for vittles, and I'll bring you somethin' up, just in case you are."

Toni slid her gaze to him. Her eyes appeared cloudy with consternation, but gradually they cleared. She quirked her mouth corners slightly, a feeble attempt at a smile. "Thank you, Lou."

Prophet tossed her a wink then headed out into the hall and drew the door closed behind him.

Chapter 6

Prophet dropped back down the stairs to the main saloon hall.

Louisa stood at the bar. Several sets of saddlebags lay atop the bar around her, as well as several stacks of greenbacks and burlap sacks of coins. While Prophet had been sorting out the bodies, Louisa had been going through the dead gang members' gear, looking for the money they'd stolen out of a bank in Wyoming.

They'd gotten away with almost forty thousand dollars and there was a 3 percent safe return fee in addition to individual bounties, which meant more bounty money for the bounty hunters.

"Well, we've gotten quite a bit of it back," Louisa said as Prophet walked around behind the bar. "They split it up but didn't have much time to spend it. Let's hope Hatchley and the others don't, as well."

"Not much to spend it on around here," Prophet said, "this far off the beaten path." He splashed whiskey from his bottle into a shot glass. "I reckon ole Wind River Bob didn't care to share any of it with Jiggs or his girls. You're tighter'n a heifer's ass in fly season,

Bob!" he yelled over the bar at the outlaw lounging on the sofa, his injured leg drawn up, the other one on the floor.

"Why buy the cow when you can have the milk for free?" Bob threw his head back and howled with delighted laughter, slapping the sofa back. He laughed for a long time, eyes squeezed shut.

Finally, his guffaws dwindled to hiccups and chuckles.

"I tell you what, you Confederate devil," he said, brushing tears from his cheeks, "I'll pay you full price for a bottle of that liquor you're makin' sure I know how much you're enjoying over there."

Prophet threw back the rye. He smacked his lips and shook his head. "Mmmm-Mmmmm! That there is nectar of the gods. Makes me feel sooo good! Why, it take all the soreness out of my joints—you know, the ones you tried to pulverize with that Appy?"

"Spare a bottle—damnit, Prophet!" Bob punched the sofa back.

"I tell you what, Bob," Prophet said. "I'm gonna do just that." He pulled a bottle down from a back bar shelf. Walking around from behind the bar, he said, "Maybe this will silence your infernal caterwaulin'. It ain't a labeled bottle, you understand. It's probably tarantula juice old Jiggs brewed out in a stock tank in his barn, complete with strychnine and rattlesnake venom, maybe a dead lizard for seasoning. I see no reason to waste good liquor on a raping, thieving killer like you, Bob."

"Keepin' the good stuff for yourself—eh, Lou?" Bob accepted the brown, unlabeled bottle. He pulled the cork out with his teeth and spit it toward the leaping flames of the fire.

"An' why shouldn't I?" Prophet tramped back over to the bar.

He stopped near where Louisa stood, still counting money and penciling figures onto an open notepad, and turned his head to see Toni coming down the stairs on the room's opposite side. The young doxie held the same quilt as before around her slender shoulders, drawing the corners up tight beneath her chin.

"Sorry, honey," Prophet said. "I said I was gonna bring you some vittles. I reckon I got sidetracked."

"That's all right." Toni moved from the bottom of the steps toward the bar. "I ain't hungry, after all. Couldn't sleep, either. I keep seein' . . ." She shook her head as though to nudge troubling thoughts away.

She moved up to the bar near Louisa.

"I reckon I didn't feel like bein' alone up there," the girl said in a thin, faraway voice.

"We're all alone," Louisa said, absently, scribbling figures on the pad. "Either up there or down here."

Prophet nudged her left boot with his right one. When she turned to him, brows arched, he gave her an admonishing look. Louisa hiked a shoulder and returned to her figures.

"Ha-ha!" Bob laughed. "Ain't that just like the Vengeance Queen? As philosophical as she is purty."

Toni turned toward the sofa. "That him?" she asked. "That the last one?"

Prophet splashed more whiskey into his shot glass. "Pretty close to the last one. Four more are still running off their leashes but not for long."

Toni pushed away from the bar and, holding the quilt taut beneath her chin, walked over to the end of the sofa. She stopped and faced Bob, standing near his left boot resting on the hemp rug on the floor before the snapping hearth. She shook the thick ribbons of her red hair back from her eyes.

Bob looked her blanket-wrapped body up and down, slowly, leeringly.

"Hello, sweet thing," the outlaw grunted. He quirked half of his mouth in a mocking grin. "You miss ole Bob?"

The girl stared at him dully, shook her head slowly.

"No, I haven't been missing you, Bob. I'll likely smell your stench, just like Hatchley's, till the day I die."

Bob chuckled.

"I'll tell you who's calling for you, Bob."

"Oh?" Bob said, arching one brow. "Who's that?"

"The devil." Toni opened her hands, releasing the quilt. It dropped to her bare feet. In her right hand was a .38 caliber, elaborately engraved, Merwin & Hulbert revolver. "You should go see him, maybe."

"Whoa now!" Bob said, sitting straight up and holding both his hands toward the girl, palms out. "Stop! Stop! Sto—"

The pop of the little pocket pistol cut off Bob's last plea.

Bob howled and snapped his right hand down, falling back against the sofa arm behind him. He held his hand up in front of his face, mouth wide in astonishment. The bullet had drilled a bloody hole through his palm. It had drilled a second one into his chest from which blood was now beginning to ooze.

"Stop her!" Bob wailed, looking down in horror at the blood bubbling out of his chest. "Stop her! For chrissakes, stop the crazy little polecat!"

Holding the pocket pistol in both her small hands,

Toni fired again, again, and again. She blinked with every shot, gritting her teeth.

With each shot, Bob jerked violently back against the arm of the sofa. As he rolled to his left and fell off the sofa to the floor with a heavy thud, Toni fired twice more. She would have fired one more time, but the pistol's hammer pinged benignly against the firing pin.

Lou and Louisa stared in shock from the bar.

Toni stared down at Bob. Smoke from the Merwin & Hulbert wafted around her.

"There," she said, finally, reaching down and pulling the quilt up around her shoulders again. "I think I'll sleep better now."

She padded barefoot across the room toward the balcony stairs.

Prophet turned slowly to Louisa, his lower jaw hanging.

Louisa raised her brows and dipped her chin in appreciation. "She'll do."

Prophet dragged Wind River Bob outside and added him to the carnage in the barn.

He also hazed the horses into the barn from the corral, for the wind was really howling now, and more snow was coming down. It was damn cold and would likely get colder. Horses needed shelter from such weather as much as people did.

Prophet knew from previous experience how cold it could get here. And how much snow could fall, choking the ravines. This wasn't the first time he'd gotten caught in Dakota Territory this late in the year, when he should have been close enough to the Mexican border that he could smell the tequila and pulque, the carnitas enchiladas, the salt tang of the Sea of Cortez, and the beguilingly gamy aromas of the dusky-skinned señoritas who plied their artful trade in those balmy climes.

When he'd gotten the dozen or so horses into their stalls, he heard Mean and Ugly kicking his own stable door and whickering darkly, customarily spoiling for a fight. Most of the other horses just glanced sidelong at him over their stall partitions, their eyes glistening in the darkness, skeptically pricking their ears.

"Look how well behaved these killers' horses are, Mean," Prophet admonished his ewe-necked hammer-head. "Ain't you ashamed?"

With that, he closed the barn doors and ran to the roadhouse, holding his hat on his head with one hand and watching his footing. It was true dark now and about all he could see before him was murky darkness stitched with swirling snow.

Once back in the roadhouse, he ate some of the beans Louisa had cooked from a tripod over the fire, then brought a bowl up to Toni. The doxie was sound asleep in her bed, snoring softly. Prophet smiled at that. He vaguely wondered if Toni and Louisa weren't somehow related, for nothing made the Vengeance Queen sleep so well as killing men who needed killing.

He left the beans on the doxie's chest of drawers, banked her fire against the cold night, then went back downstairs and polished off the whiskey in his labeled bottle. He was too exhausted to talk. Louisa appeared that way, as well.

She sat staring into the fire, sipping her coffee. They both had a good long ride ahead of them tomorrow, possibly in several feet of snow, so Prophet shrugged out of his coat and hat, kicked out of his boots, and plopped down on the same sofa on which Wind River Bob had met his well-deserved, bloody end. He drew his blanket roll up over him, against the chill wind howling through the broken windows.

Louisa sat up for a while, staring into the fire.

Finally, she banked the fire in the hearth, nudged Prophet as far back against the sofa as he could get his tall, brawny frame, and then stretched her slender, willowy body down against his, facing away from him. He wrapped his arms around her, sniffed her hair, nuzzled her neck, and kissed her left ear.

"Thanks for breaking out those windows," he growled, shivering against the unabated breeze.

"Don't mention it."

She put his right hand on her left breast, snuggled back against him, groaning luxuriously. She ground her round rump against him then glanced over her shoulder at him, frowning.

"Take your gun off."

"I did."

Louisa's frown became an exasperated scowl. "After this long day and a whole bottle of whiskey?" Louisa lay her head back down with a sigh. "Men!"

Chapter 7

A low growling nudged Prophet from the depths of sleep.

The growling stopped. Prophet didn't know how much time passed, for he was falling back into sweet slumber once more, before the growling came again—longer, sharper, more angry.

The sound pulled him out of his slumber again, all the way out this time. He lifted his head from the sofa and slitted one eye to see a large, round, shaggy head with a long black snout and two mud-black eyes, ears angling back and quivering. Leathery, whisker-bristling lips rose from the beast's mouth, showing bone-white, peglike teeth framed by long, curved fangs.

The dark eyes, flat with wild savagery, glared at Prophet from three feet away. Lou could smell the sweet, dead-meat fetor of the beast's breath.

The bounty hunter jerked his head farther up with a start and an involuntary, clipped yell.

The wolf wheeled with a frightened yelp, ran toward the saloon's far wall flanking the stone hearth, and leaped up and through the broken-out window in which granular snowflakes swirled. The beast was a mottled gray and blue blur in the dingy shadows. There was a soft thump as the four feet hit the snowy ground outside the roadhouse, and then soft, frantic thuds faded as the wolf ran away, breath rasping.

"What is it?" Louisa said, lifting her head and looking around, her hair in her eyes. "What's the matter, Lou?"

"You sure sleep sound for a bounty hunter!" Prophet exclaimed, his heart still pounding. "There was a wolf in here!"

"I always sleep sound when I'm with you, because I know you don't. What are you talking about? A wolf? *Inside?*"

"Sure as hell!"

"You were dreaming. Go back to sleep." Louisa stared toward the window, touched with the grays and blues of the early dawn. "Sun's not up yet. And it's cold and snowy. I need another hour. Build up the fire, will you?"

"Hell, I can't go back to sleep after that." Prophet crawled over his slender partner and rose, staring at the window through which the wolf had disappeared and through which snow swirled, dusting the floor several feet in front of it, around the now-cold hearth. "We was wolf bait. That beast likely smelled the carrion in the barn. Couldn't get in the barn but he could get in here through them windows. I should've boarded 'em up."

"What's that horrible smell?" Louisa said, curled in a ball beneath Prophet's bedroll, eyes closed but frowning as she sniffed the air. "First thing you should do when you get to Indian Butte, Lou, is take a bath."

"That's the wolf stench!"

"Hush." Louisa turned over with a groan, giving her back to him. "I need another hour. Occupy yourself, please, Lou. *Quietly.*"

"'Occupy yourself, Lou,'" Prophet mimicked, sitting in a chair and pulling on a fur-lined moccasin. "'*Quietly.*' Miss Uppity Britches."

Louisa snored softly into the back of the sofa, sound asleep.

Prophet pulled on his other moccasin. "Wolf bait is what we was. Here, I survived the War of Northern Aggression and a dozen years on the wild and woolly frontier, hunting the baddest men for the highest bounties, and I was damn near ate by a damned wolf while sleeping in a backwater Dakota watering hole!"

He moved to the cold hearth, muttering, "'Occupy yourself, please, Lou. *Quietly.* Take a bath when you get to Indian Butte, Lou!'"

He took an iron poker and poked at the remnants of last night's fire until a flame licked up from a bit of burned log. He added paper and bark to the flame, growing it, then added twigs and branches and finally a couple of stout, split logs. Soon, a fire was once again licking up through the chimney, panting like a baby dragon and putting up a fight against the bone-splintering chill in the room.

The perfume of the smoke warred against the sweet, gamy stench the wolf had left behind.

Prophet buckled his cartridge belt and Peace-maker around his waist. He tied the thong around his thigh. He shrugged into his heavy buckskin coat, pulled on his knit gloves and then his wool-lined, buckskin mittens over the gloves. Having been caught up here in similar weather before, he'd be damned if he'd leave any fingers behind. His oysters, maybe, but not his fingers. He tramped lightly back along the bar then headed out the roadhouse's rear door and into the chill air of early morning.

He paused on the wooden stoop, looking around.

The cold air nipped at his nose and cheeks. It was cold, all right, but it could get a hell of a lot colder in these climes. The air was now as still as that inside an abandoned church though a few small flakes were still falling, lazily, like afterthoughts. Sweeping his gaze around the yard, Prophet thought that only an inch or so of the white stuff had fallen overnight, not the good two feet he'd expected.

A rare bit of good luck.

The light was growing, the eastern horizon blushing like a Lutheran bride. Peering up at the sky, Lou spied a few stars flickering wanly between the parting, ragged-edged clouds. He'd be damned if it didn't look like the sun might make an appearance once it had heaved itself out of the eastern plains. As he dropped down off the stoop and began tramping toward the big log barn, a single crow, larger than some hawks, cawed at him from atop the corral to the barn's right, shuffling its feet and sending the light dusting of snow from the corral's top slat to the ground.

The snow glittered like stardust.

Prophet threw open the barn doors and stood staring down at the dead men he'd laid out in the barn's main alley, shoulder to shoulder and hip to hip, starting just a few feet beyond the door. "Don't get up, gents," Prophet said. "It's just me—Lou Prophet, ex–Confederate freedom fighter from the hills of north Georgia." He pronounced the last two words, "Nawth Joe-jahhhh," playfully accentuating his drawl.

He wasn't mocking the dead. Prophet had just

enough hillbilly superstition in him to know to never mock a dead man and risk attracting a possible hex from the dead man's ghost or from one of the many unknown but very real hoo-doo specters that prowled the earth. In fact, even after all the men Prophet had killed or seen killed on Southern battlefields as well as out here on the western frontier, dead men still made his spine tingle.

That's why, as he went to work saddling the outlaws' horses and then hoisting the dead men over the saddles and tying cold wrists to cold ankles beneath the horses' bellies, he joked aloud and whistled while he worked. He was relieved to finally lead Mean and Ugly out of the barn and into the weak sunlight of the early morning.

Sure enough, it would be a sunny day. Sunny but cold . . .

Five horses, tied tail to tail, followed behind Mean and Ugly. Prophet led the lead horse of the second set of five by the lead mount's bridle reins.

Also in his right hand were the reins of the spare horse he'd saddled and over which no dead man lay, as well as the reins of Louisa's brown and white pinto.

The day was cold but clear. A breeze had picked up, swirling the freshly fallen snow so that it glittered in the clean-scoured air like crushed sequins. The horses clomped heavily, slowly behind him, several whickering anxiously at the dead men draped over their backs.

As Prophet pulled up in front of the roadhouse, just off its snow-dusted front porch, the front door opened. Louisa stepped out holding two steaming tin cups in her gloved hands.

She came down the porch steps and held one of the cups up to Prophet.

"Figured you might want some mud before you start for Indian Butte."

Prophet dropped the reins of Louisa's horse as well as that of the spare horse and accepted the cup. He salivated at the welcoming smell of the freshly boiled belly wash in his hand, the warm steam wafting up around him. "You're good enough to marry."

"Yes, I am," Louisa said with customary insouciance. "Unfortunately, you're not."

Prophet gave a wry chuff. "Ever the charmer." After he'd taken his first couple of sips of the coffee, blowing on its tar-black surface, he said, "Well, we got ten dead men here. I figured we'd each take five. You take the money. I'd likely get drunk and head straight to Mexico with it."

Louisa had walked back up onto the porch. Now she turned toward the yard and glanced over the rim of her own steaming cup. "Who's the calico for?"

Prophet glanced at the spare mount over which he'd strapped a spare saddle he'd found in the barn's side-shed tack room. "Well, I figured . . ."

"Is that one for me?"

Toni stepped through the open door behind Louisa. She was bundled in a thick blue wool coat too big for her, a gray wool hat, red wool muffler, and matching red knit mittens, the bright red of the muffler and mittens fairly glowing in the crisp sunshine. She held a carpetbag in one hand. On her feet were heavy, wool-lined, deerskin boots that had seen better days but would do just fine, keeping the girl's toes from freezing. One of the dead hardcases had likely left the boots upstairs, maybe the rest of the gear, as well.

"Yes, ma'am, it is," Prophet said.

Louisa frowned at the pale redhead moving up to stand beside her. "I don't understand."

"She can't stay here all by herself," Prophet said. He glanced around at the sunlit, empty yard fogged by windblown snow. "There's nothin' here now. Jiggs is dead. Besides, the windows are broken out. And whether you saw it or not, we was almost eaten by a big blue wolf one short hour ago."

"We could board up the windows before we leave," Louisa said.

"No." Toni moved up to stand beside the female bounty hunter, gazing pleadingly at Prophet. "I don't want to stay here. I can't run this place myself. I don't want to. Besides . . ." She glanced around apprehensively. "Lots of bad men in these parts. Almost as bad as them."

She pinned her gaze on the dead men riding belly down across their saddles, and she hardened her jaws in renewed anger.

"You must know some good folks in these parts," Prophet said. "I figured one of us, Louisa or me, would drop you off on the way to Indian Butte or Sundown. Some nice rancher? Mayhaps a nice farmer in need of a cleanin' girl?"

"I know few people in these parts, Mr. Prophet. The few I do are probably not looking for a maid."

"Nice people are in short supply everywhere," Louisa said to Toni. "But there must be someone you can . . . I don't know . . . trust, at least."

"Trustworthy folks are in short supply, too, Miss Bonaventure. I was hopin' I could ride with you to Sundown. I won't be alone there, at least. And I could maybe get a job working for Mr. Emory. Adam Emory. He's the banker there. Came last year from Bismarck,

I heard, thinking the town would grow with the coming of the spur line. I heard he has a nice new house but no wife and no children. I'm thinkin' he might need a girl to help him clean an' cook."

A pink flush touched her cheeks, and she dropped her eyes with vague self-consciousness.

Prophet and Louisa shared a fleeting, meaningful glance. Toni was likely hoping in the back of her mind, or maybe even in the front of it, that the new banker in Sundown might need a young wife, as well. There was nothing unreasonable about that. Many a girl had married for far more nefarious reasons than to have a shelter over her head, food on her table.

Louisa looked at Prophet, frowning. She sucked her cheeks in, not liking the situation. She didn't want the girl tagging along with her, but she saw no solution to the problem.

"If that's what you want to do," she said with a sigh. "Let's get a move on. We're burning daylight."

"Thank you!" Toni set down her carpetbag. "I'll be right back. I just have one more small bag."

When the doxie had gone back into the roadhouse, Prophet frowned curiously down at Louisa. "What's the matter with you?"

Louisa tossed the dregs of her coffee into the snow and set the empty tin cup on the porch rail. "She should ride with you."

Louisa stepped back inside the roadhouse and returned a few seconds later with her saddle, saddlebags, sheathed carbine, and blanket roll. A second set of saddlebags contained the loot the gang had stolen from the bank in Wyoming.

"Why should she ride with me?" Prophet said, still

scowling down at his comely but moody partner. "She wants to go to Sundown. I'm headin' to Indian Butte."

Louisa leaned her rifle against a porch post then moved down the steps and over to her pinto. "Indian Butte's the larger town. I saw it on the map. Sundown is practically just a water stop for the spur line. Besides, you're better with people than I am."

"You can say that again. But the banker's in Sundown. She wants to work for him."

Louisa tossed both pairs of saddlebags over her pinto's rump, behind her saddle. She shook her long, honey-blond hair over her left shoulder and began strapping her bedroll to her saddle. "She shouldn't get her hopes up about the banker."

"How do you know?"

"I just know, that's all."

"You're some authority on bankers, now, are you?"

Louisa cast him a wry look then retrieved her rifle from the porch.

"What's got your bloomers in a twist?" Prophet asked. "Don't you like that girl?"

"I don't know her enough to like her or dislike her. I just prefer to ride alone, that's all."

"She needs help, fer cryin' in Grant's moonshine! That's what you're all about—helpin' women an' children who've been savaged by outlaws like them!" He hooked a thumb over his shoulder, indicating the dead men behind him.

"I have helped her," Louisa said, glancing at the dead men. "That's all I can do. The rest is up to her."

"I don't understand you. I know I've said that before, but I'll say it again. I purely do not understand you, Miss Bonnyventure."

"It's Bonaventure," Louisa said automatically,

tightly, pulling down on the rifle with one gloved hand as she adjusted the set of her scabbard with the other. "There's no *y* in it."

Prophet chuffed and shook his head. "Just get the girl to—"

He cut himself off as Toni came back out of the roadhouse, carrying another, smaller carpetbag. "I'm ready," she said, stopping at the top of the porch steps, where her other bag leaned against a post. She stared down at Louisa, who was sliding her rifle back and forth in its oiled sheath, making sure of a quick draw if needed.

"I haven't ridden a horse in a while," Toni told her. "I've pretty much been cooped up here for nigh on three years now. You won't ride too fast, will you?"

Louisa didn't respond to that. Without even looking at the girl, she said crisply, "Get mounted up so we can get a move on, girl. Like I said, we're burning daylight!"

Toni approached the spare horse tentatively.

"I'll help." Prophet swung down from Mean's back and walked over to where Toni stood beside the spare calico, which had turned its neck to sniff the redhead curiously.

Prophet gave Toni a hand up into the saddle then handed her carpetbags up to her.

"Thank you, Mr. Prophet."

Prophet pinched his hat brim to her then leaned toward her, muttering with a conspiratorial air, "Don't mind her." He jerked his chin toward the Vengeance Queen. "Louisa never did sleep in a bed she didn't get up on the wrong side of. She'll come around once the coffee hits her veins and you're well along the trail. Sittin' still is what gets to her. As soon as she gets another man in her rifle sights, she'll be sweet as fresh apple pie."

Toni glanced at Louisa and gave the ghost of a smile.

As cool as the freshly fallen snow, Louisa scooped up the reins of the first lead horse then swung up onto her pinto's back. She turned the pinto away from the roadhouse, jerking on the reins of the lead packhorse, and said to Toni, "Come on, if you're coming."

"I know, I know," Toni said, rolling her eyes. "We're burning daylight."

Louisa touched spurs to the pinto's flanks and went loping toward the mouth of the southern trail leading away from the roadhouse. Toni glanced back at Prophet, who said, "Hang on, now!"

He slapped the calico's rump, and the horse lurched forward, lunging after Louisa. The sudden movement took Toni by surprise. She leaned far sideways over the right stirrup, throwing her left arm high. Prophet winced, thinking she was about to lose her seat. But then she managed to grab the horn and pull herself upright. She hunkered low, holding on for dear life, as the calico bounded after Louisa and the pinto.

They turned around a bend in the southern trail and disappeared behind a clump of snow-dusted brush, only the thuds of their horses' hooves and the rattle of the bit irons lingering in the cold, sunlit air behind them.

"Go with God, girl," Prophet said. "Go with God."

He didn't mean Louisa.

Chapter 8

Louisa trotted the pinto and her five packhorses down a shallow rise. At the bottom of the rise, she stopped and glanced over her shoulder. The redhead was not behind her.

At least, the redhead wasn't in sight behind her.

Louisa sighed, waited, tapping her left thumb against her saddle horn, looking around. She was in relatively open country now—the heart of a massive prairie, low, rolling hills carpeted in the fresh ermine of last night's snow. Fawn-colored weeds poked up above the fresh coat of white, like a man's tawny beard stubble through shaving soap.

The sun was high and bright, but it was also the color of unpolished brass, a customary hue for this time of year. A depressing hue, to her mind. Depressing, too, was the vast, lonely prairie over which shone the occasional small clump of grazing cattle and the straight line of some rancher's barbed wire fence, some artist's ever-thinning pencil line foreshortening into the distance of a vast, empty canvas.

Louisa hipped around in her saddle to cast a look over her shoulder. Just then a lone rider, not the girl, appeared at the crest of a distant hogback. It appeared to be a man. He continued riding up over the top of the hill and then down the near side, heading in Louisa's direction.

Fifteen or twenty feet down the slope of that hill jutted a single, spindly cottonwood. The rider drew rein beside the cottonwood, pulling his reins up tight against his chest. He was a good two hundred yards away, but Louisa thought he stiffened in his saddle a little. He sidled his horse closer to the spindly cottonwood, as though he thought he could merge his figure with that of the tree, and Louisa wouldn't see him.

"Oh, but I do see you," Louisa said softly to herself, narrowing her eyes at the distant rider. "I saw you back a ways . . . and I see you now."

When she'd first spied the man, she'd wondered if he were trailing her and the redhead. Or maybe he was only heading in the same direction. She'd kept an eye on him for several miles as he'd pretty much matched Louisa's and the redhead's pace, staying about a quarter mile behind. Now, however, he'd gotten closer. He must have gigged up his horse when he'd been out of Louisa's view, on the far side of a bluff well behind them now.

He must be intending to overtake them.

Louisa's pulse quickened slightly. But only slightly. He was only one man, after all. She'd dealt with such men before. In fact, five such men lay slumped over the saddles of the five horses tied tail to tail behind her.

Louisa swung her head around to stare off over

her right shoulder. Still no sign of the girl. What was her name again?

Toni?

Louisa cursed. She dropped the reins of the lead packhorse, hoping it was trained to stay with its reins, then swung the pinto around and galloped up and over the top of the low rise down which she'd just ridden. At the bottom of the rise, the girl was having a devil of a time trying to mount the calico. She had her left foot in the left stirrup, and she was hopping on her other foot as the calico turned slowly away from her, a devilish gleam in its eyes.

As the calico turned more sharply, snorting playfully, Toni gave a loud, groaning cry as her left foot slipped out of the stirrup. She fell in a heap. The calico gave its tail a satisfied switch then casually dropped its head and began to crop grass growing up around a cedar post from which three nasty-looking strands of barbed wire stretched.

Louisa reined up before the girl, who, sitting on her butt in the snow, leaning back on her hands, looked up at her angrily, narrowing one eye.

"He stopped to eat grass," she said bitterly. "I pulled his head up firmly, just like you said to do last time he pulled that. He didn't lift his head a bit. It was his rear end he lifted. He bucked me off! Then, when I tried to mount again—"

"That was quite a dance you two were performing." Louisa leaned forward, arms crossed on her saddle horn. She rolled her eyes slightly right to see the rider she'd seen before now riding slowly down the hill, heading toward her.

"He seemed to be enjoying it," the girl said of the calico.

Louisa sighed and stepped down from the pinto's back. She grabbed the calico's reins and pulled its head up sharply by the bridle's cheek strap. Chewing a mouthful of grass, the calico stared at her with a contrary gleam in its eyes. Louisa swatted its snout with her open palm.

"Don't think you're going to defy me, you cayuse!" she warned.

Toni heaved herself to her feet. "He's contrary."

"Of course he's contrary. He's male. Just like males of the human race, he's dumb and stubborn. You have to show him who's boss. Once he knows, when you tell him to jump, he'll ask you how high. Until then, he'll think he can do whatever he wants to you, and he'll laugh while he's doing it."

Again, Louisa swatted the calico's snout. The horse jerked its head up and whickered. The contrary gleam in its eyes disappeared and it stared at her slightly askance, warily, ears straight up.

"Mount your horse," Louisa ordered the girl.

The girl gave a grunt as she hiked her skirts and poked her left foot into the left stirrup. Holding the horn with her left hand, she swung smoothly up into the leather.

She looked down at Louisa and shook her long red hair back from her face. "You know men right well."

"Well enough to know the lot of 'em deserve to be gut-shot and left to howl."

"Wow!" Toni exclaimed. "You really don't like men. Is it because of what they did to your family?"

"Be quiet."

Louisa glanced at the rider still moving toward them down the slope of the hill to the northeast.

"I read about that," the girl persisted. "In a newspaper story about you and Mr. Prophet. I'm sorry about how your whole family was—"

Louisa snapped a sharp-eyed look of pure rage at the girl, hardening her jaws. "Shut up about that!"

The words were like a slap, causing Toni to lurch back in her saddle.

Louisa turned again to the rider. He was coming along slowly, hesitantly, head cocked to one side, holding his reins up close to his chest, clad in a bulky gray winter coat. He wore a broad-brimmed hat tied to his head by a plaid muffler, which was knotted beneath his chin.

Toni turned to follow Louisa's gaze. She gasped slightly and said, "Who's that?"

"I don't know." Louisa looked sharply up at the girl. "You think you can stay in that saddle, or do I need to tie you to it?"

"I'm going to try!" the girl said in exasperation, her pale cheeks, already rosy from the cold, turning as red as apples. She had a temper almost to match Louisa's, but the Vengeance Queen stifled any empathy she might have felt for the girl.

"See that you do."

As Toni gave an enraged chuff, like a young student unduly harassed by her schoolteacher, Louisa swung away and mounted the pinto.

"Come on!" The Vengeance Queen put spurs to her mount and loped up the hill, hearing the girl behind her clucking to her horse.

Fifteen minutes later, Louisa and her charge rode through a fringe of winter-naked trees near the edge of a frozen slough ringed with cattails. Louisa glanced behind. The rider was still on the other side of the last rise they'd crested. He wouldn't be for long. She'd been keeping a close watch on the man, for he was shadowing them, staying about a city block behind but slowly closing the gap.

Louisa turned to Toni, said, "We're going to take a little detour," then swung her mount off the trail's left side and into the trees.

"What? What're you—?"

Louisa pressed two fingers to her lips, scowling at the girl, and booted her pinto deeper into the trees, climbing a low hill. Another glance behind her told her that Toni had managed to get the calico off the trail and was shambling along with the packhorses, clinging to her saddle horn but looking as though the next stiff breeze would fling her from her saddle.

When they were roughly thirty feet from the trail, Louisa said, "This is far enough."

She stopped and curveted the pinto, so that it stood parallel with the hill and the trail below.

Toni stopped her horse several feet down the slope from Louisa.

"Come on," Louisa said, tossing her chin. "Get behind me."

"I don't understand. What're you—?"

"You don't need to understand," Louisa told her sharply. "All you need to do is what I say and keep your mouth shut."

The girl drew a deep breath, averted her offended gaze, and batted her heels against the calico's ribs. She put the calico up the slope above and behind Louisa, stopped, and turned the horse back around until it and she were facing Louisa, who was looking down toward the trail and the white expanse of the slough beyond it.

Louisa dropped the reins of the lead packhorse then removed her right mitten and shoved it into her coat pocket. She reached forward with her right hand and shucked her Winchester from its scabbard. Quietly, she pumped a cartridge into the action then off-cocked the hammer and rested the rifle across her saddle horn.

She thrust her index finger through the trigger guard, ignoring the sting of the cold air—it must have been down around ten degrees—and waited.

Shortly, the thuds of horse hooves sounded on the chill air. Growing gradually louder, they came from the right. Louisa saw the rider moving down the hill, just now entering the trees. Horse and rider were obscured by the bur oaks and box elders. The hoof thuds grew louder and louder until the man was nearly directly below where Louisa waited with the girl and the five horses packing the dead cutthroats.

The man had his eyes to the ground. When he reached the place where Louisa and the girl had left the trail, he drew back on the reins of his apple bay and said, "Whoa, now—whoa." His voice was clear in the crisp, clear air.

Holding his reins taut, he leaned out slightly from his saddle's left side, eyes scouring the trail. He turned his head toward the slope rising with the trees, following the scuff marks Louisa's horses had left in the freshly fallen snow.

When he turned his face up toward where Louisa waited on her pinto, rifle resting on her saddle horn, surprise flickered across the stranger's eyes behind a pair of small, steel-framed spectacles. "Oh, uh . . . hello, there."

Chapter 9

Louisa caressed her Winchester's hammer with her cold, bare thumb as she studied the stranger staring up at her from the trail.

He appeared an older man—late fifties, early sixties—with a thick, light gray beard and a long, slender, hawk's nose. The round, steel-framed spectacles perched on that nose slightly obscured his close-set, pale blue eyes. A rifle jutted from a saddle scabbard on the far side of the apple bay. Louisa thought she glimpsed a bulge on the other side of the man's coat, indicating a holstered hogleg.

As his eyes flitted to Louisa's carbine, which was generally aimed at him, his right, mittened hand began to slide up his thigh toward the bulge beneath his coat.

"It's a losing proposition," Louisa said matter-of-factly. "One, it's too far under your coat. Two, you're wearing a heavy mitten. Three, I don't need any more encouragement than I've already received to blow you out of that saddle, you tinhorn peckerwood."

"Holy cripes!" the man exclaimed. "That some way for a girl to talk!"

"I know of only one other." Louisa lifted her Winchester slightly above the pommel of her saddle.

The man held up a hand, palm out. "Don't get an itchy trigger finger, pretty lady. I'm not a bad person."

"What kind of a person are you?"

"I'm not sure how to answer such a question. The name's Clayton. Edgar Clayton."

"Why are you shadowing us?"

"I wasn't, uh . . . *shadowing* you, pretty one."

"Stop calling me that. It's annoying. For that alone, I'm liable to trim your wick." Louisa nudged the barrel of the carbine up from her saddle horn again, this time resting it over the top of her left arm.

"Christ, you're contrary!"

"Bein' shadowed makes me more than contrary."

"I wasn't shadowing you," said Edgar Clayton, raising his voice in frustration. "We happen to be headed in the same direction, is all. I spied you from Bear Butte when I was makin' my way cross-country to the main trail. Saw your packhorses from a distance. They made me curious. My curiosity was welcome, for this is rather dull country. There ain't much to occupy a man's thoughts while traveling through it, so I occupied myself by wondering what you could be packing over them horses—five in a row.

"As I gradually closed the gap between us, I saw that you were . . . well"—he gave an ironic smile—"two young women. Pretty young women, at that. One a blonde, one a redhead. And that you were packing"—now he frowned as he turned his gaze to the five packhorses flanking Louisa and the girl—"dead men. True enough, I see now. I'll be damned. Two pretty young women trailing five dead men. Hmmm."

Clayton returned his frowning, curious gaze to Louisa and scratched his chin. "How could that be?"

"None of your business." Louisa jerked her head. "Ride on."

"I was only trying to make polite conversation."

Louisa gave a caustic chuff and booted the pinto on down the hill, the packhorses lunging into awkward motion behind her, the dead men jerking stiffly down their sides, their hair sliding around in the breeze.

Louisa steered the pinto through the trees. When she bottomed out on the trail, she turned her mount to face the stranger, who eyed her warily from beneath the floppy brim of his dark felt hat. Louisa saw now that a thin, tightly bound gray braid slithered out from beneath his hat to hang down the back of his coat. Either his cheek was swollen or he had chaw tucked against his jaw.

"Who are you, Mr. Clayton?" Louisa asked pointedly, keeping her carbine aimed at the annoying stranger.

"What do you mean?"

"What do you do for a living? Maybe you're a bounty hunter."

"What?" Clayton widened his eyes in shock. "A bounty hunter? No, no!"

"Are you sure about that?" Louisa kept after him. "Maybe you saw five dead men . . . five men from the Gritch Hatchley bunch . . . and were sort of wondering if you might be able to wrangle them away from the two pretty females whose possession they are in. Perhaps you considered turning them in for the bounties yourself."

Clayton glanced behind Louisa at the packhorses. "Gritch Hatchley, you say? Those men are from his bunch, eh?" He whistled his amazement, shaking his head. "Imagine that!"

"Don't act so surprised. You keep up the charade, Mr. Clayton, and I'll blow you out of your saddle."

"You sure are eager to blow another man out of his saddle!"

"Don't worry, Mr. Clayton—it's not personal with her." Toni was riding down the slope, clinging to her saddle horn. When the calico stepped onto the trail, the girl pulled it up to where Louisa sat facing Clayton. "It's how she communicates regular, that's all."

Clayton raised his shaggy eyebrows in surprise at the girl. "Toni? What in tarnation are you doin' out here? You're a fair piece from Jiggs's place!"

Toni glanced at Louisa. "He is who he says he is. He's not a bounty hunter. He's not after your bounty money, Miss Bonaventure. Stand down."

Clayton shifted his gaze back to Louisa. "Bonnyventure, Bonnyventure. Where have I heard that name?"

"If not in the newspapers, then maybe in your nightmares," Toni said with subtle irony. "Some call her the Vengeance Queen. She is that and more. She rides with Lou Prophet."

"Prophet rides with me."

Toni said to Clayton, "Her and Prophet cleaned those vermin back there out of Jiggs's place but only *after* they'd killed Greta an' Grace and blew out Jiggs's lights because he balked at servin' up free whiskey and mattress dances."

"Burt Jiggs is dead?" Clayton's bearded face acquired a pained look. "Ah, that grieves me. Purely, it does." He shook his head then looked at the doxie. "Where are you off to, Miss Toni?"

"Sundown. I don't want to stay at the roadhouse. Not with Jiggs dead. He may have had his faults, but he gave me a home when no one else would. Now I reckon I have to find another roof, but I'll be damned if I'll ever work the line again."

"I don't blame you a bit."

"I didn't mean no offense, Mr. Clayton."

"None taken, none taken," Clayton said, flushing sheepishly. "I realize those times with you an' me at Jiggs's place was just business arrangements."

"You were nicer than most, Mr. Clayton."

"Why, thank you, Toni. I hope I always treated you respectful-like."

"You did. Say, how is Rose, anyways?"

"Listen, I'd love to sit here and listen to you two chin the morning away," Louisa said, cutting off Clayton's response, "but I'll be heading up the trail." She glanced at Toni. "If you're comin' with me, get your horse turned around."

Louisa started to rein the pinto around then stopped when Clayton said, "You headin' for Sundown, too, Miss Bonnyventure?"

Turning her mouth corners down, Louisa said, "It's Bonaventure. If you'd listen closely, you wouldn't hear a *y* in it. And . . . so what if I *was* heading for Sundown?"

Clayton held up his mittened hands in supplication.

"Please don't shoot me for askin'. I was just making polite conversation."

"I don't care for conversation—polite or otherwise."

"Jesus!" Clayton said.

"There you have it." Louisa booted the pinto on up the trail, jerking the packhorses into line behind her.

Toni shrugged at Clayton and then batted her heels against the calico's ribs, urging the feisty mount along behind the Vengeance Queen.

Clayton spurred his horse up beside Louisa. He rode in silence for a time. Louisa didn't look at him. She didn't want to encourage any more of his so-called polite conversation. She couldn't get rid of him short of shooting him, but she didn't have to talk to him.

Clayton drew a deep breath, filling up his chest beneath his coat. "I am hunting a man."

Louisa glanced at him sidelong. "But you're not a bounty hunter . . ."

"No, no, no. I'm hunting no bounty. Just the man. The no-account Ramsay Willis isn't worth a damn cent either alive *or* dead."

"You're hunting Ramsay Willis, your hired man?" Toni's eyes widened in shock as she rode behind Louisa and Edgar Clayton. "You two must've had one nasty fallin'-out, Mr. Clayton."

Clayton dipped his chin and bunched his lips. He narrowed his eyes until a sudden light in them shone like miniature bayonets. "We did, indeed," he said slowly, letting the words hang ominously in the chill air around his head.

He drew a deep, calming breath. "Well, I'll ride on ahead." He glanced at Louisa. "Don't want to nettle the Vengeance Queen with all my polite conversation."

He glanced back at Toni, pinched his hat brim to the girl. "Be seein' you, Miss Toni."

"See you, Mr. Clayton."

"Be well, now."

"You, too."

He touched spurs to the apple bay's ribs and galloped up the trail.

"I wonder what they had words over," Toni wondered aloud behind Louisa.

"They must've been some loud words," Louisa opined with an ironic snort.

When Clayton was nearly out of sight around the far side of the slough, riding through thick timber, Toni urge the calico up beside Louisa. She looked at the Vengeance Queen and turned down her mouth corners.

"Well, now I know it ain't just me, anyways," she said.

"What isn't just you?"

"It ain't just me you got it in for. You hate everybody equal."

Louisa glanced at her. "I don't hate you. I just . . ." She paused and stared ahead, as though searching the distance for the right words. "There's only so much one person can do for another, is all. Each one of us is alone in this world, and we might as well face up to that cold fact."

"We're alone, maybe, but that don't mean we can't be friends."

Louisa turned to her again, her face expressionless. "Most of my friends are dead. Except for Prophet. But even he has one foot in the grave."

She glanced at the sky across which low, gray clouds were sliding again, blotting out the sun. It looked as though more bad weather was on the way. She spurred the pinto into a rocking lope. "Come on," she called. "We're—!"

"I know, I know," Toni said. "We're burning daylight!"

At the same time but roughly thirty miles northeast of Louisa and Toni, Lou Prophet followed a two-track wagon trail up into a crease between two haystack bluffs and halted Mean and Ugly.

The hammerheaded dun turned his head slightly to one side, sliding an incredulous glance at the big rider on its back. Mean rippled his withers, whickering, his breath frosting in the air before his leather-tipped, whisker-bristling snout.

"Get your neck out of a hump," Prophet growled, leaning back to pull a spyglass from a saddlebag pouch. "I know you got your hat set on hay and oats and a nice warm barn. Hell, I got mine set on beer and grub and a nice warm girl. But, me?" He slid the brass spyglass from its leather sheath, dropped the sheath to his lap, and raised the glass to his right eye. "I like to look a town over before I ride in."

Slowly, Prophet adjusted the focus, bringing the little town of Indian Butte gradually into magnified view before him. "A fella—especially one like myself, who's acquired him plenty of enemies over the years—never knows what he's gonna ride *into*."

In the circular field of magnified vision, the town clarified in the broad hollow about a quarter mile away from the rise upon which the bounty hunter sat. Prophet had found himself in this neck of the upper Midwest before, so he knew a little about the place.

Indian Butte, named after the rise itself, had originated as a hide hunters' camp back before the War of Northern Aggression.

When the buffalo herds had been turned to little more than piles of bleached bone and baled hides stacked along western railheads, or natty coats sheathing the figures of eastern dandies, the hiders had disappeared from Indian Butte. A saloon/hotel remained, serving mainly wandering pilgrims and occasional cavalry patrols. It remained down there now, at a curve in the wide main drag of the small town that had grown up around it when the country outlying the town had been homesteaded off into a scattering of large and small ranches, which the town now supplied and which gave it its sole reason for existence.

Now there were a half-dozen business establishments—most either log or wood-frame affairs, hunkering close to the saloon/hotel, a sprawling, hodgepodge of a place—part log, part wood frame, part mud brick—which unoriginally was called Indian Butte Saloon & Hotel. The name was announced proudly in large, red, ornate letters brightly painted across its second story.

The hotel gave its back to the twin iron rails that curved into the town from the south, bisecting the flat area between the town and a sharply twisting creek choked in scrub brush and deciduous, winter-naked trees. The rails came from the blur of nowhere in the south and disappeared into a similar blur to the north, ending just twenty miles up the line, in a town called Devil's Lake, near which lay an Indian agency to which beef and other supplies were shipped by the new spur rail line.

A long, low depot building ran parallel to the rails in

Indian Butte, on its ragged southern end. On the rails sat a train complete with black iron locomotive with a diamond-shaped stack, a tender car stuffed to brimming with split wood, and several other cars, including what appeared to be passenger coaches, a freight car, and a stock car before the obligatory red caboose at the tail end.

The train, more substantial than what Prophet had expected, was aimed south.

That fact warmed Prophet's cold, cold heart. Genuinely cold, not just figuratively cold. He was bonedeep cold. Ticker-deep cold. In fact, he hadn't heard the old turnip beat a single hiccup in his chest since leaving the blood-washed roadhouse locally known as Jiggs's Place. He half thought the blood-pumping organ might be frozen to the texture of stone by now, just like his feet inside his fur-lined moccasins and his fingers inside his mittens and gloves.

He took a good, slow look at the town through the spyglass, sliding the piece gradually from right to left and then back one more time, bringing in the shacks, shanties, stock pens, and corrals at its ragged outer fringes. He saw no obvious signs of anyone lying in ambush for him.

He could never be too sure, however. He'd been hunting bounties a good long time, and it was only natural that he'd acquired more than a few enemies here and there. A couple of raggedy-assed-looking drifters had passed him a ways back along the trail, giving his freight load of stiff cadavers as well as himself the woolly eyeball. They hadn't said anything, just looked the dead men and himself over real good, glanced at each other in silent communication, then ridden on ahead.

Prophet hadn't been sure, but he thought he might have recognized one of them—a tall, slender fella with a droopy right eyelid. Prophet couldn't remember the man's name or where he'd seen him before. That was the problem. The fella with the sleepy eye might be trouble. He and his partner—a younger, blond man with a coyote face—might be waiting somewhere down there in Indian Butte with a rifle. Or two rifles. Maybe they'd talked to Prophet's quarry down there— Gritch Hatchley and Weed Brougham—and given them the lowdown on the bounty man heading this way with the dead men tied belly down over their saddles.

Hatchley and Brougham might be waiting to greet him with a hail of hot lead, as well . . .

Prophet drew a deep breath, wincing at the cold air chafing his tonsils, burning his nostrils, and grieving his lungs, and reduced the spyglass.

No, there were no obvious signs of trouble in Indian Butte. That didn't mean there would be no trouble, of course. But all he was doing, sitting out here where it was colder than a banker's heart, was turning more and more of him to stone and further piss-burning Mean and Ugly, though that didn't take a whole lot of doing.

Lou narrowed an eye as he glanced at the sky. Gunmetal clouds had slid over the blue bowl. There was no longer any sign of the sun. It was so gone it might have gone out. In its place, a fine snow was falling again. A building wind was swirling it around, howling morosely.

Damn Dakota . . .

"All right, Mean," Prophet said, leaning back to return the spyglass to its saddlebag pouch. "Have it your way." He clucked to the horse.

As he and Mean and the five horses bearing the dead men started down the hill toward the town, he said, "Just keep your eyes skinned. I'm too cold to die today. Why, if I died today, Ole Scratch would have to wait a good year to thaw me out before he could put me to work shovelin' coal!"

He chuckled at that. Not because the joke was funny but because he was nervous.

Chapter 10

It was the cold that was making Prophet nervous. Leastways, that's what he told himself.

As Mean and Ugly thudded his hooves down the broad main street of Indian Butte, the five packhorses trudging along behind, the big bounty hunter shivered inside his coat and looked around carefully at the buildings spaced widely apart on both sides of the trace. If he saw a man aiming a rifle at him from one of those stock pens to his left or from behind a barrel of the sprawling mercantile store on his right, and he had to throw himself from his saddle to keep from being perforated, his frozen bones would likely shatter like the delicate china you'd find in a preacher widow's cupboard.

The door of Madame Montrose's Ladies' Fineries opened. Prophet jerked suddenly back on Mean's reins, reached for the Peacemaker he'd shoved into his left coat pocket, butt forward, for a faster grab. An old woman clad in a thick mountain lion shawl poked her crowlike head out the door. She jutted her pointed chin at Prophet, her dark, beadlike eyes taking in the big bounty hunter and the dead men hanging over the saddles of the horses behind him.

Returning her disapproving gaze to Prophet himself, the crone leaned farther out the open door and expertly spat a long, black stream of chaw over the front porch rail before her and into the frozen stock trough on the other side with a dull, wet plop.

With that she gave an audible harrumph, pulled her head back into her shop, and closed the unpainted, Z-frame door.

Prophet removed his hand from over the Peacemaker's grips. The gun wouldn't have done him much good, anyway, as he'd forgotten to remove the mitten. You couldn't shoot a pistol wearing a mitten. He quickly pulled the mitten off his right hand with his teeth and stuffed it into his coat pocket. Flexing his right hand, covered in a thin, knit glove that in this severe kind of cold was almost like wearing nothing at all, he cursed the weather and this extreme northern territory, and rode on.

"Please, Scratch, get me the hell to Mexico," he muttered beseechingly as he swerved Mean and Ugly toward a two-story livery barn on his left, sitting kitty-corner to the Indian Butte Saloon & Hotel, which occupied the opposite side of the street, on the far side of a narrow cross street on which a shaggy dog was just then ripping a dead jackrabbit to bloody shreds, holding the body down with its front paws, snarling and growling, thoroughly reveling in its meal.

Raucous piano and accordion music was reverberating from inside the hotel. There was the collective, metronomic clapping of many hands, as well, and the stomping of many pairs of feet. Occasionally there rose a jubilant, victorious bellowing wail and then raucous laughter.

A single wagon was pulled up in front of the sprawling hodgepodge of a building. The wheeled contraption was sort of a cross between a chaise and a hansom cab. It was constructed of some sort of expensive-looking, dark, polished, ornately scrolled wood appointed with brass window frames and fittings, including a brass gas lamp mounted on the near side, and high gold-painted wheels. No horse stood in the traces, but Prophet bet that when one did, it was a fine one, sure enough. The empty yellow shafts sagged onto the ground that was collecting a fresh, fuzzy layer of new-fallen snow.

The fancy wagon—as fancy as Prophet had ever laid eyes on—was the only contraption sitting on the town's main street—or on any street in Indian Butte, as far as Prophet could tell from his vantage. The townsfolk appeared to have secured themselves away from the nasty weather, the purple clouds roiling over Prophet portending even nastier weather still ahead. The fragrant smoke from many warm fires peppered the bounty hunter's nose and made his bones fairly scream for warmth.

"It's a savage world, ain't it?" The rhetorical question came from the skinny oldster standing between the livery barn's open doors, pensively smoking a corncob pipe while watching the dog devour the jack, the festivities throbbing from inside the hotel just beyond it.

"You Schofield?" Prophet asked the old, pipe-smoking graybeard, whose long, blue-gray hair hung down his back from the round bear fur hat perched on his wizened head. A tangled gray beard hung to his chest. The sign above the man, tacked to the barn's second story, announced POP SCHOFIELD'S LIVERY & FEED.

The oldster turned to study the five, cadaver-burdened horses behind Prophet, pensively puffing his pipe. "That depends."

"On what?"

"On what you got slung over your horses."

"What's it look like? Dead men."

"That's what I thought they were."

Prophet swung down from Mean and Ugly's back. "Then why'd you ask?"

"A man wants to be sure."

"Well, now you're sure. I need a place to house them until the train leaves for Bismarck. The horses, too. Do you know when that will be?"

The old man seemed a little distracted. "When what will be?"

"The train leaving for Bismarck."

"Oh, that." Frowning apprehensively, the old man continued to puff his pipe while studying the dead men. "Tomorrow, I think, maybe. If them fancy Dans and the princess is ready to pull out by then, I reckon. They got dibs on the train, don't ya know."

"What fancy Dans? What princess?"

The oldster lifted his scrutinizing gaze up to Prophet, who stood a whole two heads taller than he. He looked Prophet up and down several times, nostrils flaring slightly as he drew on the pipe, smoke slithering like gray snakes from between his thin, loosely compressed lips. "The ones the senator and his son is entertainin'. They brought 'em out here to hunt. The princess, too. She's purtier'n a speckled pup. Don't look like butter would melt in her mouth. But she's got the blood fever, I hear."

"Another one, huh?" Prophet chuffed, reflecting on his comely partner.

"Another one?"

"Never mind. Did you say 'princess'?"

"Leastways, I think that's what they called her," the old man said.

"You say they got dibs on the train?"

Prophet held Mean and Ugly's reins out to the old man, who looked at them as though he were being handed a handful of fresh dog crap. Stepping back uncertainly, the oldster said, "Yeah . . . yeah . . . that's right." He took another step back. "Don't get too close to me, will ya, son?"

"Huh?" Prophet scowled down at him. "Why not?"

The old man stiffly shifted his apprehensive gaze toward the hotel and winced slightly around his pipe stem. "'Cause . . . 'cause I don't . . . I don't think you got long to live, partner."

Prophet turned his head to follow the old man's glance toward the hotel. Good thing he did, too, or the bullet that curled the air against his left cheek would have connected the canal of his right ear with the canal of his left ear, out of which his brains likely would have dribbled like corn chowder from a broken soup bowl.

Instead, the bullet slammed loudly into the livery barn's open door an eighth of a second before the ripping screech of the rifle that had fired it reached Prophet and the old man, echoing.

Mean and Ugly reared and whinnied, clawing the gray, snow-stitched air with his front hooves, his eyes wide and white-ringed. The horses behind him followed suit, whinnying shrilly and dancing, pulling against the ropes tying them to the tail of the horse in front of them.

Meanwhile, the man standing on the roof of the Indian Butte Hotel & Saloon's broad front veranda stared through his own wafting powder smoke toward the livery barn, showing his teeth as he spat a curse that couldn't be heard above the din in the building below him. He also angrily worked his Winchester's cocking mechanism, racking a fresh round into the breech.

For some reason, Prophet's first impulse was to save the old man.

"Get down, you old devil!" The bounty hunter bounded forward and hammered the heel of his left hand against the old man's upper chest.

The old man gave a squeal and, opening his mouth and losing his pipe, flew backward against the edge of the right open barn door, slamming the door back against the barn and falling to his ass with an indignant yelp.

Prophet dropped to a knee as the shooter on the hotel's porch roof loosed another chunk of hot lead, the rifle smoking and stabbing yellow-orange flames from its maw. The shooter was frustrated now, and harried. That and Prophet's sudden crouch caused that bullet to fly wide, also hammering the open barn door behind Prophet, ripping out several long wood slivers about six inches to the right of the first gouge.

Prophet rose to his feet and ran out to where Mean and the other horses were dancing in the middle of the street. Prophet grabbed the dun's reins out of the air, where they were swaying in time to the hammerhead's movements, and pulled the horse back toward him.

He reached across his saddle pommel and jerked

his Winchester '73 from the leather scabbard strapped
to the saddle's right side. As yet another round screeched
over his head to break a window of another shop
behind him, Prophet dropped to a knee, bit off his left
mitten, spat it into the street, and rammed a cartridge
into the Winchester's breech.

He quickly lined up his sights on the murky, gray-
black figure on the hotel's porch roof, whom he instantly recognized by the man's battered cream Stetson
as the droopy-eyed man from the trail. Lou drew a
sharp breath, held it, and as he started to let it out
slowly, he squeezed the trigger.

The Winchester bucked against his mackinaw-
padded shoulder.

"Damn!" he spat through gritted teeth, seeing
through his wafting powder smoke that his bullet had
merely shattered the left knee of the curly wolf on the
porch roof.

The man showed his teeth again as his left leg
jerked backward. He dropped to the porch roof on his
right knee, dropping his rifle and clutching his bullet-
torn knee with his left hand.

When he looked up at Prophet, gritting his teeth
and likely cursing like an Irish gandy dancer though
Prophet still couldn't hear above the din in the building beneath the man, Prophet drew a bead on the pale
square of the man's head—specifically, on the narrow
strip between the man's wide nose and his dark hairline, which was clear now that the man had lost his hat.

Prophet cursed as he drew a breath. He held the
breath and squeezed the trigger, enjoying the reassur-
ing kick of the Winchester's brass butt plate against his
shoulder. He also enjoyed seeing the droopy-eyed
man's head jerk backward then bob forward. When it

jerked backward again, as death spasms gripped the bushwhacker, Prophet could see the dark hole in the pale strip between the man's nose and his hairline.

The bushwhacking devil sagged forward then rolled down the sloping roof. He dropped over the roof's edge and turned a single forward somersault before crashing through the roof of the fancy carriage standing directly below him on the street. The whole carriage leaped as though with a start off all four wheels then settled back down as the bushwhacker made himself deathly comfortable inside.

"Don't tell this Georgia boy he can't shoot straight in cold weather!" Prophet bellowed. He gave a raucous laugh, throwing his head back.

That sudden movement probably saved him, also. This time from a bullet that came hurling out of the dark depths of the barn itself. The bullet trimmed the several days' worth of beard stubble along the nub of his chin before making a wet smacking sound as it drilled into the back of the head of one of the dead men hanging down the side of one of the horses prancing in the street behind him.

"There's . . . there's a second one!" rasped the old man, down on his side in the snow and straw-flecked dirt just outside the barn's open doors. "I'm sorry! They told me they'd burn down my barn and cut my ears off, shoot all the stock! I had to play along!"

Prophet ran crouching to the left open barn door. From far back in the barn's dark depths, a gun flashed.

The bark came as the bullet screeched through the air to Prophet's left and broke out yet another shop window with a dull clink followed by a man's bellowing curse. Cocking the Winchester, Prophet edged a look around the door's right side.

Again came the flash. Prophet pulled his head back just as the bullet hammered the edge of the door, flinging slivers, the loud smack making his ears ring.

Cursing, Lou snaked his Winchester around the door and fired several times quickly down the barn's dark alley, aiming generally at where he'd seen the flash. Empty cartridge casings arced over his right shoulder, smoking, clinking together in the snowy dirt behind him.

He pulled his head and rifle back behind the barn door.

He waited.

Nothing.

He glanced at the old man lying to his right, on the other side of the opening. The old man frowned, puzzled.

"You get him?" he whispered.

"Stop!" came a wail from inside the barn. "Stop! Stop!"

Prophet edged a look around the barn door. A vague shadow moved around toward the rear of the barn. There was a slice of gray light as a rear door opened. The man-shaped shadow blotted out the light for a second as the man stumbled through it and out the back.

Prophet heaved himself to his feet and strode purposefully into the barn. "Old son," he said loudly, angrily racking another round into his Winchester's breech, "we're just gettin' started!"

Chapter 11

When Prophet's eyes had adjusted to the murk inside the barn, which was relieved by only two small windows in the wall to his left, he broke into a jog. Stalled horses whickered to his right, anxious eyes glistening over stall doors.

A mule brayed raucously.

"Sorry for the noise, pards," Prophet said as he approached the rear door, which stood half-open, gray light and flecks of snow oozing through the gap. "I'll be out of your hair in two jangles of a whore's bell."

He doffed his hat and edged a cautious look around the door frame. Instinctively knowing he was about to have a third eye drilled in his forehead, he pulled his head back behind the frame. Sure enough, a bullet smashed the frame's edge, flicking sharp slivers against Prophet's cheek. At the same time, the shooter's rifle report reached his ears.

Prophet jerked his head around the door again, casting his gaze into the weedy, rubble-strewn yard behind the barn. Smoke was just then wafting and tearing on the breeze to the left of a small, dark log cabin hunched against the weather, brittle weeds jutting up high around its stone foundation. A man's head slid out away from the cabin, to where the gun smoke was being dispersed by the breeze.

Prophet saw the coyotelike eyes gazing at him from beneath a cap of matted dark blond hair, and the bounty hunter grinned malevolently, triggering the Winchester that was snugged up against his right shoulder.

On the heels of the '73's buck and roar, the blond head jerked back out of sight against the cabin with a sharp yowl. It reappeared a second later atop the short, slender figure of the man himself. The droopy-eyed hombre's coyote-faced sidekick, clad in a red and white plaid mackinaw, stumbled out away from the barn. He held his hat in his left hand, his carbine in his right hand.

He gave another yowl as he triggered the carbine into the ground near his right boot. Dropping his hat, he slapped his left hand to his bloody left cheek.

"You shot me!" he cried, stumbling farther out away from the cabin and glaring at Prophet striding up to him, holding his Winchester '73 out from his right hip. "You shot me in the face, you son of a buck!"

The blond coyote stumbled around and tried running away but his right boot came down on a stray chunk of split firewood, partly hidden by the snow-dusted grass. He tripped and dropped to his knees, clutching his left cheek with one hand, clamping his other hand against his right side, just above his shell belt.

Prophet reached down and pulled the bone-handled Colt from the man's holster and tossed it away. He pulled a skinning knife from a second sheath, on the blond man's left hip, and tossed that away, as well. He walked around to stare down at the top of the man's blond head, as the wounded ambusher writhed in pain, holding each of his wounds from which blood dribbled liberally.

White lice clung to strands of the man's matted hair that had been pressed flat against his head by his hat, revealing a small, round bald spot at the crown.

Prophet flared his nostrils. "Who are you, you gutless, bushwhackin' privy snipe?"

"You shot me!" the wounded man bellowed, lowering his head toward the ground.

Prophet lowered his '73's butt, hooked it under the wounded man's chin, and raised the man's face until the two coyote eyes glared up into his. "You shot me in the face, you big bastard!" the wounded bushwhacker bellowed, half sobbing, spitting blood.

"Couldn't have happened to a more deserving cur! Tell me who you are, who your friend is, and why you were both out to liberate my soul, or I'm going to take your own knife and go to work on ya *slow.* You'll forget all about your face and that bullet in your liver. Trust me on that one, old pard."

The blond coyote's eyes sparked with both fear and exasperation. He spat another gob of blood. "Chauncey Nettles. My pard is Arlen Piper."

"Okay . . . ?"

"You sent us both up the river, you big ape! Three years ago! West Texas!"

Prophet furrowed his brows, thinking back, sifting through the remembered faces in his mind, riffling through names. "Nettles an' Piper," he said. "Nettles an' Piper. Oh yeah . . . now I remember." The names were familiar but the face staring up at him was that of a stranger. "That was you two?"

"Sure as hell!"

"Damn, you don't look nothin' like how I remember. Maybe the sharp nose a little, and your cow-stupid eyes. But . . ." Prophet shook his head, befuddled.

"Yeah, well that's what two and a half years in the Texas State Pen, turning big rocks into little rocks, does to men, you big, ugly rebel son of a buck!"

"If you don't stop insultin' me an' the glorious South, I'm going to cut your ears off an' feed 'em to you."

The man's pain-bright eyes widened a little, as though he believed Prophet would actually make good on his threat. He spat blood to one side. He was breathing hard, panting. His left cheek looked like freshly ground beef.

"So that's what this was about."

"Of course, that's what this was about! We seen you along the trail, an' . . . You know how long Arlen an' me been wantin' to settle up for what you done to us?"

"Five, six years, I'd fathom."

"Sure as tootin'!"

"You didn't get much satisfaction, though, did you? Arlen's dead as a post inside that once-fancy buggy, and you appear to be headed that way yourself."

"Christ!" Nettles sobbed as he jerked his chin out from under Prophet's rifle butt and slowly lowered his head to the ground, jerking as he cried. "I'm gonna die!" he wailed. "I'm gonna die!"

"I'll get you to a sawbones pronto if you tell me one more thing."

Nettles stopped sobbing. That was the only way Prophet knew the ambusher had heard him. Nettles hung his head over his knees, his forehead only inches above the ground.

"Do you know Gritch Hatchley?"

Nettles wagged his lowered head.

"How 'bout Weed Brougham?"

Again, Nettles wagged his head.

Since outlawry was at times a tight fraternity, Prophet had wondered if Nettles and Piper had headed here to meet Hatchley and Brougham. Or had maybe talked to them after the former pair had come to town ahead of Prophet and told the latter about the bounty hunter headed toward Indian Butte.

Hatchley and Brougham might have suspected Prophet's dead freight was men from their own gang. In turn, they might have suspected Prophet had come to Indian Butte to add more dead men to his pack train—namely, them.

"All right," Prophet said, jerking Nettles to his feet by his coat collar. "Rise and shine, boy!"

"Oww—it hurts!"

"Stop whining!"

"You take two bullets—one to your liver the other to your cheek and see if you don't whine, you rebel swine!"

Prophet slammed his right fist into the small of the coyote-faced ambusher's back. Nettles screamed and dropped to his knees again.

"All right—hold it right there, you big galoot!"

The order had come from behind Prophet.

The bounty hunter sighed and said, "I sure wish everyone would stop impedin' my progress here in this little town." He turned to see a young man crouched over a long-barreled, double-barrel shotgun, both large round maws aimed at Prophet's belly. "I need a whiskey and a hot bath, gallblastit!"

The young man before him was maybe nineteen, possibly twenty. His fair-skinned face was nearly hairless save for a soot-stain mustache and a just as insignificant goat beard curling from his chin. He was maybe five foot seven, mean eyed, bucktoothed, and wearing a five-pointed deputy town marshal's star on his patched, butterscotch-colored coat. He wore a red wool cap and a bright green muffler.

He sucked up some snot dribbling from his nose and said, "Stop beatin' on that fella and drop that rifle, you big galoot, or I'll blow a hole through your guts big enough to drive a train through!"

"Oh, for chrissakes!" The kid had gotten so close to Prophet, wagging the shotgun barrel tauntingly beneath the bigger man's nose, that all Prophet had to do was quickly nudge the shotgun aside with his left arm.

Both barrels discharged skyward with a cannonlike roar as the kid's fingers jerked back on both triggers. Prophet grabbed the gun with his left hand and wrenched it out of the startled kid's grip.

The kid screamed as he stumbled sideways, half turning. As he did, Prophet grabbed the hogleg poking out of the kid's coat pocket. He tossed the shotgun good and far and followed it up with the old Bisley .44 trimmed with baling wire holding the cracked walnut grips in place.

"What . . . what're you doin'?" the kid cried in exasperation. "Those is my guns! I'm the deputy town marshal!"

"Yeah, well, I'm Lou Prophet, bounty hunter, you wet-behind-the-ears little polecat. You're lucky I don't take you over my knee and thrash your backside raw for wagging that gut-shredder at me like that! You try it again, and I will!"

"Ah, *Jesus!*" the kid cried, throwing up his hands and then running off in search of his weapons.

Again, Prophet jerked Nettles to his feet. The outlaw grunted, yelped, and snarled.

Prophet shoved him brusquely ahead. "Get goin'!"

Prophet stayed about ten feet behind the outlaw, in case Nettles tried anything. He didn't look capable, however. He was stumbling on the toes of his boots, leaning forward and to one side, clamping his right hand to the wound above his shell belt, his left hand to his bullet-torn cheek. Prophet thought the bullet must have torn through the flesh without penetrating the bone, or the coyote-faced bushwhacker would be fussing even more than he was.

Or he'd be dead.

As it was, he left a very clear trail of blood on the snowy ground behind him.

Prophet followed Nettles around the barn's right corner. Nettles stumbled forward then dropped to his knees, grunting and writhing. Prophet stopped near his charge and slid his gaze toward the open bar doors.

The old liveryman who'd sold Prophet down the river to Nettles and Piper was talking to another man a few years younger than the oldster, but only a few. The second man was a little bigger than the graybeard, and he wore a cinnamon beard liberally flecked with gray as well as a high-crowned, broad-brimmed Stetson. As he turned toward Prophet, Prophet saw the town marshal's star pinned to the lapel of the man's dark wool coat.

"There!" the liveryman cried, lifting an arm to point accusingly at Prophet. "There he is now. Trouble!

Pure-dee trouble—all two hundred pounds of him!
Damn near got me killed!"

"I saved your life, you old coot! You sold me down
the river!"

"Ah hell!" said the man wearing the badge, scowling
up at Prophet.

Prophet studied him closely, recognition suddenly
dawning on him. "Sheldon? Sheldon Coffer?" He
smiled. "What the hell are you doin' this far north? I
thought you was down in Nebraska. Last time I seen
you, you was sheriff of . . . of . . ."

"Cottonwood Springs," Coffer said, still scowling
at Prophet as though the bounty hunter were a two-
hundred-plus pound of dog plop someone had left on
his front porch. "I married a woman up here. Followed her up here, in fact, from down there. Didn't
know we was gonna stay, but then her pa died and left
her a little house . . . an' they needed a marshal . . . an'
Brandy was homesick, though how any woman—or
man, for that matter—could be homesick for anyplace
in Dakota Territory is beyond me."

He beetled his eyes again at the bounty hunter.

"Anyways, back to you. What in the hell are you
doing up here, Prophet? This time of year, no less! You
know one thing I thought I'd never see again when I
left Nebraska was the big peck of trouble known as
Lou Prophet, who skinned through town from time to
time, either on the heels of some dastardly owlhoot or
with one or two in tow, smellin' up the place! That was
the one thing that almost made the move this far
north worthwhile to me. In spite of the skeeter-bit
summers and the ass-grindingly cold winters, I thought
at least—at the very *least*—I'd surely never ever have to

run into *you* again and deal with the seven kinds of trouble you're always packin'. *Always!*"

"Jesus, Sheldon," Prophet said, tipping his head back and scowling down at the badge-toting Coffer. "If you ain't careful, I'm gonna get the notion you ain't happy to see me!"

Chapter 12

Marshal Coffer shaped a constipated look. He lowered his gaze to the man groaning and writhing on the ground near the bounty hunter, and shook his head. "Do you ever ride into a town without shooting a man . . . or *men* . . . within the first ten minutes, Lou?"

He glanced over his left shoulder, toward the fancy carriage parked before the Indian Butte Hotel. Several folks had gathered around the contraption with a caved-in roof. The people, mostly men, had apparently spilled out of the hotel. Several stood out on the hotel's broad front veranda, as well, staring down at the carriage through the roof of which Arlen Piper had made landfall, ruining the fancy contraption in the process.

Indignantly, Prophet said, "I'm the injured party here, Shell!"

"Huh?"

"I can't help it if within the first ten minutes I ride into a town and someone . . . like these two low-down, dirty, back-shootin' dogs . . . tries to send my soul haulin' its freight to the golden clouds. That one over there in the fancy carriage tried to do so from the roof of the hotel. This here back-alley rattler tried to do it from inside the barn. Piper must've been the better shot—that's why he took the first one. This little coyote-faced jasper wasn't much of a shot at all—fortunately for me. He must have been Piper's backup. Not much of a backup. If he had been, you'd be hauling me off to get fitted for a wooden overcoat, Sheldon!"

The bounty hunter glared at the town marshal scowling at him skeptically. "Where's the law an' order in this town? When a feller can't ride into your fair town without gettin' shot at within the first ten minutes, *you* got a *problem*!" He pulled his head back and to one side, narrowing a curious eye. "Brandy, did you say?"

Coffer frowned. "Huh?"

"The girl you married. Her name is Brandy?"

"That's right." Coffer's frown became a defensive scowl. "So what?"

Prophet grinned insinuatingly.

Coffer's scowl deepened, and his face turned redder than it already was from the cold. "She was a singer! And that's all she did. She sang!"

"Oh, I see, I see," Prophet said, chuckling. "Calm down, Shell, I didn't mean to climb your hump."

Running footsteps sounded from the side of the barn. Prophet glanced behind him, raising his Winchester defensively, as the young deputy ran around the barn's front corner. He stopped abruptly, slipping in the snow. Breathless and red-faced from exasperation, he jutted his chin and pointed an angry finger at Prophet.

"There he is! There he is, Uncle Shell! The man causin' all the trouble!"

"Easy, Ham," Coffer said.

"He threw my guns away!" the kid said, spittle flying from his lips and snot stringing from his nose.

"Stand down, Ham," Coffer said, holding up his right, thickly gloved hand, palm out. "Everything's under control." He glanced at the coyote-faced Nettles on the ground near Prophet. "That fella there tried to clean Lou's clock."

"No thanks to the liveryman." Prophet had turned his angry gaze to the old man sort of shrinking back against the edge of the open barn door, looking as sheepish as a schoolboy who'd put a snake in the girl's privy. "Pop Schofield, I take it?" He glanced at the sign stretching across the barn, just over the big open double doors.

Coffer turned to the long-haired, bib-bearded old man. "What's this all about, Pop?"

"I would very much like an answer to that question myself, Marshal Coffer!" The speaker was one of the two nattily dressed young men striding toward the livery barn from the direction of the hotel, where several men in heavy fur hats and coats were still inspecting the wreckage of the fancy carriage while two others wrestled the slack body of Arlen Piper out of the carriage's busted door, from beneath the collapsed roof.

The young man who'd spoken hardened his clean-lined jaws and hooked a thumb over his shoulder. "The carriage. It's ruined!" He spoke with what Prophet recognized as a phony English accent, common among the moneyed elite.

He appeared in his early twenties with a delicate,

even-featured face some might call handsome though
in a feminine sort of way. His pale, flawless skin appeared to have never known the caress of direct sunlight. A dark red mustache of the handlebar variety
complete with waxed ends and a carefully trimmed
goatee made the popinjay resemble a pretty young
lady with a glandular vexation—or whatever caused
facial hair on females. The man's little eyes appeared
yellow.

The man beside him, slightly taller and leaner,
though dark haired and mustached, was the same cut
of man—a preening dude hailing from what he himself
would call "good blood" and toting around a corncob
stuck so far up his pale, bony behind that a sawbones
could see it when he examined his tonsils.

The first young man, who appeared the alpha of
this two-man sissy wolf pack, turned angrily to the marshal. "Did you hear me, Marshal? That carriage—that
expensive carriage—is ruined! It was my father's gift
to the countess!" He turned his fiery yellow gaze on
Prophet. "Is this big ruffian the culprit?"

"Who the hell is this?" Prophet asked Coffer.

The young man jerked his head back, as though
he'd been slapped. His lower jaw hung in shock.
"*Excuse* me? Who the hell are *you*?"

"The one you just called a big ruffian. It's true I
crap a bigger pile than you standin' there, but you best
talk nice and grown-up when addressing me, Dan, or
I'll drag you off to the nearest woodshed for a lesson
in manners."

"Oh, you think so, do you?"

"I think so."

The young man's face turned as russet as a baked
yam. His nostrils flared to double their normal size.

Stepping forward, he removed his thick glove from his right hand, clenched that hand into a tight fist, and grimaced as he threw that fist up from behind his right hip toward Prophet's face.

"Oh hell!" Coffer lamented.

Prophet had seen turtles withdraw from their shells faster than this kid could throw a punch. He had ample time to raise his left hand up in front of his left cheek.

Fancy Dan's fist slammed into it. Prophet closed his fingers around it, squeezed.

Fancy Dan yipped, rising onto the toes of his high-topped fur boots. His face turned even redder, puffing up, as the fop stared in anguish at his hand, the little bones of which Prophet ground together in his own fist, bunching his lips, his eyes sparking angrily.

"Prophet!" Coffer barked.

"You ever want to use this hand again, Junior?" Prophet asked the fancy Dan.

"Release me, damn you," the kid chortled, tightly. He rolled his eyes to one side, glancing back at the second fancy Dan—the one with the dark hair and dark beard, the one who appeared just now like he'd swallowed something he not only couldn't digest but which was trying to claw its way out of him.

"Leo!" said the fancy Dan whose hand Prophet was grinding. "Do . . . do something . . . before he breaks my *hand*!"

Leo stumbled forward, eyes blazing, jaws hard. "Unhand him! Unhand him this instant or . . . or you . . . you'll be tangling with me, as well!" He raised his fists, crouching, feinting.

Prophet squeezed the fancy Dan's fist harder, grinding the bones more aggressively. His victim yipped louder. "No! Stay . . . stay back, Leo! This devil's going to break my hand!"

The young peacock's knees buckled as Prophet angled his hand back toward the his face, threatening to snap his wrist, which he could do with one small jerk toward the young man's chin. It would be as easy as snapping a dry twig.

"Release him this instant!" demanded Leo, hoarsely.

"Prophet!" Coffer bellowed. "Let him go, you crazy rebel!" He pulled up a flap of his coat and shucked a Smith & Wesson Model 3 .44 revolver from a black leather holster.

Prophet stopped grinding the blustering fool's bones together. He shoved the kid's fist as well as the kid himself straight backward. The yellow-eyed, red-mustached dandy gave a cry as he stumbled, twisted around sideways, and fell to a knee.

"Big galoot!" he cried, clutching his injured hand in his left one, glaring up at Prophet.

"You're lucky I didn't twist that little hand of yours around behind your back and shove it up your behind. The curly wolf who caved in your fancy wheeler tried to perforate my hide. So I shot him. I didn't have no say in where he landed."

"Are you all right, Rawdney?" Leo asked, dropping to a knee beside the groaning fop. "Let me see your hand. Do you think it's broken?"

"It ain't his wheeler," Coffer told Prophet, holstering the Smith & Wesson. "It's the princess's."

Rawdney shoved the doting Leo aside and turned a glare on the marshal. "How many times do I have to tell you she's not a princess, you old hooplehead? She's a *countess*!" He turned his glowering, hard-jawed stare at Prophet. "Countess Tatiana Miranova. Daughter of

Count Ilya Miranova, who, along with his daughter the countess, are guests of my father and myself!"

"I'll be damned!" Prophet said, ironically. "Imagine that. The count and countess himself! Guests of yourn!"

The dandy heaved himself to his feet, again brushing aside his overly devoted pal, Leo. He gritted his teeth at Prophet once more. "You will be paying dearly for that carriage, you rube. As well as for this!" He held up his hand, the fingers curled toward the palm like claws. "Mark my words!"

Still holding his injured hand against his chest, like a delicate kitten, he glanced at Coffer again. "Why don't you do your job, Marshal, and lock this brigand up? He assaulted me!" He jerked his head toward Prophet.

Coffer turned to the bounty hunter and, a vague humor gleaming far back in his brown eyes, said, "I'll get right on that, Mr. Fairweather. Yes, sir, I'll turn the key on this big rebel—you can count on that. Awful cold out here. You best get back inside the saloon, where it's warm. Have you a toddy on the town of Indian Butte."

Rawdney stared at him, vaguely incredulous, as though wondering if he were being made fun of. Maybe it was too cold for him to wait to come to a conclusion, or maybe his hand hurt too badly. Whatever the reason, he gave a shrill curse, wheeled, lips quivering with rage, and stumbled back in the direction of the hotel.

Leo shot an angry look between Prophet and the town marshal. Then he, too, wheeled and ran to catch up with Rawdney, placing a hand on his friend's arm, guiding him gently back to the hotel. Staring after them, Prophet's gaze flicked toward the sprawling building's high front porch. His gaze started back toward the two popinjays then shot back to the porch itself.

Or, rather, to the rather well-set-up young lady standing atop it, staring out over the front banister toward Prophet. In fact, as the bounty hunter stared at her, he could see that her large, lustrous, ink black eyes were riveted on him. As cold as it was, his belly warmed instantly, and he felt a tingling in his frozen knees. For the first time in a long while, he felt his heart beating, sort of hiccupping inside his chest.

She was a delicate little thing, maybe five feet two inches tall. The heavy but stylish cold-weather clothes she wore made her appear even smaller inside them. Still, he could see that behind her sleek black bear fur coat was the rise of an ample bosom. She wore black fur boots that rose to her knees, clad in what appeared to be heavy deerskin lavishly embroidered. The breeches were probably lined with fleece.

On the girl's beautifully shaped head was a large, black fur hat, the fur ruffling in the snow-laden breeze, the snow dusting it lightly. Her face was delicately carved beneath the large topper—vaguely heart shaped and boasting a short but assertive nose and plump red lips sheathing a wide, sensuous mouth. Even from this distance, Prophet could tell that the lashes of her button-black eyes were long and exquisitely curved.

"Holy moly," Prophet heard himself wheeze out on a breath he didn't realize he'd been holding until now as he released it, growing a little faint from lack of oxygen.

"What is it?" Coffer said.

"Not what. Who?" Prophet shaped a friendly half

smile at the chocolate-eyed little siren standing atop the porch. "Who, Coffer, is *that*?"

Prophet thought the little goddess was about to smile back at him. He thought he detected the faintest parting and curving of her lips. But then the two popinjays, one crouched over his hand, mounted the veranda steps, and she moved over to the top of the steps, saying something to the two dandies that Prophet couldn't hear from this distance though the din in the hotel had gone silent.

He could see her lips moving, though. Seeing them moving, he couldn't help imagining how plump and full and pliable they would feel, mashed against his own.

"Oh, that?" Coffer chuckled. "That there is the owner of the carriage you destroyed. Senator Fairweather gave it to her. It's hers, all right. Ever since that party came up here by train from Bismarck, whenever they been in town and not huntin' out in the hills, she's been shuttled around in that fancy contraption, just like the queen of Sheba, don't ya know. Not no more, though!" The marshal laughed again. "I reckon you took care of that, Lou!"

He turned to look in amazement at the big, Southern bounty hunter standing beside him. "My God, man, wherever you go, destruction follows, don't it? Wherever you go! Sort of like the plague. Walkin', talkin' smallpox is what you are. And here I thought by followin' my dear Brandy all the way up here to this frozen pimple on the devil's backside, I'd gotten shed of you once and for all!"

"Ah, throw a rein on the drama, Shell." Prophet dipped his chin to indicate the hotel. "That there— that's the countess, you're sayin'?"

"That there's the countess, I'm sayin'," Coffer said, following Prophet's gaze again to the hotel. The girl was just then standing with the two fancy Dans in the middle of the porch. She held Rawdney's hand in her own two mittened hands and was looking down at it, moving her mouth, speaking to him. Likely consoling the wretched little rube.

The bounty hunter's wild heart fluttered once again. Oh, how he would love to hear the music of the girl's voice in his own ears, preferably in a room of their own, a fire dancing in a big stone hearth . . .

Almost as though she'd read his thoughts, the countess turned her head to glance over the porch rail at Prophet once more. Seeing him staring back at her, she turned away quickly, but not before—had that been a slight flush rising in her perfect, alabaster cheeks?

One of the other, larger men standing on the porch opened one of the hotel's two front doors, and the girl and the two fancy Dans walked into the hotel and disappeared, making Prophet's heart quicken with longing. The big man who'd opened the door for them followed them inside, and the door closed behind them all.

"The countess Tatiana Miranova," Coffer said, staring at the porch on which only big, bearded, fur-clad men stood, smoking and talking. There was something soldierly in the big men's bearing. "Daughter of Count Ilya Miranova," the marshal continued. "Some mucky-muck from Russia. Big, noble family, kin to the country's head honcho, I hear tell, though, uh, not in those exact words.

"I've heard the count talking of a night over there in the saloon, at the end of their huntin' days. Little bearded blowhard. The countess, though, she seems a sweet little thing though I hear she's got some sand in her. Loves to hunt wolves and grizzly bears. Guts and skins 'em herself.

"The count and countess and their entourage—I've heard them big men who shadow both her and the old man are Cossacks—tough, half-wild tribal fighters from the back country over there—are here as guests to that squarehead whose paw you mangled. And the squarehead's old man—Wilfred Fairweather—is territorial senator from Bismarck. Rawdney's his son. Leo's Rawdney's personal assistant, though I don't even want to think what he assists him with. In my opinion, men shouldn't pester each other like that!"

Coffer chuckled.

Continuing, he said, "Apparently, Wilfred Fairweather met the count in Washington at some big powwow the president held at the White House. Turned out the count was itchin' to come over to the New World and hunt the game we got in these parts. He wanted to shoot buffalo but since they all been shot out, he and the kill-crazy little countess settled for grizzly bears, wolves, elk, wildcats, moose, birds of all feather, and anything else they see out in the hills and creek bottoms around Indian Butte."

"Christalmighty," Prophet said, shaking his head as he imagined the bloodbath. He hated sport hunting in the worst way possible. Animals should die only for their meat, not so some popinjays could mount their heads on parlor walls, showing off for their friends. "How long they been here?"

"A week. They was out farther west first, but then they heard we got some nice-sized game in these parts, so they came up here. The senator's got him his own private train coaches—parlor cars, sleepers, gambling car, dining car. You name it, they got it."

"When are they pullin' out?"

"Tomorrow, I hear tell. Likely shot all the game out of this part of the territory, the square-headed devils. Those of us who live here will probably have to live on jackrabbit for the rest of the winter."

Prophet blew a sigh of relief at his good fortune. "Do you think a raggedy-heeled fella like myself could board that train, Shell?" He winced. "Even if I wrecked the little princess's purty wagon?"

Coffer chuckled. "I reckon you'll have to ask them." He chuckled again, as though imagining the scene of Prophet getting his hat handed to him by those big, bearded Russians Prophet had seen inspecting the wagon and milling on the hotel porch.

"Crap," Prophet said.

"Not to worry, Lou," Coffer said, clamping a hand on the big bounty hunter's shoulder. "The spur line has one of its own passenger cars in that train's combination. For lowly folks like yourself. You tell me if Birdie down at the depot gives you any grief over buyin' a ticket." He winked. "I'll make sure you're aboard that car when it's time to head south. Trust me on that one, ole son!"

Coffer laughed.

When he finally sobered, he scowled at Prophet and said, "So . . . tell me, Lou—what brings you here, anyway, so late in the year? You tellin' me you was after him an' the gent in the princess's wagon?" He glanced at Nettles slumped forward against the ground, turning the snow pink beneath him.

"Piper an' Nettles?" Prophet shook his head. "Pshaw! I got bigger fish to fry here in Indian Butte." He shuttled his gaze around the ragged-looking settlement growing darker now as the afternoon waned and the snow continued dancing on the chill breeze.

Gritch Hatchley and Weed Brougham.

Where in hell did he suppose they were holed up? Had to be here somewhere, either waiting out the weather to head north or for the train to head south. Just like Prophet himself was. If they intended to hop the train, little did they know they'd have a two-hundred-plus-pound, ex-Confederate, bounty-hunting chaperone . . .

Again, Prophet shook his head. "No, I got much bigger fish to fry here in Indian Butte, Shell. Much bigger."

"Well, that's good."

"Why's that?"

Coffer placed a boot on Nettles's shoulder and shoved the coyote-faced bushwhacker over on his side. Nettles gave no resistance. He lay staring straight up at nothing, lips slightly parted.

"Oh, Lordy me!" Ham intoned, leaping back with a start.

"This one here's as dead as the other one over there!" Coffer said.

Chapter 13

"Thank God," Toni said as she and Louisa rode up out of a dry wash and saw the town of Sundown sitting along the tracks before them.

It was getting late. The sun would be gone in another hour. A light snow was falling out of a moody, purple sky.

"Here we are," Louisa said, sizing up the town before her. "End of the line."

The town, if you could call the small, rough collection of tracks along the twin spur line rails a town, didn't look all that welcoming. There were maybe half a dozen shacks and shanties crouched around a few two-story business establishments and a long, low, wooden structure hugging the rails. That was likely the depot station.

Near the depot was a large pile of split cordwood for feeding the locomotives that passed through Sundown, as well as a big wooden water tank on high stilts, also for feeding the trains. The town was so new that as Louisa and Toni approached it from the north along the trail that just ahead became the town's main street, Louisa could smell the pine resin in the green wood the place had been built from.

Squinting against the fine grains of snow catching in her eyelashes, she could see a broad, unpainted building on the far end of town, on the street's right side. A sign poking into the street identified it, easily the largest building in town, as the TERRITORIAL HOTEL. On the town's near end, stood the train depot and a livery barn and corral just beyond it. The small, stone, cracker box–like structure of the Stockman's Territorial Bank sat just beyond the livery barn.

Aside from three other, much smaller business buildings between the depot and the hotel, there were five or six small, randomly arranged frame houses and a couple of log huts. That was pretty much the entire town of Sundown. All around it stretched flat, nearly featureless prairie—fawn-colored grasses slowly being consumed by the snow.

"I'm surprised this place has a bank," Louisa muttered half to herself.

"It'll grow," Toni said, riding off Louisa's right stirrup. "It's along the spur line now, so it'll grow. Good grazing country up here. The country's growing. This will be a wealthy place one day." There'd been a definite note of hopefulness in the girl's voice as she stared ahead at the town into which they now rode.

"Yeah, well," Louisa said, leaving her opinion of the place's future at that. She checked down the pinto as well as the five packhorses behind her in front of the small, wood-frame train depot on her left. "You go on ahead, stable your mount at the livery barn."

Toni stopped the calico. She'd gotten pretty good with

the horse. It minded her without balking overmuch, without fighting the bit. Turning to Louisa, she said, "What're you gonna do?"

"I'm going to see when the next train is due." She paused, then looked at the girl. "You flush?"

Toni's cold cheeks turned a shade darker red, and she glanced down at her saddle horn. "I'll make do."

"Here." Louisa bit off a mitten and reached into a pocket of her denims. She pulled out a coin and handed it over to the girl.

Toni shook her head. "Like I said, I'll make do."

"You're going to need a roof over your head tonight, food in your belly. Until you can hogtie that banker, anyway."

"I'll see about getting a job," Toni retorted bitterly, offended by the Vengeance Queen's irony.

"You can see about getting a job tomorrow. Until then, take this." Louisa shook the hand in which she held the coin.

Drawing a deep breath, Toni reluctantly held out her own mittened hand. Louisa pressed the coin into it. Toni drew it to her, looked at it. She looked up at Louisa, frowning. "This is a double eagle. I can't take twenty dollars from you."

"You're not taking it from me." Louisa glanced at the dead men behind her. "You're taking it from them." That was a lie. The double eagle was from the jingle in her own pocket.

Toni studied Louisa critically. Finally, she closed her mitten around the coin, slipped it into a coat pocket. "I'm obliged, Miss Bonaventure."

"No reason to be." Louisa glanced up the street. Saddled horses stood at the hitch rack fronting the hotel. Returning her gaze to the girl, she said, "Watch yourself. Men here." But then, Toni knew all too well what that meant.

The girl nodded, pressing her lips together. She batted her heels against the calico's ribs and rode on up the gradually darkening street.

Louisa swung down from the pinto's back and tied it and the lead packhorse to the hitchrack fronting the depot. The brick cobbles surrounding the humble building were lightly snow dusted but cleared here and there by the swirling breeze. A mountain lion hide was tacked to the building's front wall, just left of the door. The head had been left on, and it snarled, glassy-eyed, at Louisa, long curved fangs showing inside its open mouth.

The shingle announcing simply SUNDOWN DEPOT ratcheted back and forth on its rusty chains, beneath the building's broadly overhanging eaves.

Lifting her gaze to the stovepipe protruding from the shack's shake-shingled roof, the Vengeance Queen saw that the place was occupied though it didn't otherwise appear to be. Smoke lifted from the pipe to get pressed low against the roof by the breeze before it was quickly torn and dispersed. It was perfumed with the smell of cedar and pine.

Louisa stepped up onto the brick platform, removed her hat and muffler, and shook her hair so that it spilled loosely about her shoulders, shedding the snow that had clung to it. She stepped to the front door and turned the knob.

The door squawked open on unoiled hinges. She stepped inside, slowly pushed the door closed behind her, latching it. As she did, she instinctively stepped to one side, not allowing the light from the door to outline her.

A soft whistle sounded to her left. Louisa jerked her startled gaze to see two men sitting on the bench on that side of the door, running the length of the front wall. They had all manner of gear, including saddles and saddlebags, piled around them. They wore their heavy coats open, and the larger of the two, a tall, fat, bearded, blue-eyed man in a quilted elk-hide coat, wore a battered black felt hat. The smaller man—lean and wiry and rolling a matchstick around between his thin lips—was bareheaded, his hat hooked over the horn of the saddle resting on the bench beside him.

"Look at that, French," said the little man. "Ain't she purty?" He smiled at Louisa. It was more of a leer, revealing one missing front tooth.

The big man, French, shoved his saddle away, clearing a spot on the bench to his left. He patted the cleared spot on the bench. "Come on over here and sit down beside me, pretty girl. If you're here for the train, you got a long wait. Ain't gonna get here till to-morrow afternoon, most like. And *that's* only if the tracks don't get blocked by the snow."

"So a train is on the way?" Louisa asked hopefully, ignoring the leers in the men's eyes. Or trying to, anyway. She almost succeeded despite the way their eyes turned glassy as they raked her up and down.

"Certain-sure," said the smaller man, his eyes on the rise where her breasts were pushing out her coat. "Might as well take a load off." He cleared a small spot beside him on the bench and grinned. "Sit down beside me. French ain't had a bath since last Fourth of July. He stinks to hog heaven!"

"That's a lie an' you know it, Cully," accused French, his big, bearded face turning crimson. "I took a bath just the other day over at the Territorial." He glowered at Cully. "Just before Tutwiler kicked us out on account o' you cuttin' that half-breed swamper he had workin' for him!"

Louisa rolled her eyes at the seedy pair of hardtails—likely ranch hands laid off for the winter and heading toward warmer climes. They'd spend the winter fighting, gambling, getting drunk, and mistreating the doxies they'd badly underpay.

Louisa glanced at the ticket cage to her right. It was vacant, though what appeared to be a solitaire hand was laid out on the pine counter just inside, near a whiskey bottle and a shot glass. A quirley lay at the edge of the counter, its burning coal hanging over the edge, sending a curl of gray smoke into the air of the shadowy niche that also housed a telegraph key.

Louisa turned to the two men now arguing on the bench to her left, and said, "Where's the stationmaster? Hey, you two—pipe down! Where's the—?"

"Here, I'm here!"

Louisa turned to see a stocky man with longish dark brown hair struggling through a trackside door in the far back wall of the place. He, too, wore a thick beard. Louisa judged him to be in his late thirties, early forties, once a hard worker, judging by a layer of thick muscle, but gone to fat. He had an armload of split wood in his arms, which were clad in a grimy striped blanket coat with a torn and dangling pocket.

He drew the door clumsily closed behind him and strode into the waiting room, shivering, shaking his long, greasy hair back away from his face, revealing his doughy, rawboned features including a nose like a door handle.

He shivered, cursed the cold, and walked over to the big potbelly stove sitting in the middle of the room. As he did, he glanced at Louisa.

He glanced away and then glanced back at her again. He stopped dead in his tracks and looked her up and down. His eyes widened, turned glassy, glistening in the gray light angling through the two windows in the wall behind the pretty, hazel-eyed blonde.

Cully, who had stopped arguing with French, chuckled seedily. "Me an' French—we got us a new friend, Jerry. See what happens when you leave?"

"Somethin' special happens," French said, his voice low but teeming with sleazy laughter.

Jerry's coal black eyes raked Louisa up and down, a smile gradually growing on his mouth.

"French and Cully tell me a train is due tomorrow afternoon," Louisa said to Jerry. "That right?"

Jerry's eyes brightened even more. He smiled even wider. He turned away from Louisa and dropped the wood from his arms into the bin beside the stove, glowering at French and Cully and saying, "This ain't no hotel. If you two are gonna hole up here till the train pulls in, you can at least split wood and keep the stove fed, damnit!"

He turned to Louisa again, and his unctuous smile was back in place, his eyes roaming across the swollen top of her coat. He brushed his hands together. "What's your name, pretty lady?"

Louisa smiled stiffly. "The train."

Cully chuckled through his teeth. French gave a snort.

"What about it?" Jerry said.

"One is pulling through here tomorrow afternoon?"

"That's right. If the weather holds."

"Can I purchase a ticket?"

"Why, sure you can," Jerry said, planting his fists on his hips. "But first you gotta give me a smile."

Louisa stared at him blankly.

Cully chuckled through his teeth again. Again, French snorted.

"All right, all right," Jerry said, glowering at Louisa as he pushed through a Dutch door to enter his cage. "You're purtier'n a speckled pup, but you sure are a sour little thing. A pretty girl should cheer a place up. A storm's on the way, don't ya know. That's what the old man said."

Staring through his cage now, over the playing cards, whiskey bottle, and shot glass, he plucked the quirley off the counter and stuck it in his mouth. He slid his eyes from Louisa to Cully and French, now sitting behind Louisa as she stood in front of the cage.

"The old Injun who lives down by the creek says so," Jerry continued. "That old dog-eater's bursitis starts actin' up somethin' fierce when a storm's on the way. He goes through twice as much wood in his old shack, keepin' the place warm. When he starts howlin' about his bursitis, you know you're in for one hell of a storm!"

"I'm sorry about your Indian's bursitis," Louisa said. "Tell him to grind up some mint and lavender and liberally apply the paste to his joints. Now, it's getting late and I have horses to tend, so I'd like to purchase a ticket for Bismarck and be on my way."

Jerry sat on the high stool fronting the counter inside the cage and squinted his eyes as he took a deep drag off the quirley. "Bismarck, eh?"

"Right."

"What you got goin' in Bismarck, pretty lady?" Another sleazy smile tugged at the agent's mouth corners as he blew smoke out his nostrils at Louisa through the cage.

"That's none of your business, Jerry. Just the ticket, please."

"Just the ticket, huh?"

Cully and French snorted and squirmed around on their bench. Louisa heard one of them take a pull from a bottle. He chuckled, choking a little on the tangleleg, and drew the bottle down sharply, coughing. The other man squealed hoarsely.

Louisa removed her mittens and gloves and set them on the counter. "Just the ticket."

"All right," Jerry said, drawing on the quirley again and holding the smoke in his lungs as he said, "that'll be twenty-five dollars."

"Twenty-five dollars?" Louisa shuttled her gaze to the various ticket prices chalked on a board on the cage to her left. "The board says it's three seventy-five to Bismarck."

"Oh, that," Jerry said. "That's summer prices. I ain't gotten around to changin' 'em yet. Yeah, in winter the cost goes up. You know—on account o' the weather an' such. Costs more to run a train in the winter."

"It sure does, that's true!" laughed Cully.

There was the sloshing sound of either him or French taking another drink from the bottle.

Louisa pulled her mouth corners down.

"Is that too much?" Jerry asked.

"I don't have twenty-five dollars," Louisa lied. She looked up at him again and injected feigned beseeching into her gaze. "Please, Jerry. I have to get to

Bismarck. I can't afford twenty-five dollars, but I have to get to Bismarck just the same. Oh, please, Jerry— you *must* help me!"

"Help you?" Jerry said, his eyes brightening like those of a wolf smelling fresh meat.

Chapter 14

Louisa raised her brows in mock helpless pleading. "Please, Jerry. You have to help me. I have to get to Bismarck!"

"Of course, of course," Jerry said, nodding slowly, eyeing her cagily. "How could I not help such a purty girl in need? Such a pretty girl on the run—now, ain't that right?"

"On the run?"

"Yeah. Maybe from a husband out on some ranch around here. You got mail-order bride written all over you, sweetheart."

"She does got mail-order bride written all over her!" French said, slapping his thigh with the sudden realization. "I'll be damned but you're good, Jerry!"

"Sure, sure," Jerry said. "I know how it goes. You prob'ly came in on the train this summer. Up from Bismarck or God knows where. Answered the ad of some lonely rancher. Married up with him. Ate his food, enjoyed the shelter he put over your head. But now when it starts turnin' a little cold, an' maybe he slapped you around a little bit, teaching you how it is, you think you can just turn tail and run back home to Ma an' Pa—leavin' the poor old rancher high an' dry!"

Louisa stared at him, as though both amazed and taken aback by his insightfulness. "How . . . did you . . . know?" she cried softly, making her upper lip quiver.

"This ain't my first rodeo," Jerry said. "I seen it all."

"Please, Jerry . . ."

"I'll tell you what I'm gonna do," Jerry said.

"What's that?" Louisa asked, again hopeful.

"I'm gonna go ahead and let you pay the summer price for the ticket to Bismarck."

"Oh, thank you so much, Jerry. I can't tell you how obliged—"

Jerry held up his hand. "Hold on, hold on!"

Louisa feigned a puzzled look.

Jerry stared at her darkly, his lips fashioning a dark smile. "But you're, uh, gonna have to stay right here with me an' Cully an' French tonight. Gonna be a long, lonely, stormy night, don't ya know."

"Sure is," French said, walking slowly up behind Louisa. He was a big man, Louisa saw now, glancing over her left shoulder at him. Almost as tall as Lou, but with a large, round gut. His neck was as thick as a bull's neck, and the hands he held down at his sides were the size of hams. "Gonna be a long, cold, lonely night. We could use a girl to purty the place up a bit."

"Uh, fellas," Cully said after clearing his throat behind French.

Ignoring him, French stopped behind Louisa and placed his hands on Louisa's shoulders. He drew her back against him. He closed his hand over her shoulders.

"Wait," Louisa said. "I . . . I really . . . I don't think this is at all fair. It's not right to take advantage of a poor, defenseless young woman down on her luck!"

"Oh, it's fair, all right," Jerry said, rising from his stool and pushing back out through the swinging Dutch door. "You be good to us or we'll kick you out in the cold. If the man you're runnin' from catches you, he'll likely bullwhip you and leave you out in the snow to die slow, wolves feedin' on your purty parts. We're doin' you a favor. You just gotta pay us back, see."

"Oh God!" Louisa cried in a pinched, little-girl's voice. "Please don't let him find me!"

"Don't you worry, purty one," French said, pressing his nose to Louisa's neck and taking a long, deep, animallike sniff. He himself smelled like sour sweat, stale whiskey, and cheap tobacco. "We'll protect you. You'll be right here. With us."

"Fellas," Cully said again, tentatively.

Again, French and Jerry ignored him. Jerry beckoned to French, grinning, then walked toward a closed door just beyond the cage.

French closed his hands even more tightly on Louisa's shoulders, turned her away from the cage, and, keeping his hands on her shoulders, shoved her toward the door through which Jerry now stepped.

"Please don't do this," Louisa said, making her voice quaver. "All . . . all I want is a ticket to Bismarck!"

"We'll get you that ticket to Bismarck," Jerry said. "In due time, li'l girl!"

"Uh, fellas . . ." came Cully's voice once more, pitched with singsong warning.

French pushed Louisa into the room, which appeared to be Jerry's private, sour-smelling sleeping quarters with a small cot covered in animal skins, a chest of drawers, a washstand, and not much else. A lamp burned low on the chest, casting a weak, fluttering light about the small room. Jerry turned to Louisa, grabbed the front of her coat, spun her around to put her back to the bed, then slammed the back of his hand savagely against her left cheek.

The scream that vaulted out of her throat was as real as the sudden blow that sent her sailing backward onto the lumpy cot.

Her head struck the cot's hard wooden frame, and her vision dimmed. Her cheek was on fire. She could feel the welt swelling hotly. She lifted her head. As she did, she looked up to see two gauzy images of Jerry laughing and crouching over her, bringing his right hand back toward her face.

This time his hand connected with her mouth, tearing the left corner of her bottom lip.

The second blow set up a loud ringing in her ears. It dimmed her vision further. It may have even caused her to pass out briefly. The next thing she was aware of, as she lifted her head from the cot, was blinking her eyes to clear the cobwebs.

Giving a lusty wolf's howl, Jerry threw his thick body on top of Louisa. Abruptly, the howl died in his throat. He turned his face to hers. His eyes were wide, glazed with apprehension.

His mouth was half-open. His breath smelled like a dead fish rotting in the sun. It made Louisa's eyes water. She blinked them clear and returned Jerry's gaze with a threatening one of her own.

She quirked the corner of her mouth into a knowing half grin.

"What?" Jerry croaked. "What's . . . what's that?"

Louisa said, "Twin Colts."

She'd shoved her pistols into her overlarge coat pockets before entering the depot station. She'd positioned them for the cross-draw. She was so good with the little ladies, and so instinctual, that even in her addled state, she'd pulled them as Jerry had hurled off his heels and onto the bed. She hadn't quite gotten them turned forward before he'd jumped on her, but she did so know, feeling Jerry's soft belly yielding to the barrels pressing into it.

She cocked both pistols. The clicks, muffled by Jerry's body, sounded little louder than the twin croaks of baby frogs.

Jerry stared into Louisa's eyes, wincing and shifting his weight to accommodate the shooting irons. Louisa stared back at him, trying to ignore his fetid breath blowing against her own mouth, from which she could feel the cool wetness of blood trickle.

A sweat bead popped out just off the corner of Jerry's left brow and began to slowly make its way down through the three-day growth of beard stubble on his ugly, pitted face.

"Hold on, now," Jerry said tightly.

He grimaced, nearly closing one eye. Slowly, keeping his gaze on Louisa's eyes, he pushed his bulk off her until he knelt over her, straddling her. He raised his hands, palms out, his face slack, eyes wide with fear. Clumsily, he slid his feet back behind him and off the bed to the floor. Keeping one hand raised in supplication, he pushed off the bed and straightened, staring down at her, slack-jawed.

"Ah hell!" French said when he saw the guns in Louisa's hands, resting on each of her hips, the in-

tricately decorated barrels aimed at Jerry. "What in
tarnation . . . ?"

"Fellas?" came Cully's voice again from the waiting
room. It sounded far away, tentative.

Jerry backed away toward the open door. "Don't
now . . . don't . . ."

Louisa sat up on the edge of the cot, extending
both cocked pistols straight out before her. She could
feel her right cheek swelling hotly. Blood continued to
dribble from her torn lower lip. She stared unblink-
ingly, stone-faced at Jerry, who slowly, slowly backed
toward the door standing open behind him.

French stood to Louisa's left, staring wide-eyed at
her twin Colts.

"Easy," he wheezed, slowly raising his hands. "Easy . . .
easy . . ."

Louisa canted her head toward her right Colt, narrowed that eye as she aimed down the barrel.

"No, no, no, no!" Jerry cried.

The last "no" was drowned by the explosive roar of
Louisa's right-hand .45.

Jerry screamed and slapped his right hand to his
left, bullet-torn shoulder. He'd no sooner made the
motion than Louisa's left-hand Colt roared, punching
a hole through Jerry's right shoulder. He flew straight
back through the door and hit the waiting room floor,
howling.

"No!" French bellowed.

He'd just made it to the door before Louisa's
bullets began chewing into him, the flashy Colts bucking in her hands. She'd punched four bullets into
French's side and his back—she wasn't beneath shooting such a devil in the back—before she stopped and

peered through the powder smoke wafting before her, peppering her nose.

French was down on the floor about five feet beyond the door, to the right of Jerry. Jerry was on his back, writhing. French was on his belly, also writhing and bellowing loudly.

Louisa rose from the cot. She crouched to retrieve her hat from the floor. She set it on her head then strode purposely out into the waiting room.

She turned her glance to see Cully standing by one of the two windows at the front of the building, hands raised toward the rafters, eyes squeezed shut, shaking his head resolutely from one side to the other and back again.

Louisa looked down at French. Blood welled from two bullets in the man's back, spaced about eight inches apart. More blood welled from a hole in his side, six inches below his armpit. Another wound oozed the thick, dark red fluid from the back of the man's raised right arm.

"Oh God, oh God!" French cried, trying to crawl forward but not having the strength to rise onto his hands and knees. He just flopped on his belly like a fish in the grass.

Jerry howled as he stared stricken-eyed up at Louisa, his eyes widening as she turned to him, raising the twin, smoking Colts in her hands.

"Oh God," Jerry pleaded. "Please . . . stop!"

Louisa stared mildly down at him. "I begged you to stop, Jerry."

"I know you did," he said, sobbing. "I'm sorry!"

Louisa shot him in the right kneecap. Then she shot him in the left kneecap.

Now he was really bellowing and sobbing, thrashing like a bug on a pin, his face a crimson mask of pure, wailing agony.

"*Now* you're sorry," Louisa said. "And *now* you have every right to be."

She looked at French. The big, bearded man stared in horror over his left shoulder at her, eyes bright with misery. *"No!"*

He turned his head away from her and began squirming across the floor as though trying to make it to the rear door. He was moving only a couple of inches at a time, however, leaving a broad swath of blood in his wake. He'd never make it to the door before he ran out of blood and strength.

Louisa turned to Cully, who stood as before, slowly shaking his head, eyes squeezed shut.

"How 'bout you?" Louisa asked, aiming down her raised Colt at him. "Do you want some of this?"

He drew his head back. "No! Now . . . please!" He kept his eyes squeezed shut. There was a soft ticking sound that Louisa could barely hear against the sound of the wind outside. She glanced down to see water dribbling down from the inside of the man's right pant leg to patter onto his boot before rolling onto the floor, a small pool of urine growing there beneath him.

He opened his eyes, turned his head slightly to the window. "I looked out the window to see what you was ridin' an' I seen the hosses. I seen the pinto an' . . . an I seen the five hosses packin' dead men. It was then that I realized who you was. From the stories. You know—the one folks tell about you, the ones I heard about in the papers. I don't read myself, but . . ."

Keeping his hands in the air high above his head,

his fingertips raking the ceiling, Cully gave a slight, knowing smile. "Shoulda . . . shoulda known . . . it was you—the Vengeance Queen her ownself." He smiled again.

Louisa kept her guns aimed at him. She kept one eye narrowed threateningly at him, as well. Above the men still howling behind him not quite as loudly as before, she said, "You're the new station agent."

He frowned, his gaze becoming dubious.

"That's right. Congratulations. You'll be selling the tickets now, manning this place."

"Uh . . ." Cully looked around, turned his gaze back to Louisa. "Really?"

Louisa tossed a glance over her shoulder. "Jerry's not long for this world. You leave him as he is, though, you hear? Don't tend him. Don't fetch a doctor for him. You don't tend French, either. You let them both die slowly, howling. Even that is too good for them."

Cully winced, a muscle leaping in his cheek beneath his right eye.

"I'm going to show a rare bit of mercy here tonight. But you leave them alone, you hear?"

"Yes, ma'am—I hear you."

"And when they're dead, you drag them out into the cold. You leave them out there in the snow and the cold, to the wolves. That's what they would have done to me—after you three had finished with me."

"All right. I will. Yes, ma'am. It's what they deserve, all right."

"It's better than what they deserve."

"Yes, it is. It's better."

"Take your hands down."

Obediently, Cully lowered his hands. "Am I really the station agent now?"

"Yes, you are. Once you learn how it all works, you can write me out a ticket. I'll fetch it in the morning, before the train arrives. I'm going to have a free ride to Bismarck—understand?"

"Oh yes, ma'am. I understand. Of course!"

Louisa lowered her Colts, off-cocking the hammers with soft clicking sounds. "Good. Now, before I go, I have a question for you."

"All right."

She stuffed her pistols into her coat pockets, turning the butts forward and then lowering the pocket flaps over them, concealing them. She touched a finger to her lip, glanced at the blood.

Turning to Cully, she said, "Did a man and a woman ride into town recently? Say, yesterday sometime?"

Cully rolled his eyes around, pondering the question. "Well, yes. Yes, they did. A man and a woman. Late yesterday afternoon." Realization dawned on him. "Ohhh," he said, "you're after them, ain't ya? Sweets DuPree and Pima Quarrels." He gave an eager, expectant smile, and whistled.

"You know them?"

"Not me. French did. He recognized 'em. He rode with Quarrels once down in Texas. He knew Quarrels's woman, Sweets DuPree, by her description an' reputation. Got a long, white streak running through her hair"—he lifted a finger to his left eye—"and a scar over her eye. They say Quarrels himself gave it to her."

Cully chuckled.

"Yeah," Louisa said. "I've heard they have a real sweet relationship."

Cully chuckled again, louder, nervously.

"Where are they?"

"Over to the Territorial. They came in when me an' French was just leavin'." He gave a fated, defeated expression and a sigh. "They're probably holed up in one of the rooms upstairs, waitin' out the storm, waitin' for the train, most like."

Louisa considered the information. She glanced behind her at Jerry, who was sobbing and gasping. The blood pool around him had doubled in size over the past few minutes. French was still trying to crawl to the door, but he was making even slower progress than the last time Louisa had looked. He was still six feet away from it.

Even if he made it outside, where could he go?

"Well," Louisa said, jauntily, turning back to Cully. "Congratulations on the new job."

She flashed an affable smile, retrieved her gloves and mittens from the ticket counter, then strode to the door and went out.

Through the door behind her, Cully said, "Th-thank, you, ma'am!"

Chapter 15

SCRAW! SCRAW! SCRAW!

The cry same so suddenly and loudly out of the forest that Lou Prophet's heart nearly burst out of his chest and heavy buckskin mackinaw.

"What in *thunder*?" exclaimed Sheldon Coffer, drawing sharply back on his mare's reins, just off Prophet's right stirrup.

"Owl," Prophet said, stopping Mean and Ugly and staring up at the big, winged creature beating upward through the skeletal aspen branches, a black silhouette against the dark charcoal sky. Something dropped to the trail about twenty feet ahead of Prophet and Coffer.

The owl's wings made a windy, rushing sound. It gave another piercing *scraw* and then flapped on over the trees and out of sight.

"Hoot owl," Prophet said, staring ahead along the trail. His heart had hammered his ribs so hard they ached. Now it was slowing but he could still feel the lightning in his blood.

"Great gray," said Coffer, staring at the gray tops of the trees where the bird had disappeared.

Prophet glanced at the local lawman. "That's what I said."

Coffer snorted, his breath frosting the air before his bearded face, beneath the black brim of his big Stetson trimmed with a braided rawhide band into which a square chunk of turquoise had been woven, snugged against the front of the crown.

"Let's see what it dropped." Prophet gigged Mean and Ugly ahead a ways then stopped again and swung down from the saddle.

Holding his reins in one hand he walked ahead. He could see a small object lying in the snow, in the middle of the two-track trail. It had rolled after it had hit the ground, leaving a three- or four-inch track to its left. That small a track wouldn't have been noticeable if the snow hadn't been fresh, and if it were just fifteen minutes later in the afternoon.

Prophet frowned down at the object, which resembled a bauble of some kind, then chewed off his mitten and glove, dropped to his haunches, and picked the curious article up between his right thumb and index finger. A couple inches of what appeared to be a ragged, red thread was attached to the object. Prophet held it up in front of his face.

"I sure wish I would have known what this was before I picked it up," he said, stretching his lips back from his teeth distastefully, continuing to stare at the round object, which was roughly the size of a pullet egg, in his hand.

"Why's that?" Coffer asked, riding up behind Prophet.

"Because I never would have picked it up."

"Why not?"

Prophet tossed the object up to the marshal, who caught it awkwardly against his chest, leaning back in his saddle. Coffer held the object in his gloved right hand, angling the piece to catch the last, dirty light from the cloudy sky, and looked at it closely.

"Jesus!" He tossed it away like a hot potato. "Christalmighty, why'd you give me that damn thing, Lou? Why, it's a human eye!"

Prophet rose from his haunches, turning his head to peer into the fast-darkening woods to his left. "Smells to high heaven out here." He sniffed the sickly sweet fetor emanating from the woods.

"Yeah, I smell it," Coffer said. "Helkatoot—that's a might whiffy on the lee side!"

Prophet dropped Mean's reins and moved slowly into the woods, stepping carefully through the snow-dusted brush and bramble. He wended his way through the trees for about twenty feet, the stench growing stronger, before he stopped. The brush had been knocked around just ahead of him, the new-fallen snow scuffed. Animals had been moving around here recently. Just ahead and to his right lay something that didn't appear natural.

Prophet stepped over to it, dropped to a knee beside it, and stared down at it.

He picked it up. It was a man's badly scuffed leather boot crusted with dried blood.

Prophet dropped the boot when something else caught his eye. He walked over to the second object, dropped to a knee beside it. From recent experience, he knew not to pick it up. Clearly it was a man's hand and part of an arm to the elbow. Bits of a blue shirt-sleeve clung to it. On the man's hand, which was badly swollen, was a small, flat-faced gold ring, on the pinky finger. To either side of the bauble the finger itself was swollen to nearly the size of a small breakfast sausage.

Yet another object caught Prophet's eye. This thing was shiny, glistening in the last rays of the sun concealed by the low, stormy gray clouds from which a light, breeze-whipped snow continued to fall. Prophet stepped over to the shiny thing, snow-dusted vines and branches snapping beneath his boots. This object he picked up and scrutinized.

A five-pointed chunk of nickeled tin into which the words DEPUTY SHERIFF GRANT COUNTY had been engraved.

"I'll be switched!" said a voice behind Prophet.

The bounty hunter's heart thumped with a start, and he dropped the badge. He whipped his head around to see Sheldon Coffer standing behind him, bent over to inspect the badge.

"Christalmighty!" Prophet exclaimed indignantly. "You sure move quiet for a fat old geezer!"

Coffer smiled at Prophet's dismay. "What—this fat old geezer sneak up on you, man-hunter?"

"I was deep in contemplation," Prophet said. "Otherwise you'd be tryin' to digest a .45 round about now."

Coffer gave a fateful sigh and glanced around. "I do believe we done found Chester Thom."

Prophet looked around at the other scattered remains of a man—mostly predator-gnawed bones and bits of torn, bloody clothing, much of it well concealed by the snowy shrubs and fallen tree limbs.

"Who's Chester Thom?"

"One of Dwight Pierson's deputies. Pierson's the sheriff over in Devil's Lake. He rode out to Indian Butte last week, lookin' for Thom. Said he'd sent Thom out to investigate whiskey peddlers who may or may not have been makin' an' sellin' busthead to the Injuns on the reservation. Pierson told me to keep an eye out for Thom. Thom passed through Indian Butte a couple weeks ago.

"He always felt like he was too good to check in with me, a lowly town marshal. So he laid up with the girls in a local cathouse, drinking the bar dry, and left early the next morning—with one hell of a hangover, no doubt. When Pierson said he was missing, I had me a suspicion he might have rode out here to snoop around that woodcutters' camp where I believe them toughnuts of yours, Gritch Hatchley an' Weed Brougham, is probably holed up, since I ain't seen 'em in town."

Coffer shook his head darkly as he stared down at Chester Thom's pinky ring. "Bad element out here, Lou. French Canadian misfits. Half-breeds. Outlaws of a very bad stripe. It was like that even before Hatchley an' Brougham came, if they're out here, that is. I'm just glad the place, bein' out of town, is also out of my jurisdiction, so I don't have to mess with it. I'm too old for that kind of savage business. Whoever's holed up out here must've killed Thom and left his carcass to the coyotes an' wolves an' that big gray owl."

Prophet rose from his haunches and tugged his mitten and glove on over his right hand. "Well, I didn't think I was ridin' out here to a Saturday-night hoe-down."

Coffer gave a dark laugh and shook his head.

Prophet looked at him. "What's funny?"

"Sheriff Pierson told me he investigated out here, didn't find Thom. I don't think he came out here at all. Just told me he did. He plays the big cock of the walk of the whole county, ole Dwight does. But the only reason he's sheriff is because no one else was stupid enough to run for the office. Not out here. There's more outlaws up here than law-abidin' citizens. Besides, Dwight's damn near as old as I am and twice as fat!"

Coffer spat a wad of chaw to one side. "No, sir—I don't believe he even came as near to the place as you an' me are right now. Thom must've been foolhardy enough to investigate the camp. Prob'ly found a couple stills and had his candle snuffed in the process."

Coffer looked around at the grisly mess before him and Prophet. "And everything else . . ."

"Looks that way."

Prophet walked back out to the trail. He stared off up the two-track trace, which curved just ahead and was lost in the growing murk of dusk and falling snow. He glanced at Coffer, who was breathing hard now as the old marshal trudged out of the snowy brush and ambled over to where his mare stood beside Mean and Ugly. The hammerheaded dun, who didn't realize he'd been gelded, was making eyes at the mare, who was having none of it.

"How much farther is that camp?" Prophet asked him.

"Less than a mile. Straight on. The trail dips into a hollow. There's a big shack and a barn and a corral by Little Sioux Creek. It's run by a French Canadian half-breed. There's a half-dozen woodcutters' cabins nearby. The woodcutters are likely also peddlin' whiskey, which probably pays better than firewood, even when the spur line's buyin'."

Coffer shook his head. "Forget it, Lou. If Hatchley and Brougham are out there, there's gonna be a whole lot more of their stripe out there with 'em. You won't have a chance."

"I'm gonna check it out," Prophet said, grabbing Mean and Ugly's reins.

"Hell, there ain't no point. Hatchley an' Brougham'll probably catch the train tomorrow. You can take 'em both down then when they won't have no one else backin' their play."

"I don't know that they're gonna catch the train," Prophet said, swinging up into his saddle. "They're both Canadians themselves. I heard they might be headed for Canada. Now, Sweets an' Pima Quarrels— I think *they're* headed south." He shook his head. "I don't know about Hatchley and Brougham. Those two hardtails ain't gettin' away. They got too big a bounty on their heads, an' . . . besides . . ."

He let his voice trail off as he stared up the trail, a sheepish set to his shoulders.

"Besides what?" Coffer asked, settling his heavy bulk in his saddle.

Prophet winced, gave the old marshal a sidelong glance. "What would I tell Louisa?"

"You'd be alive to tell her *somethin'*!"

Prophet pondered on that, chuckled. "Nah," he drawled. "That girl can shame a man worse than any preacher. Besides, I need the money them two got on their heads. In a month, I wanna be in Mexico, and there ain't no way unless I bring them two to the U.S. marshal in Bismarck first—dead or alive. I hope alive, because they're worth more alive, but I'll perforate 'em if I have to an' haul 'em back like the others."

He glanced at Coffer. "You go on back to town, Shell. You showed me where the camp is. You've done your duty. Go on back home an' let Brandy warm your feet." He winked and grinned. "And you know what flavor of brandy I'm talkin' about, you old reprobate."

"I'm gonna do just that!" Coffer began to rein his horse around, casting Prophet a defiant gaze.

"There you go."

"I *am* goin'. Back to town. You're gonna be alone out here, Lou."

"See you back in Injun Butte," Prophet said, touching spurs to Mean's loins and moving ahead along the trail. "I hope to be over to the jailhouse later with my prisoners in tow."

Coffer continued to turn his horse back in the direction of town. "No, you won't, neither. You'll be out there keepin' Chester Thom company!"

"I'm gonna miss you, Shell," Prophet said, chuckling softly as he trotted Mean in the direction of Little Sioux Creek. He'd spoken too quietly for the marshal to hear. It was time to be quiet. Time to watch his back. Time to have his Winchester handy.

He did just that as he followed the bend in the trail, sliding the '73 out of his saddle boot, cocking the piece one-handed then easing the hammer down to half-cock and resting the barrel across his saddle horn.

The hair on the back of his neck pricked against his coat collar as he remembered that big, round eye in his hand. It had been the clear blue of a spring lake. He couldn't help wondering what the last thing the poor soul, Chester Thom, had seen through that eye before they'd beefed him.

Stop thinking about it, Prophet, he told himself. *Think instead about that sneering look the Vengeance Queen would give you if instead of going after Hatchley and Brougham you rode back to town and spent the rest of the night with a couple of comely girls and a bottle of Taos lightning by a warm, popping fire, which is what you'd really* rather *do.*

He chuckled at that, but it was mostly just his nerves rattling around in his brain.

Fifteen minutes later, he'd dismounted Mean and Ugly and tied the horse to a tree. He'd crabbed to the crest of a small knoll capped with several horse tooth–shaped rocks cropping up out of the snowy earth before him, and stared down into the hollow in which the big cabin, barn, and corral sat.

The cabin's windows shone with a soft umber light. Someone was playing a fiddle inside. Not too shabbily, either.

"Someone is havin' a hoedown out here, after all," said a raspy, breathless voice behind Prophet.

The bounty hunter whipped around, swinging his Winchester around, as well, thumbing back the hammer. He dropped the rifle's barrel and eased the hammer back down as he saw Coffer crawl up beside him in the gauzy darkness, breathing hard.

"Christ!" Prophet wheezed under his breath. "I thought you went back to town!"

"I got an old fool's pride, I reckon," the marshal said, staring through a gap between the rocks at the cabin. He held a Sharps carbine in his gloved hands. "Besides . . ." He turned his dark eyes to Prophet. "Brandy left me last summer for a crazy Canuck. That worthless nephew of mine . . . of Brandy's, I should say . . . lives with me now. Hell." The old lawman sighed and shook his head. "I got a long, cold night ahead. I might as well spend it here."

Chapter 16

"Sorry about Brandy," Prophet said. "She prob'ly did you a favor, though, Shell. If she's the kind of girl who'd run off with a crazy Canuck, then you're better off alone."

"Maybe," Coffer said with a sigh. "But she sure could warm an old man's feet, that girl could!"

"There's more foot warmers in the sea, Sheldon."

"It's a pretty small sea up here, Lou." Coffer shook his head, glowering as though the conversation embarrassed him. "Anyways, how you gonna handle this thing?"

Prophet chuckled. The question made him think about Louisa, and he wondered vaguely where she was and what she was up to at that very moment. Probably raising hell in Sundown, no doubt. Of course she was. That's what the girl did. She raised hell.

"What's funny?"

"Nothin'. You stay with the horses. I reckon I'll figure this one out as I go. Plans don't work much in man-huntin', anyways. With any luck, in a half hour or so, I'll be back with Gritch Hatchley and Weed Brougham in cuffs an' shackles."

He crabbed backward down the hill. At the bottom, he grabbed his Richards coach gun off his saddle horn and slung the lanyard over his head and right shoulder, so that the sawed-off gut-shredder hung straight down behind his back. The savage, double-barreled popper cleaned up well in close quarters.

He edged a look around the shoulder of the hill toward the cabin, which was a one-and-a-half-story affair with a peaked roof and a lean-to addition at the rear. Someone was still sawing away on the fiddle. Through the curtained windows, Prophet saw moving shadows. He thought he could see two people dancing in time with the fiddle.

He glanced at the sky. Nearly all of the light was gone. It was dark out here. Dark and cold. He'd be damned glad to get back to Indian Butte for a hot bath, a steak, a few drinks, and at least a couple hours of shut-eye before hopping the train in the morning with his prisoners, living and dead, in tow.

Hatchley and Brougham were each worth five hundred dollars more alive than dead, so he hoped he could take them with their lights on. Louisa would just go ahead and cap them both and call it money well spent. In cold weather, it was more convenient to haul a dead man, as opposed to one you had to keep your eye on and feed, to his rightful destination. In hot weather, a dead man could get a mite sour.

Then again, Louisa didn't have Prophet's spend-happy habits. Nor his urge to hightail it down to Mexico—a long trip that needed ample financing.

No, he'd take Hatchley and Brougham alive if possible.

He jogged out away from the butte, heading directly toward the cabin. It didn't look like any pickets had been posted, which didn't surprise Prophet. It was stormy and dark, and apparently lawdogs tended to give this so-called woodcutters' camp a wide berth. Most, at least.

Lou's heartbeat quickened anxiously as the cabin loomed before him. He was close enough now that he could hear the hum of voices above the scratching of the violin behind the stout log walls. He was only fifteen feet from the front door, which sat back behind a very small stoop, when a latch clicked.

Prophet's heart leaped. The front door was opening, showing a slice of weak umber light reflected off velveteen curtains beyond it, inside the cabin. The curtains were obscured by a brocade-upholstered fainting couch on which two people sat, though Lou could see only their legs.

A man stepped into the door's opening—a tall, slender man, judging by his silhouette.

Prophet stopped, skidding a little in the slippery snow, breathing hard. Crouched slightly forward, he looked around.

The only cover within many square yards was an overturned wheelbarrow to his left, ten feet away. He took two broad, running steps then lofted himself off the toes of his moccasins, hitting the snowy ground with a grunt and then rolling up behind the wheelbarrow, clutching his Winchester before him.

He gritted his teeth, silently cursed.

Had the man seen him?

"Close the damn door!" someone barked from inside the cabin. "It's colder'n a gold digger's heart out there!"

The "there" was muffled by the closing of the door and nearly drowned by the click of the door's latch.

Prophet held his breath, listening. He kept his teeth gritted, awaiting a hail of hot lead. The wheelbarrow was too insubstantial for adequate cover. If the man had spied Lou, the bounty hunter would be feeding the hoot owl soon.

The man on the stoop grunted. Drew a ragged breath. A soft, liquid dribbling rose. Again, the man grunted, groaned, drew a breath.

Prophet's heart slowed a little. He started breathing again. The man had stepped onto the stoop only to shake the dew from his lily. He must not have seen Prophet. Probably, the man's eyes had been compromised by the light, weak as it appeared, inside the cabin, so he hadn't been able to make out Prophet's dark figure in the murky darkness stitched with falling snow.

Prophet drew a slow, relieved breath, released it, drew another.

He turned his head to peer over his left shoulder and over the wheelbarrow's snow-dusted wheel toward the cabin. The man was relieving himself, all right. He stood at the front end of the stoop, sideways to Prophet, listing a little from side to side. He was either writing his name in the snow or he was wobbling from drink.

Maybe both.

For chrissakes, Prophet silently complained after the man had been dribbling for nearly two full minutes, *you either better see a sawbones about your pinched flow or stop drinkin' like a fish, you damn fool!*

Finally, the man's flow dribbled to a stop.

The man grunted, drew another breath as he tucked

himself back in and buttoned his fly. He swung around
and, humming under his breath the lyrics to the tune
that the fiddle was sawing away on inside the cabin and
which Prophet recognized as "Little Brown Jug," the
man swung around and stepped to the door. He
tripped the latch, stepped inside, and closed the door
with a click behind him.

"'Bout damn time!" Prophet grunted as he heaved
himself to his feet.

But he hadn't taken one full step before a man's
voice cried inside the cabin, "*Someone's outside, fellas!*"

The door jerked open again. The tall, slender gent
ran out onto the stoop and loudly cocked the rifle in
his hands.

Prophet threw himself to his right.

The rifle in the man's hands thundered, flames lapping from the barrel. It thundered two more times,
flashing brightly, sending bullets screeching through
the air over Prophet's head. He hit the ground and
rolled as the rifle belched again, a slug pluming the
snow just ahead of him.

He rolled up on his left shoulder, clicked his Winchester's hammer back, aimed quickly, and threw three
quick shots at the cabin. The man standing on the
stoop, and who'd been cocking another round into his
own rifle's breech, was punched back inside with a
scream, leaving the door standing wide behind him.

Glass clattered in the window left of the door. Another
rifle flashed in the broken-out window. As two slugs
tore into the ground just beyond Prophet, Prophet slid
his rifle to the left and sent two rounds hurling toward
the shooter silhouetted in the window there, against
the wan light behind him.

One of the bullets plunked into the window casing.

The other made a wet crunching sound, which meant it had hit its target.

The man standing there wailed and leaped backward, dropping his rifle out the window and clamping both hands to his face. "My face!" he screamed. "The devil shot me in the face!"

"You're surrounded!" Prophet shouted. "We got twenty lawmen out here! Another twenty armed and ready soldiers, you sons o' devils! Come out with your hands up or die wailin'!"

He thought the lie was worth a try. It might freeze the owlhoots for a few valuable seconds.

"Law!" a man inside the cabin shouted. "Soldiers!"

"Oh hell!" lamented another.

There were the sounds of more breaking glass as more windows were knocked out. More rifles started belching.

Prophet emptied his Winchester into the two windows on both sides of the now wide-open door, evoking a couple of exasperated curses, then heaved himself to his feet and took off running. He tossed the Winchester aside then slid the Richards coach gun around to his chest, grabbing the double-barreled cannon in both gloved hands.

Rifles were belching inside the cabin but the fire must have been directed out other windows besides the front ones, because Prophet saw no flashes and was met with no lead. Maybe his lie about the lawmen and soldiers had worked and the tough nuts inside the cabin thought they were sure enough surrounded and were shooting at shadows.

Prophet gained the stoop, thumbing both the shotgun's rabbit-ear hammers back to full cock. He bolted through the door like a bull through a chute, lifting a

raucous rebel yell he hoped would further send ice
water through the veins of his quarry. When he was
two steps inside, he vaulted off his heels, propelling
himself straight into the cabin in a high arcing dive,
absently opining that he was lucky to have such a nice,
big, thick Oriental rug beneath him, to soften his fall.

The two men shooting out the windows to either
side of him, one man to each window, swung around
bellowing, swinging their smoking rifles around, as well.

"Company!" the man on the left shouted, pressing
his back to the window he'd been firing out of.

He hurled a round at Prophet.

He'd been slow to track the flying bounty hunter,
however, and instead of plunking the lead into his intended target, he hit the man on the opposite side of
the room from him. That man wailed and also fired
his own rifle at Prophet. His aim was no better than
the other man's. No sooner had his partner's bullet
drilled into his brisket, he drilled a hot one into his
partner's neck.

Both men bounced off the walls behind them, bellowing like gut-shot mountain lions.

Prophet hit the rug and rolled just as the man to his
left screamed again and fired his rifle at him. The
bullet tore into the rug just in front of Prophet, who
rolled up onto his left shoulder, quickly aimed the
Richards at the man who was now on his right, as
Prophet faced the front door and tripped a trigger.

The fist-sized spread of double-ought buck lifted
the curly wolf two feet up off the floor while opening a
pumpkin-sized hole in his belly and hurling him straight
back through the busted-out window behind him.

Just like that, he was gone.

All that remained was his rifle, which clattered onto

the floor at the base of the window through which he'd disappeared.

"Damnit!" a man shouted behind Prophet as boots thundered loudly. "What in the hell is—?"

Prophet swung around to see a man running down the stairs to the right of the short plank bar ahead of Prophet and on his left. The man wore only his long-handles, hat, boots, and the cartridge belt he just then finished buckling around his broad, flat waist. The man stopped, eyes widening as he saw the big bounty hunter on the parlor area of the large, timbered room.

The man facing Prophet had long, stringy red hair and a broad, freckled, hairless face. He was maybe five foot seven, but he was nearly as wide as he was tall.

"Howdy, Weed!" Prophet bellowed, his voice echoing in the cavernous room. "How the hell has life been treating you, anyways?"

Brougham dropped his chin. His eyes turned dark. He was thinking through his options. He must have concluded he didn't have many. He snatched the bone-handled hogleg from the holster hanging down his stout right thigh.

Before he could clear leather, Prophet said, "Damnit," and tripped the Richards's second trigger.

KA-BOOMMMMM!

Weed Brougham flew straight back against the stairs, which were already plastered with bloody bits of his heart, which the twelve-gauge buck had shredded as they'd punched the pieces out of his back, along with flesh and bone from his spine. He slammed against the steps with an indignant grunt, his body twisting around and then rolling wildly, limbs akimbo, all the way to the bottom.

Prophet tossed away the empty Richards and cursed again. He'd just lost five hundred dollars.

He'd heard footsteps on the balcony running along the second story on his right, hanging suspended above the first-floor parlor area. He grabbed his Peacemaker from the coat pocket he'd stuffed it into, for an easier reach, and swung his head to his left.

Two men were coming at him from opposite ends of the balcony—one from his left, one from his right. The one on his left had a Colt's revolving rifle. The one on his right had a big-assed Buntline Special which he was just then cocking as he stopped, dropped to a knee, and rested the barrel on the edge of the balcony rail, narrowing an eye as he aimed down into the parlor at Prophet.

Prophet vaulted off his heels and onto a table covered with coins, bottles, glasses, and playing cards. The Buntline followed him, chewing three lead slugs into the table, each one not more than three inches behind Prophet's rolling torso. Cards and coins flew in all directions.

Lou rolled off the table and thumped to the floor on the other side, coming up with the Peacemaker talking in the only language it spoke:

Bang! Bang! Bang-Bang!

Both the Buntline and the man who'd been wielding it tumbled straight forward over the balcony rail. The man turned a forward somersault and then landed crossways on the fainting couch, behind which Prophet had just a seen a girl pull her head, her eyes wide and frightened. The man's back snapped like several dry twigs under a heavy foot and he lay groaning as he died fast but hard.

Prophet had seen the second shooter, the hardtail with the rifle, out of the corner of his left eye. The man had snaked the rifle over the balcony rail. Prophet pulled his head down under the table as the rifle thundered twice, blasting two big holes through the table and scattering what cards and coins Prophet hadn't dispersed when he'd rolled across it.

When the Colt had fallen silent, the bounty hunter thrust the Peacemaker above the table, narrowing one eye as he aimed down the still-smoking barrel. The man with the rifle, big and shaggy and clad in only a bear claw necklace and longhandles, widened his eyes a quarter second before Prophet's .45 round blew away his right temple. The big, shaggy man flew back against the wall of vertical, unfinished pine planks behind him, gave a guttural rattling sigh, then slid slowly down the wall to sit on his butt on the balcony floor.

He tipped his chin to his left shoulder then rolled over onto that side as though he'd just gotten the notion it was time for a badly needed nap.

Prophet looked both ways down the upper-floor balcony. No more movement.

In fact, there appeared no more movement anywhere in the building. At least, nowhere he could see it or hear it.

The only sounds were the fire in the stove in the middle of the room and the wind moaning through the broken windows. A man's agonized voice said softly, "My face . . . my face . . . the devil shot my face . . ."

Prophet rose.

Quickly, continuing to look around the big, lofty room, at the stairs at the rear and at the second-story balcony above, he flicked open the Peacemaker's loading gate. He shook out the spent cartridges then reached under his coat for five fresh loads from his cartridge belt. He thumbed the bullets into the chambers, closed the loading gate, and spun the cylinder.

It made a sound like an angry rattlesnake.

He walked over toward the window to the right of the open front door. The man he'd shot in that window lay on the floor at the window's base. He wore a shabby, mismatched suit and two pistols on his hips. He was in his late twenties with short, dark red hair and a hooked nose. He'd been trying to grow a beard with little success.

He writhed on his back, clamping both his bloody hands over his bloody right cheek.

Prophet pressed the Peacemaker's barrel against the hardcase's left, closed eye. "How 'bout I shoot you on the other side, make ya even?" He clicked the hammer back. "Where's Hatchley?"

Chapter 17

The stocky, bald, apron-clad man with a bushy, upswept mustache and a face as red as a prairie sunset looked Louisa up and down from behind the rough-hewn bar in the Territorial Hotel's large but crudely appointed saloon.

His brown eyes sparkled. "Hello, there." He frowned a little when he saw the welt on Louisa's right cheek and the swelling cut on the left corner of her lower lip. "Looks like you got taken to the woodshed."

"I'd like a cup of tea and a rag."

"Tea and a rag," the barkeep said, deep lines of consternation cutting across his red forehead, beneath his egg-shaped bald dome. "I got whiskey an' beer. Might be able to scrounge up a bottle of tequila, but . . ."

Louisa grabbed the rag wadded up on the bar to her right, snugged up against a gallon jar of pickled pigs' feet. "Just the rag, then."

She swung around and headed back out onto the Territorial's small front porch. It was nearly completely dark. The snow was moaning and groaning around the small prairie settlement hugging the spur line tracks. The snow was still falling though not heavily.

Mainly, it was cold. Bitterly cold.

The chill wind bit at Louisa's torn lip as she walked over to a covered rain barrel that sat on a corner of the porch. She removed the lid, punched a hole in the ice with a stick provided for that purpose, then dipped the rag into the cold, slushy water. She wrung out the rag then headed back into the saloon, ignoring the lusty stares of the half-dozen men seated at various tables around the place, near the horseshoe bar that ran halfway into the middle of the room from the rear.

A narrow stairs ran up the rear wall, off the bar's rear end, to the hotel's second story. The howling wind made the hotel's spindly wood-frame walls creek and groan. The Vengeance Queen could also hear other sounds. These issued from the second floor. They were sounds you'd hear in any cheap parlor house.

A couple of the men sitting around the saloon chuckled as they lifted their eyes to the ceiling above their heads. Louisa kicked out a chair at the table she'd chosen when she'd first entered the place, after stabling her horses and the dead outlaws for the night in the only livery barn in town. She'd hid the saddle-bags, bulging with the loot that she and Lou had taken off the dead outlaws, in the barn, as well. Her bedroll, saddlebags, and Winchester were piled on a chair to her right, the rifle positioned for an easy grab from its scabbard.

She was about to take a seat but stopped when she saw Edgar Clayton sitting at a round table on the other side of a large potbelly stove. She hadn't recognized the man without his hat and scarf, both of which were on the table before him, near a whiskey bottle, a half-full shot glass, and schooner of dark ale. His hair was so thin on top that the pink top of his head shone through it. His small, round spectacles sagged on his long nose.

He stared back at Louisa. His pale blue eyes were dull, almost vacant. Suddenly, he smiled, lifting his gray-speckled beard, and raised his shot glass in salute.

Louisa said, "Any sign of your friend?"

"Ramsay Willis is no friend of mine," Clayton said, the smile abruptly disappearing, and sipped his whiskey. "But in answer to your question—no. He's out there somewhere, though. I assure you. He's waiting on the train, no doubt. Thinks he can flee his sins, escape my wrath."

Again, Clayton sipped from his shot glass then frowned at Louisa curiously. "What happened? You fall off your horse, Miss Bonaventure?"

Ignoring the question, Louisa sat down in her chair and pressed the cold cloth to her cheek. She probed her torn lip with her other hand then pressed the cold cloth to it. She pulled the cloth away and saw blood. She turned the wadded cloth around and held the cleaner side against her cheek.

Meanwhile, the barman, looking grumpy, brought a steaming mug of tea to her.

"Had to scour the pantry for that," he said.

"How much do I owe you?"

He spread his hands and gave a tolerant smile. "On the house."

"I'll take a room."

"They're filling up fast on account of the storm."

The apron glanced around at the other men in the saloon. "Likely be more now that night's fallen. Too cold for even the most seasoned grub-line rider to camp out. More folks might be comin' in for the train. You can have room six. Two dollars an' fifty cents. We'll settle up in the morning. Fetch the key from the bar when you're ready to go up. Name's Morris Tutwiler. I own this heap."

He glanced around and sighed.

Grumbling, Tutwiler started to turn away but turned back around when Louisa asked: "Who's upstairs, Mr. Tutwiler?" Still holding the cloth to her cheek, she glanced at the general area of the ceiling from which the sounds were coming.

The bartender glanced at the ceiling. "That?" He shook his head, gave a fleeting grimace. "Believe me—you don't want to know."

Tutwiler turned away with his heavy paunch and his broad, apron-clad hips, and headed back around behind the bar.

Holding the cloth to her cheek, Louisa raised the tea to her lips, blew on it, and, wincing at the pain of the cut, took a quick sip. Staring through the steam lifting from the stone mug, she saw yet another man gazing at her.

This man was a soldier with a captain's bars on the shoulders of his dark blue tunic. He was a handsome man in his early thirties with thick black hair curling over his ears and a thick, dragoon-style mustache. He was a little pale, and his eyes were cobalt blue. He was playing poker with three other men, somewhat older than he and dressed in the store-bought suits of traveling drummers.

Having caught Louisa's gaze, the captain cast her a warm, friendly smile. There didn't appear to be any leering lust in the man's eyes, but maybe he was just better than most men at disguising it.

She did not return the smile. She took another sip of the hot tea and looked away from him. She was in no mood to parry unwanted advances.

Louisa sat with her back to the wall, facing the bar ahead and on her left, the stove and Clayton about ten feet straight ahead of her. The door at the front of the room was ahead and on her right.

Now as she heard it open, she turned her gaze to it, her right hand tingling in anticipation of the possible need to reach for the Winchester. Her hand stopped tingling when a slender, female figure in a blue wool coat, wool hat, red muffler, and matching red knit mittens came in and closed the door behind her. Shivering, she stamped snow from her boots. The redhead from Jiggs's place loosened the muffler, removed the hat, and shook out her long, thick red hair that contrasted sharply with the delicate paleness of her face.

Just then the woman on the second story gave a long, shuddering cry.

The men in the room snorted and chuckled sheepishly.

"That's enough to make a fella wanna take his turn up there," said one of the drummers playing cards with the soldier.

"You'd better not try it," warned the bartender, Tutwiler, who was stirring a pot of stew bubbling on the stove near Louisa. He glanced around the room. "Anyone who wants some of this, it's ready. Beans and bacon. You put enough salt on it, you might be able to

choke it down. Bowls are on the bar. Dime apiece."
Anticipating objections, he threw up a thick arm and
said, "A man's gotta make a livin'!"

He dropped the spoon into the stewpot and walked
back around behind the bar.

Toni glanced at Louisa. They held each other's
gazes for a moment then Toni, holding her hat in one
hand, her red mittens in the other, walked past the
stove toward the bar.

As she passed Louisa's table, the Vengeance Queen
said, "Did you find the banker?"

Toni stopped. She didn't look at Louisa but only
straight toward the back of the room, and nodded.
"Hitched. He and his new wife aren't in the market for
a housekeeper just now but I can check back in a few
months. She's in the family way." Toni shrugged. "That's
the way my luck runs sometimes."

"That's the way it runs for most of us."

"Thank you for those words of wisdom, Miss Bonaventure," Toni snapped out bitterly.

She continued toward the bar, where she ordered
a bottle then, clutching the glass by the neck, walked
to the back of the room and climbed the stairs to the
second story, where she must have secured a room
earlier, before she'd gone off looking for the banker
and while Louisa was cleaning the rats out of the train
depot.

Another woman came down the stairs just as Toni
was going up. They brushed shoulders though neither
looked at the other. The second woman had long,
dark brown hair with a white streak running through
it, and a knotted scar at the outside edge of her left
eyebrow. Her hair was badly mussed. All she wore
was a striped blanket wrapped loosely about her body,

angling down low enough on one side to reveal her left shoulder.

It was obvious that she wore nothing beneath the blanket.

She wasn't a pretty woman, but she wasn't ugly, either. There was a feral hardness about her face, even now with her cheeks flushed. She appeared in her late twenties, but the lines spoking out from her eyes and etched around her mouth bespoke the roughness of those years, of burning the candle at both ends. Her eyes were darkly smug, and thin, colorless lips were stretched in a catlike grin.

She held a long-barreled Smith & Wesson revolver down low in her right hand, along her right leg. She held the gun casually, almost as though it were as much a part of her person as the several rings Louisa could see on her fingers.

She might leave a room without her clothes, but never without a gun.

She dropped to the bottom of the stairs and padded barefoot to the bar.

"Hello, Morris—how are you?" she asked as she set the pistol atop the bar then leaned forward, ever the coquette, well aware that all eyes in the room were directed her way. Her thick, dark brown hair fluffed against her cheeks, concealing her face from the sides. The white streak ran down over her left ear.

The fact that she was being watched seemed to delight her while also embarrassing her, making her feel shy.

"What can I get you, Sweets?" Tutwiler asked with a tolerant air, setting his big, red fists on the edge of the bar.

"Another bottle of your best." Sweets glanced toward

the stove then turned back to the barman, who was dusting off the bottle he'd just pulled down off a high back bar shelf. "Are the beans ready?"

"The beans are ready."

"We'd like a couple of bowls delivered to our room."

"I don't got no room service, Sweets," said the barman with a resolute shake of his bald head, staring obstinately down at the bar.

Sweets threw her head back and laughed. She grabbed the bottle off the bar and in the process nearly lost the blanket. She laughed again.

"Tonight you have room service, Morris!" she announced, her laughing voice pitched with subtle warning.

She adjusted the blanket about her shoulders and started padding back toward the stairs, the bottle in the hand holding the blanket closed at her chest, the Smith & Wesson in her other hand hanging low at her side. "We'll settle up with you in the morning."

As Sweets padded back up the stairs, Louisa realized that someone else had entered the hotel via the front door, which the man was just then closing carefully against the wind and blowing snow. He was a tall man in a dark blue wool coat to which the snow was sticking, mottling it white. His collar had been raised against the storm but now as he turned to the room, he jerked it down. He removed his hat and batted the weathered cream Stetson against his wool trousers, the cuffs of which were shoved into the tops of mule-eared, black leather boots.

A town marshal's badge was pinned to his coat.

He was a blond man with a fair, weathered-pink, clean-shaven face with high, tapering cheekbones. At least, what little hair he had was blond. The hair was confined to a band running around the sides of his head, leaving the crown as bald as Tutwiler's.

The lawman looked around the room. His gaze settled on Louisa, and he turned his head slightly to one side, scrutinizing the Vengeance Queen from a distance, frowning.

Louisa turned away and sipped her tea.

She had no time for lawmen.

It was as though her aversion summoned the man. Out the corner of her eye, she watched him walk toward her. He stopped at her table, stared down at her. He smelled smoky and cold.

"You an' me," he said tightly, tossing his wet hat onto her table. "We gotta talk."

Chapter 18

"Forgive me, but I'm feeling rather antisocial at the moment." Louisa dabbed at her torn lip with the cloth that was no longer cold, only wet.

The lawman pulled out a chair and sat down by his hat. He leaned forward, arms on the table. "I'm Del Rainy, town marshal."

Louisa set the rag down on the table and sipped her tea.

"I know who you are," Rainy said.

Louisa didn't say anything but only blew on her tea and sipped, staring off toward the stairs at the rear of the room.

"I know who you are," Rainy said again. "I seen you ride to the livery barn with them five men tied over their horses. I'd heard the shooting over at the depot. I checked *out* the depot."

Louisa turned to him now, blankly. "Did you introduce yourself to your new depot agent?"

"You go to hell," Rainy said in frustration. "I know who you are, I'm sayin'!"

Louisa sipped her tea again. "Good for you. I'm still feeling rather private, so if you'll excuse me, Marshal."

"Look, you can't just ride into my town throwing your weight around, Miss Bonaventure. I know who you are. I know your reputation, and I don't care. I'm the lawman here." Rainy poked himself in the chest. "You follow the laws here in Sundown just like everyone else. I don't doubt those fellas over to the train station gave you that split lip and swollen cheek, but in Sundown, I'm the law!"

Louisa looked at him again. "Are you saying that when they dragged me into your depot agent's sleeping quarters, I should have excused myself to come fetch you?"

She sipped her tea.

Rainy flushed a little. He stared at the Vengeance Queen, his eyes hard.

"Why are you here?"

"For the train."

"Who're the men in the livery barn?"

"They're from the Gritch Hatchley bunch."

"Damn!" Rainy gritted his teeth and slammed his right fist into his left hand, looking around. He pondered the situation for a moment then turned back to Louisa. "Them two upstairs—the woman and the half-breed. They're part of that bunch, aren't they? You followed 'em here."

"I'm here to catch the train."

"Damn!" Rainy slammed his fist into his palm again. "I knew it. I recognized 'em. I was here when they come in yesterday. I seen their faces on wanted dodgers over to my office. The sheriff wired me last week the

Hatchley bunch might be headed this way and to keep my eyes open."

"Forget about them, Marshal Rainy."

"What? Oh." Rainy smiled, nodded slowly. "I see. You want to take them down yourself, that it? Them two up there"—he pointed at the ceiling—"both have good money on their heads. You want it all for yourself."

"It is what I do for a living," Louisa said. "And if you'll forgive me for bragging, I do it rather well."

"Good money for each." Rainy sank back in his chair, his eyes glazing dreamily. "That would be one nice stake, I bet. How much we talkin', exactly?"

"You're a lawman. That makes you ineligible to receive the bounty."

Rainy looked at her. "You know that ain't true. Lawmen can take a bounty just like any civilian bounty hunter can." The marshal smiled, his eyes dropping to Louisa's open coat. "Just like any bounty hunt*ress* can." He smiled. "You sure are purty. Just like I heard. In a few minutes, I'll buy you a drink."

"Leave those two to me, Rainy." Again, Louisa pressed the cloth to her cheek and stared toward the stairs at the back of the room. "*Muy* bad folks up there."

"They're up there together, ain't they?" Rainy said. "That's what Morris said is all they been doin' since they rode into town yesterday, takin' a little time now and then for a meal."

"Leave them to me, Rainy."

The marshal's eyes hardened and his tapering cheeks flushed. He leaned toward Louisa. "This is my town. I'm the law here. I enforce the laws here in my town." He slid his chair back, rose. "You got the five in the barn. Them two upstairs is mine. They're each worth a thousand, at least. Just the stake I need to get me the hell out of here."

Absently, as though mostly to himself, he rubbed his jaw and added, "Don't know what I was thinkin', comin' up here in the first place. Me, a farmer! Got crowded out by the cattlemen so now I'm a town marshal makin' twenty-five dollars a month and havin' to sit here takin' grief from a female bounty hunter."

Rainy shrugged out of his wet wool coat, hung it over the back of his chair. He set his hat on his head, released the keeper thong from over the hammer of the Colt Army on his right hip, and turned toward the back of the room.

"You stay there an' sip your tea, purty girl. I'll buy you a real drink later." Rainy grinned and winked at her.

He strode down the long room toward the stairs. As he passed the bar, Tutwiler said, "Where you goin' Del?"

"Haul me down a bottle of the good stuff, Morris." Rainy continued toward the stairs.

"Don't go up there, Del."

"Haul me down a bottle of the good stuff. Pop the cork, pour it up." Rainy mounted the stairs, one hand on the banister, and began climbing. "I'll be down in three shakes of a pig's tail."

"I'm all out of the good stuff!"

All eyes in the room were on Rainy. When he'd gained the top of the stairs and stepped into the second-floor hall, several men muttered darkly. One chuckled. Clayton turned to Louisa and raised his freshly refilled shot glass, smiling behind his little spectacles, and said, "Here's to the good marshal."

Louisa looked away from him then swung her gaze to the front of the room when boots thumped on the porch. The door opened and a large draft of cold air blew in with large, swirling snowflakes that instantly dusted the floor and began melting. Three men came in, raising a raucous din with their boots thumping, spurs rattling, the men talking loudly, the wind howling in the street behind them.

"Shooo-weeee!" said the man entering first, doffing his hat and batting it against his woolly chaps. "Colder'n a banker's heart out there!" He chuckled and glanced at the other two men moving into the room behind him, the third one closing the door on the storm.

They were all dressed in rough trail gear. They had the seedy looks of market hunters. Blood stained their clothes. All three appeared to be in their mid to late twenties, and they owned the devilish, twinkling eyes of firebrands. Especially the first man who'd entered, who was tall and whipcord slender and with long, stringy blond hair hanging to his shoulders. He had a skull and crossbones tattooed on his neck, Louisa saw now as he unbuttoned his blanket coat.

His wild eyes, glassy from drink—the trio must have been passing a bottle as they'd ridden to Sundown— swept the room several times, each time coming to rest on Louisa, whose belly tightened in dread of having to parry more unwanted, drunken advances.

Keeping his eyes on Louisa, who did not look back at him directly but only out of the corner of her eye, not wanting to encourage him in the least, the blond firebrand said, "Hey, Morris, how 'bout a bottle?"

Tutwiler said, "What the hell you boys doin' in town, Vink? I thought you was huntin' game fer the railroad down in Bismarck? And you know I don't walk that far. You want a bottle, come an' get it!"

"You fat, lazy son of an old she-lion!" said the second young firebrand—shorter than the blond, and dark haired. He owned a roosterlike strut.

Tutwiler didn't react to the insult, which seemed to have been spoken only half seriously, mostly in a dry kind of joking though the dark-haired man wasn't smiling. He had three days' worth of beard stubble and close-set, mean little eyes. Tutwiler only said, "There's beans on the stove. Bowls are up here—a dime apiece."

"It's free if we're drinkin', ain't it?" asked the dark-haired little man, bellying up to the bar.

"No, it ain't free if you're drinkin'," Tutwiler mocked him, setting a bottle of unlabeled busthead onto the bar before him.

"Hi, little lady!" said the tall, blond Vink.

Louisa had shrunk deep inside herself as out of the corner of her right eye she'd watched him saunter up to her table. Now he stood over her, thumbs hooked behind his cartridge belts, the flaps of his blanket coat shoved back behind the pistol holstered on his right thigh and the handle of the silver-capped bowie knife jutting on his left hip, from a bloodstained sheath.

"What's your name?" the blond wanted to know.

Louisa brought her mug to her lips, sipped the tea. "Go to hell."

"Go to hell?" the blond said with a high-pitched squeal of laughter. "Well, hello there, Miss Go-to-Hell. My name's Ray. Ray Vink. These is Mose and Nasty Ralph."

He'd glanced first at the short, dark-haired man just now chewing the cork out of his bottle at the bar, and then at the third man who'd walked into the saloon with them and who was kicking out a chair at a table between Edgar Clayton and the bar.

Clayton sat broodingly over his shot glass and beer, appearing so preoccupied by his own thoughts— thoughts of Ramsay Willis, most likely—that he wasn't even aware of the newcomers. The third newcomer stood over the chair he'd kicked out, unbuttoning his coat and staring lustily toward Louisa. He was big and rawboned, with a full cinnamon beard carpeting a round, fleshy face. A large, dark wart grew out of the side of his nose, near the stubby tip.

"I'm Nasty Ralph," he said, stretching a smile at Louisa. "I won't be nasty to you, though, Miss Go-to-Hell, if you ain't nasty to me." He smiled more broadly and winked.

"Shut up, Nasty Ralph," Vink said, gazing dreamily down at Louisa. "I seen her first."

"Hell," said the short man, Mose, carrying the bottle and three shot glasses over to the table where Nasty Ralph was sagging his bulk into a chair, "she's the only woman in here. Hey, Tutwiler, you got any girls upstairs?"

"I don't have any workin' girls no more," Tutwiler said. "I done already told you boys that several times. Runnin' sportin' girls is worse than herding cats, an' I'm just too damn old to herd cats. If you want girls, Clarence Gray Wind has girls down at his place along the creek."

"It's too cold for the creek," Vink said, still staring with simpleminded fawning down at Louisa. "Besides, one of the half-breed's girls gave me the pony drip last fall. I spent the winter on mercury!" He laughed at that. "Tincture of mercury," he explained to Louisa, who still did not look at him. "The sawbones over to

Devil's Lake gave me some. Nasty stuff but it did the trick." He paused. "Hey, how 'bout if I sit down here with you, Miss Go-to-Hell?"

"Can't you see the lady isn't interested?"

The man who'd spoken was the handsome, blue-clad soldier sitting at the table nearer the bar, playing cards with the drummers. He was hipped around in his chair, his cards in one hand, glaring at Vink.

"Who're you?" the blond firebrand inquired, sneering. "Her lord an' master? Or . . . maybe you just wanna be." He grinned insinuatingly.

Ah, Jesus, Louisa thought, her gut tightening.

The soldier slid his gaze to her then back toward Vink, who turned to face him now. The soldier laid his cards down, near a cigar smoldering in an ashtray, and rose from his chair.

"It's all right," Louisa called, fashioning an affable smile. "He was just joking. Even if he wasn't, I'm not offended. Come on, fellas. It's a cold and stormy night, and we're all friends here. Friends staying warm. Let's be friendly!"

The captain was having none of it. He left the drummers at the table, staring at him expectantly, and strode over to where Vink stood near Louisa, facing him. The captain was the same height as Vink, and he wore an army-issue Colt in a flap holster positioned for the cross-draw on his left hip. He wore a bone-handled bowie knife in a sheath on his right hip.

His cobalt blue eyes glinted in the light of several smoky lamps guttering from ceiling support posts.

He stopped three feet away from Vink and said, "Apologize to the lady."

"Please," Louisa said, "let's all just—"

"No." The captain kept his eyes on Vink. "This man insulted you. I won't let him get away with it." To the blond firebrand, he said, "Apologize to the lady."

"Go to hell, soldier boy!"

"That's *Captain Yardley*, you uncouth bastard. Apologize to the lady!"

"Go to hell, soldier boy!"

Captain Yardley jerked. It was such a quick jerk that he became a blur for half a second. When he stopped moving, Louisa saw the man's right fist buried in Vink's solar plexus. Vink gave a great "*Gnahh!*" as the air was punched out of his lungs, and he jackknifed forward, eyes wide, face swelling and turning dark red.

As Captain Yardley pulled his fist back, straightening, Vink dropped to his knees, groaning.

His two cohorts, Mose and Nasty Ralph, had gained their feet when the captain had walked over to Vink. Now they both leaped forward but froze when a gun blasted at the room's rear, the sudden explosion making everyone, including Louisa, jerk with a start.

Louisa quickly shuttled her gaze to the back of the room. A man stood on the stairs just far enough down from the top that Louisa could see his entire body, his hat crown grazing the ceiling above his head. Marshal Del Rainy held his smoking Colt down low in his right hand, aimed at the floor.

Rainy just stood there, staring straight ahead. At least, he appeared to be staring straight ahead. His body was nearly entirely in shadow, his eyes deeply shaded by his hat brim. Louisa kept expecting the man to order the men before her to stand down, but it didn't come.

Everyone in the room watched him, waiting.

Finally, Rainy dropped his left foot down to the next step below him. It was a sudden, violent movement. His head bobbed as though he hadn't been ready to take the step, as though his own movement had caught him by surprise.

Rainy continued down the stairs, taking the steps faster and faster until near the bottom he was nearly running. He dropped his gun, which struck the second step from the bottom with a loud thud. He dropped to the saloon floor on both feet, twisted around as though drunk, and fell on his back near the bar without breaking his fall.

Louisa had already gained her feet. She ran out from her table, pushing past Yardley and Vink, who remained on the floor, groaning. She ran down the bar to stand staring down at Rainy.

The marshal lay flat on his back, staring up at her, his eyes glazed. His expression was blank except for one eye twitching spasmodically. Louisa raked her gaze down the man's body and parted her lips, drawing a breath when she saw the blood oozing out from between the fingers of his left hand, which he'd placed on his belly.

As the men in the room slowly converged on her and the marshal from behind, Louisa dropped to a knee beside the dying lawman. She slid his left hand aside and winced down at his belly. She drew another slow, deep breath as she studied the stab wound just above the square buckle of the lawman's cartridge belt.

Rainy's dull-eyed stare found Louisa. He opened his mouth but was slow to speak. When he did, it came out as a raking, barely audible whisper. "Sh-she-devil buried a bowie in my guts."

Louisa lifted her head. All the men in the room

except Vink stood around her and Rainy, quiet as church mice. They were so silent that Louisa could hear only the beans bubbling on the stove and the wind outside the saloon . . . and the snickering laughter, male and female, issuing from the ceiling.

Chapter 19

"I'm gonna ask you one more time," Prophet told the young hardtail lying at the base of the window through which the cold wind blew. "Where's Hatchley?"

He pressed the Peacemaker's barrel more firmly against the young hardcase's right cheek. The hardcase flopped on his back on the deep, sour-smelling Oriental rug, kicking his legs defiantly. Blood oozed from the ragged hole on the other side of his face.

"I don't know, you son of the devil!" he screamed.

Another scream sounded somewhere in the bowels of the remote whorehouse/saloon, beneath the wind moaning through the broken windows. This scream, a girl's, had been muffled.

"You go to hell!" the one-eyed hardtail bellowed.

Prophet pulled the Peacemaker away from the young man's cheek. Slowly, staring up at the balcony, he rose and started striding toward the stairs. The scream had come from the second story.

When Prophet was halfway across the room, he heard soft scuffling and grunting sounds behind him. He wheeled.

The kid was just then pulling a hideout pistol from the well of his right boot. Prophet whipped up the Peacemaker, cocking it, and squeezed the trigger. The kid was knocked straight back against the floor, where he lay flopping, dying fast.

"Fool."

Clicking the Peacemaker's hammer back again and holding the big .45 barrel-up in his right hand, Prophet continued across the room and mounted the stairs angling up the back wall, running parallel to it and the balcony. It was a steep staircase with a rail made of woven aspen saplings.

Prophet moved slowly up the stairs, as quietly as possible then walked just as slowly along the balcony, listening behind each door as he passed. When he was three-quarters down the balcony, in deep shadows that wavered with watery light reaching weakly up from the first story, something sounded behind a door off his right shoulder.

Prophet stopped, wincing as a floorboard squawked faintly beneath his left boot.

From behind the door came a clipped, muffled cry and then the sound of someone saying, "Shhh" very faintly. A click followed the admonition.

Prophet took a quick step forward. Before he'd even set his boot down again, a loud explosion assaulted his ears, making the balcony leap beneath his boots. A hole the size of a squash was blown through the door from the other side, the buckshot blasting the wood slivers out over the balcony and into the saloon below.

Another concussive explosion sounded close on the heels of the first, plugging one of Prophet's ears and doubling the size of the hole in the door.

Prophet stepped back in front of the door and

slammed the flat of his right boot against it, near the latch. The door with the gaping hole burst open, and before it could slam back against him, Lou stepped into the small room and caught the door with his boot as he extended his cocked Colt straight out from his right shoulder.

The man standing before him—six feet, broad, long haired, pale skinned, and clad in only wash-worn balbriggans—had just lowered his smoking, sawed-off, double-barreled shotgun and was smiling as he aimed a Bisley .44 straight out from his own right shoulder, lining up his sights on Prophet's forehead.

Prophet was about to cut loose with his Colt but then the face of the man before him crumpled in sudden horror, chocolate eyes turning wide as silver dollars, his mouth opening to nearly the size of the hole he'd blown in the door. There was a girl on the bed to his right. She appeared to be a small, plump Mexican, and she had long, dark brown hair. She pulled a stiletto out from between Hatchley's legs, from behind him.

She must have stuck him in his backside. She appeared very satisfied with her work, too, for she slid her plump lips back from her gritted teeth and shrieked, "¡No sabes cómo tratar a las chicas, loco!"

Prophet, who knew just enough Spanish to get himself into deep trouble south of the border, roughly translated the puta's exclamation as: "That's no way to treat a girl, you crazy fiend!"

Hatchley had dropped to his hands and knees, bellowing. He dropped the Bisley and reached down to cup his hand over the gash whose placement Prophet still hadn't pinpointed.

The girl vaulted her small, dark, plump body off the

bed and onto Hatchley's back and went to work, screaming and punching his head, slamming her fists against his ears, the back of his neck and the crown of his skull, making his dark brown hair, which was nearly as long as the girl's hair, fly like a muddy tumbleweed in the wind.

Hatchley glared up at Prophet and yelled, "Get her off me!"

Prophet lowered his Colt as he stepped farther into the room.

"All right, señorita," he said. "I'll take over from here."

She continued to punch and slap the wounded hardcase, screaming Spanish epithets, for a good half a minute. She likely would have continued the assault if she hadn't gotten winded and if she hadn't looked up and seen the big man in the buckskin coat holding the .45 low in his right hand, his funnel-brimmed Stetson tied to his head with a ratty green muffler.

She didn't know if Prophet were friend or foe. For all she knew, he was just as bad as Hatchley. Breathing hard, muttering curses under her breath and sobbing now, as well, she climbed down off the hardcase's back and brushed past Prophet as she ran out of the room. She gave a scream in the hall, and Prophet turned to see that she'd run into Marshal Sheldon Coffer, who'd just stepped into the room's doorway.

She bounced off Coffer and then ran down the balcony to her right, the padding of her bare feet dwindling behind her. Another door opened and slammed shut, and she was gone.

Coffer held his old Remington barrel-up, and looked first at the howling Gritch Hatchley and then at Prophet. Coffer's face was red from the cold outside, and his nose was running. "You clean up right well, Lou." He nodded at the cursing hardcase, who now sat on his butt against the washstand abutting the room's back wall, to the right of the bed. "Who's your friend here?"

"This here's Gritch Hatchley," Prophet said. "Damn near thought I wasn't gonna be able to take him alive. If that little girl had had her way, I wouldn't have. She really worked him over." He raised his voice. "How you doin', Gritch? Feelin' all right, you old bank robber?"

Hatchley's face was as broad as an Indian's. In fact, he looked Indian though Prophet had heard he hailed from French coal-mining stock up in Canada. He wore long, black mare's tail mustaches down past his chin, long sideburns, and a silver stud shaped like a cross in his right ear. His left earlobe was missing. Only a grisly white knot remained. His face looked as though it had been hammered crudely out of dark granite though the rest of his body was as white as salt.

"That loco señorita cut me good!" The outlaw spat through large, square, gritted teeth. "I'm bleedin' bad!"

"She cut off anything important?"

Hatchley glared at Prophet, dark eyes shiny from both drink and exasperation. "You'd like that, wouldn't you, Prophet?"

The bounty hunter had never met the man before though he'd heard plenty about him. Hatchley had probably heard plenty about Prophet, in turn.

"No, I wouldn't," Prophet said, shaking his head. "Because that'd mean you're likely gonna bleed to death here in a few minutes, and that would cost me five hundred dollars. Me? I'm a thrifty son of the old rebel South. I'd just as soon tote your livin', cussin' corpse into Bismarck for the full two thousand."

The bounty hunter canted his head, trying to get a

look at how bad his prisoner's wound was, but all he could see was way more than he wanted to see and not the wound itself. Plenty of blood was oozing onto the floor between the man's pale legs, however. He had his right hand cupped under his upper left thigh.

"She missed the important stuff," Hatchley hissed, "but she come close! I'm bleedin' bad! Fetch me a sawbones before I bleed dry!"

Prophet dragged a pair of girl's pantaloons off a chair back. He tossed them to Hatchley. "Wrap it up and get dressed. We're ridin' back to Indian Butte."

"In this weather? It's stormin' outside, fool!"

Coffer stepped forward. "Storm or no storm, we'd best light a shuck, Lou. Several men skinned out the back when you went in the front. They probably lit out for the woodcutters' camp, which means they'll likely bring more men back here soon. They prob'ly think we're federal"—he raised his brows significantly— "and after their whiskey."

He shook his head. "They won't want to part with their whiskey."

"I've had about enough lead swappin' for one night, anyways. I'm plum tuckered out." Prophet turned to Hatchley. "Don't make me tell you again, Gritch, or I'll sic that little Mex on you again. Wrap it up and get dressed. We're burnin' starlight!"

It was a chilly ride back to Indian Butte.

In the barn flanking the whorehouse Prophet had saddled a horse for Gritch Hatchley and tied the man's handcuffed wrists to his saddle horn. Not that Hatchley would have strayed far without the cuffs and the ties. It was a cold, snowy, windy night, and he'd missed being gelded by the width of a cat's whisker.

The plump señorita had, however, buried her stiletto deep in the killer's left inner thigh. At least, judging from the amount of blood Hatchley had left on the girl's floor, she must have buried it deep. Due to the location of the injury, Prophet felt no compunction to scrutinize it overly closely. If the outlaw died, he died. The hell with him and the extra five hundred. Prophet had lost that much money in a half hour at a poker table.

Still, he summoned a sawbones once he, Hatchley, and Sheldon Coffer reached Indian Butte, after the horses had been turned over to the livery barn's slightly pie-eyed hostler, Pop Schofield. Horses first, Hatchley second.

Indian Butte's venerable surgeon, an older gent named Karl Hassler, who'd been the medico at the nearby Fort Totten Agency and who, like the liveryman, had been keeping the stormy chill out of his bones with a goodly portion of who-hit-John, continued to sip from a small, flat brown bottle while he sutured Hatchley's leg in one of the three cells forming a line along the rear stone wall of Coffer's jailhouse two blocks east of the Indian Butte Hotel.

"You're one lucky feller, I'll give you that," the mossy-horned medico announced from time to time, pinching up the groaning killer's skin and running his curved needle through the torn flesh.

Each time he drew the catgut taut, he took a drink, extending one beringed, age-gnarled pinky then smacking his lips as he returned the bottle to the floor. "If your girl had slid that blade a hair to the right, she would have perforated the circumflex fibular branch

of the anterior tibial artery, and your goose would
have been cooked."

"That sow," Hatchley grunted, panting and swill-
ing whiskey against the pain as he lay belly down
against the padded iron cot. "That crazy little sow! I'm
gonna cut her tongue out, cut her ears off, cut her
nose off . . ."

And on and on he went while Prophet, yawning, sat
in a chair in the cell's open doorway, keeping his
Richards gut-shredder trained on the miserable killer's
head.

It had been one hell of a long day. It was damn near
midnight, and Prophet wanted nothing so much as to
head over to the Indian Butte Saloon & Hotel, rent a
room with the softest, least louse-ridden bed in the
place, order up a steak, a bottle, and a hot bath. After
soaking himself into near unconsciousness, he'd throw
himself into the bed and plummet deep into a restful
if all too brief slumber.

As soon as the sawbones had finished sewing up the
growling, snarling killer, Prophet closed the cell door
on him, twisted the key in the lock, turned the key
over to Coffer, who looked as weary as Prophet felt,
then slogged through the several inches of fresh snow
to the sprawling flophouse, which sat at the opposite
end of the main street from the marshal's humble
little jail.

Not much snow was falling, but the wind was a blue,
howling devil. The cold bit Prophet deep. It seemed to
bite him even deeper than before, coming again so
violently after he'd so recently thawed himself out in
Coffer's jailhouse, heated by a roaring potbelly stove.
He slipped and slid in the fresh white stuff that lay like

a two-inch-deep bed of feathers on the boardwalk fronting the hotel.

He climbed the steps, grumbling, hunkered down inside his coat, hearing music resonating from inside the place—strange music to his ears, but damned lively music, as well.

He stomped snow from his moccasins then pushed through the heavy storm doors inside of which the batwings, used in warmer months, were tied back against the wall to either side. He closed the storm doors but not before a cold breath laden with large snowflakes had swept in around him, causing several people in the saloon beyond to give him the woolly eyebrow.

Prophet shrugged guiltily as he turned to face the room, untying the muffler knotted beneath his chin and removing his hat. He stood several feet above the room, which was sunken five steps down from the door, so he had a good view of the layout.

Broad and deep, the room was lit with several well-placed bracket lamps. It was heated by two large, black, bullet-shaped Windsor stoves. There were a good twenty men in the room, occupying two long tables running along the room's far-right wall and several scattered tables nearer to Prophet and the front of the room. The men were smoking and drinking but what they were mainly doing was watching the dark-eyed little countess dancing about ten feet from the stove to Prophet's right, to the right of the bar that ran along the rear wall.

Prophet had never seen such a dance. And he'd never seen a young lady—or any woman of any age—decked out in such billowing, brightly colored finery as was the dancing countess.

Her dress was snow-white with a pleated skirt, and it was trimmed in gold and red velvet, and there was even some spruce green in it. It looked almost like a fancy Spanish ball gown, for it was low cut, leaving the pretty, olive-skinned little damsel's shoulders bare, its brocade bodice jostling as she moved, hopping and skipping and turning lithe pirouettes that caused her long, thick, dark brown hair to fly out wildly around her head.

Just watching such a scrumptious, sensuous female move in such an exotically enticing fashion made the bounty hunter's heart twist.

"If that don't beat a pig a-flyin'!" he heard himself mutter beneath the jubilant strains of the happy, raucous music to which the dark-eyed countess kicked and hopped, flinging her arms about and even, at one point, crossing them straight out in front of her chest while she kicked her knees up nearly to her chin.

"Holy moly," the bounty hunter said, pensively scratching his chin.

Chapter 20

The music the buxom little countess danced to was being played by instruments Prophet had never before encountered.

There was a five-man band. No, a five-man-and-one-*woman* band.

The light was weak at the room's rear, and Prophet hadn't noticed the stout, older, black-haired woman seated in an upholstered armchair and playing a strange-looking stringed instrument laid flat across her lap. Her hair was pinned severely atop her head, which she lowered and sort of rolled from side to side with the oddly sonorous twanging sounds that rose from her fingers as they flicked across the strings.

One of the men was playing a guitar with a triangular body! The others were playing a fiddle and various wind instruments, one of which resembled a very long meerschaum pipe with a broad, ornately flared bowl. The men were all decked out in gaudily embroidered costumes with high, red velvet, conical caps, and they bent their knees and jostled to and fro as they played. The old woman played the flat, stringed thing on her broad thighs from her chair, moving only her hands and her head.

Prophet found himself staring so long at the dancing countess, intoxicated by the girl's smoldering sensuality not to mention the thrilling way she moved, the inadequate bodice of her colorful dress jostling enticingly, that only when his knees began to buckle did he realize he was about to pass out from exhaustion.

He didn't think any other man in the room was conscious of his presence. All eyes were on the girl.

The men at the long table along the far wall appeared to be in the countess's party. There were a good dozen of them, maybe more. They were dressed more fashionably than the others, their mustaches and beards immaculately clipped. Most were from the countess's home country. Prophet recognized several of the large, dark-bearded, straight-backed men from the veranda earlier. Even sitting, they owned a military bearing.

Prophet saw the fancy Dan sitting there—Rawdney Fairweather—between an older, bespectacled man Prophet assumed was the Dan's father, Senator Wilfred Fairweather, and the younger, dark-haired and neatly bearded gent, Leo, who'd accompanied Rawdney on the street earlier, when he'd confronted Prophet about the countess's carriage.

About its demise, to be exact.

All of the men at the table over there, dressed in dark suits, with fur coats hanging from their chair backs, a heavy cloud of tobacco smoke billowing over their heads, clapped their hands in time with the music and thumped their feet on the floor. They smiled with admiration touched in no small amount with leering lust. Even the old senator, whose craggy cheeks were flushed above his thin, charcoal beard, was no doubt imagining the countess dancing in his private quarters sans the fancy dress, clad in only that earthy, bewitching smile.

The old man—as old or even older than the senator—who sat at the end of the table nearest the front wall and smoked a long-stemmed, brass and ivory pipe, was likely the count himself. The countess's father. There was a distinct family resemblance though he must have been pushing seventy.

Leaning forward, elbows on the table, he appeared short and squat, but his bearded face was regal, the eyes the same liquid black as the girl's. Long, thick, coal black hair was combed straight back over his head and tucked behind his ears. There wasn't a thread of gray in it, as far as Prophet could tell. Shiny with pomade, it licked down over the back of the collar of his fine, metallic red coat richly adorned with gilt stitching, including two golden eagles spreading their wings high on each breast.

Prophet lifted his right boot, about to drop down the steps and head toward the bar, then stopped. He saw now that at least one of the men at the table of the countess's party was aware of his presence.

None other than Rawdney himself was glowering at him, eyes narrowed, his pale forehead glistening like polished pearl in the light of a guttering lamp hanging low above his head. Prophet smiled, pinched his hat brim to the fop. Rawdney curled one half of his thin mouth in a silent snarl.

Adjusting the saddlebags and rifle sheath hanging heavy on his left shoulder, and the Richards hanging down his back, the bounty hunter dropped down the five steps to the main floor and strode heavily toward the bar.

As he did, he glanced at the countess once more. Her dark eyes were on him. They seemed glued, in fact, their expression unreadable. She turned away suddenly, blushing ever so slightly, as she performed another acrobatic leap and pirouette.

Prophet gave a lusty groan as he turned his own gaze from the girl's ravishing succulence and continued to the bar at the back of the smoky room, the music and the girl's dancing reverberating through the floor beneath his boots. A barmaid, the only one in the place, it appeared—a rotund, dour-looking young Indian woman—was just then making her way toward the count's table with a tray of frothy beer schooners.

A beefy man with a beard but no mustache stood behind the bar, smoking and watching the countess while yet another fellow—a full-blood Indian with long, scraggly black hair—stirred a pot on the big range behind the bar.

The barman eyed Prophet a little warily as the bounty hunter approached, bristling as Prophet was laden down with weapons, including the Richards poking up from behind his broad back.

"Room," Prophet said, noting the tingling in his toes as they began to thaw once more. "A hot bath. A steak. Rare. And a bottle. No, make that two bottles of your best firewater."

The barman scowled at Prophet. He canted his head toward the count's table then slid his gaze toward the four or five other tables at which rough-hewn townsmen sat, also enjoying the entertainment.

"Can't you see I got a full house tonight? I got one room left but no time to haul water to it. You can have it for three dollars. I'll sell you the stew Henry is cooking and I'll sell you a bottle of good liquor. Grub an' whiskey's five dollars. Eight dollars total." The barman extended his pudgy palm. "Payable up front."

"You're gouging on account of the storm. Rooms in a stink hole like this likely go for a dollar, maybe six bits on any other night."

The barman smiled.

"And I bet your best whiskey goes for seventy-five cents."

"Ain't you the wise man? If you're looking for baby Jesus, he's out in the manger."

Prophet gave a wry chuff. He reached into his coat pocket and flipped a coin in the air. The barman jerked his hands up with a start and caught the coin against his chin, flushing with annoyance. He opened his hand.

He arched a shaggy brow at Prophet. "That's an eagle."

"There'll be one more ten-dollar gold piece *after* I've had my bath and eaten my steak." Prophet had scavenged the money off one of the dead men, who no longer had use for it now that he was sleeping the last, long sleep, likely frozen up as solid as a tombstone out in the livery barn.

The bounty hunter extended his hand across the bar. "Key."

The barman looked at Prophet's hand. He glanced behind him at the big Indian, who, with a corn-husk cigarette dangling from between his lips, returned the glance with a shrug and then turned back to his pot.

Ashes from the cigarette tumbled into the pot. The barman reached under the bar for a key and set it in Prophet's hand.

"Fourteen. Third floor. Far, far end," he added with a satisfied snarl.

"Thunder juice."

When the barman had handed over two labeled bottles, Prophet stuffed them into his coat pockets. He made his way along the bar to the broad staircase opening at the far right end of it, near where the countess had been dancing.

She'd stopped now and, flushed from exertion, stood near the long table, Rawdney Fairweather hovering over her, fawning shamelessly. He held one of her small hands in both of his hands, patting it and fairly sniveling over the girl, rising anxiously up and down on the balls of his feet.

Just as Prophet turned to mount the stairs, the girl, who must have been watching him out of the corner of her eye, swung her head toward him. Again, their eyes met. They held briefly. Rawdney saw the quick, furtive exchange and raised his own gaze to Prophet, his eyes and mouth hardening.

Prophet pinched his hat brim to the dandy, chuckling, and mounted the stairs, climbing up into the shadowy bowels of the creaky old building, which groaned and shuddered against the gusts of the cold Dakota wind.

An hour later, he dozed in a hot tub, his hunger sated by an entire bottle of whiskey as well as the succulent steak that Henry had delivered to him, after the Indian had brought the copper tub and filled it with near-scalding water. Prophet dozed despite the raucous music still hammering through the floor from the main drinking hall below.

Footsteps sounded on the hall outside Prophet's door, rousing him slightly.

The footsteps stopped. There was a light tap on the door. He barely heard it above the music from below.

Prophet lifted his head, frowned at the door. He hadn't had an opportunity to lock it, as he'd been soaking in the tub the last time Henry had come and gone.

Prophet blinked sleepily, half-drunk. "Who is—"

He hadn't had time to finish the question before the door was thrust open. The little countess waltzed straight into the room, followed by two big men in gaudy red uniform tunics and deerskin trousers stuffed into the high tops of fur-trimmed leather boots.

The little countess stopped before Prophet, planted her fists on her hips, and glared down at him, eyes blazing. In badly broken English, she shrieked, "Are you the *bol'shoy ublyudok* who broke my carriage?"

"Hey, now!" Prophet said.

He automatically completed his reach for his Peacemaker, which he'd hung from a chair near the tub, always in close reach. But he was so sluggish from steak, whiskey, and fatigue that he'd moved too slowly. One of the big men who'd entered with the girl reached around Prophet and grabbed the pistol before Prophet could close his hands around the grips.

The big man, ginger bearded and with frosty gray eyes set beneath thick ginger brows, barked something in a foreign tongue, which Prophet figured was Russian, and rapped the barrel of Prophet's own revolver across the bounty hunter's forehead.

"Ow!" Lou pressed his hands to his head, just below his hairline.

Scowling against the pain from the bruise the frosty-eyed Russian had tattooed him with, Prophet looked up at the little countess still glaring down at him with her fists on her hips. Now she was smiling, eyes slanted like a devilish cat's.

Prophet drew a breath and let it out with: "*Get the hell out of my room, you little polecat!*"

The countess's eyes snapped wide again, fairly stabbing bayonets of pure rage at the naked man in the tub. She glanced at the men to each side of her and stepped back, pursing her lips in a savage, menacing smile.

The man to each side of Prophet closed on him. As he placed his hands on the edge of the tub, trying to hoist himself up and out of the now-tepid water to where he had a better chance of defending himself, each big Russian grabbed one of his arms. They pulled him up out of the water.

Prophet leaped out of the tub, raging, trying to fight, but they held his arms fast, one on each side of the tub. While the ginger-bearded Russian stepped behind him and wrenched both his arms behind his back, the second man, wider and shorter than the first and with one brown eye and one eye that was eggshell white, drew his right fist back, bunching his lips with fierce determination.

Prophet canted his head to one side, accidentally timing the move perfectly. The one-eyed Russian's fist glanced off his left jaw. With an enormous explosion of indignant rage, Prophet bulled forward and, before the one-eyed Russian could cock his fist for another blow, Lou slammed his head against his forehead.

As the man howled and stumbled backward, slapping his hands to his left temple, Prophet heaved his torso forward, giving a bearlike roar. He jerked his arms up and around from behind him. Since his arms, like the rest of him, were wet, they slipped easily from the ginger-bearded Russian's grip.

Wheeling, Prophet swung a hard right cross that smashed savagely against the ginger-bearded man's left cheek, sending him barreling sideways into the room's front wall. Prophet wheeled again to see the one-eyed Russian rushing toward him, bringing his right fist up again, that determined look compressing his mouth.

Prophet ducked. The ginger-bearded Russian's fist whooshed through the air where his head had just been.

Prophet was big—two hundred–plus pounds on a frame nearly six and a half feet tall. But even tired and drunk, he was as lithe as a cat, especially when he was raging with as much fury as he was now. He stepped forward and slammed his right fist into the one-eyed man's left ear.

"Oh!" the man said, his head jerking to one side, eyes snapping wide. His head shook, reverberating from the blow. His ear turned snow-white then rose-petal pink.

Prophet slammed his fist into the same ear again, again, and again, driving the man across the small room to the front wall. As the one-eyed man slumped there, stunned, blood issuing from his torn ear, Prophet hammered his head three more powerful times.

Prophet turned. The ginger-bearded man stood before him. The Russian was smiling despite the blood leaking from the left corner of his mouth. A broken tooth appeared between his lips. He spit it out then bolted forward, snarling like a rabid panther and closing his big hands over Prophet's face, trying to work his thumbs into the bounty hunter's eyes.

Prophet tipped his head back, keeping the man's thumbs out of his eye sockets. He tried to shrug out from under the man's solid grip to no avail.

Both men bellowing and snarling and cursing in their own native tongues, they struggled there against the wall for nearly a minute, hands clawing at the other's face, before Prophet finally jerked his arms up, breaking the ginger-bearded man's grip on his head.

He head-butted the man then smashed two left jabs against his mouth.

The man stumbled backward, lips smashed, giving a shrill cry as he fell into Prophet's tub crossways, making the water splash up and over the edges and onto the floor. Prophet walked over to him, leaned down, and smashed the man's face twice more—first with his left fist, then with his right.

That turned the man over sideways, and he wallowed lengthways in what remained of Prophet's bathwater, blinking rapidly, eyes rolling back in his head.

Breathing hard, Prophet straightened. He stumbled backward then regained his balance. He looked around, saw the countess sitting in a chair by the door, her left leg crossed over the knee of the other leg, beneath her frilly skirt.

She had her arms crossed on her lovely bodice. Her eyes raked him up and down. Her expression was unabashedly brazen, ripe lips slightly parted, olive-colored cheeks tipped with pink. She returned her gaze to Lou's and quirked her mouth corners up into a beguiling, ambiguous half smile.

Suddenly self-conscious, he grabbed a towel off a near chair and held it over his privates.

The countess glanced at her fallen accomplices—one in the tub, one on his knees to Prophet's left, pressing his forehead against the floor. The girl's face colored up like a stormy sky. She shot up from her chair, and, bent slightly forward at the waist, sliding her accusatory glare from one man to the other and back again, bellowed loudly in Russian.

Prophet couldn't have distinguished her harsh tongue from the language of the wildcats, but he could tell she was berating both men roundly. By the furious flush rising in her perfectly formed cheeks, she was likely castigating their bloodlines and manhoods, to boot.

The man in the tub, wincing against the verbal bombardment, hoisted himself out of the water. He fell over the side to the floor then worked himself to his feet. His face was badly smashed, nose turned sideways. His wet uniform tunic was spotted with soapsuds. He gave Prophet an indignant but also a faintly admiring glance then stumbled over to the door.

Slumped under the countess's unrelenting denouncements, he slogged out.

The one-eyed man finally maneuvered his head, which appeared to be a heavy burden for him, up off the floor near the front wall. While the countess continued to harangue him, he trod heavily to the door, tripped over the tub, then stumbled into the hall and disappeared.

The countess turned her beautifully flushed cheeks and angrily crossed eyes to Prophet, standing seven feet away from her, holding the towel over his privates.

"You have beaten two Cossacks senseless," she said, her tone coldly accusing. "Do you know what this means?"

Prophet had no idea. He was still searching for an answer when the countess extended her right hand out to her side, grabbed the door, and slammed it.

"It means I am yours for the rest of the evening!"

Chapter 21

Louisa stared down at the glassy eyes of the Sundown marshal, Del Rainy, who lay spread-eagle on the saloon floor, between the stairs and the bar. The thick, dark red blood pool grew wider beneath him, leaking out of the stab wound in his belly.

Rainy stared plaintively up at Louisa. He moved his lips as though trying to speak.

The lawman's eyes turned opaque. They rolled upward until he was staring at the ceiling directly above him. His final breath rattled across his lips, making his mouth flutter. His chest contracted. Then it stopped moving. It did not expand again. The man would never draw another breath.

"That's a damn shame," lamented the red-faced barman, Morris Tutwiler. He shifted his gaze to the top of the stairs down which Rainy had come. "Rainy never was much of a lawman, but I always liked Del. He didn't deserve a knife in his guts!"

Slowly, Louisa rose from her knee. Staring down at the lifeless body of Del Rainy, she unsnapped the keeper thong from over the hammer of her right Colt and, closing her hand around the cool, smooth pearl handles, shucked the .45 from its holster. She slid her gaze up the stairs and then scuttled it along the ceiling, in the direction from which the sounds had issued earlier and now from which came delighted snickers and unrestrained laughter.

Louisa turned slowly around. She stepped away from Rainy.

All the men in the saloon—Tutwiler, Ray Vink, and his partners Mose and Nasty Ralph, the three drummers, the handsome cavalry captain, Yardley, and the grave-faced Edgar Clayton—stood in a ragged semicircle around her. Now they shifted their positions, frowning at her, making way for her, as, holding her Colt straight down along her right leg and peering up at the low ceiling, she strode back along the bar toward the front of the room.

She followed the snickering in the ceiling around the front end of the bar and toward the far side of the saloon, moving back down along the bar's opposite side, kicking chairs out of her way. There was another customer over there on that side of the bar, one that Louisa hadn't seen until now. The reason she hadn't seen him was that he'd been on the opposite side of the bar from her and he hadn't spoken or even moved much since she'd come in out of the storm.

Obviously drunk, he was slumped forward across his table, arms flung straight out above his head. His left cheek was pressed against the table, and he snored softly. An empty bottle, a half-empty shot glass, and an empty beer mug stood on the table around his head and outstretched arms and overturned black felt hat. A ragged winter coat hung off his narrow shoulders.

From what Louisa could see of his darkly wrinkled face, he was an older gent. Sixties or seventies.

Louisa stepped quietly around the sleeping drunk and stared up at the soot-stained, pressed-tin ceiling at the southeast corner of the room, near a large oil painting depicting a hefty blond woman lounging semi-naked on a red velvet fainting couch.

In the ceiling there, Louisa heard a man's voice, doubtless the voice of Pima Quarrels, say something in a laughing tone. The woman, Sweets DuPree, laughed in response and said loudly and clearly enough for Louisa to hear:

"Did you see the look on his face when I shoved the blade in?"

She squealed with laughter.

Her lover, Quarrels, guffawed. There was the clink of a bottle nudging a glass, refreshing a drink.

Louisa hardened her jaws. She clicked her Colt's hammer back, raised the gun, angled it up above her head, aiming at the ceiling beyond which Sweets DuPree and Pima Quarrels were likely lounging together in bed, drinking, smoking, making love—if you could call it love—and delighting in their murder of Marshal Rainy.

They'd probably celebrated their murdering of the two young female tellers, whom they'd kidnapped from the bank they'd robbed in Wyoming, in much the same fashion. After they'd taken their pleasure from the poor, unwitting girls and cut their throats.

Bang! Bang!

Louisa's Colt bucked in her fist.

The old man who'd been sleeping at the near table lifted his head with a start, wailing, "What, ho? What, ho?"

He turned to Louisa, his dark eyes shiny and wide. He had a bony, wizened face and short, greasy, dark brown hair. He just stared at Louisa and her smoking Colt, his lower jaw hanging in shock.

For a moment, silence. Then, beyond the ceiling, Quarrels said: "What . . . the . . . hell . . . ?"

"Christ!" exclaimed Sweets DuPree. "I'm hit!"

Bang!

"Pima!" Sweets screamed.

"What the *hell*?" Quarrels bellowed again, louder.

Bang! Bang! Bang!

Both Quarrels and Sweets DuPree screamed as they stumbled around in the room over Louisa's head. Louisa emptied her first Colt into the ceiling then shucked the second Colt from the holster on her left thigh and sent another six rounds of .45 caliber lead into the floor of Quarrels and DuPree's room. By the time the second Colt's hammer had clicked benignly down on the firing pin, there'd been one heavy thud, like that of a large body hitting the floor.

The screaming had stopped but someone was still stumbling around up there, grunting, groaning in agony.

Quickly but methodically, calmly, Louisa shook the spent cartridges out of both Colts and replaced them with fresh from her cartridge belt. The old man at the near table stared at her in shocked silence, lower jaw still hanging, holding his bony, arthritic hands over his large, elongated ears.

As Louisa thumbed the last shell into the last empty chamber of her right-side Colt, she strode back around the bar, keeping an eye on the ceiling in which she was following the stumbling of bare feet as they moved down the hall toward the stairway. The men were still over there, staring at the Vengeance Queen in mute silence and wide-eyed incredulity.

They moved quickly out of her way as she strode back down the bar toward the stairs at the top of which Sweets DuPree emerged from the second-floor hall. Half-naked and bloody, wearing only a pair of men's longhandles, the outlaw woman dropped clumsily down the stairs, leaning hard against the rail. She had a revolver in her right hand. Wailing shrilly, her hair wild, she stopped about halfway down the stairs and raised the Smith & Wesson.

Louisa stepped over the sprawled figure of Del Rainy and raised the Colt in her own right hand. Sweets triggered a shot that went screeching through the saloon to plunk into the front wall, making the men behind Louisa duck.

Sweets's eyes found Louisa. She must have recognized the Vengeance Queen.

She took one more step down, screaming, "*Witch!*"

Calmly, Louisa triggered three shots, one after the other, spaced about one second apart. The slugs tore into the outlaw woman's already bullet-torn body. They threw her backward against the stairs. She twisted around, groaning, and rolled wildly down the steps to pile up at the bottom, her head resting over Rainy's ankles.

Sweets stared up at Louisa, blinked once. "Go to hell," she said, then died with a ragged sigh.

Louisa turned to the men once more standing around her in a semicircle. They all regarded her in shocked silence, including the handsome captain Yardley. Louisa holstered the Colt and stepped forward, in the direction of her table, then switched course suddenly, turning toward the bar.

The tall, blond hardcase, Ray Vink, was in her way. He stepped aside quickly, muttering, "Ex . . . excuse me."

Louisa dropped a coin into the shot glass atop the bar, grabbed a bowl and a spoon, and strode over to the potbelly stove on which the beans bubbled.

Behind her, breaking the pregnant silence, the barman, speaking overly loudly, said, "Well, uh . . . why don't a couple of you fellas help me with this fresh beef? We'll drag the bodies out to the woodshed, and I'll figure out what to do with 'em come spring."

Louisa ladled up a bowl of beans. The barman and the handsome captain and two drummers went upstairs and dragged the bullet-riddled body of Pima Quarrels outside.

They returned for Sweets DuPree, and once they'd disposed of her, they returned for Rainy. The barman and the two drummers came back in on a chill breath of stormy, snow-laced air, stomping snow from their boots, batting it from their hats. Tutwiler, breathless from exertion, walked back around behind the bar and strode back out a minute later.

He set a mug of fresh tea on the table where Louisa, one pistol on the table to her right, was finishing her beans. Louisa reached into her pocket for a coin, and the bartender raised his hands, palms out.

"No, no, no," he said, smiling down at her and then running his hands nervously down his stained green apron. "This round's on the house. Truth be known, it's kinda old. Not too many folks drink tea around here. My wife did. She was English, don't ya know. She liked it good and strong. With milk. She never cleaned the teapot. Said cleanin' the teapot's a badness, accordin' to English ways. Norma Jane, she's been gone nigh on five years now, so I reckon that's how old that tea is. If it tastes old, I'll throw it out and see if Mrs.—"

"It's fine."

"Oh, okay. Good."

Louisa looked up at him. The look was intended to excuse him but he apparently didn't read it correctly.

"I, uh," the barman said, leaning forward to rest a hand on a chair back. "I, uh . . . reckon I didn't know who you were. You know . . . not until I seen you shoot."

"Well, now you know." Louisa spooned up the last bit of beans in her bowl. "Good beans, Mr. Tutwiler."

"Morris."

"Good beans, Morris." Louisa sipped from the fresh mug and said, "And good tea."

"Oh, thank you, Miss Bonnyventure!"

"It's Bona-venture," Louisa said. "There's no *y* in it."

"Oh, I bet there's not. Well, just the same, Miss Bona-venture, it's an honor to have you here, and if there's anything you need . . . any more beans or tea or anything else, you just let me know."

"I think I'll be turning in after I finish my tea. It's been a long day, Morris."

"Gonna be a long night, too," Tutwiler said. "You can take room nine. It's nice and roomy and it's got a real good fireplace in it. I don't rent it out 'cept to special guests, but I reckon you're one o' them, all right. I'll make sure there's fresh wood in the box right now, and I'll leave the key in the door for you."

With that, Tutwiler swung his bulk around and waddled breathlessly back toward the bar.

Louisa sipped her tea.

Bonnyventure.

She wondered where her partner was. She hoped

Lou was having a better time of it over in Indian Butte than she was having here in Sundown. Lou wasn't going to like the fact that she'd beefed Sweets DuPree and Pima Quarrels, both of whom were worth more alive than dead.

Louisa didn't care about the extra money. She didn't need it. She was far thriftier than her ex-rebel partner, Prophet. She didn't drink and carouse and gamble until her pockets were empty, like Lou did.

She kept focused. She remained on the blood trail. After all, the world was full of bad men . . . and bad women . . . badly in need of killing. Maybe someday they'd all be dead. Maybe someday no more good, innocent people, like her own family, would be murdered by the wolflike gang of Handsome Dave Duvall. Maybe someday all bloodthirsty wolves like Duvall . . . and Sweets DuPree and Pima Quarrels . . . would be scoured from the earth.

Of course, deep down Louisa knew that would never happen, people being who they were. But she knew that with only one part of her heart, with only a remote part of her brain. The rest of her brain and her heart, her entire being, in fact, was determined to keep trying . . . and trying . . . and trying until she herself had run out of time.

The satisfaction of killing two bloodthirsty killers like DuPree and Quarrels was worth every penny of what she'd lost in bounty money.

Louisa finished her tea. She shoved her pistol down into her holster then grabbed her rifle and saddlebags and began to rise from her chair. She stopped when the front door opened and the handsome captain walked into the saloon, shivering and stomping snow from his boots, the draft from the door dousing several lamps and sending a deathlike chill through the room.

The captain removed his kepi, brushed snow from his fur coat, and glanced at Louisa. He cast her a winning smile and strode toward her.

Louisa set her Winchester down and sank back into her chair as she watched the handsome soldier approach. It was going to be a long, cold night, after all.

Chapter 22

Captain Yardley stood over Louisa's table. He gazed down at her with an ironic smile. "Mind if I sit down?"

Louisa shrugged a shoulder. It was never wise to look too eager. Yardley was handsome. Dashing, even. But even handsome, dashing soldiers might be black-hearted devils. You just never knew.

"It's a free country, Captain."

Yardley tossed his hat, wet from the snow, onto a chair, shrugged out of his thick bear coat, and hung it over the back of another chair, this one directly across the table from Louisa. He sat down in the chair, scooted it inward, and leaned forward, wringing his hands together.

He stared down at his hands, that sheepish half smile lingering on his dragoon-mustached mouth. Louisa noticed that what appeared to be dry blood streaked his left thumbnail—a gift from one of the bodies he helped haul outside, no doubt. He must have noticed the blood himself just then, because he covered that thumb with the other one.

"What is it?" Louisa asked. "What has you tongue-tied, Captain?"

Yardley looked across the table at her. "I must say . . . I feel a little silly, having rushed to the honor of one who so notoriously didn't need it."

"Don't feel that way. I was flattered."

He arched a brow at her. "Really?"

"Really. It's been a long time since a man has come to my rescue."

"Oh? What about your partner, uh . . . ?"

"Prophet?"

"Yes, Prophet."

Louisa smiled. "He might have a different story, but I believe I've had to save his honor more times than he's had to save mine."

Yardley's cheeks dimpled and his cobalt eyes flashed as he smiled more broadly. "I don't doubt that a bit." He cleared his throat. "Tell me, Miss Bonaventure . . . you and Mr. Prophet . . . uh . . ."

"We're partners."

"*Just* partners?"

"Officially, we're partners. For as long as we can stay together on the same trail without shooting each other. Unofficially . . ." Louisa sighed and glanced around the room before letting her gaze stray back to the soldier. "Well, let's just say the nights can get very long and lonely out there on the hunting trail."

Yardley seemed pleased by the answer. "I see, I see." He nodded slowly. "They do tend to get rather long and lonely here in Dakota, as well. Especially over the winter."

"Are you stationed at Totten?"

"Yes. A crude, lonely place. I'm from back East. I'm furloughing out, heading home for the holidays."

"Congratulations."

"And you?"

"Headed for Bismarck. Lou is coming in on the train tomorrow. He went after two killers, and I went after two killers."

"Well, you'll find them out in the woodshed."

"Mr. Tutwiler will be glad to have to bury only Rainy in the spring."

Yardley winced. "Terrible thing what they did to the marshal. Seemed a decent man."

"Decent people are killed all the time, Captain. Surely you know that. That's why I do what I do."

Yardley studied her, staring deep into her eyes from across the table, his dark brows beetled critically. "You are rather efficient at it, aren't you? And merciless."

Louisa glanced at the dozen bullet holes in the ceiling, toward the back of the far wall. "You mean that?"

"Yes." Yardley chuckled. "I mean that."

Again, Louisa shrugged. "Getting shot through the floor while they lay in bed, making love after butchering a man who was only trying to do his job, was an appropriate way for them to go. They showed Rainy no mercy. Why should I have shown them any? A hanging in a public square in Bismarck would have been too good for them." She paused, ran a finger around the rim of her tea mug. "They deserved being shot like rats in a privy."

Yardley was studying her again, lips drawn wide beneath his mustache. "My God, you are beautiful. As beautiful as all the scribblers have written about you. And just as . . ." He seemed to struggle for the right word.

"Just as cold-blooded as they write about me?"

The captain chuckled. "Yes, just as cold-blooded as they say."

They smiled into each other's eyes.

"Can I buy you a drink, Miss Bonaventure?"

Keeping her eyes on his, Louisa shook her head. "Never touch anything stronger than tea. I have once or twice. Don't like to lose my edge. And, trust me, you wouldn't like what I become after a few sips of the tarantula juice, as Lou calls it."

"Hmmm," Yardley said, canting his head to one side, tapping his fingers along his jaw. "Intriguing."

Louisa laughed then leaned intimately forward, toward the dashing young soldier. "Tell me, Captain, would you like to share my bed this evening?"

Yardley's lower jaw dropped. He sank back in his chair. For a moment, he just stared at her, not knowing what to say. Finally, he laughed. "You, uh . . . you don't like to beat around the bush—do you, Miss Bonaventure?"

"You never know when you've beaten the last one, Captain. I find you attractive. You find me, well, intriguing. Cold-blooded. So, I say we head up to my room and get down to business. Mr. Tutwiler has likely filled my wood box and laid a nice fire in the hearth."

Yardley continued to stare at her as though suspecting she might only be teasing him. Finally, convinced her proposition was genuine, he said, "Miss Bonaventure, I would like nothing more than to go upstairs with you and, uh, 'get down to business,' as you say."

"Well, then . . ." Louisa slid her chair back.

"Wait!" Laughing, Yardley reached across the table to close his hand over hers. He glanced around at the other men in the room, including Tutwiler behind the bar, and said, "Shouldn't we be discreet? Perhaps you should go up to the room first. Then, after a fair amount of time, I'll—"

"That's silly, not to mention cowardly."

Again, Yardley's jaw dropped "What?"

"Why on earth would you care what anyone in this room thinks of you?"

"Well . . . it wasn't so much myself I was thinking about."

"Okay, now, Captain," Louisa said, giving him a remonstrating, sidelong stare. "Your chivalry is beginning to wear a little thin. If you want to share my bed, you'd best show a little more—"

She stopped as boots thundered suddenly on the stoop outside the saloon, muffled by the snow but still loud. The front door opened quickly, but not before Louisa had shucked her right-hand Colt from its holster and whipped it toward the old man just then entering on a windy blast of snow-laced air, and clicked the hammer back.

The old man looked at the pretty blonde aiming the Peacemaker at him, narrowing one hazel eye as she aimed down the barrel. He frowned, blinked. He wasn't holding a weapon in either wool-mittened hand, so Louisa depressed the Colt's hammer and lowered the weapon.

Yardley glanced at her dubiously, his mouth corners lifting in a wry, knowing smile.

The old man closed the door, glanced once more, cautiously, at Louisa, then turned to the bar behind which Tutwiler was standing, saying, "Well, well— Lester Johnson. What're you doing out in this weather? I figured you'd be snuggled up with your cats, a long book, and that bottle I sold you earlier."

"Where's the marshal?" the old man asked, leaning forward, hands on his knees. He was trying to catch his breath.

"Dead," Louisa said.

Johnson looked at her. He had a broad face nearly as dark as an Indian's, and a full, snow-white beard. He was short, lean as a flax stem, and bowlegged. A large, liver-colored wart sprouted from one of his shaggy, white brows. "Who're you—Annie Oakley?"

"Close." Standing beside Louisa, Yardley smiled.

Still crouched forward, breathing hard, Lester swallowed and looked at Tutwiler again. "What happened to Rainy?"

"Two tough nuts did him in. Upstairs. He's out in the woodshed, where he'll likely remain till spring. What's the matter, Lester? You look like a ghost of one of your dead wives came back."

"Worse than that." Johnson straightened, widened his eyes beneath his shaggy white brows. "Someone took a hatchet to the banker, Emory. That's what I came to fetch Rainy for!"

"The banker?" Louisa glanced around the room, looking for Toni, but then she remembered that the girl had gone upstairs and hadn't come down again. Not even after all the fireworks.

"Yeah, the banker," Johnson said, glancing at Louisa again, curiously. He strode forward in his bull-legged fashion, heading toward the bar, removing a mitten and brushing an arthritic hand across his nose. "That's what I came to fetch Rainy for."

"Emory's dead?" Tutwiler asked in disbelief. "You sure, Lester, or has this cold weather just got you hittin' the bottle extra hard?"

Johnson turned to rest an elbow atop the bar. He

shook his head in shock and consternation. "Seen him myself. I was fetchin' firewood outside my shack—you know, over close to where Mr. and Mrs. Emory got their new house—and I heard the woman scream. She screamed several times. Really scared-like. Crazy-like.

"I throw on my cold-weather gear and I walk over there and I see her sitting down outside the back door beside Mr. Emory himself. Emory's got a hatchet in his back, right up close to the back of his head. Laid his spine wide open! And it was still in there, lookin' like a pump handle, when I come up on him and that poor woman. She was just cryin' an' kickin' and screamin' an' really carryin' on! I didn't think I was ever gonna get her settled down and inside out of the cold!"

Johnson turned to the barman, his eyes bright, stricken. "Give me a whiskey—will you, Morris? Make it a big one."

As Tutwiler grabbed a bottle from beneath the bar, Louisa walked over to stand facing Johnson. "Do you have any idea who might have killed Emory, Mr. Johnson?"

"Hell, no. But, then, I don't know him that well. He ain't been here long, and I'm just an old hermit livin' alone in my shack, readin' an' tendin' my cats an' such. And that's just how I like it!"

"The woman's still over there?"

Johnson nodded as he watched Tutwiler fill a water glass. "Of course, she's still over there. I was just gonna fetch Rainy an' leave it up to him. I ain't the law. I was just gonna have me a coupla drinks to calm my nerves." He lifted his glass in salute to Louisa. "And that's just what I'm gonna do, too!"

Louisa glanced at the other men in the room. None

looked eager to face the cold. Most of them turned away from Louisa's vaguely accusing gaze.

With a disgusted chuff, she strode back over to her table and shrugged into her coat.

"What're you gonna do?" Yardley asked her.

"I'm gonna see to the banker's wife." Louisa cast old Johnson an incriminating glance. "Her own life could very well be in danger."

"It's started," said Edgar Clayton. He sat at his table, staring over his shoulder toward the front of the saloon, his eyes dark, round, and ominous.

Buttoning her coat, Louisa frowned at him. "What's started?"

Clayton turned his head slowly to face her. "The killer of the banker, Emory, is Ramsay Willis. He's started killin' here in Sundown."

"Ramsay Willis?" said Lester Johnson. "I haven't seen Ramsay Willis in town since it turned cold. Don't he still work for you?" He paused, scowling deeply at Clayton. "In fact . . . what're you doin' in town, Clayton? It's stormin' outside."

Clayton returned his dark gaze to the front of the room, sliding his eyes quickly along the windows and door, as though expecting the nightmare specter of Ramsay Willis to gain entrance at any moment. "I'm huntin' Ramsay Willis. Gonna shoot him down like the loco wolf he is."

"Huntin' him?" The bartender and Lester Johnson said at the same time. "Why?"

"He's gone mad." Clayton turned to give both Tutwiler and Johnson a grave, direct look. "It's the winter fever. It's got him. He's mad with it. He killed Rose. He killed the three old woodcutters at the camp on the Cannonball." He swung his head back around to face the front of the room. "Now . . . he's come to town to keep right on killin'."

"What's the winter fever?" Louisa asked.

"Old wives' tale," Yardley told her. "It's said that some men go mad at the start of the winter up here. They can't stand the thought of the next five, six months of cold, of being socked inside a small prairie cabin with nothing around, not even any trees to look at, so they go mad and start killing folks." He smiled wisely and shook his head. "The notion itself is madness."

"It happens," Johnson told the captain. "I was here when this place was still only a hiders' camp. It happened a time or two. Men stayed on here through the winter 'cause maybe they didn't have nowhere to go, or maybe they'd married up with a squaw from around here. In November, with all those hard, cold, lonely months starin' 'em in the face, they'd go mad and start killin'. It's like a demon took hold."

Tutwiler nodded slowly. "I've seen it, too. I was trappin' once up on the Mouse River, just across the border in Canada. We had us a small camp, and . . ." He let his voice trail off as he stared at the saloon's front door. He gave a barely perceptible shudder. "Yeah. Yeah . . . I've seen it."

Louisa felt a chill crawl up her spine. She looked from Johnson to Edgar Clayton, staring darkly at the door beyond which the wind moaned like a lonely witch.

"Nonsense," said the captain. "It only happens to those men who already have cold-blooded killers living inside them. Then, when the itch to kill gets so strong they can't control it any longer—and some men . . . and even some women . . . are born with it, unfortunately— they go mad, pick up the weapon of their choice, and blame the weather for causing them to leave one hell of a blood trail."

"There ain't no nonsense to it," said Clayton with stubborn defiance.

"It's all nonsense. Oh, a few men . . . possibly even some women," Yardley added for Louisa's benefit, "have gone mad this time of year and started killing people. But that doesn't mean that's what's going on here. Now, because of the legend that has grown from a very small but all too fertile seed, men on the prairie have come to fear it the way children fear the grim reaper."

"Well, I seen my dear Rose lyin' dead on my cabin floor with my own eyes," said Clayton.

"Rose?" Tutwiler exclaimed in shock. "Rose is *dead*?"

Clayton nodded slowly. "He killed her. Ramsay Willis did. I was off huntin' a wildcat that was pesterin' my cows down along Porcupine Creek. Ramsay stayed home with Rose because he wasn't feelin' right. Took to his bed several days ago. Couldn't sleep. Paced the floor at night. I come back and found the cabin awash in blood . . . and Rose dead with a hatchet through her head. Ramsay was gone. Saddled a horse and headed this way . . . to Sundown . . . but not before stoppin' at the Cannonball to kill them old woodcutters."

Tears glazed Clayton's eyes, dribbled down his cheeks. A sob welled up from his throat and it sounded like the utterance of some poor, bereaved, unearthly soul. "Now he's here, in town," Clayton said, clearing his throat. "And he's started with the banker." He paused, then added in a low, menacing trill, "He'll work his way over here . . . sooner or later . . . and continue the carnage."

Clayton rose from his chair and grabbed the rifle

lying across the table before him, near his half-empty bottle. "If I don't hunt him down and kill the son of the devil first, which I surely aim to do!"

He stomped across the saloon and went out into the cold.

Louisa grabbed her own rifle and pulled on her gloves and mittens.

Yardley stepped up to her. "What're you going to do, Louisa?"

She scowled up at him. "What do you think I'm going to do? I'm going to check on the banker's poor widow, and I'm going to see to finding the killer who widowed her."

Louisa knotted her muffler beneath her chin and followed Clayton out into the cold, howling night.

Chapter 23

"That was wonderful!"

The countess Tatiana Miranova placed her hand on Prophet's cheek and turned his head toward hers, giving his nose a tender peck. "You are better than Cossack!"

Prophet snuggled down in the surprisingly soft bed in his room in the Indian Butte Saloon & Hotel, and nuzzled the girl's neck, chuckling. "Well, I reckon I don't know how a—"

"I think I will take you home with me, Lou. Back to Russia!" Tatiana wrapped her arms tightly around his neck, drew him taut against her, entwining her legs with his.

"Not that I even know where your home country is." Prophet chuckled. "But I doubt your old man the count would go in for haulin' my raggedy behind back to your castle or palace or whatever it is you folks live in, Miss Tatiana."

She frowned at him, curious. "I don't understand. What is . . . 'raggedy behind'?"

Prophet thumbed his chest and laughed. "Me!" He

laughed again. "What I mean is I don't think your pa would go for that."

"No. Probably not." The countess sighed. She snuggled against him, burying her nose in his armpit and sniffing, savoring his manly smell. "But I think I will spend the night right here in your arms. I never want to leave your bed, Lou Prophet!"

"That may not be such a good—"

Prophet stopped. He pricked his ears, listening. The music downstairs had fallen silent and now there was a low rumbling of footsteps and concerned male voices.

Prophet's heart quickened. *Uh-oh.*

Before he had time to voice his concern at the sudden change in the atmosphere of the sprawling hotel, a deep, heavily accented male voice shouted from somewhere below: "Tatiana! *Tatiana!* Where are you, my daughter?"

"Ach!" The countess jerked her head up and stared wide-eyed at the door. She exclaimed in what could only have been Russian, adding for Prophet's benefit, "My aunt, Sonya Drubatskoya, must have checked my room and found my bed empty!"

Prophet sat straight up in bed, his heart thudding. "Who the hell is Sonya Drub . . . whatever-you-called-her?"

"Drubatskoya. She was the big woman playing the gusli downstairs! My mother's sister! She is my chaperone on this trip to America!"

Just then a woman's chortling, angry, exasperated voice shot up the stairwell at the end of the second-floor hall: "TAT-I-ANAHHHHHHH!"

"Ah, shit!" The big, severe-looking woman who'd been playing the flat, boardlike stringed instrument downstairs had cut a rather imposing figure. She had not looked like a woman who would take lightly the compromising of her niece's honor. Especially not by a hard-tailed western bounty hunter!

In a flash, Prophet saw himself being held down by a half-dozen big Russian Cossacks while Aunt Sonya beat him silly with her gusli . . . or whatever Tatiana had called it.

Several pairs of boots pounded the stairs, growing louder as what sounded like the countess's entire party—a whole posse of Cossacks—was thundering toward Prophet's room in which he'd just despoiled their young charge, the countess.

I'll be damned, Prophet silently reflected, staring at the door shuddering in its frame from the resonations of the thundering herd rushing toward it, toward him. *I survived the War of Northern Aggression and a dozen years bounty hunting across the wild and woolly western frontier to be killed in Indian Butte by Russians for despoiling a countess.*

"Them two Cossack friends of yours must've told your old man where they last seen you!" Prophet said, dropping his feet to the floor and reaching for the sawed-off Richards hanging from the near bedpost.

"I don't think so." Tatiana was on her knees on the bed, sitting back on her heels, staring anxiously at the door. "They would have been too embarrassed to tell my father what happened. They are likely cowering like dogs in their rooms!"

"Still . . ." Prophet rose from the bed, the sawed-off in his right hand. "He'll turn this place inside out. He'll find you sooner or later. I might have to shoot my way out of here. Don't worry—I've done it before!"

"No, no!" Tatiana leaped off the bed and began climbing into her pantaloons. "I will crawl out a window, make my way to the ground. I will enter through the back door. I will tell Papa that I stepped out for some fresh air and got turned around. Don't worry, Lou—if I told Papa I flew away to have a few quiet moments on the moon, he would believe me!"

She chuckled throatily as she grabbed her gown and the rest of her undergarments and shoes and padded toward the room's single window.

"You can't go out there, Tatiana!" Prophet glanced from the door to the girl then back again, the voices and the footsteps growing louder in the hall. He could feel the reverberations through the floorboards beneath his bare feet. "You know how cold it is out there! You'll freeze your pretty little . . . not to mention your feet!"

"Cold? Hah! You have never been to Russia in the winter, Lou."

"No, I haven't. And if this cold is to scoff at, I reckon I never will, neither!"

The footsteps fell silent outside Prophet's room.

A fist thundered on the bounty hunter's door. "Prophet! Lou Prophet, are you in there, you scalawag?" It wasn't a voice Prophet had heard before.

The countess drew a sharp breath through gritted teeth and cast her bright, anxious gaze at the door. To Prophet, she said just loudly enough for the bounty hunter to hear, "That's the senator. Maybe you were right, Lou—Papa must have gotten Ivan and Dmitri to tell him where they last saw me!"

"Either that or that damnable Rawdney had his suspicions!"

The pounding came on the door again—three loud thuds, making the door leap in its frame. *"Prophet?"*

Wearing only her white cotton pantaloons, holding

her shoes and gown in a large ball before her, the countess ran back to Prophet, rose up onto the tips of her toes, and kissed his cheek. "All will be well, Lou. Don't you worry. I am as strong as a bear and lithe as a monkey!"

She kissed him again, giggled, apparently delighting in the excitement, then ran back to the window, which she'd already opened. Windblown snow slithered through the gap.

Three more hard whacks on the door. "Mr. Prophet, open this door or I will have it broken down!"

"Don't break down my door, Senator!" the barman begged from farther off down the hall. "Doors don't grow on trees around here. Hell, hardly any *trees* grow around here!"

The countess, perched on the sloping roof outside Prophet's window, grinned through the window at him. She blew him a kiss then quietly closed the pane.

"Prophet!" came the voice of the senator's nancy boy son, Rawdney. "We know you're in there, Prophet. The barman told us. If you have the countess in there, you'd better not have harmed a hair on her head!"

The Russians were anxiously conferring in their own tongue around the senator and Rawdney Fairweather.

"Let her go, Prophet!" bellowed the senator. "Her father is right here, and if you've harmed that girl, I am going to leave you to the count's men to do with as they see fit! It will not go well for you!"

"Oh, for chrissakes!" Prophet pulled on his long-handles and socks. As the senator and Rawdney and the Russians continued milling around outside his room, pounding on his door and threatening him, he buckled his Colt and cartridge belt around his waist and set his hat on his head. Somehow, the hat seemed to make up for his lack of pants, which he didn't want to take the time to put on.

Besides, he wanted it to look as though they'd awakened him from a dead sleep.

"Hold on!" he bellowed, feigning a loud yawn. "Don't get your bloomers in a twist, Senator. I'm comin'. You keep poundin' on the door like that, you're gonna turn it into toothpicks!"

He turned the key in the lock and slid the bolt free of the frame.

He opened the door just as the senator threw his fist at it once more, and the man stumbled forward into the room, bulling into Prophet. Prophet was an unmoving mountain. The senator, a foot shorter, bounced off him and stepped back into the hall, scowling up at the brawny bounty hunter clad in only longhandles, gun belt, socks, and hat.

Fairweather's son flanked him on his right, drawing his father back by one arm.

The stocky, bearded old count stood to his left, glaring up at Prophet through a monocle.

Rawdney's assistant, Leo, and a half-dozen big, bearded Russians in their crisp red uniform tunics and deerskin trousers stood behind the count, the senator, and Rawdney, looking like wild grizzlies fixing to bust out of an inadequate zoo cage.

"Let her go, you animal!" yelled the senator.

"You heard my father," Rawdney intoned, holding a small, silver-plated, pearl-gripped over-and-under derringer in his beringed right fist, aimed at Prophet's heart. "Let her go right now!" He bolted forward, poking his head into the room. "If you've hurt that girl, so help me!"

"Hold on, hold on!" Prophet said, holding up his hands, palm out. "Will someone please tell me what in the hell is goin' on here? You woke me out of a dead sleep, and I got a big day tomorrow!"

Count Miranova stepped forward, monocle dangling by a thread from his left lapel, and cut loose with a tirade of gibberish the likes of which Prophet hadn't heard since traveling through a mining town populated by Prussians in the San Juan Mountains of southern Colorado. This particular spiel was directed at him, along with a good deal of spit.

Prophet held up his hands again and shook his head. He cut the old Russian off with: "Friend, I don't understand a word you're sayin', so you might as well save your gas!"

Again, Rawdney poked his head into Prophet's room, sniffing like a dog. "What's that I smell?" He sniffed again. "Why . . . why, that's the countess's smell, you mangy Southern dog! I'd recognize her fragrance anywhere!" The dandy stepped back and aimed the derringer up at Prophet's head, hardening his jaws and brightening his eyes. "What have you *done* with her, you Confederate scalawag?"

"Did someone say my name?" It was the voice of the countess herself, rising from somewhere behind the knot of mostly large, uniformed, bearded men gathered before Prophet's open door.

All heads turned as though on a swivel.

The old count exclaimed in his own language and pushed through the small crowd of big Cossacks, hurrying over to where the countess was just then padding along the hall, wearing her gown, arms crossed on her splendid bodice, shivering. Prophet was relieved to see that she'd put on her shoes. Russian or no Russian, even the countess's toes would turn to stone after only a few minutes exposed to the frigid winds of Dakota Territory.

"Countess!" Rawdney yelled, and rushed over to stand with the pretty young woman and the count, who had just then taken his long-lost daughter into his arms, hugging her tightly and speaking in his guttural tongue that was all gibberish to the bounty hunter's ears.

The senator and all the others rushed over to hover around the countess, also. After conversing with her father in their own harsh, nonsensical language, she turned to the senator and his dandified son to explain in broken English and in a pinched, frightened little girl's voice, "I stepped out to get some air—I was so hot from dancing—and . . . and I must've gotten turned around."

Tatiana's gaze drifted fleetingly toward Prophet, who could have sworn a devilish little grin tugged at her mouth corners and flashed in her eyes.

Continuing, she said, "As I stepped out, there was a great gust of snow, and suddenly I found myself by the barn. The snow was so thick that I couldn't find my way back, until . . . until . . . well, I don't know how I managed it. I guess the snow cleared, and I saw the lights in the windows, and—"

"Oh, thank heavens, Countess!" exclaimed the senator, placing a relieved hand on the girl's arm. "However you managed to make it back, we're all soooo glad you did. The snow can get quite thick up here at times."

The count turned his wizened head to yell down the hall. Presently, the stout woman whom Prophet had seen downstairs bounded out of a room at the hall's far end. The count yelled again in Russian, and Aunt Sonya, the countess's rain barrel–shaped chaperone, returned to her room before bounding back out a few seconds later, this time with a thick quilt in her arms. She'd obviously been crying; her fat cheeks were red and swollen.

She'd thought the countess had been gobbled up by the big bounty hunter and spat to the wolves.

Cooing and clucking and pattering in Russian, breathless, the big woman rushed over to where the countess stood shivering with her father, the senator, and Rawdney. Meanwhile, Leo and the Cossacks, who saw that their assistance was no longer required, drifted off down the stairs to the saloon's main drinking hall, muttering and chuckling among themselves.

Prophet had seen by the brightness of the men's eyes that they were all, to a man, pie-eyed. Headed as they were back to the saloon, they were apparently in no hurry to sober up despite the lateness of the hour.

They were on vacation, after all . . .

The gently cajoling aunt Sonya wrapped the countess in the quilt, picked the girl up in her stout arms, ordered the men out of her way, and hustled down the hall toward Tatiana's room. As they passed Prophet, the countess turned toward the big bounty hunter still standing in his open doorway. She gave him a furtive wink and pooched her rosebud lips out in a fleeting kiss before she was hustled away in her aunt's suety arms.

When the pair had disappeared into a room next door to Aunt Sonya's, the senator patted the count's back in relieved congratulations and, conversing jauntily, chuckling and wagging their heads, the older men drifted back down the stairs and likely to a couple of hot toddies.

Rawdney Fairweather, however, remained.

The priggish little mucky-muck turned toward Prophet, looked the bigger man up and down, critically, disdainfully, then sauntered toward him, swaggering a little on the heels of his black, high-topped, fur-lined riding boots. Again, he poked his head into Prophet's room, sniffed.

He turned to Prophet, who stared dubiously down at him.

"Don't think I don't know what went on here, Mr. Prophet." Fairweather jabbed two fingers against the bounty hunter's chest. "And don't think your taking advantage of the countess, an innocent and romantic young woman in a foreign land, will go unpunished." He jabbed Prophet again, wrinkling his nose and narrowing his priggish little eyes.

Prophet sighed.

"Rawdney," he said, "let me share some words of rarefied wisdom once expressed by none other than my dear old mother, Ma Prophet, her ownself, may her wise and lovely soul rest in peace."

"Oh, please, do share your mother's words of wisdom, Mr. Prophet!" Rawdney said, snickering.

"'Never dance in a graveyard,'" Prophet recited. "'And never mess with a Prophet!'"

With that, he rammed the first two fingers of his right hand against Rawdney's chest, sending the little dandy stumbling backward with a startled grunt. Lou slammed his door, locked it, skinned out of his hat, gun, boots, and socks, and went to bed.

Chapter 24

Louisa followed the tracks of Edgar Clayton down off the saloon's front porch and into the street. It wasn't snowing hard, but the hard-blowing wind was quickly filling in Clayton's tracks, dark dimples in the freshly fallen snow angling across the street.

She followed the tracks through the snow that was around three or four inches deep. It wasn't the snow that made for hard going. It was the brutally cold wind. In fact, as she peered up at the sky, she could see the dull glow of a pale moon between thinning, parting clouds. The snow would likely cease soon, but Louisa had grown up in the Midwest—albeit farther south, in Nebraska—and from that she knew that savagely cold temperatures often followed a storm.

The wind made the cold doubly bad.

She followed Clayton's path between two buildings on the north side of the street. The man's tracks led out behind the buildings and then angled again to the right, toward where a lone, two-story house with a peaked roof sat near a small barn and stable—vaguely outlined against the dark, stormy sky brushed with pale moonlight. As Louisa headed toward the house, a man's ragged breaths sounded behind her as did the crunching of running footsteps.

Louisa wheeled, taking her rifle in both hands, and quickly racked a round into the action.

The man heading toward her—an inky silhouette against the paleness of the snow lit by the feeble moon—stopped suddenly and raised his gloved hands. "Captain Yardley!"

Louisa lowered the rifle, turned, and continued striding toward the house. Yardley ran up beside her and kept pace with her. She could hear him breathing beneath the wind; she could hear her own ragged breaths, as well.

"You don't need to be out here, Captain," Louisa said. "It's not your game."

"It's not yours, either."

"Yes, it is."

Yardley looked at her and she looked back at him. She couldn't read his expression in the darkness but saw only the shimmer of the moonlight in his eyes beneath his thick, dark brows.

Louisa stopped and turned to him. He stopped, too, facing her, his pale breath frosting around his head upon which he wore a round hat made of the same fur as his coat.

"If you're out here to impress me, you're wasting your time. It's not going to happen. *We're* not going to happen. Not tonight."

Yardley flashed his perfect white teeth in a smile, chuckling. "You flatter yourself, Miss Bonaventure. You're not the only one concerned about justice, you know."

Louisa wasn't sure how to respond to that. So she

didn't. She merely turned and continued following Clayton's dwindling tracks in the snow. She was baffled by the man's behavior. Most men had ulterior motives. If Yardley did not, he was a rare breed, indeed. She shook her head, ridding her mind of the useless reflections. She had more important things to think about.

Just as she broke into a jog, Clayton's voice sounded beneath the howling wind, from dead ahead: "Ramsay?" A pause, then: "Ramsay Willis?"

Louisa stopped. She and Yardley shared a look. Louisa broke into a run again, and the captain did, as well.

As Louisa approached the house, which sat sideways to her, she could see a shadowy figure standing behind it. The figure moved off toward the barn and the stable to Louisa's left, flanking the house, which was a modest, brick, two-story affair. Small and tight but stately, with dormer windows and a shake-shingled roof. Just the kind of house a small-town banker would own.

The figure stopped. Clayton appeared to lower his head slightly and tip it to one side. He raised his rifle.

"Ramsay?" he called, the words ripped by the wind. "I know you're out here, Ramsay Willis!"

The rifle in Clayton's hands flashed, stabbing flames in the direction of the barn. The report reached Louisa's ears a quarter second later, sounding little louder than a twig snapping beneath the moaning, rushing wind.

Louisa quickened her pace. As she drew within twenty or so yards of the rancher, she yelled, "What are you shooting at, Mr. Clayton?"

The man turned to her. His voice was shrill, hoarse

with emotion. "I seen him! I seen Ramsay Willis! He just ran around behind the barn."

"How do you know it was him?"

"Don't you worry—I know! You best go in and see to the woman. I'll get Ramsay. He's mine. He murdered Rose. He's all mine!"

Louisa looked around for tracks in the snow. The only ones she could make out were Clayton's own. Yardley ran up behind her as Clayton ran off toward the barn.

"Where's he going?" the captain asked Louisa, raising his voice above the wind.

"He thinks he saw Willis run behind the barn. Why don't you check it out? I'll go inside and see how the banker's wife is doing."

Yardley nodded and reached under his coat for a long-barreled Colt Navy revolver. "Right!"

As he jogged off after Clayton, Louisa walked over to the house's back door. Firewood was stacked five feet high against the back wall. More lay farther out from the wall. That stack, twenty feet long, was covered with several tarpaulins. Between the two stacks of wood was what appeared to be a chopping block now mantled with snow. Near the small wooden porch angling down from the back door were several deep scuffmarks that the wind had not yet filled in with snow.

That must have been where Lester Johnson had found the banker, Emory, before dragging him into the house.

Louisa mounted the stoop, tapped on the door. No response.

She tapped again, harder this time.

Still, no response.

Louisa turned the knob. The latching bolt clicked.

She eased the door slowly open, the hinges creaking softly. She stopped when she saw a man lying just inside, the man's feet shod in brown ankle boots maybe three feet from the door's threshold.

A light shone to Louisa's left. Sidling through the quarter-open door, she peered toward where a lamp burned on a table.

The room she was in was a kitchen—well appointed and neatly arranged, with a black cooking range abutting the back wall, to Louisa's hard left. What caught the brunt of the Vengeance Queen's attention was the woman sitting on the floor against the far wall, beyond the range and near a wet sink with a pump and several well-stocked shelves, pots and pans dangling from hooks in the bottom of a finely crafted wooden wall cabinet.

She was a plump young woman, possibly in her midtwenties, with light brown hair pulled up in a bun, though the bun had come partly undone and had tumbled down the left side of her head. Her face was round and even-featured with a small nose and thin lips, scars from a bout of pimples when she was younger showing faintly on her forehead. She wore a plain cambric housedress, buttoned to the throat, and a white apron.

She stared without expression toward the table, as though trying to make out something that lay on the floor beneath it. Atop the table, two loaves of freshly baked bread were cooling on a rack beside a bowl of red apples.

The kitchen was smoky and rife with the smell of the stew that had been burning atop the stove until the fire in the stove's firebox had burned down. Apparently, the young woman had been preparing supper when her husband, the man on the floor—the banker, Emory—had gone out for more wood. When he'd returned, it had been with the assistance of Lester Johnson, and Emory had been sporting the ax in his back.

He still was.

Johnson had been right. The ax resembled nothing so much as a half-lifted pump handle.

Emory was a lean man of medium height, in his midthirties. There were a few strands of gray in his dark brown hair combed straight back from a severe widow's peak. Wire spectacles dangled from his left ear. His eyes stared vacantly at the floor, glazed in death. He wore broadcloth trousers, a white shirt, and a fawn vest from which a pocket watch drooped to the floor, dangling by a gold chain.

Emory hadn't been robbed—that much was plain. The watch looked expensive.

Louisa closed the door on the howling wind. She felt her belly tighten when she inspected the ax, the head of which was nearly entirely embedded in the banker's back, revealing the grisly mess of his ruined spine and several ribs, the shards of which shone inside the bloody gash. There had been nothing tentative about the attack. Whoever had wielded the ax had been resolute in his endeavor to kill the banker, and he'd gotten the job done without question.

He, if the ax-wielding killer had been Ramsay Willis, as Edgar Clayton was insisting. However, Louisa couldn't help entertaining a vague suspicion concerning the redhead from Jiggs's place. Could it be a mere coincidence that the banker had ended up dead— murdered—only a few minutes after turning away the young woman who'd come inquiring about a job with the longer-range hope of someday marrying the man?

Louisa turned to Emory's wife. The woman continued staring in a daze at the floor beneath the table. She had her knees drawn up toward her chest and angled slightly to one side, the skirt of her dress tenting over them. She had her hands on her knees. She was in shock. She didn't even appear aware of Louisa's presence. The only thing real to her was the horror inside her own head.

Louisa knew all too well how she felt. She herself had been in shock for nearly three days after she'd watched her own family butchered in the yard of their farm in Nebraska.

When she'd come out of it, she'd buried her family one by one, and then she'd strapped on her father's old pistol and slid his old rifle into her saddle scabbard and set out after the men—the Handsome Dave Duvall gang—who had killed her parents and siblings, shooting her father and brother and raping her mother and sisters while Louisa had looked on in horror from the brush.

No, not when she'd come out of it.

Because she knew that she had never fully come out of the shock of such an experience, and she likely never would.

She leaned her rifle against the wall by the door and walked slowly over to where the woman sat on the floor. Louisa removed her mittens and gloves and stuffed them into her coat pockets. Crouching beside the banker's wife, she slowly waved a hand in front of the young woman's face.

Mrs. Emory didn't react. She didn't even move her eyes.

Gently, Louisa said, "Can you tell me your name?"

Nothing.

Louisa dropped her butt to the floor, beside the stricken young woman. Louisa leaned back against the wall. She studied the woman's profile, the expressionless face with lips slightly parted, the unblinking, staring eyes.

Gradually, a cold darkness crept into Louisa's bones. Into her very soul. It was like poison. Snake venom. She was well acquainted with this darkness. She'd gotten fairly good over the past couple of years at holding it at bay. She must have let her guard down too low, however, because suddenly it grabbed her like a giant fist, squeezing, making her heart race, oozing cold sweat from her pores, and she was right back in that brush at the edge of her family's farm in Nebraska.

She heard her mother pleading with her tormentors, begging them to take her and to leave her daughters alone.

"Please . . . please don't you savage my girls!" she screamed.

Two gunshots. A man yelled. That was Louisa's father.

"Oh God, no!" he bellowed as Louisa's brother flew back off his heels with a bullet in his chest. *"Noooo—not my boyyyyyy!"*

Handsome Dave and the other gang members were whooping and yelling and passing bottles, two members wrestling Louisa's mother into the brush behind the springhouse. Two others had Louisa's sisters. Her sisters were screaming at the top of their lungs, one being dragged by one ankle as she fought to free herself, grabbing at the brush with her flailing hands. Her captor held her ankle with one hand, and he took pulls from a bottle with his other hand.

There was another gunshot.

Louisa leaped nearly a foot up off the floor of the dead banker's house in Dakota Territory and slammed her head back against the wall. In the brush at the border of the Nebraska farm, she watched her father drop to his knees. He knelt there for a moment then looked down at the bloody wound in his chest. He fell forward without breaking his fall and lay facedown in the weeds, quivering.

Meanwhile, Louisa's mother screamed, *"Not my baby girls!"*

She screamed . . . and screamed . . .

Louisa rolled onto her belly, lay flat against the floor, writhing with the screaming in her head and the daggers of grief and terror in her heart, grinding the heels of her hands against her temples as though to knead away the sights and the sounds that were more real than the cold wooden floor she lay upon.

A hand closed over her shoulder. A man said, "Louisa?"

She thought she recognized the voice. Louisa rolled over. She placed both her hands on the man's arm, squeezing, half sitting up and yelling hopefully, "Lou?"

It was Captain Yardley staring down at her with concern, on one knee beside her. Lou's absence was nearly as palpable as that of Louisa's family. Suddenly, she wanted to scream the bounty hunter's name, to call to him across the cold miles between them, for it was only he who could comfort her, settle her down when the black claws of terror engulfed her.

But he wasn't here.

It was the handsome, cobalt-eyed Captain Yardley. She felt tears slither into her eyes, felt her lips tremble with longing. Her disappointment must have been plain on her face.

Yardley gave a regretful smile, his brows forming a V above his nose. "Sorry. Just me." His eyes probed hers. "Are you all right, Louisa?"

Quickly, she brushed her hands across her cheeks, rubbing away the tears that had started to dribble down from her overfilled eyes. She sniffed, nodded, her face warming with chagrin. "Did you find Clayton?"

Yardley shook his head. "Dark back there. I lost his tracks. I think he headed for some woods north of town but I couldn't be sure. I thought I'd come back and check on you . . ." He glanced at the banker's wife to Louisa's left. "And Mrs. Emory."

"She's been sitting like that since I came in," Louisa said.

"Poor woman."

"Does she have family around here?"

Again, Yardley shook his head. "I wouldn't know. I only pass through here from time to time."

Still flushed with embarrassment over her un-seemly emotional display, Louisa rose with a grunt. What horrified her almost as much as the memories of her family's murder was Yardley having witnessed her breakdown. If only she could go into the captain's brain and clear his memory of the past few minutes. Only Lou had ever seen her like that. Only the big ex-rebel knew how to comfort her.

If only he were here. If only they could get along, stay together . . .

She suppressed the trembling in her hands and knees and looked down at the banker's wife. "We'd best get her over to the saloon. We can't leave her here. Not with a killer on the loose. Can you carry her?"

"Sure." Yardley glanced at Emory. "What about him?"

"Leave him here," Louisa said, walking over to the door and picking up her rifle. "Let the town deal with him once the storm breaks."

Quickly, feeling the walls of the banker's house closing in on her, Louisa glanced once more at the dead Emory still lying with the ax embedded in his back, then swung around and went out.

Chapter 25

Tipping her hat brim low against the storm, Louisa headed back in the direction of the saloon, the cold engulfing her, the wind sucking the breath from her lungs. She was maybe halfway there, lost in thought, her own horrors slow to retreat, when she stopped and turned back to stare toward the Emory house.

More chagrin assaulted her.

She should have helped the captain with Mrs. Emory. She started walking back toward the house but then a figure materialized out of the darkness and the blowing snow. She'd started to raise her rifle when she recognized the tall captain in his dark coat and hat. He was carrying the banker's wife. Obviously, without Louisa's assistance, he'd found a quilt to wrap Mrs. Emory in.

Not one for apologies—to accept or to offer them— Louisa swung back around and continued heading back toward the hotel. Yardley was just behind her as she mounted the stoop and pushed through the heavy winter door, causing all faces in the room to snap toward her, apprehensive looks in the men's eyes. In the eyes of one woman, as well. Toni was working behind the bar.

Louisa held the door open while Yardley passed through it then she closed it and said, "Take her over to the fire. We'll get her warm before we take her upstairs."

The barman, Tutwiler, sat at a table near the bar, a bottle and a steaming coffee mug before him.

"Is there a doctor in Sundown?" Louisa asked.

The blond hardcase, Vink, was playing cards with his rough-looking pards, Mose and Nasty Ralph, at a table near the barman. Vink chuckled wryly and threw down a card.

"A doctor?" Tutwiler said. "Sure, we got a doctor." He tossed his head to indicate the little, wizened oldster asleep at the table on the opposite side of the bar, near where Louisa had shot Quarrels and DuPree through the ceiling. "For all the good he does."

The doctor was snoring softly, his head buried in his arms.

Louisa inwardly cursed and went over to where an old, faded brocade armchair sat against the far wall, under a cracked leather harness, a ragged duster, and a moldering gun belt housing a rusty pistol—paraphernalia that customers had likely left on the premises long ago. There was even a badly faded dodger for a traveling Shakespearean theatrical troupe from Memphis.

Louisa brushed it all onto the floor then dragged the chair over to her own table, positioning it between the table and the crackling, sighing woodstove, the orange flames inside showing through the slight gaps around the brass-handled door.

Yardley eased the addled woman into the chair.

Mrs. Emory sat with an expression very similar to the one she'd had in the house—staring into space as though she were trying to remember something that stubbornly evaded her. It was as though her mind, unable to comprehend the horror she'd witnessed— the ax embedded in her husband's back—had simply shut down.

Louisa understood only too well the condition.

She removed her mittens and gloves and shrugged out of her coat then made her way to the bar. All eyes in the room slid between her and the banker's wife.

"What happened to her?" Vink asked as Louisa strode past his table. He was staring at Mrs. Emory.

"Shut up."

Nasty Ralph and Mose shared a smirk and chuckled. Vink curled his nose at the Vengeance Queen. "I was just askin'," he said.

Louisa walked up to the bar, where Toni stood unpacking bottles from a box and stacking them on back bar shelves. When she turned to Louisa, Louisa said, "You found a job."

Toni shrugged. "Didn't much care to stay upstairs. Not after all the shooting and hollering." She gave Louisa a vaguely ironic look. "So I came down and asked Mr. Tutwiler to put me to work."

She glanced at Tutwiler, who sat sipping his coffee and smoking a loosely rolled quirley, looking as apprehensive as all the other men in the room. The consternation was understandable, given that a killer was apparently running loose in Sundown.

"He figures it's going to be a long night and needed a hand," Toni continued. "If I work out, he might keep me on." Again, she hiked a shoulder. "No promises.

But, then, I'm not accustomed to promises, anyway. What can I get you, Miss Bonaventure?"

"Two cups of tea." She glanced at the bottles lining a shelf behind Toni then added as an afterthought, "And a bottle of whiskey. Something that's not going to burn the skin off my tonsils."

"I knew you'd come around, Miss Bonaventure," Tutwiler said with a knowing smile, raising his own coffee laced with whiskey in salute. "It's that kind of night, ain't it?"

"It's looking that way."

"Is . . . is he really dead?" Toni asked Louisa, frowning in befuddlement.

"He's really dead."

Louisa stared at her. Toni stared back at Louisa, the dawn of recognition growing in her eyes. Indignation grew there, as well. "You don't think I had anything to do with it."

"I don't know," Louisa said.

Toni glanced around. Several men, including Tutwiler, were staring toward her and Louisa. Toni leaned over the bar and said in a rasping voice barely audible above the wind outside, "You think I would kill the man merely because he didn't offer me a job?"

"We both know you were over there for more than a job," Louisa said, keeping her own voice down but also keeping her previous frankness in it. "But, then, I guess if you wanted one of them dead, it would most likely be the woman he married." She glanced toward Mrs. Emory, staring down at the floor near her feet, then turned back to Toni. "And I don't suppose you would have had the strength to hammer that ax as far into his back as someone did."

Toni gave a caustic snort. With open contempt, she studied Louisa across the bar. Louisa stared blandly back at her.

Tightly, Toni said, "You can sit down. I'll bring your tea and your whiskey. And I'll add them to your bill."

"Two cups."

"Two cups."

"Obliged."

"On the house," Tutwiler said, again raising his coffee to Louisa. "Under the circumstances, I for one am glad to have you here, Miss Bonaventure. If anyone can run that crazy man down, it's you."

He shivered as he rose from his chair. "Damn, it's a cold night. Gotta keep the stove a-roarin'!" He shambled heavily toward the back of the room.

Louisa turned away from the bar and started back to her table.

Ahead of her, Vink sat staring darkly over his shoulder at Mrs. Emory. "She's a purty woman," he said, as though mostly to himself. "Right fine-looking woman, the banker's wife."

Louisa stopped by the tall, lanky blond, who was slowly closing a quirley as he stared toward where Mrs. Emory sat in the brocade armchair, near the stove and Captain Yardley, who had taken a seat at the table now, as well.

As Vink turned his head to face Louisa, his eyes shone, bright as newly minted pennies, with drink. His nose was bright red. He seemed to have a mood on, as though after a few more drinks he'd considered Louisa's treatment of him earlier, and he was stewing about it.

Stewing himself raw.

He had set a pistol on the table, up close to his right hand.

He glanced over his shoulder again then turned back to Louisa and said over the quirley he was rolling up near his chin, "Look at her sittin' over there . . . all nice an' quiet. The banker's wife. Very quiet an' polite. The kind I like. I hear she came all the way from Council Bluffs. Mail-order bride. Poor woman's without a man now, though, ain't she? That's an awful shame. It purely is."

He glanced at his partners sitting to his right. "Ain't that right, boys?"

Mose and Nasty Ralph smiled up at Louisa.

Also grinning at Louisa, Vink fired a match to life one-handed. "Maybe she needs me to step in an' take care of her."

Louisa took one step toward him, hardening her jaws and flaring a nostril. "I liked you better when you were smart enough to keep your mouth shut."

Vink gave a crooked, faintly jeering half smile. "I'm just sayin' I could—"

Louisa's hand whipped forward. It cracked against the blond's left cheek so sharply and loudly that one of the three drummers leaped in his own chair with a start.

"*Je-zuzzz!*" he exclaimed.

One of the other drummers laughed softly, derisively.

Vink dropped his quirley and closed his right hand over the Colt on the table. Louisa slapped him again, harder, and he spun the Colt across the table. It dropped over the side and hit the floor with a thud.

Vink glared up at her, a bright red welt blossoming

high on his left cheek. The blow had knocked his hat off, and his hair hung in his eyes. Mose and Nasty Ralph, also glaring up at Louisa, had dropped their hands beneath the table. She smiled down at them in bald challenge, holding both her hands straight down over her holstered Colts.

Both men's faces slackened. They glanced at each other sheepishly then slowly lifted their hands above the table, resting them on the cards and coins piled before them. They sat in their chairs, heads hanging like those of cowed schoolboys.

Louisa returned her gaze to Vink. "If you so much as look at Mrs. Emory again, I will shoot you through your heart." She arched a brow. "Understand?"

Vink only stared at her, the corner of one eye twitching.

"I'll take that as a yes."

Keeping her face to the man as well as to Mose and Nasty Ralph, Louisa backed over to her own table then sagged into her chair, where she could keep all three hardcases in full view. Louisa glanced at Yardley. He smiled. Mrs. Emory sat looking as stricken as before, hunched as if chilled.

When Toni had brought two mugs of tea and a bottle, Louisa popped the cork and splashed a little whiskey into each mug.

"I thought you didn't drink the hard stuff," Yardley said, lifting his own shot glass to his lips.

"Cold night," Louisa said.

She slid one of the mugs toward the banker's wife, who sat to her right. "Here," she said. "You need to drink this. It'll warm you some, make you feel better."

Louisa was surprised when the woman turned to

her slowly and seemed to meet Louisa's gaze directly.
She studied Louisa for a time and then her lips moved
for several seconds before any words came out.

"Is . . . is . . . my . . . husband . . . dead . . . ?" She'd
asked the question barely loudly enough to be heard
above the wind and the fire in the stove as well as the
low rumble of conversation that had risen in the room
now on the lee side of the Vengeance Queen's slap
down of Ray Vink.

Louisa shared a quick look with Yardley, sitting
across the table from her. Then they both returned
their mildly surprised gazes to the woman.

"Yes," Louisa said. "But everything is going to be
all right."

The woman looked down at her steaming tea and
slowly shook her head. "No, it's not."

Louisa didn't have a reply to that, so she said nothing. She just sat slowly sipping her tea laced with
whiskey while Yardley sat across from her, nursing his
own drink.

Finally, he looked across the table at Louisa once
more and said, "You needn't be embarrassed, you
know."

Louisa glanced at Mrs. Emory to her right. The
woman seemed preoccupied with her tea, holding it
in both her hands close to her chest and taking small,
frequent, but tentative sips. Louisa hoped it would put
her to sleep soon and give her some relief from her
angst. When it did, Louisa would take her upstairs, to
her own room.

Louisa turned back to Yardley. "I'm not embarrassed." Of course it was a lie, but she found it impossible

to talk about her past with anyone but Lou Prophet, damn his big, roguish Confederate hide, anyway.

Yardley gave her a warm smile and reached across the table to place his hand on hers. He squeezed it gently. The warmth of his supple flesh was like a lightning bolt that shot right to her heart. She looked at the man smiling at her from the other side of the table, and then she could hardly see him through the tears in her eyes.

What the hell was happening to her?

She tried to pull her hand away, but he squeezed it all the tighter. Leaning across the table, he said, "There's no shame in being human, Louisa."

She felt a tear dribble down from her right eye to roll coolly along her nose to the corner of her mouth. Self-consciously, she looked around the room and found Vink looking over his shoulder again at the banker's wife. The man's dark eyes seemed to be boring into the stricken woman, who sat near Louisa, lifting her mug with quivering hands to her lips.

Reading the thoughts going through Vink's small, mean, stupid mind, understanding that the savage brute smelled weakness and opportunity in the woman whose husband had been so brutally taken from her not yet an hour ago, the sorrow that had welled up in Louisa for her own family was automatically shunted into the raw, blazing fury she knew almost as well.

The Vengeance Queen pulled her hand out of Yardley's. She quickly brushed the tear from her jaw, slid her chair back, and, heart pounding with iron-hot fury, she stood and closed her hand over the pearl grips of her right Colt.

"Vink!" she shouted.

The hardcase shunted his eyes from Mrs. Emory to Louisa, who slid her Colt from its holster and clicked the hammer back.

Vink's eyes snapped wide. "Now, hold on!" He lurched up out of his chair and turned to face Louisa, hands up, palms out.

Louisa narrowed an eye and fired three times, drilling three neat, round holes into the blond hardcase's chest, directly over his heart. The roar of her six-gun sounded like dynamite explosions, causing every man in the room, including Yardley, to leap to his feet, yelling.

Vink gave a shrill scream and flopped back atop the table on which he, Mose, and Nasty Ralph had been playing poker. Both men leaped to their feet, away from the man dying before them.

"Shit in a bucket!" shouted Nasty Ralph, jerking his fear-bright eyes to Louisa.

"Want some?" Louisa shouted back at him.

Nasty Ralph thrust his hands high above his head and dropped his chin to his chest. "Nope! No, ma'am, I don't!"

Louisa slid her Colt toward Mose. He threw his hands in the air and shouted, "Same!"

Keeping her Colt raised, Louisa looked around the room through the thick cloud of her own pungent powder smoke. The three drummers looked as though they'd each swallowed a snake. Toni stood behind the bar, a ragged towel draped over her shoulder, arms crossed on her chest. She stared at the dead hardcase with ironically arched brows, sucking her lower lip.

Turning to Louisa, she said, "She does clean the rats out of a place."

Closer by, Yardley stared at Louisa with a vague apprehension, as if he half feared she was going to keep her pistols dancing, emptying both her six-guns into the men around the room. Mrs. Emory sat to Louisa's right, staring up at the gun-handy blonde in glassy-eyed disbelief, stretching her lips slightly back from her teeth, holding her tea mug up close against her chest.

Slowly, Louisa lowered her smoking pistol.

Silence hung like a pall over the room. A log dropped through the stove's grate with a thump.

Outside, the wind moaned. The walls creaked against it.

Boots thumped on the front stoop—clumsy, scuffing sounds. The door opened. Louisa raised her Colt again, swung it toward where Edgar Clayton stumbled into the saloon, grunting and groaning. He dropped to his knees, panting, leaving the door standing wide behind him, the wind blowing a mare's tail of snow over him.

"Clayton!"

Yardley ran over to where the rancher knelt, holding one hand to his head. In his other, gloved hand he held his rifle. Yardley closed the door on the wind and snow and dropped to a knee beside the rancher.

"What the hell happened, Clayton?" the captain asked the man.

Clayton dropped his rifle and raised his head, a gash in his temple dribbling blood around his eye and into his bearded cheek.

Breathing hard and stretching his lips back from

his teeth in a grimace, Clayton raised his head and bellowed, "*Ramsay Willis!*"

Louisa hurried over to him, dropped to a knee. "Where, Clayton? Where's Willis?"

Just then more heavy footsteps sounded from the rear of the room. Louisa turned quickly, bringing her Colt around and cocking it. She eased the tension in her trigger finger.

Another familiar figure had just entered the room, moving up along the stairway from the room's rear. Morris Tutwiler shambled toward the bar. The draft through the open rear door behind the stairs was wreaking havoc with the lamps.

The barman was breathing even harder than Clayton. With each ragged breath, he puffed out his quivering lips. His face was mottled red, and his eyes were bright with misery.

As he neared the large bloodstain marking where Del Rainy had lain dead only a little over an hour before, Tutwiler stopped. He lifted his chin, throwing his bald head back and loosing a grizzly-like bellowing wail that echoed around the cavelike room. He hooked an arm behind himself as though to scratch his back.

The arm dropped to his side. He raised his other arm, pointing an accusatory finger toward Louisa, as though blaming the Vengeance Queen for the recent catastrophes. He tried to speak but the words gave way to another agonized wail.

The arm dropped and then the big barman himself fell straight forward to hit the floor with a heavy thud, landing on his face.

"Good Lord!" cried one of the drummers, leaping

back from his table and closing a hand over his mouth in horror.

Toni looked down at Tutwiler and screamed.

Then Louisa, standing with Yardley at the other end of the room, saw it, too.

Angling like a pump handle up from Tutwiler's back, a hatchet handle jutted out from the steel head embedded in the big man's spine.

Chapter 26

Despite having been ridden hard and put up wet, as the saying went, Prophet was awake if not at dawn's first blush, then at least at its broadening grin.

He rose, groaning against the stiffness in his muscles and bones, his bewitching tussle with the countess seeming nothing more than a half-waking dream now in its aftermath, and took a quick, frigid bath from the slushy water left in the pitcher on his washstand. He didn't bother with a fire in the little monkey stove in the corner. It would no sooner start heating up the wintry air in which his breath frosted plainly, than he'd be pulling his picket pin.

He cut loose with more than a few blue curses when that cold, cold water—so cold that he'd had to bust through the frozen rime on top with his Colt's butt—hit his extremities. Panting and wheezing against the chilling misery, he vowed for one last time to never let himself get caught in Dakota Territory again after, say, the Fourth of July.

If he were fool enough to ever again let money, even money as good as that which the Hatchley bunch

had on their ugly heads, lead him north of, say, the
North Platte River.

He dressed in his several layers of cold-weather
attire, tied his Stetson to his head with his moth-eaten,
mouse-chewed green muffler, and gathered his gear.
The Richards hanging down his back by its leather lanyard, his saddlebags draped over his left shoulder, his
Winchester secure in his right hand, he stepped out
into the hall filled with the night's lingering shadows.

As he stepped lightly toward the stairs, he could
hear men from the countess's party stretching and
groaning behind closed doors, murmuring in their
odd, barbaric-sounding tongue. He flashed on the
image of the countess herself, still curled in slumber
beneath her loving quilts. He recalled several blissful
seconds of their own primitive struggle, and groaned.

He made his way to the stairs and stopped above the
first step. He'd heard a door latch click behind him.
He started to turn his head to one side, to see along
the murky corridor, but then the latch clicked softly
again as the door was furtively closed.

Prophet frowned into the hall's dingy shadows.

The countess?

Or her doting friend Rawdney Fairweather?

With a dismissive grunt, the bounty hunter strode
down the stairs and bulled his way out the main door
and into the blistering cold of a new Dakota morning.
The pale sky looked as clear as a dawn mountain lake.
That meant the cold would likely be even more intense
than the previous night.

There would probably be no more snow, but that
cold scratching his cheeks like coarse sandpaper was
a bitch on high red wheels. He'd almost prefer the

snow. Then, again, in Dakota you never had to name your poison. You'd get a good dose of whatever the crotchety Dakota gods were passing out at any given time.

In summer, it was mosquitoes as large as horseshoes, ticks as large as tarantulas, and mile-wide cyclones that could drop out of a sickly yellow sky, pluck a man up in their devilish arms, and hurl him along with a whole herd of cattle all the way to Canada.

It was a hell of a place any day of the whole damn year!

Prophet hailed a boy in a torn coat and immigrant hat tramping past the saloon and holding a snow shovel, and offered him a dollar to fetch his horse over to the jail office.

"Careful, though, he's mean as a snake, son, and that's the god-awful truth!"

When the boy had pocketed the silver coin and run off in the direction of the livery barn, feeling as rich as Jay Gould, Prophet tramped north along the snowy street. He followed his own ghostly breath, the devilish Jack Frost chomping down on his nose.

He walked a block and saw Marshal Coffer standing on the freshly swept boardwalk fronting his jail office, staring toward the northwest. The marshal was all bundled up in his big blanket coat and mittens, his high-crowned Stetson tied down on his head like Prophet's, with a muffler knotted beneath his chin.

"Good morning, Marshal Coffer," the bounty hunter greeted the older man, wheezing against the cold as he drew up before the squat, stone jailhouse from the tin stovepipe of which a skein of gray smoke unfurled. "Out enjoying the soft spring zephyrs, are you? Is that agave blooms I'm smelling, or do I just need a stiff shot of tequila to remind me the devil has done called me home to his frozen-over hell?"

Turned away from Prophet, scouring the northwestern sky as though for geese to shoot, Coffer said, "Your prisoner is still sawing logs in yonder. I tried to wake him but he told me to do something to myself I truly wish I could now that my bed is once more empty and likely will be from here on in."

"Women are overrated, Sheldon. Don't you know that?"

"Easy for you to say."

"You need to join me on my journey to Mexico. I'll introduce you to some young ladies I know down that way."

"They'd kill me."

"But what a way to go!"

Coffer turned to Prophet, the marshal's cheeks rosy above his gray-streaked beard. His face was drawn, his eyes red-rimmed. He'd likely just hauled himself out of his lonely mattress sack, his feet hard as rocks.

He smiled insinuatingly. "How'd you sleep, Lou? Surely, you must have found some harlot to curl your toes."

Prophet hadn't thought it possible, but his cheeks actually warmed with chagrin. "It's too cold to palaver out here. Let's get inside and wake Hatchley from his beauty sleep—if he's still alive, that is. I got a train to catch, and . . ."

He let his voice trail off when Coffer turned his back to him to stare straight north along the street. Following the lawman's gaze, Prophet saw horseback riders just now enter the town, materializing gradually from the dawn's misty shadows. There were three of them, and they were all riding spotted ponies—two pintos and a paint.

As the trio drew closer, Prophet saw that the riders were decidedly dark-skinned and hawk-nosed. They wore hand-sewn robes stitched together from trade blankets. Long, coal black hair drooped from thick fur hats. Deer hide, fur-trimmed moccasins rose to their knees. The pintos were not outfitted with leather saddles but only blankets, and the bridles were fashioned from rope.

Indians.

"What the hell?" Prophet said.

Coffer glanced at him, saw him lower his Winchester from his right shoulder.

"Easy, Lou. They're Sioux. Cut-Heads. Hell by the half pound at one time, but they've had their horns filed."

Prophet looked at the raised Winchester in his hand then returned it to his shoulder. "Old habits die hard," he said with chagrin.

"That first man there—the old one," Coffer said, returning his gaze to the three Indians now approaching on their slow-walking mounts, the lead rider craggy faced and with gray liberally streaking the hair flowing out from under his rabbit fur hat. "He was once a chief, before his people were hazed onto the reserve at Fort Totten. Now he's just a pathetic old beggar, like the rest of them."

Coffer's face broadened with a toothy smile as the old man angled toward him, his pinto's hooves thudding in the fresh snow. "Good morning, Leaps High! What brings you out in such cold?"

The old man, his face like a dried-up raisin, his nose

like a sharp-tipped, crooked stick poking out from beneath the brim of his fur hat, cracked a wry grin of his own, showing a single front tooth—a badly chipped one, at that. "Just 'cause it's cold don't mean the people don't eat." He glanced at the dead bobcat lying slack across his horse's rump behind him. "Trapped that one there. Gonna take him over to Ripley, see what he'll give me for him. Need coffee, molasses for sweet. Good winter hide." He patted the bobcat behind him. "Make warm hat!"

As the two other, younger Indians reined up behind Leaps High, one of them jumped down from his saddle, grinning broadly, brown eyes flashing in the growing dawn light. He was a slender lad in his late teens, but the folly in his eyes bespoke a squishy thinker box. He jogged up onto the stoop before Coffer, laughing as he removed his thick, rabbit fur mitten and extended his bare hand to the marshal.

He laughed as though at the funniest joke he'd ever heard.

"Hello there, Little Fawn," Coffer said, chuckling as he removed his own glove to shake the young man's hand. "How are you this crisp winter morning? Still like to shake, do you? All right . . . there you go. I'll shake your hand."

Shaking the laughing youngster's hand, Coffer winked over his shoulder at Prophet. "Little Fawn loves to shake hands. Learned it from us white folks. The gesture is totally foreign to him, as to most Indians, and he thinks it's as funny as a fart in church. Can't get enough of it."

When Little Fawn had pumped Coffer's hand up and down a good dozen times, giggling like a school-girl, he pulled his hand away from Coffer and then leaped down off the stoop to stand before Prophet, bare hand extended. He stared up at the tall bounty hunter, slitted eyes flashing delightedly, spittle collecting in the corners of his mouth as he laughed.

"Go on, Lou," Coffer urged. "Shake his hand."

Prophet switched the Winchester to his left hand, bit off his mitten and inside glove, and closed his hand around the small, russet, femininely delicate hand extended toward him.

"All right," Prophet said, chuckling a little with embarrassment as he let the strange Indian boy pump his hand. "Pleased to meet you, Little Fawn. Yes, sir . . . damn tootin'."

Little Fawn laughed and laughed . . . and laughed . . . and when he finally had enough of pumping the bounty hunter's big paw, he ran off to the west and mounted the boardwalk where the barber was sweeping snow from the steps of his stoop and shook hands with the barber, too, laughing his fool head off. When he was done with the barber, he ran laughing across the street to where a man was splitting wood out front of the land office.

Smiling after the boy, Leaps High urged his horse east along the street, saying, "Good day, Marshal." He nodded to Prophet as he passed, and he and the other young man—this one taller and older than Little Fawn, and sober as a judge—angled over toward the mercantile just beyond where Little Fawn was pumping the hand of the man who'd been splitting wood.

"I don't think I'll ever look at a handshake in quite the same way again." Chuckling, Prophet mounted the jailhouse stoop and stomped the snow from his boots. "Well, I reckon I'll be takin' my prisoner off your hands, Marshal."

"I'll be sad to see him go."

Chuckling wryly, Coffer followed Prophet into the small, stone building warmed nicely by a small potbelly stove standing near the front wall, thumping and fluttering softly, flames dancing behind the soot-stained glass in the iron door. The musty place boasted a battered desk, a map of the county on one wall, and three steel cages running along the back.

Loud, guttural snores sounded from the middle cell in which Gritch Hatchley lay belly down, one arm and one leg hanging down off the side of his iron-framed cot toward the stone floor. The outlaw's long hair was thrown back behind his right ear, revealing the small, silver stud in the lobe. A whiskey bottle lay overturned on the floor near his dangling hand, which bore the tattoo of what appeared to be a butterfly.

Prophet snorted. He wouldn't have taken Hatchley for a nature lover.

"Damn, that heat feels good!" Prophet leaned his rifle against the wall. He set his saddlebags on the floor and turned to the stove, jerking off his mittens. He tossed the mittens and gloves down with his saddlebags and held his hands out to the stove, the soothing warmth pushing against him, battling out the cold and thawing the ice chunks he imagined floating in his veins as in a snowmelt mountain stream in the springtime.

He glanced over his shoulder at Hatchley. "Come on, Gritch. Rise an' shine, ole son. You've done been invited to a necktie party down in Bismarck." The bounty hunter winked at Coffer, who was hanging his hat on a tree by his desk. "Don't wanna be late. This one's bein' held in your very own honor, don't ya know!"

He and Coffer chuckled.

Hatchley stopped snoring. He smacked his lips, muttered, "Go 'way. I'm sleepin'." The snores resumed.

Prophet gave a wry snicker then grabbed a tin coffee cup from a shelf on the wall near the stove. He winked at Coffer again then tramped over to Hatchley's cage and raked the cup across the door, drawing it back and forth across the iron bands several times, lifting a ringing racket while bellowing, "*Wakey, wakey, little one! Time to rise and shine an' meet the train that's gonna haul your worthless ass to the hangman, Gritch!*"

Chapter 27

Hatchley lifted his head and bellowed as though someone were prodding the stab wound near his groin with a glowing hot poker. "Stop it! Stop it! Stop that infernal racket, Prophet, you crazy rebel son of Satan!"

Prophet lowered the cup to his side. "Just tryin' to get your attention, Gritch. Haul your bloomers!"

Hatchley turned his head to glare over his shoulder, dark eyes glistening with fury. "Go to hell! I'm gonna stay right here an' sleep till I feel well enough to travel. And that, you dog-diddlin' rebel devil, is that!"

He laid his head back down on his pillow. He closed his eyes and smacked his lips.

Prophet sighed. He turned to where Sheldon Coffer lounged back in his swivel chair, grinning with his hands locked behind his head.

Prophet extended his hand to the marshal, palm up. "Key, Sheldon?"

Ten minutes later, Gritch Hatchley bounded through the open jailhouse door like a mortar round from a cannon's maw. His hands cuffed before him, he stumbled across the stoop and down the steps and into the street, where he dropped and rolled, yelling like a gut-shot renegade Comanche.

He turned his head toward Prophet, his right eye red and swollen from its recent introduction to the butt end of Prophet's Colt. As the bounty hunter stepped through the door behind him, Hatchley assaulted Lou with a fresh string of curses ribald enough to make the ears of even a ten-cent doxie turn as red as liquid steel.

The boy who stood near the base of the stoop, holding the reins of Mean and Ugly, lowered his shocked eyes to the ground and blushed. He lifted his gaze to Prophet and said, "Did your mother really . . . really—?"

"Don't listen to him, boy," Prophet said, dropping down the steps to where Hatchley remained cursing in the street. He shoved his rifle into his saddle scabbard. "This one's bad. As bad as they come. Thank you mighty kindly for fetchin' my broom-tailed hay-burner for me. I hope he didn't nip you none." He hoisted the howling outlaw to his feet. "If he did, I'm purely sorry. That hoss is the animal version of this man, I'm afraid. As mean as a striped snake crossed with a scorpion!"

The boy turned to Mean and Ugly and, backing away cautiously while caressing his right shoulder with his mittened hand, said, "He's still got some green in him, don't he?"

He swung around and ran eastward along the street, probably heading off to the snow shoveling job he'd been heading toward when Prophet had waylaid him.

Mean watched the boy, owlishly twitching his ears.

Prophet shoved Hatchley against the saddled cayuse. "Mount up or I'll give you another big, wet kiss with my .45!"

Hatchley leaned against the saddle, sobbing. "You're a devil, Prophet!"

"So I been told."

"I think you opened up my wound again. I'm bleedin', damnit! I can't climb up onto this hoss, you crazy fool!"

Prophet rapped the barrel of his Colt against the back of the outlaw's head. It was a glancing blow. Still, Hatchley howled. "Oh, now you've really hurt me!"

"Get up there!"

Yowling and sobbing, the outlaw hooked his cuffed hands around the saddle horn. He tried several times to poke his left boot into the stirrup, hopping on his right foot. Finally, he stuck his boot into the stirrup and pulled his thick bulk into the leather, the horse giving an angry whinny as the weight of the foreign rider settled on his back.

He turned his ugly head to get a look at Hatchley, showing his large, ivory teeth, like an angry cur.

"Easy now, Mean," Prophet said, holding the horse's reins taut in his left fist. "Can't you see this poor soul is injured?" He chuckled.

"Here you go, Proph," Coffer said, and tossed the bounty hunter's saddlebags from the stoop.

Prophet caught the bags with his free hand and slung them up over Mean's rump, behind Hatchley, who was crouched over the horn, grunting and cursing.

"See you later, Sheldon!" Prophet said, waving at Coffer as he pointed Mean and Ugly eastward, in the direction of the train station.

"Not if I see you first!" Coffer chuckled as he strode back into his warm office and closed the door.

"Yeah, I get that a lot," Prophet said, laughing as he

tramped down the street, Mean and Ugly clomping along behind him, Gritch Hatchley moaning as he hunkered over the saddle horn.

"Stop your caterwauling, Gritch," Prophet admonished the outlaw. "Such carryin's-on ain't seemly in a man of your stature!"

"Diddle yourself!"

Prophet wagged his head. "Such language."

As he approached the hotel looming on his left, the front door opened and none other than the countess Tatiana Miranova stepped out onto the broad front porch, speaking quietly in Russian to someone remaining inside the hotel behind her. She moved out onto the porch, drawing the door closed, and turned to the street.

Prophet's heart warmed at seeing the beautiful young lady again, cloaked in a heavy black fur coat with matching fur hat on her lovely, black-eyed head. He also felt his cheeks flush a little with embarrassment over their carnal doings of only a few hours earlier. As her eyes found him leading his horse with the grunting outlaw on its back, Prophet pinched his hat brim to her.

"A hearty good morning to you, Countess!"

She stepped up to the porch rail, her rich lips shaping a delighted smile. "A hearty good morning to you, as well, Mr. Prophet." She glanced furtively behind her, chuckling throatily, then turned to him once more and said, "How did you sleep?"

Prophet gave a choking laugh as he continued tramping along the snowy street, feeling more warm blood congeal in his cheeks. "Not well at all, not well at all."

"No," the countess said, smiling broadly. "Me, neither!"

Prophet glanced at the fine wagon with its caved-in roof still sitting in front of the hotel, tongue drooping into the snow. "Oh, uh, once again I sure am sorry about your wheels there."

"That's all right." The countess chuckled throatily, glancing furtively behind her once more before leaning toward Prophet and smiling alluringly. "You made up for it!" She winked at him.

Prophet was about to bid her a nice trip home to Russia but then the door behind her opened, and her father the count and the senator and several beefy, bearded, fur-clad Cossacks clomped out onto the porch behind her.

Tatiana turned to them, and Prophet scowled and swung away, heading over to the livery barn where he spent the next fifteen minutes saddling the five dead outlaws' horses and then tying the dead outlaws over their horses' saddled backs. Bidding the somewhat sheepish-acting Pop Schofield adieu, Prophet and Hatchley were once more on their way to the train station, Prophet leading both Mean and Ugly and the lead horse of the five-horse pack team.

As his boots crunched in the new snow, the bounty hunter stared straight west toward the wooden depot building that sat roughly two hundred yards from the edge of Indian Butte, the tracks curving toward it from over Prophet's left shoulder, along the south edge of the town, to curve away again on his right, heading southwest toward Bismarck.

The station appeared little more than a small brown box from this distance, with the dark caterpillar of the train itself slouched on its far side. A finger of gray

smoke rose from the stovepipe poking up from the
station's shake-shingled roof. Darker smoke unfurled
from the diamond-shaped stack of the black iron locomotive sitting ahead of the tender car. Apparently, the
engineer and fireman were heating up the boiler in
anticipation of the journey south.

South. Oh, what a lovely word!

Ahead, several horses and men were gathered near
a couple of winter-naked trees along the trail between
the town and the train station, in a swale in the otherwise featureless prairie. One of the men was crouched
slightly forward, like a photographer over his camera.
But then Prophet saw the man wasn't taking a photo-
graph. No, he was crouched over what appeared to be
a rifle mounted on a tripod, its barrel aimed north, to
Prophet's right.

Judging by his diminutive stature and garish attire,
the man crouched over the rifle appeared to be the
senator's foppish son, Rawdney.

Prophet could hear Rawdney speaking to the others
gathered around him, for sounds carried well in the
crisp, infernally cold, post-storm air. Besides, Rawdney's voice was raised. He was boasting about his prized
sporting rifle to the Russians and his assistant, Leo,
gathered around him, admiring the long-barreled,
fancily carved piece bristling atop its brass tripod.

As the bounty hunter continued striding forward,
Mean and Ugly matching his stride, Hatchley groaning
atop the horse's back, Rawdney crouched over the rifle
again. The others stepped slightly back from Rawdney
and the gun, tensing slightly, staring off toward the
northwest in expectant anticipation.

Flames stabbed from the big rifle's maw. The long
gun bucked against the dandy's right shoulder. The

report reached Prophet's ears a second later—a loud, belching report that reverberated in the cold air, the echoes caroming over the town, gradually fading.

Rawdney fired the heavy gun again. Again, the report rocketed over the prairie and the town, sounding like a near thunderclap.

Turning the rifle on its swivel and working the trigger guard cocking mechanism, ejecting the spent cartridge and seating fresh, the senator's son picked out another target through the sight poking up in front of the rifle's silver breech. He fired again, reloaded, fire again, reloaded, and fired yet again, the heavy, thundering, echoing booms causing Mean and Ugly to arch his neck and tail, snorting apprehensively.

The five packhorses didn't like the racket much, either. They whickered and pranced, the lead horse tugging on its reins in Prophet's hand.

"Easy, fellas," Prophet said, keeping a firm hand on the lines, not breaking stride. "It's just the nancy boy showing off for the Russians. Next, they'll be breaking out the rulers and dropping their pants."

He snorted at that.

The men clumped under the winter-naked cottonwoods were a hundred yards from Prophet now. Rawdney was clad in pale, fringed, Indian-beaded buckskins complete with broad-brimmed buckskin hat with an Indian-beaded band. He stepped away from the rifle and swung his head this way and that, grinning, crowing to his friends about his German-made, custombuilt Scheutzen sporting rifle bored in the .56 caliber "and accurate—in the hands of an expert marksman, of course—up to five hundred yards!"

The others stood around, smoking cigars, some drinking from silver flasks, looking impressed. As

Rawdney's head turned toward Prophet, the priggish fop suddenly fell silent. He stared toward the bounty hunter for a few seconds. He grinned, his lips stretching back to show the white line of his teeth against the plump, pink paleness of his face beneath the outlandish buckskin hat. His entire costume was like something out of a silly Wild West traveling show.

Rawdney said something to the others too quietly for Prophet to hear.

Whatever he'd said, it struck the other men's funny bones. They all turned toward Prophet and laughed.

Rawdney stepped up to the rifle again. He swung the gun around on its swivel, which chirped like a bird in the cold air. Prophet felt a tingling in his chest when he saw that the rifle's slender, dark maw was aimed directly at him. Leastways, it appeared to be aimed at him.

Nah. Couldn't be.

Still, the hair on the back of the bounty hunter's neck pricked. He frowned, staring at the rifle and the ridiculously attired dandy crouched over it from behind.

Flames lanced toward Prophet. There was a screeching whine. The whine grew quickly louder until Prophet felt a sudden burn across the outside of his left cheek then heard the thud of the bullet plowing into the ground behind him.

Mean and the lead packhorse jerked back on their reins and lifted shrill whinnies.

Prophet stopped, crouching. He brushed his left mitten across his cheek and looked at it. There was a thin streak of red on it.

Maybe seventy yards away from Prophet now, straight ahead of him along the trail, Rawdney and the other men threw their heads back, laughing.

Unbridled fury burned through Prophet as he glared across the cold distance at the foppish bastard surrounded by the burly Russians and his ass-kissing assistant, Leo. The smarmy assistant threw his head back again with laughter and then lifted a silver flask to his lips with his black-gloved hand.

Rawdney spoke to the others, chuckling, and crouched over the rifle, again directing the maw toward Prophet.

The red-faced, fiery-eyed bounty hunter lurched forward and flung his right arm out, pointing furiously. "Don't you dare!"

Again, bright orange flames lapped from the Scheutzen's maw.

The rifle bellowed.

The slug chewed into the ground two feet in front of Prophet, sort of between him and Mean and Ugly.

"Oh *hellll*!" Hatchley screamed.

Mean had already been prancing around, tugging at the reins so hard that Prophet was having a hard time maintaining a hold on them. Same with the lead packhorse. Now, as the German rifle's echoes rocketed skyward, Mean gave a ferocious tug, jerking the reins free of Prophet's mittened hand.

The lead packhorse jerked its own reins free at the same time. With raucous whinnies, all six mounts wheeled and galloped away to the north, some kicking out their rear hooves in anger, the packhorses tied tail to tail.

"Mean!" Prophet barked.

To no avail.

Loosing another shrill whinny, Mean bucked again, nearly unseating its cursing rider.

"What the hell?" Hatchley bellowed, the chain between the cuffs drawn taut around the horn. He crouched low over the mount's billowing mane, looking back desperately at the bounty hunter. *"Proph-ettttt!"*

As Mean buck-kicked violently, lifting another shrill whinny, Hatchley's boots came free of the stirrups. His cuffed hands rose up and over the horn, and the man himself gave a screaming wail as Mean bucked again, throwing Hatchley forward against the horse's left wither.

Hatchley flopped there for a moment, crouched forward, but after two more of Mean and Ugly's lurching, pitching strides, the outlaw rolled down over the left stirrup.

He hit the ground on his side then bounced and rolled in the snowy sagebrush, yowling and bellowing.

Prophet slid his glance from Hatchley and the fleeing Mean and Ugly toward the men clumped beneath the cottonwoods. Again, Rawdney grinned and crouched over the tripod-mounted rifle.

"Watch this," Prophet heard him say, causing a stone to drop in the bounty hunter's belly.

Chapter 28

Toni screamed again and lurched back against the back bar shelves, closing a hand over her mouth in shock at the sight of Morris Tutwiler lying dead on the floor near the stairway, in nearly the same spot that Del Rainy had died.

The hatchet angled up out of the big barman's back.

"Christalmighty," said one of the drummers, in a hushed tone of awe. All three drummers stood at their table, eyes bright from drink, mouths drawn wide in horror.

The two hard-eyed market hunters, Mose and Nasty Ralph, had been standing at their own table near the bar ever since Louisa had trimmed Ray Vink's wick. That had happened just before the injured Edgar Clayton had stumbled into the saloon. Right after Clayton had stumbled in the front door, bleeding from his temple, Tutwiler had ambled in from behind the stairs, wearing that hatchet in his back.

"Christalmighty," Captain Yardley said, standing over Clayton, who knelt on the floor, holding a hand over his bloody right temple. "What in the name of God is going on here?"

Slowly, Louisa stepped away from Yardley and Clayton. She walked down the length of the shadowy saloon, down past the bar, and stood over the bloody, lumpy figure of Morris Tutwiler.

"I don't think it has anything to do with God."

One of the drummers—the shortest of the three and wearing a thick, brown handlebar mustache peppered with gray—quickly crossed himself. "You can say that again."

Another drummer, a tall, thin man in a gaudy, orange checked suit, slurred his words as he said, "What . . . what the hell's goin' on?" His voice trembled slightly. "Who's . . . who's out there . . . killin' folks?" He turned toward where the back door stood open behind the stairs, letting in a near-steady draft of cold wind laced with snow. "Who killed the barman?"

Louisa stepped over Tutwiler. Drawing her right Colt, she walked around behind the stairs and stood in the open doorway, peering into the snowy darkness. She could see nothing but the snow and the indefinite edges of several piles of split wood and the privy standing about fifty feet straight out from the saloon. The snow was scuffed near the door, where Tutwiler had stumbled away from the wood when the ax had been plunged into his back, but the storm was quickly filling in the marks.

Louisa felt a wave of frustration mixed with fury rise inside her. She squeezed the Colt tighter in her right hand. She didn't like being hunted. She was the hunter. Having the tables turned enraged her. But she felt that for some reason on this stormy night, she was being hunted, sure enough.

She didn't know why. Maybe that's what made it all the more frustrating. Maybe her hunter didn't know why he was hunting her. He was just hunting. His mind turned to mush for one reason or another, and he was out for blood.

Louisa walked outside and stopped just beyond the woodpiles clad in downy snow. The wind whipped against her, pelting her with snow falling from the murky sky. She endured the cold ripping into her and suppressed her need to shiver.

Her heart thudding angrily, she yelled, "Are you out here, Willis?"

Nothing but the wind's moans.

"Willis?" Louisa called. "Are you out here?" She paused, holding her Colt in one hand, sliding her windblown hair from her eyes with her other hand, the anger churning hotter and hotter just behind her heart. "Come to me, Willis! If you want to kill me, face me! Come to me, Willis! I'm right here! Face those you want to kill, you *coward*!"

She screamed that last.

A hand closed over her shoulder. Louisa whipped around, clicking the Colt's hammer back and tightening her finger over the trigger. A tall, dark figure stood before her, two feet away. Louisa's Colt was aimed at a gold button of the dark blue cavalry tunic showing between the flaps of an open bear coat.

Yardley jerked his hands up, palms out, in surrender.

"You almost got a bullet through your heart, Captain!" Louisa shouted above the wind.

"I came out here to talk some sense into you. This

Willis character is off his nut. He's crazy. I know you're frustrated, but you can't call him in like a wild turkey!"

"Get the hell away from me!"

Louisa brushed past him and, holstering her revolver, walked back into the saloon. As Yardley came in behind her, she swung back toward him, the fire of rage in her eyes. "Do me a favor, Captain. Mind your own business from now on. You might think what other women do concerns you, but what I do concerns only myself. No one looks after me. You pull another stunt like that, I won't fail to bury a blue whistler in your guts."

Louisa turned and strode back along the stairs and into the saloon. All eyes were on her. Everyone in the room had heard her hand the captain his proverbial hat. She stepped over Tutwiler again and walked up past the bar on her left and the three gamblers on her right.

Mose and Nasty Ralph stared at her from over Vink's body still laid out on their table. Toni stared at Louisa from behind the bar. The redhead was in the same place she'd been when Louisa had gone out the back door.

Toni's eyes were wide with shock, her cheeks pale. She had one arm crossed on her chest. She had the other hand raised to her mouth and was nervously fingering her bottom lip.

Mrs. Emory sat in the brocade armchair at Louisa's table. She was slumped forward over her tea mug, elbows on the table, kneading her temples with the heels of her hands. Edgar Clayton sat at his table, just beyond the two market hunters. He'd gotten himself a fresh bottle, and, one eye on Louisa, was just then pouring himself a fresh drink. The blood on his right temple had congealed.

The only other man in the room, the Sundown doctor who apparently did double duty as the town drunk, sat alone on the far side of the bar, staring over his table littered with two empty bottles, a shot glass, and a beer glass—just staring toward the dark windows beyond which the wind howled and against which the snow blew.

Louisa dragged a chair out from Clayton's table and slacked into it. Leaning forward, crossing her arms on the table, she turned to the rancher. "Did you run into Willis?"

Clayton threw back half a shot of whiskey and nodded. "He ran into me, more like. The wind was blowin'. Mighty dark out there. I must've come up on him and didn't see him. Don't think he saw me till I near ran into him. He swung around sudden-like and hit me with the handle of his ax. I dropped my rifle and ran . . . ran before he could lay the blade into me. He chased me for a ways but he gave up fast."

He took another, smaller sip of his drink and said, "I think he was heading this way."

"Where was he when you ran into him?"

Clayton tossed his head. "Two, maybe three buildings to the north. In a break between Ed Lander's old barn and the barber's boarded-up shop. I was purty dazed. Took me a few minutes to get my wits about me. When I did, I went back for my rifle then came back here. He must have been out back just when I was comin' in the front, and buried his ax in Morris's back."

Clayton showed his teeth like an angry dog and shook his head. "Crazy devil. Crazy, bloodthirsty devil!"

Big Nasty Ralph hipped around in his chair to regard Clayton over his shoulder, scrunching up his big, meaty face. "Who is this Ramsay Willis fella, anyways? What the hell's his problem—murderin' folks with an ax an' such?"

"Worked for me," Clayton said, throwing the last of his whiskey back then leaning forward again to stare down at his table with his rheumy, angry eyes. "For two years. Lived in a room off the back of our cabin—Rose's an' mine. Quiet man. He—"

"Hey, wasn't there a Rose who worked here?" Nasty Ralph interrupted Clayton. "Why, sure there was! Damn, she was one nice little . . ."

Looking around the room, the market hunter saw all eyes on him, including those of Louisa and Clayton himself, whose gaze was the darkest, most castigating of all. Even the town drunk/doctor was staring at Nasty Ralph.

"Jesus, Ralph," Mose whispered.

Nasty Ralph brushed a sheepish fist across his nose and lowered his gaze to Vink, staring sightlessly up from the table.

"Kept to himself, Ramsay Willis did," Clayton continued, his voice pitched with strained patience, keeping his gaze on the back of Nasty Ralph's head. "Rarely came to town. Stayed in his room when we wasn't workin'. He got restless every winter. Couldn't take the short days. Endless gray days . . . all the cold, the snow. Took to drinkin' too much. I seen it comin' on in him this fall. That restlessness, thinkin' about another winter comin' on. Brewed his own beer, Ramsay did. Drank all of it himself. Never shared. Now . . ."

Clayton looked at Nasty Ralph and gritted his teeth. "Now he's got the winter fever. He's a killer. He'll try to kill all of us, and that's a fact. That's how it works—the winter fever. You gotta work it out, think the only way is to kill . . . kill . . . kill. Till someone kills *you*. That's the only way to stop a man afflicted like that. Kill him."

"Just like a goddamn rabid dog," said the drummer in the orange suit, sitting stiff-backed in his chair and staring wide-eyed toward Clayton.

The rancher refilled his glass from his bottle and raised it in salute to the drummer.

No one said anything for a time. The lanterns shunted thick, purple shadows wildly about the room. One fluttered out and smoked, and Toni grabbed a box of lucifers off a shelf and walked over to relight it. She moved quickly, desperately, as though worried all the lanterns would go out and leave the entire room in darkness. Leave them all exposed to the killer, Ramsay Willis.

"Well . . ." Mose rose from his chair near Nasty Ralph, staring down at the dead man on the table before him. "I for one am damned tired of starin' at Vink's ugly face. Let's get him out to the woodshed."

"Forget the woodshed," Nasty Ralph said, scraping his own chair back. "You seen what happened to Tutwiler when he went out there. Let's drag him out to the front stoop and call it good."

"Sure, call the wolves in," Toni said as she touched a flame to the lamp's wick. "That's all we need."

"Carry him out to the woodshed." Captain Yardley stood over a half-filled shot glass at the bar. "Two of you should be all right. Just keep your eyes skinned."

Nasty Ralph scowled across the room at him. "Who the hell are you, anyway, soldier boy? You think just 'cause you're wearin' that uniform you got the right to issue orders? Rainy's dead. So no one's in charge. Not even you . . . soldier boy!"

Yardley didn't appear to be in any mood to endure any more tongue-lashings. Louisa had injured his male pride. He cursed under his breath, tossed the rest of his shot back, then strode swiftly over to the table where Mose and Nasty Ralph stood over the body of their dead pard.

Yardley stopped not two feet away from Mose and glared down at the shorter man, stony-eyed.

"Take your friend out to the woodshed," he said tightly. Toni just then got the lamp lit, and the growing glow caressed the captain's left cheek and was reflected in his left, cobalt blue eye.

Nasty Ralph glared back at him, his broad forehead creasing and turning red beneath his matted cap of coarse, wavy, straw-colored hair.

Mose sidled up to Nasty Ralph, nudged his arm. "Stand down, Ralph. We got enough trouble. Let's take Vink outside. We'll be all right. We got our guns. We'll be just fine. We see that crazy bastard, we'll blow his lights out."

Still glaring up at Yardley, Ralph said, "Don't ever push me like that again . . . soldier boy. I don't take orders from no soldiers."

Yardley glanced at Louisa sitting at the table with Clayton, almost directly behind Nasty Ralph, then flushed a little with embarrassment. He strode back to the bar, where his bottle and empty shot glass were waiting for him. As Nasty Ralph and Mose began back-and-bellying their dead friend off their table, Louisa rose from her chair and buttoned her coat.

"I'll ride shotgun," she told the market hunters.

Chapter 29

Louisa pulled on her gloves and shoved her mittens into the pockets of her wool coat. She wrapped her muffler around her ears, shoved the tails down inside her coat, and set her Stetson on her head.

She picked up her rifle and, as Mose and Nasty Ralph hefted Vink up by his arms and ankles, strode back along the bar. Louisa did not glance at Yardley standing at the bar with his shot glass and bottle, one high-topped, black cavalry boot perched on the brass rail running along the bar's base. Out of the corner of her eye she saw him glance at her in the back bar mirror as he once again lifted his glass to his mustached mouth.

Louisa stepped over Tutwiler then walked around the stairs to the back door. She threw the bolt, nudged the door open. The wind caught it and slammed it back against the saloon's rear wall with a loud bang that made both Mose and Nasty Ralph jerk with starts behind her.

"Jesus," Mose said, anxiously shaking his head.

Holding her Winchester straight out from her right hip, Louisa stepped outside. She looked around and, deeming the area relatively safe though she couldn't see much farther than about fifteen feet out before her, glanced at the two men standing in the doorway behind her, and nodded.

Mose and Nasty Ralph carried Vink out the door. They followed Louisa, leading with her rifle aimed before her, around the privy and out to the woodshed.

She set her rifle down and lit a match. Cupping it carefully in the palm of her left hand, she used the wan glow to inspect the shed, which was a small pole structure with a sloping roof, open on one side. It was filled with cut logs. Atop one five-foot-high woodpile lay Rainy, on his belly, ankles crossed. On another pile sprawled Pima Quarrels and Sweets DuPree, both with their arms and legs spread, heads tipped to one side, eyes wide and staring.

The wind snuffed the match but not before Louisa saw that no hatchet-wielding killer was lurking in the woodshed.

She nodded to the market hunters and stepped aside to let Mose and Nasty Ralph pass with Vink, whom they swung back and forth a few times between them. On "four," they sailed him up onto the pile beside Del Rainy. Vink rolled off the pile, dislodging several logs before he hit the ground with a slapping thud.

"Jesus H. Christ!" Mose complained.

They picked Vink up again and sent him sailing up onto the woodpile beside Rainy. The tall blond stayed that time though he dislodged one more log, which fell onto Mose's right foot, evoking a curse.

"Now, Tutwiler," Louisa said, jerking her chin in the direction of the saloon.

"Oh Christ!" Nasty Ralph intoned. "We're not undertakers!"

"Now, Tutwiler," Louisa repeated, more firmly, flexing her hand around the neck of her Winchester.

When Mose and Nasty Ralph had hauled the big barman out from the saloon and deposited him in the woodshed with the other cadavers, Mose turned to Louisa and said, "Happy now?"

He and Nasty Ralph stomped back toward the saloon.

Louisa remained outside the woodshed, holding her rifle on her shoulder, looking around through the blowing tendrils of her blond hair. She did not follow the men back to the hotel. Instead, she stared at a footprint in the snow near the front of the woodshed, at the base of a crooked cottonwood pole supporting the roof.

The print wasn't hers and it was neither Nasty Ralph's nor Mose's. She knew because she'd spied the print before they'd entered the woodshed. The wind was slow to fill it in because of its placement there on the lee side of the building. Now she looked around and found another print on the leeward side of a shrub straight out from the shed, maybe fifteen feet to the south. The wind was gradually filling it in.

Louisa walked slowly eastward, holding her rifle with both hands across her chest, her jaws taut against the cold wind battering her. Whoever had made those footprints had made them less than a half hour ago. And he was heading south, away from the saloon at the rear of which Tutwiler had been impaled with the hatchet.

Who else could those prints belong to but the killer, Ramsay Willis?

Louisa's heart quickened as she walked slowly east in the snowy darkness, her gaze darting this way and that, frequently returning to the ground before her that was mostly dead brown grass and buck brush partly covered with snow.

Bushes cropped up to both sides of her as she moved slowly beyond the ragged outskirts of Sundown. She crossed the new railroad tracks mounted on their recently graded, cinder-paved bed nearly swept clear by the blowing snow, and continued heading east.

She almost stopped and turned back, the icy hands of the wind grinding her bones to jelly, but then she found another recent print and knew she was heading in the right direction and that she was likely close on the heels of Ramsay Willis.

Louisa's heartbeat quickened again, her blood flowing warmly despite the chill engulfing her like a giant witch's hand.

A dark, broken wall of trees moved up on both sides of her—winter-naked and creaking and moaning as the wind ripped at them. They were cottonwoods, she believed. Maybe some ash and box elder. A small copse out here on the open prairie at the very edge of Sundown.

As she moved into them, setting one high-topped fur boot down at a time, following a meandering break through the woods, she spied another footprint. It sat askance some low shrubbery matted with fresh snow.

He was here, just ahead of her, probably. He was on the run from the saloon.

Did he know Louisa was behind him, stalking him?

Louisa swallowed. She breathed slowly, taking one cold breath at a time, wincing when a gust of wind sucked it back out of her lungs and sent a chill wave spasming through her.

She stepped over a deadfall tree blocking her path, noting where snow had been brushed off it recently by her quarry, when he, too, had hiked a leg over the fallen cottonwood, likely putting a hand down to support himself like Louisa did now, removing her right hand for a moment from her Winchester's neck.

A riflelike crack sounded beneath the wind.

Louisa set her left boot down with a start on the opposite side of the deadfall, quickly returning her right hand to her Winchester. She clenched as she waited for a bullet, but then she saw a branch tumbling downward in the darkness just ahead of her and to her right.

She swallowed, drew a slow breath.

Only a branch, broken by the wind, falling from a wind-battered tree. It crashed with a muffled thud in the brush.

Louisa continued forward, sliding her gaze across the dark woods around her, keeping one eye skinned on the ground, looking for more prints left by her quarry.

A stab of flames flashed red-orange ahead and on her left. She felt the heat of the bullet's passing just off her right cheek. At the same time, the hiccupping report of the rifle reached her ears. She gasped and threw herself to the ground laced with layers of bent, snowy brush, and rolled to her left, toward the cover of another blowdown angling before her.

Icy snow slithered down beneath her coat collar, and she gritted her teeth against it.

Another stab of orange flames in the murky darkness ahead of her, maybe twenty feet away. The wind muffled the thud of the bullet slamming into the blowdown. Snow and wood slivers sprayed.

Louisa rose to a knee and rammed the Winchester against her right shoulder.

The rifle bucked as she squeezed the trigger, aiming toward where she'd seen the flash of her quarry's rifle. The Winchester belched again, briefly relieving the darkness with its red-orange flash.

She fired two more rounds, one after the other, then, ejecting the last smoking cartridge and pumping a fresh one into the action, she rolled quickly to her left, knowing that if she'd missed her target, the shooter would track her by her own gun flashes.

She couldn't roll far. A nest of shrubs growing up around a stout trunk blocked her way. She lay on her left side, staying as low as possible, holding her Winchester in both hands up close against her, trying to make a small target.

Breathing hard from both exertion and anxiousness, wincing against the cold of the snow pressing against her and the million little sharp points of brush prodding her, she waited, staring in the shooter's direction.

She lay there for nearly two full minutes, seeing only murky, snow-laced darkness before her, hearing only the wind's relentless moaning and groaning and the agonized creaking of the battered brush and tree limbs.

She'd remained in such a position before, for several hours, waiting for the coming dawn to help her with the task of revealing her quarry. She couldn't remain here all night, however. She probably couldn't stay out here another hour, or she'd freeze to death.

She drew her legs up beneath her and, using the butt of her rifle pressed against the brushy ground, slowly pushed and hoisted herself to a standing position. She suppressed the urge to shiver against the cold snow clinging to her, the stuff that had slithered down her back melting with the contact of her bare skin, causing frigid rivulets to roll down along her spine and into the waistband of her flannel-lined denims, finding the crack between her butt cheeks.

She gave a raspy curse.

Slowly, she moved ahead through the thick woods, meandering around trees and shrubs, stepping over fallen branches. When she finally made it to where she believed the shooter had fired from, she stopped and looked around.

She'd been right. The shooter had been here. She could see his dark markings in the snow, by the light of a dull blue ambience radiating out of the snow itself. Louisa looked at the scuff marks, trying to pick out a trail. She stepped quietly straight south of the tree behind which the killer had fired, her eyes scanning the uneven, snowy ground.

Several split logs lay in a loose pile before her.

She toed one of the logs, frowning down at it. Firewood?

A faint shadow slid across the snow to her right.

A breath that was part grunt sounded behind her.

Louisa whipped around, glimpsing a man-shaped shadow before her and seeing something that might have been a swinging ax angling toward her from what was now her left. She fired the Winchester, the rifle bucking and flashing and belching a wink before the thing swinging toward her plowed into her left temple.

"Oh!" Louisa dropped the Winchester, twisted around, and fell, her landing padded by the heavy brush and the snow.

Her ears rang. Stars burst behind her retinas.

"Goddamnit!" she heard herself cry—a rare oath for her. She hadn't been raised to talk like that, but her language had gotten considerably saltier since she'd started riding with a certain blue-tongued ex-Confederate.

Gritting her teeth against the gnawing pain in her head, she rolled onto her back and pushed up onto her butt in time to see the man who'd wielded the club stumbling backward, both hands pressed to his chest, over his heart. He grunted as he continued stumbling backward, then, getting his boots caught in a tangle of barely covered brush, he fell on his butt.

He sat there, grunting, writhing, and kicking his legs.

Louisa looked around for her rifle. Not seeing it immediately, she jerked up the right flap of her coat and shucked her right-hand Colt from its holster.

Aiming the big popper straight out in front of her, she clicked the hammer back.

The man before her was winding down like a top, his grunts growing more and more strangled.

He kicked a few more times, each kick more feeble than the last, then collapsed to lay back down in the brush, hands falling to his sides. His legs quivered a little and then fell still.

Louisa tried to heave herself to her feet but fell back to her butt, clamping her left hand to her temple from which she could feel blood trickling. The blow had dazed her, made her dizzy and a little sick to her stomach. She drew a breath, pushed up onto her knees, and cupped snow to her face, bracing herself.

She drew a sharp breath through her teeth. The icy snow cleared the cobwebs. At least, it kept her from passing out.

Feeling stronger but still a little dizzy, she heaved herself to her feet and, still clutching the Colt in her right hand, moved unsteadily toward the man on the ground roughly fifteen feet away. Blood from the gash on her temple slid down her cheek, becoming sluggish as it froze. She dropped to a knee beside the man she'd shot, and, keeping an eye on his hands, placed her left hand on his shoulder, shaking him.

His head bobbed. His eyes appeared closed.

Louisa saw the dark shine of blood on the front of his homemade fur coat. A heart shot, most likely. He was dead.

Louisa pulled the man's wool hat with earflaps from his head, to get a better look at him. His face was blunt, with a short, broad nose. There was nothing striking about his features, nothing that set him apart from a million other men. Several days' worth of sandy stubble spiked his cheeks. There were maybe a few streaks of gray in his straight brown hair, which hung down a short ways over his ears. He appeared to be in his middle to late thirties, maybe early forties.

Ramsay Willis?

A voice called out of the windy darkness: "Louisa?"

She recognized Yardley's voice. He'd come looking for her, likely followed her trail.

She would have been annoyed if she hadn't suddenly, grudgingly found herself needing help.

She rose and turned to face in the direction of Sundown.

"Here!" she called, trying to lift her voice above the wind. "I'm over here, Captain!" She waved her arm so he could see her better in the dark.

An orange light flashed straight out before her, from maybe thirty yards away.

She heard the bullet whoosh through the air to her right. It was followed by a revolver's crackling report.

Two more flashes.

One bullet thumped into a tree just ahead of the exasperated Vengeance Queen. She threw herself to the ground once more and, snarling more curses taken from Prophet's repertoire, lifted her Colt to return fire.

Chapter 30

It's hard not to feel the blood pool in your knees when a rifle is aimed at you—especially a fancy sporting rifle that appeared more than a little accurate and outfitted with a sliding rear sight and mounted on a tripod.

Especially when a half-pint devil with a jealous grudge is grinning down the barrel at you . . .

The barrel of Rawdney Fairweather's Scheutzen, poking out of the small clump of men gathered under the cottonwoods along the trail to the Indian Butte train station, sixty yards from where Prophet stood crouched, heart thudding, appeared to be aimed directly at the big bounty hunter's ticker, sure enough.

Lou stared back along the Scheutzen's barrel at the fop aiming through the little, vertical, rectangular sight standing up just behind the breech. Rawdney was showing a sly little grin as he adjusted the rifle slightly on the tripod, apparently placing the bead at the barrel's end where he wanted it.

Prophet curled his upper lip in an enraged snarl touched with more than a little bare-assed trepidation.

Devil's gonna shoot me and leave me here along the trail like a sack of potatoes spilled off a cart!

With an angry, bellowing wail he hurled himself off the left side of the trail just as the Scheutzen thundered, the little viper tongue of flames lapping toward Prophet. As the big bounty hunter hit the snowy grass, he heard the hiss of the bullet stitching the air if not where he'd been standing a moment before, then within a cat's whisker, no doubt, before it hammered into the ground with a hair-raising ping.

Prophet rolled onto his belly and fired a look of keen hatred at the dandy laughing with the big, bearded Russians and his natty assistant, Leo, gathered around the rifle under the cottonwoods. Leo was rocked back on the heels of his fur boots, pointing at Prophet, laughing and tipping his flask to his mouth once more.

"You son of a buck, Fairweather!" Prophet yelled, his jaws set so hard he thought they'd crack. "I'll get you for that—mark my words!"

Fairweather held up a prissy, gloved finger to the others, then crouched over his rifle once more.

"Goddamnit!" Prophet shouted.

He rose to his heels and then ran crouching toward the only cover out here—a rock humping up out of the ground ten yards to his left. Just before he reached the rock, Fairweather's bullet hammered the face of it with a snarling bang followed closely by the rifle's echoing report.

Prophet hit the ground and rolled up behind the rock, hearing the men laughing beneath the cottonwoods.

Prophet glanced to the west. Mean and Ugly was a small brown speck maybe a hundred yards away under the low gray sky, calmly grazing now in the wake of the horse's having fled Fairweather's first assault. Nearer Prophet, maybe thirty yards from the trail, Gritch Hatchley lay in the snowy brown grass, grunting and cursing.

"If only I'd grabbed my Winchester," Lou fumed to himself, glancing toward Mean and Ugly again and seeing the butt of his rifle poking up from the saddle scabbard. He looked back at Fairweather and Leo and the Russians. "I'd blow that little nancy right out of his tailor-made outfit, and I'd finish with those goddamn Russians!"

But he didn't have his rifle. He had only his .45 and his bowie knife. Each would be of equal value from this distance. So when another bullet came screeching toward him, Prophet could only pull his head back down behind the rock and grit his teeth and curse as the heavy-caliber round slammed into it, making the rock shudder against the bounty hunter's shoulders.

"Go ahead and have your fun, you prissy coward," Prophet raked out, pressing his back taut against the rock. "When you're done, I'm gonna fetch my '73 and shove it so far up your behind, you'll . . ."

He let the words die on his tongue.

The clatter of a wagon rose. He turned to see a nice two-seat leather chaise with yellow-spoked wheels rolling along the trail out from Indian Butte. Ahead and moving toward him on his left, the chaise was pulled by a handsome dun, and the man sitting in the front seat holding the reins was Pop Schofield. Prophet could tell by the long, tangled gray beard and the long, blue-gray hair spilling from the ratty bear fur hat to dangle down over the old man's spindly shoulders clad in a molting bear fur coat. Beside the liveryman on the quilted leather seat was Rawdney's father, Senator Wilfred Fairweather.

On the second seat, behind the first, sat Count Miranova. Beside him, on Prophet's near side, was the lovely countess Tatiana. The men were decked out in dark fur coats and tall fur hats, but the countess wore a thick rabbit fur coat with a high collar made of fox fur, the fox's head complete with open eyes and black-tipped snout dangling down across her left shoulder. On her lovely, dark-eyed, fair-skinned head was a hat also of long, breeze-rippled rabbit fur. Her hands were stuffed into a rabbit fur warming muff.

Prophet turned his head to edge a look around his covering rock.

Rawdney was no longer aiming the Scheutzen at him. The sporting rifle had been taken down off its tripod. Rawdney, Leo, and the Russians were walking leisurely along the trail, heading for the train depot, talking and laughing and casting glances back over their shoulders toward Prophet. One of the big Russians was holding the rifle in a fur scabbard over his shoulder while another big Russian was carrying the tripod.

Prophet turned back to the chaise rolling toward him, within thirty yards now and closing. All eyes, including those of the countess, had found the bounty hunter hunkering down here behind the boulder, like a schoolboy playing hide and seek.

Prophet's cheeks burned with embarrassment.

He winced, cursed to himself, spat to one side, and heaved himself to his feet, brushing snow from his denim britches and from the arms of his buckskin mackinaw.

Schofield smiled and shook his head, puffing a corncob pipe wedged in one side of his mouth. "I don't believe I've ever seen a man who attracts more lead than you do, Prophet." He chuckled and shook his head once more as the chaise slowly rolled past along the trail. "No, I purely don't!"

The senator turned and leaned over the seat to say something in a jeering tone to the count. Both men laughed loudly. As the buggy continued rolling on down the trail, now between Prophet and the cotton-woods from which he'd been so reprehensibly assaulted . . . not to mention humiliated . . . the countess turned her head to keep her eyes on the man she'd cavorted with in the blissful postdawn hours of the previous evening.

She was smiling at him, but the skin above the bridge of her nose bore more than a few skeptical wrinkles.

Prophet's ears blazed even hotter behind the muffler knotted around his head. "You'd be cowerin' like a dog, too, Countess," he grunted out sheepishly, "if you had that . . . that . . . that big *cannon* bearin' down on your purty pink behind!" He spat again as he strode heavy footed across the trail, heading for where Mean and Ugly stood nonchalantly pulling at the dead grass poking above the snow. "Just wait till I see that fancy snot again—the Dan probably wears pink lace frillies—I'm gonna pistol-whip him till there ain't a bit of skin left on his purty face, and then I'm gonna—"

"Prophet, I'm in a bad way here—a real bad way!"

Lou stopped. Hatchley lay in the snowy brush, on his back but half sitting up, his right hand snaked under him to hold the back of his right leg.

"Yeah?" Prophet gave an angry chuff and continued stomping toward his horse. "Join the party, Gritch!"

* * *

Mean and Ugly was second to no one, not even the Vengeance Queen, at reading his rider's mind.

The hammerheaded dun always knew when Prophet was feeling a mite off his feed, and he wasn't at all above exploiting the situation to deepen his rider's misery. He performed such calculated follies merely for fun. A typically mean kind of fun, but fun, just the same.

Today, on the heels of Rawdney Fairweather having hoorawed Prophet with the sporting rifle, the horse made himself hard to catch, edging away from Lou just when the bounty hunter, having tramped the hundred and twenty yards or so through the cold and snow, was about to grab his reins.

When Prophet had finally stepped on the reins and gotten them into his fist, the horse took the opportunity to give Lou's right earlobe, poking out from beneath the mouse-chewed muffler, a painful nip. A person who has never had a cold ear nibbled on by a horse should endure such an injury once in his life, because it makes such frivolous injuries as, say, cracking a funny bone against a blacksmith's anvil or stubbing a bare toe on a stone hearth some cold, dark night when you're looking for the thunder bucket, seem as insignificant as a brief tickle by an annoying brother.

Suffice it to say, it was a pallid-faced, weary-eyed Lou Prophet who finally led Mean and Ugly, with Gritch Hatchley in the hurricane deck and cuffed to the saddle horn once more, up to the cottonwood hitch rail running along the side of the wooden depot building nearly a half hour later. As he tied Mean to the rail, he looked around the front of the depot to see Rawdney and his fur-clad cohorts smoking cigars near the vestibule of one of the hunting party's fancy railcars, talking and laughing.

None of the hunting party appeared to have seen Prophet. They'd long since forgotten about the butt of their joke, no doubt. Well, he hadn't forgotten about them.

Lou stuffed his right-hand mitten into his coat pocket and shucked his Winchester from his saddle boot. He'd calmed down some since Rawdney had used him for target practice. Not much, but enough that he'd managed to talk himself out of marching up and shooting the dandy through his black heart at point-blank range, but only because he didn't want to face the hangman in Bismarck alongside his old friend Hatchley.

But as long as Rawdney Fairweather was within, say, a hundred square miles, Prophet wasn't going anywhere without his Winchester in his hand or on his shoulder. Let the dandy pull that sissy-looking long gun on him again, and Prophet would give him a pill he couldn't digest. Anyone who didn't want to call it self-defense would take the second round out of the barrel and follow Rawdney straight to wolf bait.

Lou snarled at the cussed fop as he stepped up to the front of the depot, leaving Hatchley grunting curses on Mean's back, and pushed through the front door. Inside was all bleak shadows and the smell of wood varnish and cat piss. It was so warm that Prophet thought he'd faint before he made it to the ticket cage behind which a little, gray spider of a blue-haired old woman slouched on a low stool, smoking a loosely rolled quirley and stroking the liver-spotted puss on her spindly shoulder.

She blinked her brown eyes through the ticket cage

at the tall man standing slumped before her, and croaked out, exhaling smoke through wizened nostrils, "You look like you been rode hard an' put up wet, you handsome devil."

The cat turned to Prophet and meowed as though in agreement with the spidery woman's assessment.

"You don't know the half of it."

The woman smiled. At least, the lines in the lower half of her face deepened and widened slightly in what appeared to be a smile. "Wanna light and sit a spell, tell me about it? I could dig us out a bottle, and we could get to know each other."

She gave a slow, lewd blink of her eyes, the lids like moth wings.

Prophet chuffed a laugh despite his sour mood . . . or maybe because it suddenly wasn't so sour anymore. "Now, what makes you think I'm that kind of boy?"

She looked him up and down, her dark eyes twinkling with devilish insinuation. "You're a tall son of a buck. My husband was tall." She stuck the quirley between her lips, if the thin pink lines running parallel to her chin were indeed lips, and sucked on the quirley, making the end turn dark orange.

She sucked a long draw of the smoke deep into her lungs, held it, and said, "He's long since dead, an' I haven't had my toes curled by a tall son of a buck like either of ya in you-wouldn't-believe-how-long."

Prophet would probably believe it but he didn't say so as he didn't want to seem impolite, and he wanted to purchase a ticket each for himself and his prisoner. He took the spidery little woman as someone who could hold a grudge. Discreetly parrying the spidery woman's advances though his mood was buoyed by the bleak humor of the old woman's brashness, he

managed to purchase the tickets—three dollars and
seventy-five cents apiece and an extra fifty cents for a
stall for Mean and Ugly in the stock car.

While the transaction was being made, the chatty
little spider informed Prophet that there was only one
coach car, as the rest of the combination was taken up
by "that damned charlatan Fairweather and his fay son
along with them funny-talkin' furriners they got up
here huntin' all the game off this prairie so the rest of
us can live off gopher an' blackbird pie for the rest of the
winter.

"So far, you an' your friend and your hoss will be the
only payin' passengers. Don't expect a conductor or,
for heaven sakes, a porter, cause there ain't no such
thing on this line, sweetie. You're lucky to have bench
seats and a woodstove. You'll tend the stove and your
hoss yourself. For that purpose, there's a stock car between your car and the first of the senator's fancy-
dancy coaches. That's on purpose. The stock car is to
keep you raggedy-heeled, unwashed heathens back
where you belong—in the passenger coach with its
hard seats and damn little else. You're not to mingle
with the hunting party. They're way above your lowly
station, hear? Or so I hear tell . . .

"There's a piss pot in the passenger coach, near the
stove. Empty it yourself. I done punched your ticket
and, less'n you've changed your mind about that bottle
an' a little slap 'n' tickle—I got a new pad in back I just
this past fall stuffed with new corn shuckin's—you and
your friend and your hoss have a nice trip to Bismark
an' come back an' visit me soon when you can stay a
little longer, now, you hear, handsome?"

Prophet assured her he would do just that, then,
pocketing the tickets and resting the Winchester on

his shoulder again, headed for the door. He stopped when, through a front window, he saw three horseback riders ride from around the building's left side and onto the platform between the station and the train waiting on the tracks.

They were the three Cut-Head Sioux Prophet had seen before—the old man, Leaps High, the hand-shaker, Little Fawn, and the other, sober-faced young brave riding a sleek brown and black pinto.

The old man and the sober-faced brave rode ahead of Little Fawn.

Just as the three Indians started walking their horses across the brick platform, between the depot station and the sitting train, the countess stepped down from the car ahead of the stock car, which fronted the shabby passenger coach, which would have been the last coach in the combination if not for the little red caboose. The stylish, gleaming fittings of the countess's sleek, black coach with red velvet curtains adorning the windows made the passenger car look like a derelict old fishing boat by comparison.

Seeing the girl, Little Fawn jumped down off his horse and ran over to the countess, extending his hand and bowing unctuously, wanting to shake. Prophet pushed through the door and out onto the platform.

"It's all right, Countess," he said when he saw the startled, apprehensive look on the black-eyed beauty's face. "He just wants to shake your hand, is all."

The countess looked at Prophet and then, turning to the Indian boy who stood only an inch or two taller than she, pulled her right hand out of the rabbit fur muff sewn onto her coat and gave it to Little Fawn, who shook it, laughing again with a combination of embarrassment and delight at the ridiculous custom.

His laughter infected the countess, who, too, broke into laughter just before the boy released her hand and went jogging off down the platform, laughing.

He ran toward where Rawdney Fairweather and Leo stood together with only one of the Russians now, the others having apparently boarded the stylish cars of the senator's private combination.

Prophet chuckled as he strode forward, heading toward the countess. He paused when he heard a voice raised in anger several cars up the train. He turned to see Rawdney Fairweather slap the young Indian boy, Little Fawn, hard across the young Indian's face with the open palm of his right hand.

Little Fawn jerked back, startled. Looking at the dandy who'd slapped him in round-eyed, wide-mouthed shock, the young brave stumbled back toward where his horse had followed him along the platform and was also sidling away from the red-faced dandy in apprehension.

The other two Indians, Leaps High and the sober-faced brave, had their backs to the young Indian and Fairweather, but they both turned to peer back over their shoulders as the priggish dandy shouted at Little Fawn, "How dare you approach me, you filthy savage! Why would I want to shake your hand, you snickering red devil! Get the hell out of here before I fetch my rifle and shoot you through your savage heart!"

Chapter 31

"That sonofabitch!"

Prophet lurched forward, heading toward where Fairweather was still regaling the Indian boy Little Fawn, as the boy leaped expertly up onto his horse and then hurried forward to catch up to the old man and the sour-faced brave, who stared coldly over their shoulders at the raging dandy.

"Lou," the countess called, grabbing his arm. "Don't!"

Prophet stopped, glanced at the countess staring up at him with pleading in her wide black eyes, then turned to glare up along the train at Rawdney. "He had no cause to do that. The boy was just wantin' to shake his hand. He meant no harm. It was all in fun!"

"I will admonish him," the countess insisted. "I will talk to him later. It is not your place. He is . . . how do you say? . . . full of vim and vinegar, and very powerful."

"That little crawdad is a green-toothed, fork-tailed devil!" Prophet scrutinized her carefully, suspiciously, canting his head to one side. "Say, now . . . did I hear you two might be gettin' hitched?"

"Hitched?" The countess threw her head back, frowning. "What do you mean—hitched to a *horse?*"

"No, no." Prophet chuckled despite the anger still burning in his ears. "Married. You know—swap vows an' such. Walk down the aisle. Don't tell me you're gonna *marry up* with that—"

"Yes. We will marry." The countess dropped her eyes demurely then lifted her head and regarded the big man bravely. "My father and Rawdney's father have gone into business together. My marrying Rawdney is . . . is . . . well, as Father says, it is my duty. My father's businesses in Russia are, well, failing, if you must know. His brothers and a couple of powerful cousins have turned against him. We were nearly bankrupt before my father and Senator Fairweather went into business together, mostly on the senator's capital. They are building several spur railroad lines across the west. They built this one, in fact." She canted her head toward the train. "They are establishing several mines. We will visit those next . . . in Colorado . . . and hunt more grizzly bear!"

She smiled brightly at the thought.

Quickly, the smile faded, and she added with a vaguely troubled but resigned air, "I must be loyal to my father's wishes. I am his only daughter. My mother, his wife of forty-three years, died last year. His own health is failing. We will move here together once Rawdney and I are married. Russia is no longer a hospitable place for us, though I do truly love it so . . . and will miss it."

She added that last with a sigh of deep longing.

"Ah hell," Prophet said, genuinely feeling sorry for the girl's plight. Sometimes it was worse to have so much and lose it than, like Prophet himself, to have ever had very little at all. "It grieves me to hear that, Tatiana."

The countess gave him a warm smile. She looked around self-consciously. The only ones on the platform were she, Prophet, and Rawdney, Leo, and the lone Russian, who'd gone back to talking and laughing, their backs to Prophet and the girl as they stared off in the direction in which the three horseback Indians had disappeared.

Tatiana began to raise her hand to his cheek but, thinking better of the gesture, stopped and let her hand drop back down to her side. Blood rose in her face, and her eyes glinted warmly. "I will remember last night, Lou. I just wanted to tell you that. And to thank you. I only hope Rawdney will turn out to be as gentle and satisfying a lover as you."

"Oh, I'll remember last night, too, Countess." Prophet chuckled lustily. "You can count on that." He would, too.

"Maybe . . . perhaps . . . we will one day find each other again, and . . ." She glanced sheepishly off toward Rawdney, who still had his back to her and Prophet, and smiled again, lustily. "And have another night as sweet as the one we just shared."

"I'd like that."

"I would invite you up to my car for lunch, Lou. But, you know . . ." Again, she cast a sheepish glance toward Rawdney.

"Oh no." Prophet held his left gloved hand up, palm out. "Don't you worry about that. A fella like me—hell, I belong back there. Born to such a ride, in fact." He canted his head to the old coach car with rusty iron wheels and in bad need of paint. It was a goat cart compared to the senator's string of varnished surreys. "Besides, I got my prisoner to look after."

Brows beetling suddenly, the countess jerked toward Prophet as though nudged from behind. "I would like to kiss you!"

Prophet backed up, chuckling wryly, glancing toward Rawdney and remembering the slugs from the Scheutzen hammering the rock Lou had cowered behind like a chicken-thieving dog. "Oh no, no, no. Don't do that! That'd likely bring down a whole cloud of trouble on us both!"

He no longer felt all that indignant about Rawdney's ill treatment. After all, he'd sampled—and thoroughly enjoyed—the dandy's bride in advance of Rawdney himself. He couldn't really begrudge the cuckolded fop a little fun with the Scheutzen, though he'd be damned if he'd ever let him do it again.

Chuckling fondly at the memories of last night flashing through his brain once more, he stepped back, pinched his hat brim to the lovely young Russian, then turned reluctantly away, regretting that he'd likely never see her again. A frown drew his mouth corners down at the sight of the ugly Gritch Hatchley sitting on Mean and Ugly's back, hunched forward and scowling, lips stretched back from gritted teeth, nostrils flared in anger.

What a contrast to Countess Tatiana Miranova!

"I hope you didn't rush your little game of slap 'n' tickle over there for me, Prophet. Just cause I'm bleedin' dry here, and freezing my ass off. Whoo-ee— she's purtier'n a speckled pup! Just as soon as I cut your throat, I'm gonna take her to the dance myself!"

"Sorry to keep you waiting, Gritch." Prophet twisted Mean's reins from the hitchrack and led the horse over to the ugly little gray car used to transport the West's unwashed minions. "I'll have you all warm an' cozy in three jerks of a whore's bell."

Hatchley went into another haranguing tirade against the bounty hunter's lineage. Ignoring the man, Prophet dropped Mean's reins onto the snow-dusted cobbles beside the car then reached up, grabbed the sleeve of Hatchley's coat, and jerked him out of his saddle.

"*Ow!*" the curly wolf cried as he tumbled down the saddle to hit the cobbles with a hard thud. "I didn't deserve that, you scallywag!" He writhed, raising his right knee and hugging his punctured thigh.

With effort, Prophet got the wounded, howling outlaw into the car. The car was shabby and dusty and it stank like an unmucked stable. A distinct sour smell radiated off the coach's sole passenger, who lay sacked out in the first seat at the front of the coach, on the right side of the aisle.

The man was snoring loudly.

The rest of the car was as empty as a Lutheran church on a Friday night. The temperature felt no higher inside than outside. Prophet's and Hatchley's breaths frosted the air around their heads.

As Prophet shoved his prisoner down the aisle, the sleeping man came awake with a grunt. He sat straight up on the green velour–covered bench, his single wool blanket tumbling to the floor where a nearly empty whiskey bottle stood near the man's piled gear, which included a saddle and a rifle. The man grabbed two pistols from the pockets of his quilted deer hide coat, extended them straight out toward Prophet and Hatchley, and clicked the hammers back.

"Whoa, now," the bounty hunter said. "Easy, partner.

No reason to get your blood up. Just headin' for our seats, is all."

"Jesus!" Hatchley said, staring at those two Colt Army revolvers and the big, dirty hands gripping both walnut grips.

The man on the bench stared down the Colts' oiled barrels at Prophet and his prisoner, the alarm in his mud-brown eyes gradually fading. His thick, black brows beetled slightly beneath the edge of his soiled and somewhat frayed red stocking cap pulled low on his ruddy forehead.

An affable light glazed his eyes. As he depressed both hammers and lowered the hoglegs, to Hatchley he said, "*Bonjour, mon ami. Je voudrais vous voir ici.*"

Hatchley's own brown eyes widened in surprise. A smile stretched his thick lips back from his scraggly teeth. "*Henri! Bonjour, bonjour, Henri! Qu'est-ce qui vous fait sortir de cette façon?*"

"Canada was getting a little too hot for me." Henri spoke nearly perfect English, with only a trace of a French Canadian accent. He glanced at the silver bracelets adorning Hatchley's wrists. "What's with those?" He slid his scowling gaze to Prophet.

"It got a little too hot for me down here," Hatchley said with a fateful sigh.

"You two know each other, I take it." Prophet glanced at Henri's Colts, which the Canadian now rested slack in his lap.

"Henri Shambeau," Hatchley said, canting his head toward Prophet. "Meet Lou Prophet, bounty hunter. Lou, meet my old friend Henri. We go back a ways, me an' Henri do."

"Bounty hunter, huh?" Henri said, wrinkling one

nostril distastefully. Then he shrugged. "Well, I reckon we all have to make a living some damn way, eh, *mon ami*?"

"Couldn't have put it better myself. Now, while I hate to break up this happy reunion, I gotta get my prisoner situated and my horse tended before the train pulls out." Prophet glanced once more at the pistols he was glad to see still resting, hammers down, on Henri's lap, then shoved Hatchley on down the aisle.

Following his prisoner, Prophet glanced over his shoulder several times, keeping an eye on Henri Shambeau, who wore a patchy black beard over his broad face cleaved by an enormous hooked nose. Shambeau smiled over the sea of velour-covered seats at Prophet, his close-set eyes vaguely mocking, enjoying the bounty hunter's discomfort.

"Christ, it's cold in here," Prophet said to Henri, shoving his prisoner down on a bench seat near the potbelly stove, which squatted in the middle of the car, its tin chimney poking straight up through the roof. "Did you ever think about building a fire?"

Henri shook his head. "I didn't need one." He reached down then raised the bottle in the air above his head. "I had this." He took a pull from the bottle then set the whiskey back down on the floor. He smacked his lips, yawned, and dropped back down out of sight. Soon, as Prophet cuffed Hatchley's wrists behind the man's back and around a strap of the iron seat frame, the Canadian began snoring again loudly.

"This ain't one bit comfortable," Hatchley complained, leaning forward and straining against the cuffs pinning his wrists behind his back. He gritted his teeth at Prophet. "You expect me to ride all the way to Bismarck trussed up like this?"

"I'm sorry you're not comfortable, Gritch—purely I am," Prophet said, dropping to a knee beside a corrugated tin washtub sitting beside the stove. The tub was filled with split firewood. "But there's a whole lot more people out there you made a whole lot less comfortable than you are here this morning. And, lookee here, now—I'm even gonna build you a fire to keep you nice and warm."

When he'd laid feather sticks and wadded up newspapers inside the stove, he scratched a lucifer to life on the stove door and cast a hard, ironic look at his prisoner. "Gonna keep you nice an' warm and ready for the hangman. We want you dancin' real good when they drop you through the trapdoor, give the good folks of Bismarck some good, old-fashioned entertainment there on Main Street."

Hatchley spat a wad of phlegm through the open stove door, making the fledgling flames smoke. "Yeah, well, the joke's gonna be on you. That tumble I took from your cayuse opened me up again. I'm liable to be all bled out by the time I reach Bismarck. You're gonna cheat the hangman."

Prophet shoved more kindling into the stove, breaking the longer sticks in his hands. "We don't have far. A couple hours, is all. First thing after we pull into town, I'll hustle you up the best sawbones in the county." He shoved several good-sized split pine logs into the stove then closed the door and latched it.

"Not gonna make it."

Prophet brushed his hands off on his denims and turned to his prisoner. "You aren't?"

"*We* aren't." Hatchley dipped his chin to indicate the window facing the open prairie. "Look at that. Damn near impossible to see."

Prophet turned to look out the window. Hatchley hadn't been gilding the lily. Snow was once again falling out of a hazy, purple sky hovering low over the train. The cottony flakes were falling at a forty-five-degree angle, the wind pelting them against the side of the passenger coach, like sand.

"Well, I'll be damned! Where in the hell did that come from? It was clear as a bell just a few minutes ago."

"That's the way it does here. Clear as a bell one minute, then a clipper rolls in from Canada, an' Katy, bar the door!" Hatchley nodded at the window again. "That's serious business there. Butte country just south of here. The wind's gonna pile that snow up over the tracks on the backsides o' them buttes, and we'll be stuck up to the windows. Happens all the time. By the time we're dug out, I'll be gone."

Hatchley sank back against his seat and shook his head, long, greasy hair dancing over and around his dark eyes. "Kilt by a little Meskin doxie in Dakota . . . middle of winter. Ain't fair." He shook his head again. "Just ain't fair—a man like me, goin' out like this, hands cuffed behind his back. Ain't dignified." He scowled up at Prophet "Ain't fair!"

"Now, now, Gritch. Rest easy, old son. Save your strength."

Prophet started striding toward the coach's front door. He had to get Mean and Ugly aboard the stock car.

"You got any whiskey?"

Prophet paused, glanced back at the prisoner, who appeared near tears with dejection. "Sure, sure, I got whiskey. Bought me a whole bottle just last night for today's journey."

"Give me some! I'm hurtin' bad here, Lou!"

"No, sir." Prophet shook his head. "That's labeled

stuff. It ain't no painkiller. Besides, the way you tell it, you'll be dead soon. I don't see no reason to waste good liquor on a dead man."

Prophet winked and went out. Despite the wind that had kicked up outside blowing the snow around violently, he could hear his prisoner cussing him at the tops of his lungs.

Chapter 32

Louisa thrust her Colt straight out through the wind-jostled, snow-dusted tangle of branches and hurled three quick shots back behind her, in the direction of Sundown.

"Take those, Captain!" she bellowed. "I hope you choke on 'em!"

She pulled her head back down behind a broad cottonwood standing between her and the soldier, holding the smoking Colt up close against her chest, the welcome heat from the gun pressing through her coat.

"Jesus—*Louisa?*" the captain shouted from maybe thirty feet away, his voice obscured by the wind and rattling branches.

"You know it's me!" Louisa returned, her own voice torn from her lips, nearly drowned by the wind. "Why did you shoot at me, Yardley? What's your game?"

"There's no game, Louisa," Yardley shouted back. "I thought I was firing at the killer." A slight pause. "Is he still out here? Are you hurt?"

Louisa didn't reply. She continued crouching behind the tree, pressing the warm Colt taut against her breast, weighing her options, apprehension raking cold witches' fingers across the nape of her neck.

"Louisa, I'm walking toward you. I've holstered my Colt. My hands are in the air."

Louisa pondered. Could Yardley really have not heard her when she'd called out to him?

Boots thudded, growing louder beneath the wind. Brush snapped under the captain's feet.

Louisa rose suddenly, extending her Colt straight out in her bare right hand, which was quickly growing numb from frostbite. The tall soldier was silhouetted before her as he moved through the trees, just then turning sideways to step over a blowdown. When he'd crossed the blowdown he turned toward Louisa again and stopped, raising his gloved hands shoulder high.

Louisa strode resolutely toward him, aiming down her Colt's barrel at him.

"What's your game?" she asked again, tightly, just loudly enough to be heard above the wind.

Yardley shook his head. "I'm sorry I shot at you. I thought I was shooting at the killer."

"I called out to you."

"What can I tell you?" Yardley said, raising his voice in frustration. "I didn't hear anything except what I thought was a scream. Your scream." He shrugged, raising his hands slightly higher. "Why would I want to kill you, Louisa? You and I hardly know each other."

Louisa kept the cocked pistol aimed at his face. Her heart thudded heavily. She wanted to believe him. Maybe she partly did believe him. But part of her did not. Part of her believed that the bullets he'd fired had been meant for her.

"Oh, for chrissakes!" Yardley said. "Look—I heard shooting. I thought I heard you scream. I thought I was shooting at the killer. Go ahead and shoot me. Just make it quick. I'd rather die from a bullet to my brain than freeze slowly out here, which is exactly what I'm doing now."

He reached toward her, nudged her Colt aside with the back of his hand.

She let him do it. She had no choice. She knew she should shoot him, but not knowing why, she couldn't do it. Not even her—the uncompromising Vengeance Queen.

Oh hell!

Louisa shoved the Colt into her coat pocket. Keeping a cautious eye on the captain standing before her, she quickly shoved her hand back into her glove, wincing against the sharp teeth of the wind chewing at her flesh. She drew the glove only partway on then clenched her hand into a tight fist inside the glove, trying to force blood into her fingers.

"Since you're out here, you might as well make yourself useful." Rapping her gloved fist against her thigh, Louisa looked at him sharply. "Just keep your hands away from your pistol. If you make another move toward it, I will shoot you, Captain. I will not hesitate again."

Yardley held up his hands again, this time in supplication. "You have my word as an officer and a gentleman. What can I help you with?"

"Over here." Louisa stepped behind the tree. She stood over the man she'd shot. "This is the man who shot at me."

"The killer?"

"I don't know. Do you recognize him?"

Yardley stopped beside her, looking down at the dead man. He dropped to one knee, crouched for a closer look at the man's face. He looked at Louisa and shook his head. "I don't recognize him. But as I told you before, I know hardly anyone in Sundown. I've just passed through from time to time."

"All right," Louisa said. "Let's get him back to the hotel. I want Edgar Clayton to have a look at him."

Yardley winced up at her, obviously knowing that her "let's" had been of the royal variety. He'd be the one carrying the dead man back to the Territorial. "That's quite a jaunt and this is no small man. Why don't we bring Clayton *out here?*"

"Doubtful we'd find the body again. By morning he'd be covered with snow. Come on, Captain. You're a big, capable man." Louisa cocked one fur-lined moccasin forward, crossed her arms on her chest, and narrowed a challenging eye. "Aren't you?"

She knew exactly how to appeal to the fragile male pride and was not above putting that knowledge to practical use.

Yardley gave a caustic snort and chuckled wryly. "All right." He drew a breath then grabbed one of the dead man's hands. Rising to a crouch, he drew the man forward and turned slightly to one side, pulling the dead man over his right shoulder. Bending his knees, adjusting the dead man's weight with a grunt, he said, "All right. Lead the way."

Louisa moved off through the trees and tangled brush. She tried to retrace her own and Yardley's steps, but already the dark, dimpled tracks were filling in with windblown snow. Twice she found herself thinking she was backtracking herself and Yardley only to end up facing a tangled snag and an impenetrable mass of blowdown trees made even more perilous by the drifting snow.

"Come on, Captain," she said the second time she stumbled into an impenetrable wall of vines and wood. "Back this way."

"We just came from that way!"

"Back this way!"

"Hold on, hold on!" Yardley complained. "I need to rest."

She let him rest only a minute or so then berated him until he crouched beneath the dead man's weight once more and they were headed again through the murk of the storm, in the general direction of Sundown. Or so Louisa thought. With the wind and the snow and the trees and bramble all looking alike, it was very easy to get disoriented.

After what must have been over a half hour of hard walking and bushwhacking, they drew up before the hotel's southwestern rear corner. The back door was locked—likely barred from the inside for good reason—so Louisa led the captain around to the front. That door was locked, too, but Toni quickly answered Louisa's knock and let them in on a gale of brittle wind and snow.

"Who the hell's that?" Toni asked, stepping back out of the wind and the snow, now wearing a stained apron around her slender waist. Her frightened eyes were on the dead man draped over the captain's right shoulder.

"Did he get another one!" asked the tall drummer in the gaudy orange suit, rising quickly from his chair where he was still playing poker with the other two traveling salesmen. His eyes were bright from drink, and he wobbled more than a little on his feet.

Every eye in the room was on Louisa, Yardley, and the newcomer as Louisa led Yardley over to a table near where Edgar Clayton sat, hipped around in his chair, also watching the newcomers with hang-jawed interest.

"Is this your man, Clayton?" Louisa asked as Yardley dropped the dead man onto the table, which groaned and squawked beneath the cadaver's weight. "Is this Ramsay Willis?"

Clayton lurched up out of his chair so fast, twisting around to see the dead man's face, that he got a boot tangled up in his chair leg. He knocked the chair over and dropped to a knee. "Damn!" He rose from his knee and stood over the dead man, staring down at him.

Quickly, scowling, he turned to Louisa. "Hell, no. That ain't Ramsay Willis."

Louisa cursed under her breath.

"Who is it?" Yardley asked Clayton.

By now, almost everyone in the room had gathered around the table—Toni, Mose, Nasty Ralph, and the three drummers. Even Mrs. Emory, a blanket draped around her shoulders, stood staring down at the dead man.

"I don't know who it is," Clayton said. "I wouldn't know him from Adam's off ox. Who shot him?"

He was looking at Yardley, who didn't say anything.

Louisa said, "I did."

"Why'd you shoot him?"

Ignoring the question, Louisa looked around at the others. "Does anyone know who he is?"

Mose and Nasty Ralph looked at each other and shrugged.

Staring down at the dead man, the drummers bunched their lips and wagged their heads.

"Wayne Skogstrum."

All eyes, including Louisa's, turned to where the

little wizened man who'd sat alone on the far side of the bar now stood to Louisa's right, about six feet away from the table, peering between Mose and Nasty Ralph at the dead man.

"Look who rose from the dead," said Mose.

"Shut up," Louisa snarled at him.

Mose's eyes blazed at her, and he tightened his jaws but held his tongue.

To the old doctor, Louisa said, "Who'd you say he was?"

"Wayne Skogstrum," the sawbones repeated. He did, indeed, look as though he'd risen from the grave. Or had clawed his way up out of one, maybe hunting for a fresh bottle.

The rims around his eyes looked like freshly ground beef. He reeked of sweat and whiskey. "Lived down the hill to the south, across the creek. With his old man, Zeke, an old buffalo hunter an' wolfer. Zeke died a few years back. Wayne's been livin' there alone. A hermit. Hardly anyone ever sees him less'n he's coming around town to beg for coins or tangleleg. He's got it worse even than I do—the bottle fever."

He'd said that last sentence slowly, with a keen air of self-recrimination and shame, rubbing the palms of his hands down the front of his grimy wool shirt.

"I've caught him stealing wood from our pile," Mrs. Emory said in a low, strange voice, as though she were half dreaming. "Caught him stealing wash off our line . . . my husband's trousers, his shirts. Once he stole an apple pie out of my kitchen window, when I set it there to cool."

"Do you think he could have put that ax—" Louisa stopped, cleared her throat. "Do you think he could have killed your husband, Mrs. Emory? Had you seen Mr. Skogstrum around your house earlier today?"

The woman bowed her head and her shoulders quivered.

"There, now," Captain Yardley said, walking around behind the grieving widow, placing his hands on her shoulders. "Let's get you upstairs, Mrs. Emory. You should be in—"

"No!" The woman pleaded with Louisa, eyes round with horror. "I don't want to be alone! I want to stay down here with you all!"

Louisa glanced at Yardley. With her chin she indicated the brocade chair at which the widow had been sitting. Yardley guided the sobbing woman back over to the chair and helped her down into it.

The town drunk/doctor continued staring down at Wayne Skogstrum as he said, "He was bad for stealin' firewood. He used to come up here from his cabin and steal wood from Tutwiler. Morris caught him more than a few times and threatened him with a thrashing. Wayne, he'd drop the wood and run. Kept close to home, mostly. Trapped a little. Cut wood a little, when he wasn't drinking. Didn't allow no one on his place. I went down there to visit him after Zeke died—Zeke an' me was friends—and he took a shot at me, told me to never come around again or I'd get a bullet for my trouble."

The sawbones lifted his watery gaze from the dead man to Louisa. "He probably shot at you because he thought you was Tutwiler out to catch him stealin' his firewood. Or maybe you was gettin' too close to his cabin. He never let anyone come on his place, no, sir."

The sawbones shook his head and moved his jaws like a cow chewing his cud.

Louisa stared at the little wizened man, but what she was seeing were the several chunks of split wood she'd spied on the snowy ground near Skogstrum's lifeless body.

"That there's your ax killer." Nasty Ralph pointed down at the dead man on the table. "Sure enough, the banker caught this sick old coon stealing firewood from him and got an ax in his back for his trouble. Same with Tutwiler!"

"Nope." Edgar Clayton shook his head certainly.

He turned, walked over to the front window left of the door, and stared out at the cold, stormy night. "The killer's still out there. He's Ramsay Willis, an' he ain't out to steal firewood or a man's breeches off a clothesline. He's got the winter fever. He's turned his wolf loose. He's out to kill every single one of us here tonight, if we don't get him first."

Clayton turned around slowly and stared darkly at Louisa.

"An' you know what?" he asked the Vengeance Queen.

"No," Louisa said. "What?"

"At this point, my money's on him."

Chapter 33

Louisa and the others in the room studied Clayton.

The rancher poured himself a fresh drink then picked up his makings sack and began rolling a smoke.

"Well, I'll be damned," Nasty Ralph said, standing on the other side of the table from Louisa, beside Mose. "We still got us a killer on the loose, don't we?"

He turned his head to stare at the door against which the moaning wind flung snow like intermittent shovelfuls of sand.

Mose looked at Louisa, his eyes bright and rheumy from drink. "An' you just popped another pill into another poor hombre who didn't deserve it. No more than Vink did."

He closed his hand around one of his holstered .44s.

Louisa smiled. "Go ahead, Mose. Try it."

Mose stared back at her. All eyes in the room now shuttled between the two. Mose appeared to have stopped breathing. His lips were pursed and white.

"Stop," Toni said. "Stop it." She came up to stand to Louisa's left, beside the table with the dead man on it, shifting her gaze from Mose to Louisa and back again.

"We can't turn on each other. If there's a crazy man out there, an ax-wielding killer, we need to keep our heads. Stand down, Mose!"

Nasty Ralph snorted a laugh and nudged Mose with his elbow. "Come on, now, Mose. She's too purty to kill."

Mose curled his upper lip at that. It was the excuse he was needing, wanting, to pull his horns in. He chuckled and dropped his hand from the walnut grips of his .44.

"Pshaw," Mose said, leering at Louisa. "Don't get your bloomers in a twist. I was just funnin' with ya." He tipped his head back and gave a jeering laugh.

"Well, I'm not funnin' with you, Mose. You an' your nasty friend here take Mr. Skogstrum out to the wood-shed with the others."

Mose stopped laughing. He and Nasty Ralph stared again at Louisa, their eyes hard with self-righteous indignation.

Nasty Ralph lifted a thick arm and pointed a finger across the dead man at Louisa. "You go to hell!"

Keeping her hands straight down at her sides, hang-ing over the twin, pearl-gripped Colts holstered on her thighs, Louisa said with taut menace, "Do it."

Slowly, Ralph lowered his arm. He and Mose contin-ued glaring at her over the table.

Once again, all eyes in the room were on Louisa as well as on both drunk market hunters. Lamplight, shunted by drafts, flickered across the room, sliding back and forth across the hats of the men and Louisa gathered around the table. It flickered across Toni's curly red hair and across her pale cheeks set with an expression of deep wariness.

The drummers dropped back into the shadows, out of the line of fire. So did the old sawbones.

Mose and Nasty Ralph stared at Louisa. Louisa stared back at them, chin low, her hazel eyes cast with dark portent, daring one or both to slap leather so she could hurl them both to hell. She was done with these privy snipes, just as she'd been done with Vink. It was their turn to die. The world would be a better place without them.

Both men's ruddy cheeks acquired a light flush, their eyes a vaguely uncertain cast. They knew what would happen if they did not do the Vengeance Queen's bidding. They were not so drunk that they thought that, in their drunken states, they had a chance of getting their pistols out of their holsters before Louisa did. They'd seen what she'd done to Vink.

True, she hadn't given Vink a chance. But even if she had, the result would have been no different. Vink would still be dead with three closely placed slugs in his heart, lying hard as a gravestone out in the woodshed yonder.

The walls creaked against the moaning wind. Snow pelted the windows. One of the lamps leaked black smoke up through its soot-stained chimney, further tainting the room's foul air with the smell of burned coal oil.

Staring at the two men, Toni said with quiet beseeching, "Don't. She wants to. You know that. Don't give her the satisfaction."

Nearly a full minute passed. A sweat bead broke out on Mose's left cheek and dribbled down into his thin, patchy beard. Nasty Ralph's thick, lumpy chest was rising and falling heavily, nervously.

Finally, the big man's body slackened. He nudged Mose again with his elbow and said, "Yeah, all right.

Let's take him outside, eh, Mose? Maybe give us a chance to shoot that son of Satan once an' for all."

Mose's body, too, relaxed though he kept his hard, dark eyes on Louisa. Slowly, he nodded. "Yeah. All right. Sure. If he's fool enough to come after us, we'll take him down, all right. Yeah, we'll bait him in. That's what you want, ain't it?" he spat at Louisa. "Sure, sure. We'll bait him in and kill him!"

He grabbed the dead man's arms. "Get over there, Ralph. Take his feet." To Louisa, he said, "You'd best stay in here so you don't get your frillies in a twist again and go off half-cocked. You should watch yourself. Runnin' around out there, scared as hell an' shootin' down innocent folks is gonna ruin your reputation, Miss *Vengeance Queen*!"

Laughing, Mose and Nasty Ralph hauled the dead man off the table and then down the side of the bar toward the back door.

When they'd gone out, the draft from the open back door sweeping through the room, Toni turned to Louisa. "Sorry to spoil your fun."

Louisa regarded her blandly but didn't say anything.

"Don't you think one crazy person running around killing people is enough?" Toni asked.

Louisa gave her a slow blink. "I'll take some more tea." She plucked her rifle off the chair she'd set it on when she'd entered the saloon with Yardley and the dead man. She walked over toward the table at which Mrs. Emory and Captain Yardley sat regarding her dubiously. "Mrs. Emory will have some more, as well."

Toni gave a caustic chuff. She strode down along the bar and into the back of the room. Mose and Nasty Ralph had left the rear door open. Louisa heard the redhead close it with a raking thump. When Toni came back and disappeared into the side room housing the kitchen, Louisa set her rifle on the table and dropped into the chair across from Yardley.

She removed her muffler and hat, tossed them onto the table, and raked her hands through her hair.

Yardley sipped from his whiskey glass and canted his head toward the rear of the room. "Well, they're baiting your trap. Aren't you going to go and watch for the killer?"

Louisa shook her head. "I think he's done for the night. Too cold out there. I think he's holed up. If he's as kill-crazy as Clayton thinks he is, he'll likely start again tomorrow, after a good night's sleep by a warm fire."

Yardley frowned at her. "Then . . . why send out Mose an' Nasty Ralph?"

Louisa frowned back at him, incredulous. "To haul Skogstrum out of here. Who wants to stare at a dead man all night?"

"We're back, Miss Vengeance Queen!" Mose bellowed ten minutes later, as he and Nasty Ralph strode up from the rear of the saloon, ensconced in a fresh draft of chill air, slapping their snowy hats against their thighs. "Hope you warn't too worried about us!"

"Didn't see hide nor hair of that killer," said Nasty Ralph, bellying up to the bar.

"No, I figured you hadn't," Louisa said, drolly, laying out a game of solitaire on the table before her. "I hadn't heard any girl-like screams."

A drummer who had just taken a sip of whiskey blew the mouthful over his table. He and the other two drummers howled.

Mose and Nasty Ralph snapped sharp looks at Louisa. She continued to calmly lay out her solitaire hand.

"Give me a bottle," Nasty Ralph barked at Toni, who was snickering behind her hand. "And stop laughin'. She ain't one bit funny."

Mose whipped around to cast his baleful gaze at the howling drummers. "You three shut up, too, gallblastit!"

The drummers could only muffle their laughter, snorting into their hands.

When Mose and Nasty Ralph had a bottle, they strode tensely over to their table, continuing to glare at Louisa, who didn't bother to look at them but continued to study only the cards laid out before her now. Soon, Nasty Ralph and Mose were involved in another poker game, which they played for matchsticks. They went through the fresh bottle of whiskey as though it were water and they were crossing a blazing desert.

Mose passed out first, simply laying his head down on his arm with a deep groan. He began snoring softly at first but then loudly.

Nasty Ralph was vocally lamenting his partner's midgame slumber just when he himself had finally gotten a red-hot hand going. He didn't lament it long. Just after pouring a fresh drink but before he could take a sip from the glass, his own head smacked the table with a sharp thud.

He groaned, broke wind, and began snoring, hands dropping straight down toward the floor.

Louisa looked over at the man. Then her gaze swept the room.

Nearly everyone else was similarly asleep—the drummers, Captain Yardley, and even Mrs. Emory, who was curled up in her brocade armchair to Louisa's left, her feet drawn up beneath her skirt, snoring softly beneath her blanket.

Toni lay atop the bar, on her side, using her coat for a blanket, a flour sack for a pillow. The only people awake besides Louisa were Edgar Clayton and the old sawbones. Clayton sat in a chair facing the door, ten feet away from it, his rifle resting across his thighs. His head drooped toward his chest. When his chin brushed his shirt, he snapped it up with a startled grunt.

The old sawbones sat at his table on the far side of the bar, remote and alone, sitting straight-backed in his chair, staring off into space while taking frequent sips from the shot glass in his age-gnarled hand. It was so quiet save for the wind and the snow and the occasional sputtering of the lanterns and the ticking of the woodstove that Louisa could hear the old sawbones sipping and swallowing his whiskey. After each sip, he set the glass back down on the table with a weary sigh and resumed staring off into nothingness.

Louisa didn't sense any fear in the man. Not of Ramsay Willis, anyway. Maybe, in fact, he was actually waiting for the killer's hatchet.

Louisa lifted her cup to her lips, not realizing she'd already finished her tea spiked with whiskey. She set the cup back down, gathered her cards into a neat deck, set it aside, and rose from her chair.

She went over and banked the stove against the cold she could feel pressing in from all four walls and even from the ceiling. The smoking and guttering lanterns attested to the multiple drafts slithering about the room like invisible snakes. She closed the stove door quietly, so as not to awaken the others, then stole quietly about the room, peering out through the windows though able to see little because of the darkness and the thick layer of frost obscuring the glass like mold.

There were spots on the walls that showed frost, as well, and the front door was nearly white with the stuff. Snow had slithered in beneath the door to form a downy layer on the inside of the threshold, melting a little on the inside edge, where the heat from the fire found it.

Louisa looked at Clayton. Now even the rancher had lost the war against the sandman. He sat slumped straight forward in his chair, head sagging toward his lap.

Snores rising all around her—some louder than others—Louisa returned to her chair. She wrapped herself in her bedroll, laid her head down on the table, atop her crossed arms, and let the warm darkness of sleep steal over her. She had no idea how much time had passed when she opened her eyes to see a small pool of drool on the table near her lips.

She sat up with a start, blinking, swiping a hand across her mouth, looking around.

She was amazed to see a pearl wash of light touching the eastern windows, weakly illuminating the room. All of the lamps had gone out.

She looked to her left. Mrs. Emory was still asleep in her chair though she'd turned around to face the opposite direction from the one Louisa had last seen her in. Captain Yardley was gone, his chair sitting at an angle to the table, vacant. He appeared to be nowhere in the room.

Louisa looked toward the drummers' table by the bar. All three men were still asleep, one curled up on a table near where the other two sat in their chairs. Mose and Nasty Ralph slept in the same positions as last night.

Toni lay on the bar. She'd rolled onto her back. The old sawbones sat on the bar's far side, chin dipped to his chest.

Edgar Clayton snored with his head down on his own table, arms stretched out before him, fingers clutching his Spencer repeating rifle as though even in sleep he was ready to snap up the weapon and shoot down the low-down, dirty, ax-wielding dog that was his hired hand, Ramsay Willis.

Louisa shivered. She just realized that she'd been shivering for a long time, dreaming she'd been wandering only half-clothed in a terrible storm, seeking shelter.

Now she rose from her chair, clutching her blankets tightly about her shoulders, and walked over to the woodstove. By the time she had it roaring once more, several others in the room were rousing from their own stupors, having been awakened by the stove door's opening and the wood being chunked inside.

They groaned, grunted, hacked phlegm from their throats.

"Ah hell," said one of the drummers.

Louisa knew how he felt. Like her, he'd obviously awakened to find himself in the same nightmare from which he'd tried to escape into sleep.

Shivering inside her blankets, putting her backside to the luxurious heat of the ticking, sighing woodstove, Louisa looked at Captain Yardley's empty chair. She walked to the door. With her thumbnail, she scraped a hole large enough in the quarter-inch frost that she could peer into the snowy street that was gradually growing lighter as the sun rose.

She could see Yardley's footprints dropping down off the boardwalk fronting the saloon and angling off to the left, to the south.

"Strange," Louisa muttered to herself, her suspicions aroused. "Where are you off to so early in the morning, Captain?"

Chapter 34

Prophet's bones were clattering like those of a skeleton hung out to dry in the wind when he returned to the shabby passenger coach.

He'd stabled Mean and Ugly in one of the two stock cars mostly populated with the blooded horses of the countess's party, tying Mean on a short line so he didn't try to harass any of those stallions who, in contrast, made him look like the lone, unruly mutt in a kennel of pedigreed hunting dogs.

In the short time Lou had been in the stock car, the wind had increased, and it was one hell of a cold wind. The snow was coming down even harder. Shivering, Prophet climbed up onto the passenger coach's vestibule. He placed his hand on the doorknob, then, remembering the French Canadian *ami* of Hatchley's, with the fast pistols, he stopped. He tried to peer through the glass pane in the door's upper half but it was opaque with frost.

He bit off his thick mitten and his glove, stuffed both into his coat pocket, then took his Winchester in both hands. He'd left the Richards with Mean and Ugly, its lanyard hooked over a nail in the stock car. He levered a round into the Winchester's action, opened the door of the passenger coach, shoved it wide, and took one long, resolute step into the car. Kicking the door closed on the cold wind and the snow, he swung the Winchester toward where he'd last seen Henri Shambeau, expecting the man to be aiming those pistols at him again with the intention of cleaning his clock and freeing his friend Hatchley.

Nope. This time the Canadian didn't even stir at Prophet's entrance. He lay beneath his blanket across the front-most seats on the aisle's right side, his head propped atop his folded saddlebags. He stopped snoring, grunted, swiped a fist across his nose, then dropped his arm back toward the floor and resumed snoring, pooching out his lips inside his thick beard with every exhalation.

Prophet looked toward where he'd left Hatchley. The killer remained where he'd left him, all right. It didn't appear that the mice had played while the cat was tending his horse. Hatchley sat on a left-side aisle seat near the stove, in the middle of the car. He sat stiffly on the thinly padded, stiff-backed wooden seat, head thrown back, gritting his teeth against the burning, well-deserved pain in his leg. He looked at Prophet and kept his head resting back against the seat but croaked out a jeering laugh.

"Did my friend spook you, Lou?"

The bounty hunter depressed his Winchester's hammer and rested the long gun on his shoulder. He strode down the aisle, his saddlebags draped over his left shoulder. The train had given its long, wailing whistle and was pulling out now, leaving the station with a series of shuddering jerks. Prophet grabbed seat backs as he moved down the aisle toward Hatchley.

"I gotta admit," he said, sitting on the other side of the woodstove from Hatchley, also in an aisle seat, facing the front, where Shambeau continued sawing wood, "I was a might impressed by that Canuck's fast draw. Never knew a Canadian to move that fast less'n they was skinnin' out of a married woman's house."

He set the Winchester and his saddlebags on the seat to his left.

"Oh, we can move pretty fast, Lou." Hatchley glanced over at Prophet and winked. "You just watch us." He cast a vaguely threatening gaze in Shambeau's direction.

Prophet opened a pouch of his saddlebags and withdrew the bottle he'd purchased at the Indian Butte Saloon and had wrapped in burlap. "You obviously weren't moving fast enough to skin back over the Canadian line before I ran you down in that woodcutters' camp. That was one fool, Canuck move, Gritch."

"Yeah, well, it was cold. I could feel this storm brewin' as far back as last week. Me an' Weed would probably still be holed up at old Jiggs's place if that damn Sweets DuPree hadn't gotten all doughy eyed over me and caused a big blowout with Pima." Again, he chuckled. "Oh boy—did them two have 'em a fight over ole Gritch! Me an' Weed thought we'd best see that as our omen to split tail for the border . . . till we seen them storm clouds roarin' in. That's why we held up in the woodcutters' camp. Leave it to a crazy rebel devil like yourself to find us there . . . where damn few lawmen ever dare to tread!"

He shook his head without mirth.

"Leave it to a woman to mess things up for a feller."

"Ain't that the truth, though?"

"I could tell you stories." Prophet was thinking about Louisa. He hoped the persnickety Vengeance Queen's hunt was going better than his own though it was probably just as cold if not colder and stormier forty miles southwest of here, in Sundown. Knowing how good luck always seemed to ride with Louisa, she'd probably taken down Sweets DuPree and Pima Quarrels ten minutes after she'd first ridden into town and was now soaking in a hot, soapy tub, awaiting the train.

Hatchley leaned out from his seat so he could peer around the stove at Prophet. "Why don't you go ahead and pop the cork on that busthead, Lou? What you waitin' for—Christmas? We'll sit here an' share the bottle and swap lies. The trip will go all that much faster!"

The outlaw had nudged Prophet out of his reverie. Lou looked down at the whiskey bottle resting on his thigh. He popped the cork on the fresh bottle and grinned around the stove at Hatchley eyeing the bottle hungrily. He glanced out the window beyond the outlaw, through a clear patch in the frost, to see the snowy countryside sliding by at about fifteen, sixteen miles per hour. "Oh, it's goin' fast enough, Gritch. Me—I'm gonna enjoy this warm stove . . . and this fresh bottle of prime, top-shelf tangleleg. Cheers!"

He winked, raised the bottle to his lips, and took several long pulls.

Hatchley cursed him roundly and told him to do something physically impossible to himself.

Laughter rose from the front of the car. Prophet just realized that Shambeau's snores had ceased. Now as Prophet poked the cork back into the bottle he saw

Shambeau sitting up and smiling over the back of his seat toward Prophet and Hatchley.

The Canadian laughed again, chuckling. He turned forward, dropped his feet to the floor, then rose, holding his blanket about his shoulders though he was wearing a heavy fur coat, and hurried, shivering, back toward where Prophet and Hatchley sat near the woodstove.

"Cold up there! *Le ciel, m'aide, mes amis!* You don't mind if I join you back here by the fire—do you, pards?"

"The more the merrier," Hatchley said, casting another taunting grin toward Prophet.

Shambeau was short but big through the chest. He wore deerskin breeches and home-sewn rabbit fur boots. His eyes were red and his broad face was ashen. "*Le ciel, m'aide, mes amis!*" he said again, plopping into the seat directly across from Hatchley and pressing the heels of his hands against his temples. "My head hurts powerful bad!"

"What you need is a shot of whiskey," Hatchley said.

"I'm fresh out, brother."

"The big man over there . . ." Hatchley indicated Prophet with his thumb. "He's got him a fresh bottle."

Shambeau removed his hands from his head and turned to Prophet. "Do you really, brother?"

"Hatch ain't just whistlin' 'Dixie.'" Prophet smiled and patted the bottle he cradled in the crook of his left arm, like a toddler in the care of its doting mother. "And you two scalawags ain't gettin' a single drop."

"See how he is?" Hatchley said to his French Canadian friend. "He's too good to share with us, and him a lowly bounty hunter."

"That isn't right, brother." Shambeau's dark eyes were leveled on Prophet, and his tone was deadly serious. "We're all traveling together here. I mean, there's only three of us in the whole car. It's cold outside. Hell, it's cold in here! Not only that, but it's close to Christmas—the day baby Jesus was born. If one of us has a bottle, he should share with the others to celebrate the birth of baby Jesus if for no other reason."

"Yeah, Henri's got it right," Hatchley said to Prophet. "Even if you think you're so much better than your traveling companions, it's only right to share, Lou."

"Well, I am a whole lot better than you two louse-infested polecats. And I ain't gonna share." Prophet caressed the bottle lovingly. "I want the whole bottle for myself."

"Tsk, tsk," Shambeau said.

"You know what you oughta do, Henri?" Hatchley said.

"What's that, *mon ami*?"

Hatchley canted his head toward the bounty hunter sitting on the other side of the stove from him. "Kill him."

"Really?"

"Sure. Kill him an' take the bottle."

Shambeau arched a brow at Prophet, who grinned back at him.

"He killed Weed," Hatchley told Shambeau. "At Duck's place along the creek."

"The woodcutters' camp?"

"That's right."

"Weed Brougham?"

"Shot him deader'n two-penny spike. Shot him in the back. Didn't give him a chance. In fact, Weed was dead asleep."

"Well," Prophet said, "which one was it—did I shoot him in the back or when he was dead asleep?"

Hatchley looked at him and flared a nostril, an angry light flashing in his eyes. "Both."

"Oh, both," Prophet said with a snort.

"Sure. He was sleepin' on his back," Hatchley told Shambeau.

Shambeau looked at Prophet. "That ain't right, doin' a man like that."

"No, I reckon it ain't," Prophet said. "You two are startin' to make me feel down in the dumps about it now."

"*Tue-le!*" Hatchley spat out at his Canadian friend, leaning slightly forward at the waist. "Kill him an' take his whiskey. He took a good pile of money off me an' Weed, too. He's probably got it in his saddlebags."

Prophet grinned again and patted the saddlebags piled beside him.

Shambeau stared at him. There was very little light left in his eyes though suddenly the sun was shining again outside the train car. Apparently, there was a break in the storm. That light did not find its way into the French Canadian's deep-set, chocolate-dark eyes, however.

His gaze burned two holes through Prophet's own. Or that was the impression the Canuck wanted to give, at least. He'd probably practiced that menacing look in back bar mirrors.

The Canadian outlaw's hands were splayed on his thighs, just beneath the butts of his pistols poking up from the pockets of his fur coat. Prophet did not look directly at Hatchley, but he could see in the periphery of his vision the killer staring at him in hushed antici-pation, unabashed delight, waiting on pins and needles to see Prophet drilled a third eye.

The train pitched and swayed as it wended its way

around a long, gradual curve, the snowy prairie sliding past the frosted windows to both sides, streamers of black wood smoke slithering back from the locomotive.

The iron wheels clacked on the rails.

Prophet could fairly hear Gritch Hatchley's heart beating. It was beating even faster than his own.

Shambeau's hands rose to his guns in a blur.

Prophet filled his own right hand from his coat pocket and fired.

Shambeau's right-hand pistol roared a half an eye wink after Prophet's, flames stabbing between Prophet and Hatchley. The bullet clanged shrilly off the wood-stove. Shambeau jerked for a second time in that half an eye wink as his own ricochet punched him back in his seat after parting the fur of his coat, almost directly over his heart. The ricochet's hole was about three inches right of the hole Prophet had just drilled in the man's chest.

"No!" Hatchley shouted.

The smoking six-gun in Shambeau's right hand tumbled straight down to the floor between his and Hatchley's boots. He'd just gotten his left-hand Colt into that hand, but he hadn't gotten the hammer cocked. Now as he cocked it, Prophet shot him again.

The left-hand gun dropped to the floor beside the right-hand gun, from the barrel of which gray smoke curled.

"No! No! No!" Hatchley bellowed. Leaning forward at the waist, he glared at the hard-dying Henri Shambeau and yelled, "You always was slower'n molasses in January, Henri, ya damn fool! Look at ya now! You're dead, dead, *dead*!"

Shambeau sat shivering and bleeding from the mouth. He opened his mouth as though to speak but only more blood came out. He looked at Prophet then sagged to his left, turned, and dropped to the floor where he lay jerking at Hatchley's feet.

"Ah hell!"

"Doggone it, Gritch," Prophet said, twirling his smoking Peacemaker on his finger then shoving the pistol back into his coat pocket, "your luck has purely gone south."

"Hell!" Hatchley kicked the dead Canuck. "Hell! Hell! Hell!"

Prophet glanced out the train window to his left and right. They were passing woods to his left. On his right, a snowy slope dropped away to the north, toward what appeared to be a broad, snow-and-ice-covered lake rimmed with winter-naked trees. He looked away then turned back toward the lake. He saw what appeared to be three horseback riders riding out onto the lake, which the train was curving along the shore of.

"Who in the hell would be out here in this weather?" he muttered to himself.

Chapter 35

Gritch Hatchley was sagging forward in his seat, snarling and pulling at the cuffs fixing his wrists to the iron seat frame behind him.

He snarled and grunted and groaned, long hair hanging down against both sides of his face. He was staring at the dead man's guns lying near his own boots, beside the body from which a steady stream of blood issued from each hole in the dead man's coat.

Prophet rose from his seat and kicked both guns away. "There, I'll get them out of your hair, Gritch. They're only badgering you. There, now—you just sit back and rest easy."

"Hell! Hell! Hell!" Hatchley bellowed like some gut-shot beast, jerking forward in his seat.

"There you go," Prophet said, crouching down to grab the dead man's ankles. "Let it out. Make ya feel better." He began dragging the dead man toward the front of the coach. "You sit tight. I'll be back just as soon as I give your friend Shambeau here a proper send-off."

"Damn!" Hatchley said, pulling violently against his cuffs. "Damn! Damn! Damn!"

"There you go," Prophet said, pulling the coach's front door open. "Let it all out, Gritch."

He dragged the dead man out onto the vestibule, the cold wind hammering against him. Immediately, he removed his hat before the wind could blow it away, and tossed it back through the car's open door.

He rolled Shambeau toward the vestibule steps dropping down to the cinder-paved roadbed showing in wind-cleared patches amidst the fresh snow. The sun was bright now and the wind was still blowing, whipping the snow around in intermittent curtains that glittered like diamond-crusted ball gowns.

As Prophet looked through one such billowing, sparkling wave of windblown snow, he saw the three riders again—three horseback men moving straight out away from him, making their way across a corner of the lake toward another line of fur- and skin-clad riders sitting their horses facing them, apparently waiting for the first three.

The two Cut-Head Sioux hunting parties were meeting out there on the lake.

Even though the three riders' backs faced Prophet and they were about fifty yards away from him, he could tell that they were the three Indians he'd seen in town, Leaps High, Little Fawn, and the third, stoic young brave whose name Prophet hadn't learned.

The train's whistle blew shrilly—three, short resounding wails as though in greeting to the three Indians.

One of the three Cut-Head Sioux turned his horse around to face the train. Prophet could tell by his diminutive size that he was Little Fawn. The friendly young Indian raised an arm and waved broadly, heartily. Prophet could see the white line of the boy's teeth as he smiled, his face forming a brown oval beneath his rabbit fur hat.

Prophet wasn't entirely aware of it, but seeing that guileless, life-embracing smile on the face of the young Indian made him begin shaping a smile of his own.

The train whistled once more.

The whistle's echo hadn't died before there was a belching sound.

Prophet shuddered.

Right away, he knew what that belching sound had been. He'd heard it before. Not long ago.

Instantly, a chunk of ice dropped in his belly.

He stared straight out across the lake in hang-jawed horror to see Little Fawn jerk violently back in his saddle, throwing both his arms high above his head. The boy sagged straight back against his horse's hind-quarters then rolled down the side of the mount to fall to the ground beside it.

Raucous laughter blew back toward Prophet on the wind from the countess's party riding ahead of him.

Heart thudding heavily, Prophet dropped to the bottom step of the vestibule, grabbed the brass rail to his left, and leaned out away from the train, gazing up toward the fancy coach in which Rawdney Fairweather was extending his fancy shooting rifle through an open window, his round face laughing behind it.

"I told you I could make that shot," the fancy Dan bellowed victoriously behind the raised rear sight. Collapsing the sight with his thumb and withdrawing the big rifle from the window, he turned to the Russians and Leo gathered around him, all laughing heartily, to yell, "I told you I could make that shot, didn't I? Pay up, now. *Pay up!*"

Turning away from Prophet, Fairweather closed the window and disappeared in a glint of sunlight winking off the glass.

Grinding his teeth with fury, Lou glanced back toward the lake falling away behind him. The other two Indians, Leaps High and the second young brave, were scrambling down from their saddles to rush over to Little Fawn, who lay unmoving in the snow beside his fidgeting horse.

The other riders galloped toward them, whipping their rein ends against their horses' hips, the lunging horses kicking up snow.

Prophet swung his head around to glare toward the fancy Dan's coach and shouted, "*You son of a bitch!*"

Seething, he pulled himself back onto the passenger coach's vestibule, tripping over the body of Henri Shambeau, who in the wake of young Fairweather's shooting and likely killing of Little Fawn, he'd forgotten about.

Now, cursing, Prophet pushed up off his knee and kicked the body down the vestibule steps. Shambeau rolled off the bottom step to the ground, bounced, and quickly disappeared as the train rumbled forward.

Prophet pressed his back against the front of the passenger coach. His mind was racing. Fury was a fully stoked locomotive raging inside him. Over and over he heard the loud, concussive report of Fairweather's fancy Scheutzen. He saw Little Fawn jerk back in his saddle and tumble to the ground. He heard the senator's spoiled son's cackling laughter.

Before he knew what he was doing, rage taking over

his mind, Prophet lunged forward and grabbed a rung of the iron ladder running up the front of the stock car in front of the passenger coach. He clambered up the ladder, stretching his lips back from his gritted teeth.

As he gained the stock car's roof, the wind hit him from the west side, on his right, like a giant fist. He staggered to his left and dropped to both knees to keep the frigid wind from throwing him off the car. The cold in the wind must have registered well below zero. It bit his cheeks like a thousand angry yellow jackets.

It sucked the air from his lungs and chewed his fingers, which were bare, for he'd left his gloves and mittens in the passenger car.

Knowing he couldn't stand without the wind throwing him off the train, he crawled forward on hands and knees. He scrambled across the stock car to the far end, where he gauged the gap between the stock car he was on and the second stock car in the combination. He rose quickly to his knees and gave a loud bellowing yell as he sprang forward off his heels.

The wind slammed him again, throwing him hard left. He dropped to his knees atop the second stock car's far-left edge.

Snow-covered ground streamed past him, perilously close over his left shoulder, the wind shoving him toward it like a sadistic enemy. His stomach lurched into his throat. He threw himself sharply right, into the blasting wind, and lay belly down against the car's cold tin roof.

Grinding his molars in desperation, he clawed his way back to the crown of the car, where he lay for several seconds, gasping and catching his breath.

He was vaguely aware of the wind shifting, of swinging around to blast him from the front. He looked ahead. The train was making a slow curve to the west, angling around the lake's southern end, the dark smoke spewing from the locomotive's stack resembling a dirty scarf pluming out from where it hung on a line. It blew back toward him now, making his eyes sting.

"Gonna get yourself killed, Prophet, you no-good crazy rebel!" he bellowed to himself, his words whipped and torn by the wind.

With a determined grunt, he scrambled on hands and knees, keeping his head down against the head-wind, to the second stock car's front end. He stopped a few inches from the edge and peered at the passenger coach from which young Fairweather had fired at Little Fawn.

"All right, you devil!"

Prophet scrambled down the ladder running up the front of the stock car and dropped to the vestibule at the rear of the passenger coach. He bent his knees, letting his feet and hips take the brunt of the landing.

Rising, he grabbed the knob of the door facing him. It turned. He threw the door open and lunged inside. He was a bull barreling through a chute, his heart thudding, the fire of his rage fighting back the cold that had so mercilessly assaulted him.

"Lou!" the countess screamed, rising from a chair somewhere to his left.

Prophet didn't look at her. Since the second he'd entered the coach he didn't look at anyone except the senator's son, whom he'd picked out of the crowd sitting or standing in the posh parlor car, warmed by a small, ornate iron stove.

Several Russians leaped from their overstuffed

leather armchairs, exclaiming their astonishment at seeing the big, red-faced bounty hunter so unceremoniously entering their private domain.

"Good Lord, man!" Senator Fairweather exclaimed, frowning at the intruder. He sat smoking a fat cigar with the old count.

Rawdney Fairweather was leaning over the rifle stretched across a table before him, on an open, fleece-lined scabbard, lovingly running a cloth down the polished stock while holding court with several men standing around him, some still chuckling or laughing over Rawdney's kill shot. Rawdney's face was still flushed from his own boastful laughter. A smile still played across his thick-lipped mouth as he turned to see Prophet striding toward him.

Prophet stopped three feet away from the murderous young dandy, yelled, "Kill-crazy fool!"

As he raised his fist, Rawdney screamed, "*Help!*"

He started to duck but couldn't avoid Prophet's large, clenched fist, which smashed into his left temple, knocking him back against the table.

"*Help!*" Rawdney screamed again. "*Help m—!*"

Prophet slammed his fist against the kid's mouth and instantly felt the wash of warm blood as Rawdney's lips exploded like ripe tomatoes. Lou slammed his fist against the kid's mouth two more times—powerful, savage blows laying waste to the kid's mouth and shattering both of his front teeth—before two or three Russians grabbed him from behind.

Prophet turned, head-butted one and punched another, shrugging out of the grip of the third, who tripped over one of his fallen comrades. Prophet turned back to his quarry, who lay back atop the table, his hands over his face, screaming. Rage a living, breathing beast inside him, Prophet commenced throwing one blow after another at the dandy's face, driving the mewling urchin to the floor.

Prophet followed Rawdney to the carpet, both fists like pistons.

Wam!

Wam!

Wam!

Wam-Wam!

"Get him, for God's sake!" he vaguely heard the senator yell. "For the love of God, get that man off my son!"

Several men grabbed Prophet from behind. One grabbed his hair and jerked his head back sharply. Still, he managed to shrug from their grips long enough to land two more hammering jabs to Rawdney's face, which was by now a mask of pulp and blood.

One of the big Russians launched himself onto Prophet's back, grunting as he wrapped his arms around Lou's neck and rolled over onto his own back, pulling Prophet over on top of him, belly up. The other two and then yet another big Russian surrounded them, dropping to their knees and punching Prophet's face while others kicked him in the ribs, hips, and thighs.

Lou tried to fight back but the big man beneath him, holding him fast against him, pinned his arms behind his back.

Prophet stared up in frustration, grunting and groaning as the Russians' big fists smashed into his face—one hammering blow after another. He felt his brows and lips split. Thick, oily blood ran down his face only to be smeared against his cheeks and jaws by more savage blows. Meanwhile, the Russians' boots were like railroad spikes hammering his ribs and belly, his hips and his legs . . .

Vaguely, as though she were standing atop the deep well at the bottom of which he lay, being pummeled by the Russians, Prophet could hear the countess screeching out protests and crying. Just as vaguely, he could see someone, probably her father, holding her back away from the fray.

The room was beginning to fade around Lou when a man, probably Senator Fairchild, bellowed in perfect English, "That's enough. You're making a mess of the place. Get him the hell out of here!"

Prophet was fading fast when the beating suddenly stopped.

Several hands brusquely pulled him to his feet. His boots dragged across the thick carpet as two men, each holding an arm, half carried him across the railcar and out onto the windy vestibule. The cold, cold wind and bright sunlight braced him a little, at least enough that he opened his eyes in time to see Rawdney's assistant, the immaculately tailored and barbered Leo, step out through the door behind him and the Russians.

"Hold on!" Leo yelled into the wind.

The two Russians dragging Prophet to the top of the vestibule steps stopped and turned him around.

His short, dark, carefully cut hair sliding around his head in the cold wind, Leo stepped up to Prophet and curled a menacing smile. With a pale, beringed hand, he removed the cap from a six-inch stiletto with a jewel-encrusted, obsidian handle. The nasty, slender blade glistened in the new-penny sunshine.

Leo snarled again and gave a prissy little grunt as he lunged forward, sinking the blade into Prophet's belly.

Prophet felt the blade's sharp bite, like a snake sinking its teeth into him, just above his cartridge belt.

"There!" Leo shouted. "Now rid this train of that Dixie vermin!"

The Russians stepped around Prophet, each holding him by an arm, then gave him a shove.

Prophet flew backward off the vestibule. His arms flopped out around him. He watched in an absent-minded sort of horror his moccasins leave the iron platform and dangle in midair. For a long, cold moment he hung there in the air beside the train, glimpsing the snowy, gravelly ground rise up around him.

The snowy ground engulfed him like a firm pillow.

"Ohhh!" The exclamation was punched out of his lungs in a burst of wind.

He went rolling, rolling down a long hill, the snow biting into him like a million cold teeth while the train's whistle blew somewhere beyond him.

"Oh!" he heard himself say. "Oh, oh, oh . . ."

In the periphery of his blurred vision he watched the train slide away . . . away . . . away along the tracks until there was only silence and a bed of ice around him and a cold night enfolding him in its black wings.

Chapter 36

Edgar Clayton snapped his head up off the table with a fierce start. Rising so quickly that he knocked his chair over backward behind him, he bellowed, *"Rosie, how could you!"*

That gave Louisa one hell of a start, as well. She'd just walked over to her table to retrieve her Winchester but now she stopped and shucked one of her Colts from its holster and wheeled toward Clayton, lining up the sights on his head and clicking the hammer back.

Everyone else in the room was similarly spooked.

Both Mrs. Emory and Toni jerked out of dead sleeps with clipped cries to swing their heads toward the rancher. The town drunk/doctor lifted his head off his own table to stare wide-eyed toward Clayton. Mose and Nasty Ralph, who'd been stretching and yawning in their chairs between Clayton and the bar, now bolted to their feet, reaching for their own hoglegs. Nasty Ralph's chair went flying out behind him to tip over backward and spin in nearly a complete circle.

All three drummers were also on their feet, staring in wide-eyed shock toward Clayton.

The bearded rancher stood facing the bar, where Toni was sitting up, legs curled beneath her, her hair obscuring her fear-glazed eyes. Her mouth hung open in shock.

Clayton's mouth was open, as well. Now he closed it slowly. The fury and exasperation with which he'd bellowed the exclamation faded from his eyes. Glancing toward Louisa, he shaped a sheepish smile and raked a hand down his face, smacking his lips and saying, "Oh, I . . . uh . . . I reckon I had me a nightmare."

"Must've been a doozy," said Mose with a caustic snort as he slowly removed his hand from his holstered revolver.

"Christ!" said Nasty Ralph, also removing his hand from his gun and glancing back at his chair.

Louisa raised her Colt's barrel and depressed the hammer. She stared at Clayton. "How could Rosie do what?"

Clayton frowned. "Huh?"

"What did Rose do, Mr. Clayton?"

Clayton shook his head and shrugged. "I . . . I . . . don't know. I was . . . I was dreamin', that's all."

"I see."

Louisa holstered her pistol. Toni swept her hair from her eyes and glanced at Louisa and Mrs. Emory stirring in the armchair to Louisa's left.

"I'll get some water heating for tea," the redhead said, climbing down off the bar, holding a blanket around her shoulders.

"Just for Mrs. Emory," Louisa said. "I won't be having any just yet."

"You drink too much of that stuff?" Mose asked her, sneering. "You got a tea hangover, do you?"

"Shut up," Louisa said wearily, and shrugged into her coat.

She donned her hat, muffler, and gloves, and lifted her Winchester off the table. Resting the rifle on her shoulder, she walked to the door, which Edgar Clayton was already at, bundled against the cold and with his Spencer repeater in his gloved hands.

"Where are you off to, Clayton?" Louisa asked him.

Clayton peered out into the street cloaked in the pearl-blue shadows of dawn, under a clear sky in which a few stars still glittered. "He'll be out again soon, lookin' for someone else to kill. He won't rest until he's killed everyone in town."

"Then what?"

"Huh?"

"What happens when he has no one else to kill?"

"Why, he'll kill himself, then, of course. That's what they do." Clayton tapped his index finger to his forehead. "It's the winter fever."

Clayton opened the door and stepped out onto the stoop fronting the hotel. Louisa followed him out and into the street. Louisa glanced at the blue tracks pocking the fresh, sugary snow, which lay over the street in arrow-shaped drifts, where the wind had sculpted it. The captain's footprints marked several of those drifts, angling to the south and across the street toward the west side.

"Well, lookee here."

Louisa stopped and turned to where Clayton stood about twenty feet up the street to her right. Holding his rifle in both hands across his thighs, the rancher stared down at a body in the street before him.

Louisa walked over and saw that it was a man lying over one of those arrow-shaped snowdrifts angling out from the street's opposite side. He wore no coat, only a wool shirt, suspenders, and corduroy trousers and boots. He had a cartridge belt and two holsters strapped around his waist. The holsters were empty.

It was hard to say how tall he was. Judging by the flecks of gray in his thin, brown hair that blew around his head like dry corn silk, he was in his late thirties or early forties. He appeared to have been lying out here a long time.

The tracks he'd made getting here had long since been obliterated by the wind. There was a stiff, frozen look about him as he lay there face- and belly-down in the drift, one knee drawn upward as though he'd expired midcrawl.

Clayton kicked the man onto his back, making it even more obvious that the man was dead. He was stiff as a board. There appeared to be a bullet wound in his chest, another in his belly. Someone had taken a good chunk out of his left side, likely with an ax, leaving a deep, ragged gash.

"Well, I'll be," Louisa said.

Clayton looked at her. "You know him?"

"I recognize him. That's French's friend Cully. He's the new agent over at the train station. At least, he was. Didn't even make it through his first night and here I thought he'd found his calling."

"Been dead a few hours," Clayton said. "Probably tried to crawl here after Ramsay Willis come callin' on him." He glanced at Louisa. "The train station, you say?"

"Must have holed up from the storm—your friend."

"Ramsay Willis is no friend of mine." Clayton turned to stare toward the north end of town, deep in thought. "Probably long gone by now, but I'm gonna check it out."

Louisa watched him walk away down the middle of the street that was growing lighter as the dawn grew over the snowy eastern prairie. Slowly, shadows retreated. The wind was picking up on the lee side of the storm, making it feel even colder than it was.

Part of the Vengeance Queen wanted to join Clayton's investigation of the train station, but the captain's whereabouts interested her more, for some reason. She couldn't quite put her finger on it. Besides, like the rancher had said, Ramsay Willis had likely lit a shuck out of the depot building by now.

Who knew where he was?

Louisa turned and, picking up the captain's gradually fading trail, followed it to the west side of the street and then straight south along the main drag. The tracks turned toward the small front door of the livery barn. They stopped at the door.

Louisa stopped and stared down at the tracks.

Tipping her head to the rickety plank door, she heard men's voices inside. She thought she recognized Yardley's voice and one more, one that she did not recognize.

She stuffed her right-hand glove into her coat pocket then wrapped that bare hand around the icy metal handle of the door. She drew the door open just wide enough to allow her to pass. She stepped through it quickly and to one side and drew the door closed behind her.

The men's voices had fallen silent. A scuffing and rustling sounded somewhere ahead, from around where a light hung from a low rafter midway between the front and the rear of the barn. Around Louisa were thick shadows partly concealing a couple of wagons, one without wheels, and great tangles of tack hanging from ceiling support posts. The smell of ammonia was heavy and cloying on the frigid air.

From the stable area beyond Louisa came the snorts and shufflings of several horses.

"Damnit!" came Yardley's voice from back near the low-hanging lamp. "It's gotta be here somewhere."

Staring toward the light, Louisa saw a man's shadow move.

The shadow stopped. There was the click of a gun being cocked.

"Where is it?"

"I told you," said a man's high, wheedling voice. "I don't know. I don't know what she done with it!"

Voice taut with frustration, the captain said, "You were here. You're always here. She left the horses and the dead men here with you. She doesn't have the money inside, so it has to be out here!"

"So help me God . . . !"

There was a gagging, strangling sound.

"Did she pay you?" Yardley asked. "Or maybe you're just afraid of . . . ?"

The captain let his voice trail off as he turned his head toward Louisa walking slowly down the barn alley toward him, aiming her rifle straight out from her right shoulder.

"Speak of the devil," he said.

Louisa loudly cocked the Winchester and continued staring at the tall, darkly handsome soldier standing about thirty feet away from her, shoving the barrel of his cocked Colt Navy into the wide-open mouth of the bib-bearded old man kneeling on the hard-packed earthen floor before him.

The bib-bearded gent was Ash Graham, owner of the livery barn. He wore only longhandles, deerskin slippers, a blue wool stocking cap, and a ratty, blue plaid robe on his round-shouldered, potbellied frame.

"So this is where you headed so bright and early . . . and so quietly that I didn't even awaken," Louisa said, walking slowly down the barn alley.

"Hold on." Yardley kept his gun in the old man's mouth, crouched slightly forward. "Just hold it right there, Louisa."

"I wondered why it took you so long, longer than the others, to return to the hotel's saloon after you'd hauled Rainy, Sweets DuPree, and Pima Quarrels out to the woodshed. When you returned, you had blood on your thumb. That made me wonder about you, Captain. I wondered if you could possibly be the killer. But, of course, you'd gotten the blood on your thumb from one of the bodies you'd hauled out to the wood-shed. You were just a little self-conscious about it because you're self-conscious about such things. You're a man who likes to impress others. You wanted to impress me enough that I'd waltz upstairs with you. Were you really thinking that after we'd spent time together in bed you'd find a way to kill me and get your hands on the Hatchley bunch's bank loot?"

"Stay back, Louisa. I'll kill this old man."

Louisa stopped about ten feet away from him and Graham, who had turned his head slightly, rolling his eyes, to look at Louisa standing in the middle of the barn alley, aiming her rifle at Captain Yardley's head.

"You don't want to get a defenseless old man killed, do you?"

"You're not on furlough," Louisa said. "You're de-serting."

"Put the rifle down, Louisa."

"Couldn't handle the army—eh, Captain? Let me

guess—you come from a once well-to-do family. One that isn't so well-to-do anymore. Still, you think you're above such rustic conditions you likely faced at Fort Totten, so you decided to haul your freight. The only problem was you didn't have much money. Oh, you might've saved a sizable stake for yourself, but nothing like what the Hatchley bunch took down in Wyoming. After you realized who I was and that I'd trailed half of the Hatchley gang into town, belly down over their saddles, you figured I had their loot, as well."

"You're pretty damn smart," Yardley said, a pink flush rising into his cheeks above his thick dragoon mustache. "Smart enough to put that rifle down unless you want to see this old man's brains splattered all over the floor."

"That's why you fired at me earlier. You saw it as a good opportunity to kill me and call it an accident. That way you'd be free to look for the Wyoming bank loot. Ramsay Willis has been a nice distraction, hasn't he? A nice distraction, that is, unless he puts a bullet or an ax into you, too."

"Come on." Yardley flashed his dimple-cheeked smile. "Just put it down. However cold-blooded you are, you're not so cold that you'd cause the death of this old duffer."

"How do you know I didn't bury the loot in the country before I rode into town?"

"In this weather?" Yardley put some steel into his voice. "Put down the rifle, Louisa." He pressed the pistol barrel harder against the back of Graham's mouth, making the old man gag violently, cheeks flushing, eyes swelling as he stared up in horror at the soldier. "I swear, I'll do it!" Yardley warned.

"No, you won't. After too many months among men you consider your lessers at Fort Totten, you might be desperate to get as far away from the Dakota winter as possible. You might also be a spineless, conniving thief. But you're no killer, Captain."

"You don't think so?" Yardley's cobalt eyes blazed with frustration and fury.

"If I know anything, I know men. Better than I'd like to. You don't have it in you to kill in cold blood, Captain. If so, go ahead. But you'll be dead before that old buzzard's brains have hit the floor." Louisa smiled as she gazed down her Winchester's barrel, drawing a bead on the captain's forehead, just below the edge of his fur hat.

"You witch!"

Louisa's smile broadened.

"You witch!" Yardley fairly screamed as he straightened, withdrawing the Colt's barrel from the old man's mouth. *"Damn you!"*

"Oh God!" Graham choked out, dropping to his hands and knees on the barn floor, wheezing, clutching his throat with one hand. "Oh God—I thought for sure he was gonna do it! I thought"—he swallowed hard—"I thought I was a dead man!"

"You're fine, Mr. Graham," Louisa assured him.

"Oh God!" Graham scrambled to his feet, face swollen and red, eyes watery. He wheeled and ran toward an open door on the left side of the barn alley. "I need my heart pills! Oh God—my *heart pills!*"

Louisa gestured toward the large stall behind the captain—the stall in which Louisa had laid out the dead Hatchley riders. Their horses and her pinto were stabled in the stalls around her. They were all watching the doings in the barn alley with dubious interest. "Toss your gun into the stall there with the Hatchley boys."

Yardley cursed again, sighed, and tossed the Colt into the stall, where it smacked a dead man. The captain stood slouched before Louisa, face drawn and pale, not looking nearly as handsome as he'd looked before. Now he resembled nothing so much as the rat he really was.

"Just tell me," he said, shaking his head miserably. "Where is it? I gotta know. I scoured every stall for it. I was sure you musta buried it in the hay."

"Sometimes, it's best to hide your valuables in plain sight." Taking the rifle in one hand, aiming it straight out from her right hip at the captain's belly, Louisa took two steps to her left. All manner of moldy tack draped with dust and spiderwebs hung from a rusty railroad spike protruding from a ceiling support post. A burlap feed sack hung from the spike, along with several cracked bridles, rotting saddlebags splitting at the seams, and a couple of hames that belonged to a former era.

With one hand, Louisa stripped the gear off the post, letting most of it drop in a pile at her feet. She peeled the feed bag strap off the post and slung it over her left shoulder, patting the lumpy bag against her hip.

"Ah hell," Yardley said.

"I was going to retrieve them when the train arrived. Now I realize they're much safer on my person." Louisa wagged her rifle at Yardley. "Come along, Captain. Back to the . . ."

She'd just spotted Ash Graham standing back in the shadows, in the nook between stalls that led to the open door through which he'd fled for his heart pills. If he had retrieved his pills, they were not the only things he'd retrieved. He'd also retrieved a double-bore shotgun, the butt plate of which he pressed against his shoulder as he aimed down both barrels at Louisa.

He rocked the heavy hammers back.

Chapter 37

Yardley looked at Louisa, frowning curiously. He followed her gaze to Graham and lurched back with a start, raising both hands. "Who-ah!"

"Yeah, I'll say *who-ah*," the bearded oldster said, sliding the shotgun from Louisa to Yardley then back to Louisa.

"Easy with that thing, old-timer," Yardley said.

"Go to hell with that old-timer crap. I got you both in one hell of a whipsaw, and I'm about to turn the blade." He narrowed a pale blue eye down the barrel at Louisa. "You, Miss Purty Pants, drop that feed sack."

Louisa stared back at him.

"If you're calculatin' up if I'm as jelly spined as the yellow-livered soldier here, take into account I've killed before. For a lot less than what you got in that bag, judgin' by the bulge."

Louisa could see that the old man wasn't lying.

"Toss that Winchester into the stall with the soldier's pistol. If it twitches one fraction of an inch toward me, purty girl, you're gonna be a whole lot less purtier pronto."

Louisa depressed the Winchester's hammer. She took the rifle in her left hand and tossed it over the stall partition. It landed with a rustle in the hay near the dead men.

"Now," Graham said, "drop the loot. Straight down."

Louisa slid the strap of the feed bag off her shoulder. It plopped onto the floor near her left boot.

Graham looked at it hungrily. He licked his lips, swallowed, and gestured with the shotgun toward the barn's broad rear doors, at the far end of the alley. "That way. Get movin'."

"What're you gonna do?" Yardley, still holding his hands up to his shoulders, asked the old-timer.

"What do you think he's gonna do?" Louisa asked the soldier. "Take us out to breakfast?"

Graham chuckled through his tobacco-crusted teeth—what few remained in his jaws, that was. "'Take us out to breakfast.' Ha-ha. I like that." He wagged the rifle again. "Get a move on, or I'll burn you both down right here!"

"Don't get your bloomers in a bind, old man." Louisa brushed past Yardley and strode back along the barn alley toward the door. Yardley fell into step behind her.

She reached the doors well ahead of Yardley and Nash. She released the locking bar, dropped it to the floor, and slid the left-side door open, grunting with the effort, for the tracks had acquired a layer of ice.

"Hey, not so fast!" Graham bellowed, hurrying along behind Yardley, who was several feet behind Louisa.

"If you're gonna trip those triggers, trip 'em, you

old reprobate!" Louisa strode straight out through the doors and into the barn's rear paddock. Six feet from the doors, a gust of cold wind pelted her with windblown snow.

She swung around in time to see Yardley step out of the barn behind her, partly obscured by the blowing snow. A murky figure moved from the corner of the barn toward Yardley, swinging something toward the captain. A second later, the captain's head was bounding through the air toward Louisa, the soldier's eyes snapping wide in surprise, blood spewing from the ragged hole at the top of his torso, where his head had been sitting a second before.

The head glanced off Louisa's left shoulder to thump onto the ground and roll.

Louisa stared in shock, her mind slow to comprehend what had just happened. Slow to comprehend the sight of Yardley's headless body taking two more steps toward her, his hands still raised, before the man's knees buckled, and the headless body crumpled to the freshly fallen snow.

Another wind gust further obscured what happened behind Yardley. Louisa merely saw two shadows move violently. She heard a man's agonized wail. The shotgun thundered. Louisa saw the flash. One of the figures jerked to the right and then wheeled and dwindled back away into the windblown snow, quickly fading from Louisa's sight.

The wind died, the sparkling snow gradually dispersing in the air before her.

Beyond Yardley's head and his headless corpse, which lay belly down in the snow six feet away from her, Ash Graham lay on his back, groaning, a hatchet embedded in his chest. One leg was curled under the other one. He lay writhing, closing his hands around the handle of the ax angling up out of his bloody chest.

His shotgun lay in the snow to his left. Both hammers were down. If he'd discharged both barrels into the killer, Ramsay Willis was one sore puppy.

Louisa walked around what remained of Captain Yardley and gazed down at Ash.

"H-help me!"

Louisa crouched to place a hand around the ax handle, just above the head embedded so deep in the man's chest she could see his heart beating. It was beating slower and slower.

Louisa shook her head. "There's nothing I can do for you."

Ash sobbed and rested his head back against the ground.

Louisa strode back into the barn. When she'd retrieved her rifle, she pushed out through the small front door through which she'd entered the place. She stepped into the snowy street, the wind blowing mares' tails of snow into the crystalline air, which the rising sun was now causing to glitter like gold dust.

She walked to the south, spying the killer's tracks where he'd run up from the side of the barn. Louisa gazed down at the boot prints which the wind was quickly obscuring. She poked a bare finger into the pink slush beside one boot track and held it up to her face.

Fresh blood.

"He got you, all right."

Louisa straightened, cocked the Winchester, and began following the tracks toward the far side of the street. The killer had fled between two buildings, heading east.

"Hey!"

Louisa stopped and turned to her left. Edgar Clayton stood in the street before the Territorial Hotel, a hundred yards away and waving an arm above his head.

"I heard the shot!" he bellowed against the wind at Louisa.

"He's out here, Clayton! He headed east! Cut around behind the hotel and I'll meet you back there! He's wounded!"

Clayton waved again then shuffled off around the far side of the Territorial.

Louisa broke into a run. She entered the wide gap between a feed store and a boarded-up ladies' fineries shop. At the rear of the gap, she stopped and studied the tracks beside which more blood turned the snow to pink slush. The tracks continued out of the gap and swung to the left.

Carefully, aiming the Winchester straight out from her right hip, believing the killer might be waiting for her just around the rear corner of the feed store, Louisa stepped out of the gap and turned sharply to her left, tightening her bare, cold finger on the Winchester's icy trigger.

Behind the feed store was only a snow-covered pile of scrap lumber, bales of feed sacks, and a water barrel also mantled with snow.

Ahead, a rifle cracked once, twice, three times.

A man bellowed as though in agony.

Another rifle returned fire, adding three more belching reports slicing the cold air, slightly muffled by the wind.

The reports were followed by the angry cawing of

crows rising from a winter-naked tree just beyond a butte ahead of Louisa and on her left, beyond a low, snow-covered hill. A man stumbled out from behind the hillock, left of the trees from which the crows had taken wing.

Louisa began to raise the Winchester but stopped when she saw Clayton's dark blue coat and his glinting spectacles. The rancher held his rifle low in his left hand. He clutched his right side with that hand.

He took two more stumbling steps toward Louisa then dropped to his knees.

He threw his head far back and bellowed a curse before stretching his gaze out to Louisa and yelling, "The crazy devil done shot me! He's on the run! East toward the creek!"

"How bad you hit?"

Clayton dropped forward onto his hands and knees and shook his head. "Get after him!"

Louisa jogged forward and into the brush east of town. She crossed the cold gray rail line then a dry creek and jogged up and over the shoulder of another low bluff. At the top, she dropped to her belly and peered cautiously over the crest to the other side.

The crease between bluffs, cut by another shallow creek, was vacant save three spindly cottonwoods and a wagon-sized boulder the wind had blown clear of snow. Louisa gained her feet and moved quickly down the hill, hurrying, knowing she was exposed here on the hill, where there was little cover.

When she reached the bottom of the hill, she dropped to one knee and peered northward along the shallow creek bed between buttes. Nothing moved ahead except blowing snow. Fifty yards beyond was another stand of cottonwoods and then more trees along the creek tracing a serpentine course from north to south through low, rolling hills.

She was at the south end of the woods she'd been in the previous night, when she'd shot Wayne Skogstrum. If Willis was in those woods, she'd never find him. Unless he wanted her to find him. But then he'd have the upper hand.

The Vengeance Queen rose and continued along the crease between buttes, heading north toward the woods. The wind blew, howling like a thousand angry witches, occasionally creating whiteouts of blowing snow before her. On the heels of one such blast, just as the snow was ticking back to the ground, glittering brightly, she stopped suddenly and sucked a sharp breath.

A figure had just stepped out from one of those cottonwoods ahead of her and on the creek's left side. Louisa snapped her Winchester to her shoulder a quarter second after the shooter's rifle stabbed orange flames. As she triggered her own rifle, a bullet burned across the outside of her right thigh.

Cursing, she flung herself to her right, rolling up behind a small boulder as the shooter slung two more slugs toward her, one curling the air off her left ear, the other pounding the face of the boulder behind which she now crouched, grinding her back teeth against the burn in her right thigh.

She looked down at her leg. Blood oozed from the long tear in her denim trousers. Some of the snow around her was pink with her own spilled blood. The sight made her queasy. Without blinking an eye, she'd spilled the blood of enough men to fill a canyon. The sight of her own made her feel as though she'd eaten tainted beef. It used to be worse. It used to be she'd turn white and pass out.

"No more of that nonsense," she grunted, taking her Winchester in both hands, suppressing the throbbing burn.

A bullet sliced the wind with an eerie whine and slammed the face of her covering boulder. On its heels came the belch of Willis's rifle. Another bullet smashed the boulder. She could feel the reverberation through her shoulder.

Louisa slid over to the rock's right side. Assuming she was right-handed, the killer might think that that would be the side she'd return fire from. She waved her hand out from that side of the boulder then pulled it back toward her chest.

She smiled as another bullet ripped the wind to slam the rock on that end.

Louisa slid the Winchester around the boulder's left side. She'd taught herself to shoot almost as accurately from that side as from her right, in the event of just such a situation as that confronting her now. She took quick aim at the shooter, who'd stepped out around the tree, revealing his right shoulder and right leg and that half of his face, beneath the brim of his hat. She couldn't see him clearly because of the bright sunshine and the shadows cast by the tree, not to mention the blowing snow, but she saw enough of Ramsay Willis to lay a bead on.

As the crazed killer hurled another round toward the right side of Louisa's boulder, Louisa triggered her own Winchester. She cocked quickly, let three more bullets fly, and watched the slugs punch into the tree, sending bark flying in all directions. One slug must have hit pay dirt. The man jerked back sharply. He staggered, got his feet beneath him, then ran off through the trees flanking the cottonwood.

Louisa rose to her knees and hurled several more rounds, her bullets merely snapping small branches and ripping more bark.

"Coward!" she shouted into the wind.

Quickly, she reached into her coat, ripped off her neckerchief, and stuffed a handful of snow into the bloody wound to stem the blood flow. She tipped her head back, loosing a string of curses blue enough to make Lou Prophet proud.

Sucking air through her gritted teeth, Louisa wrapped the neckerchief taut around her thigh, used her rifle to hoist herself to her feet, then took off at a shuffling, limping run toward Ramsay Willis. The pain in her leg bit her hard, but she was accustomed to pain, both mental and physical. She suppressed it, placated herself with the imagined image of putting Willis down like the rabid cur he was.

When she gained the tree from which he'd fired at her, she dropped to her left knee and looked around carefully, wary of another bullet. Spying nothing in the woods beyond—nothing but Willis's blue tracks marking the snow—she rose with a pained grunt and resumed limping after her quarry.

She moved carefully through the trees, following the fresh tracks that meandered through the woods. Many of those tracks were splashed with the pink of fresh blood.

"Good—you're carrying some of my lead," Louisa muttered to herself.

She stepped over deadfalls and followed the blood-spattered path to the west, back in the direction of Sundown.

She paused, frowning.

Why was he heading back toward town?

Louisa drew another deep breath and set out once more, following the path through the trees, across the train tracks, and back into the outskirts of the town. A couple of gray cabins and stock pens moved up around her. She walked through a gap between the train station on her right and a gun shop on her left.

Willis's fresh tracks led straight through the gap and out into the town's broad main street where the fresh, sugary, sun-glittering snow was being blown every which way by the cold wind.

Carefully, holding her rifle up against her right shoulder, aiming straight out before her, she limped up through the gap. She kept her right finger, which she couldn't feel anymore, taut against the Winchester's trigger. She waited for Willis to poke his head and his own rifle around a corner of a building on each side of her, and snap off another shot.

When she reached the mouth of the gap, she sucked back the pain in her leg once more and bolted forward, swinging her rifle first right then left.

No Ramsay Willis.

She swung her gaze back to Willis's tracks. They led out of the gap and swung left, heading south, in the direction of the hotel.

Louisa lurched back one step with a start.

A horseback rider was moving toward her slowly, emerging from a thick curtain of swirling snow. Louisa raised the Winchester, tightened her finger across the trigger again. But then she lowered the weapon slightly, frowned at the man riding toward her.

Wrapped in a heavy blanket, which was draped over his head as well as his shoulders, he slouched lower over the mane of his obviously exhausted horse. The horse's eyelids were drooping, and ice from its breath had formed over its snout. Frost lay like a pale blanket over its dun withers. It moved very slowly, on wobbly legs, blowing feebly, its breaths raking like a bellows.

Finally, ten feet away from Louisa, the horse gave another ragged blow and dropped to its knees. The man jerked his head up sharply, eyes snapping wide. The horse's head sagged to one side and then its body sagged, as well, rolling over, throwing its rider into the snow beside it.

With an agonized groan, the man landed in the street.

Louisa strode over beside the dying horse to stare down at the man who appeared on his own last legs.

"Who're you?" she asked.

The blanket had fallen away from the man's head. He lay shivering violently, his face pale, staring up at Louisa, moving his lips but not saying anything. He appeared somewhere in his thirties. He had thick, wavy, dark red hair with a matching mustache. His broad face was lightly freckled.

He gazed sharply up at Louisa and stretched his lips back from his teeth. He tried to say something but he was shaking so hard that the only sounds were the clattering of his teeth.

Louisa dropped to a knee beside him. "Try again," she urged. "Who are you?"

The man gazed sharply up at her, cleared his throat and said, "I'm . . . I'm . . . R-R-Ramsay Willis!"

Chapter 38

Prophet chuckled. "Say now, that tickles."

Again, he felt something warm and bristly caress his left cheek.

Again, he chuckled. "You're ticklin' me, you naughty girl."

In a vague half dream, he saw a half-dressed señorita sitting on a bed beside him, in a room with a view through large open windows of dark sand sloping down to the Sea of Cortez shimmering in the hazy afternoon sunshine. The emerald green water was ruffled by white waves unraveling up on the shore with relaxing regularity.

He could smell chili peppers and carne asada cooking on a near fire. There must have been an open bottle of tequila nearby, as well, because he could also smell the tang of that fiery Mexican elixir.

Sitting on the edge of the bed where the bounty hunter took his dreamy siesta, the girl, cool and brown, was slowly brushing her long, dark brown hair, with each stroke letting it dance across his face. After every two or three strokes of the brush, she leaned down and pressed her plump lips to his cheek. He could feel the soft puffs of her warm breath, which also owned the tang of tequila and the peppery aroma of strong Mexican tobacco.

Again, Prophet chuckled from where he hovered in that dreamland suspended between wakefulness and slumber. "You're a playful one, ain't ya? Say, honey," he said, shivering, "would you mind closing the windows? I feel a chill comin' on."

He waited.

The chill grew. Without opening his eyes, he reached for the blankets, wanting to pull them over his cold, naked body, but he couldn't seem to find them.

The chill grew until he felt as though he'd been submerged in cold water.

"Say, honey, I think it must be . . ." He sat up suddenly, looking around. ". . . rainin'," he finished the sentence only because the word was still sliding across his lips though he could see now that it was not raining.

No, it wasn't a Mexican rain vexing him. In fact, he was nowhere near Mexico.

What was vexing him was the two or three feet of deep, pillowy, freshly fallen snow that lay beneath him and even on top of him. All around him!

Shivering violently, sensing another presence, he whipped his head to his left. There was no half-dressed señorita here with him, either. The chocolate-eyed beast staring back at him, slowly chewing its cud, was a white-faced beef cow with rubbery black lips bristled with long, coarse whiskers. The cow eyed Prophet curiously, chewing, then lowered its head to pull some wiry, brown grass up from where it jutted above the snow on the other side of the barbed wire fence between itself and the bounty hunter who sat in the deep snow at the base of the railroad bank deep in the frozen bowels of Dakota Territory.

The beast's breath frosted in the cold air, heavy with the smell of not south-of-the-border tequila and chili peppers but with the musky smell of summer-cured grass.

Prophet's body ached from head to toe. He was a two-hundred-plus-pound exposed nerve. A nerve with frostbite.

"Oh Lordy," he groaned, hugging himself. "Oh Lordy, Lordy, Lordy! It's cold out here, cow! Really, really cold out here!"

Studying him closely, the bovine stopped chewing for a moment, as though trying to understand what she'd just been told. Then, as though realizing the man was speaking only to himself, it twitched an ear and continued chewing. Several more cows flanked him, also eyeing Prophet curiously, chopping their hooves at the snow to get at the grass below.

Prophet looked around. He felt as though he were squinting, for his field of vision appeared compromised. Then he realized the problem. His eyes were swelling closed from the pummeling he'd taken aboard the train.

He wondered if any bones had gotten broken aboard the train, which appeared to be long gone. He wondered if he'd broken any during his tumble down the embankment. Probably not. The snow that had drifted up over the slope had made a good, soft pillow.

Most of the damage done to him had been done aboard the train.

He shifted position in an attempt to stand. Something pinched hard in his belly. He looked down at his coat. Blood had seeped into his buckskin. He remembered Leo's pretty little stiletto.

"Ah hell."

Had the cold numbed the pain of the stab wound to his midsection?

He unbuttoned three buttons of his coat from the bottom, an awkward maneuver, given that he could just barely feel his hands. What he could feel of them ached like hell. Dread lay heavy in him. Something told him that when he opened his coat he was going to see his own innards bulging out of the hole that the depraved cuss, Leo, had opened in his belly.

He pulled the coat open. He frowned. At least, he thought he did. With his eyes so swollen, it was hard to tell. What he could tell, however, was that there were no innards oozing out of him. His wool shirt was torn slightly just above his belly button, but there was only a silver dollar–sized bloodstain around the hole. He poked a numb finger through the hole then glanced at the square buckle of his cartridge belt.

He grinned. He fingered the nick alongside the large, round, brass buckle.

"That prissy-boy's blade skidded off the buckle. It nipped me but no worse than I've cut myself shavin'."

Prophet chuckled again as he pressed a finger against his belly to make sure he was right and that he wasn't on death's doorstep.

He jerked his head up suddenly.

He'd heard something.

Pricking his ears, he studied the snowy, brightly sunlit prairie around him. He heard it again.

Whooping sounds drifted toward him from ahead and on his left. At first, he thought it must be wolves or coyotes. But then as the sounds continued to roll toward him across the snowy prairie to the southwest, he realized what was making those sounds.

Indians.

Warriors on the blood scent.

The Cut-Head Sioux hunting party.

Prophet closed his coat and heaved himself to his feet. Balling his bare hands, he shoved them into his coat pockets. He looked around, found a relatively easy way back up to the railbed, and took it. As he climbed, his moccasins slipping and sliding in the shin-deep snow, guns began belching and popping from the same direction from which he'd heard the coyotelike yammering.

Finally, having fallen onto his hands and knees twice, burying his already-cold hands in the deep snow, he gained the top of the railbed, breathing hard, snot dripping from his nose. His ears were as cold as his hands, for he'd left his hat and muffler aboard the train.

As he stood atop the railbed, he gazed off in the direction from which the howling and yowling continued to swirl on the harsh wind. The sunlight glinted off the snow like millions of tiny javelins, piercing his retinas. He removed one hand from a pocket to shield his gaze from the sun.

Another frozen lake, smaller than the other one he'd passed aboard the train, lay to the southwest. Cows grazed along the near shoreline. On the far side of the lake, he saw the stalled train. Or most of it. From his vantage, he couldn't see the locomotive and tender car. The railroad line ran around the east end of the lake and then around its southwest shore, between the lake and several tall buttes. The train had just started to turn around the western side of one of those buttes and continue south when it had stalled.

For whatever reason, it sat stalled on the tracks, little larger than a caterpillar from this distance. What appeared a dozen men, the size of ants from this vantage, were milling around it—on top of it and around the near side, some on horseback, howling and yowling and triggering rifles into the coaches' windows.

Prophet couldn't help quirk his mouth corners in a grim smile. "They ran you down, did they?" he said. "Gettin' even for Little Fawn."

The Cut-Head hunting party had taken off across the lake, shortcutting, catching up to the train when it stalled. Prophet didn't know if the Indians had stopped it or if it had stopped for another reason. It didn't matter. They had it now.

Lou couldn't tell, but it appeared they'd taken the countess's party by surprise. He didn't think anyone was returning fire from the train. At least, he couldn't see any gun flashes in the windows. He couldn't hear the distinctive pounding of Rawdney Fairweather's big Scheutzen sporting rifle.

A scream slashed across the frozen lake, thin and high with agony. It was a girl-like scream but it was not a girl who'd made it. It was a man's scream. A young, horrified man.

Prophet fashioned another satisfied half smile. The screams, which continued, high and shrill and desperately beseeching, belonged to none other than Rawdney Fairweather, his own deserving self . . .

Another scream joined the first.

Prophet's heart thudded. When the scream came again, drowning Rawdney's, Prophet could tell it was a girl's scream.

"Ah no." Slowly, Lou shook his head, eyes widening as he stared across the lake toward the train the Indians were milling around and on top of, like ants on a succulent feast. "Ah no. No," he said again. He found himself moving back down the slope, wading through the shin-deep snow. "She didn't . . . she didn't have nothin' to do with Little Fawn!" he bellowed into the wind.

The countess's scream came again, shorter and shriller. It careened toward Prophet again, again, and again, likely through a blasted-out window.

Prophet stumbled in the deep snow, dropped to a knee. He heaved himself to his feet, a hundred aches and pains lancing him, his head throbbing from the beating the Russians had given him. Still, heart thudding, dread searing him, he found himself breaking into a shambling run out onto the lake, kicking through the finger drifts, sliding on the cracked, lumpy ice between the drifts.

Several hundred yards stretched between him and the train. Of course, he'd never make it in time to save the countess, but he had to try. Even as incapable as he was of doing much about it . . . of even making it the entire way in his battered condition . . . he had to try.

In his mind's eye, he kept seeing Countess Tatiana's girlishly devilish smile, the mischievous glitter in her eyes . . .

Again, she screamed in raw torment and horror, and Prophet lurched into a faster run.

As he ran, slipping on the lumpy ice between drifts, more yowls and hoof thuds rose from the direction of the train. He turned his swollen-eyed gaze toward the far end of the lake now maybe a half a mile away. The Sioux were pouring from the train, leaping off the platforms between coaches, and swinging up onto their waiting horses. They were hauling out loot in burlap sacks, which they hastily draped from their saddle horns.

Prophet stopped, dropped to a knee. He was glad to find that his Peacemaker was still in his coat pocket. There was a good bit of snow in the pocket, as well. He pulled the gun out of the pocket, brushed the snow away with his numb hands, and wrapped his right hand around the neck. He was as ready as he could be if the Indians saw him out here and rode toward him, intending to clean this white-eye's clock, as well.

Relief touched his anxious heart. The Indians went galloping straight up along the train, following the tracks around the butte to the south. They were soon out of sight.

"Tatiana," Prophet said to himself, a little taken aback by the wariness he heard in his own voice.

He stuffed the pistol back into his coat pocket, stuffed his hands into his pockets, as well, and continued running, if you could call his shuffling, slipping-and-sliding amble a run . . .

When you're as sore, cold, and exhausted as Prophet was, time somehow speeds up and slows down at the same time. The bounty hunter had no idea how much time had passed, or even what time of day it was, when he finally gained the far lakeshore. He scrambled over rocks abutting the steep bank and gained the railbed, having to drop to his knees beside the caboose to catch his breath.

The ground pitched around him. He was queasy, dizzy. Every bone and muscle barked out in anguish. A cracked bell tolled in his ears, every ring thrusting a sharp lance into the exposed nerve of his brain.

He gave a great grunt of rallied energy as he heaved himself back to his feet.

He shuffled up alongside the rear coach car—the passenger coach in which he'd been riding with his prisoner, Gritch Hatchley. He fumbled his way up onto the rear platform, stumbled through the rear door, and staggered to where he'd left Hatchley on the seat near the woodstove.

His prisoner was where he'd left him.

But now Hatchley's blood mingled on the floor with the blood of his old pard Henri Shambeau. Hatchley sat in the plush-covered seat, hands still cuffed behind his back. He leaned forward slightly, attached to the seat back by the cuffs. His eyes and mouth were drawn wide in bald horror.

The prisoner stared sightlessly. His throat had been cut and the blood had run down to form a thick, red bib over his chest. He'd also been scalped, leaving a grisly, bloody mess at the top of his head. His scalp rested bloody side up on his lap.

"Well, there goes another five hundred dollars," Prophet said.

The stove was still warm. Lou groaned as he dropped to his knees beside it, holding his hands out to it, grimacing as he entwined his fingers, working blood back into the half-frozen flesh. As he did, he looked around for his Winchester. Surely, the Indians would have taken it.

No.

It lay on the floor with the rest of his gear, likely

thrown there when the train had stopped. The Cut-Heads must have gotten so much more valuable plunder from the Russians' cars that they hadn't bothered with Prophet's prized Winchester '73. Or maybe they hadn't seen it over there.

For whatever reason, the rifle remained in his possession.

When he had worked some feeling into his fingers, he reached over for the trusty long gun, picked it up, and caressed it lovingly as he heaved himself to his feet with another weary groan.

"Come on, old buddy," he told the rifle, staggering toward the front of the car, where the door hung open. "Let's go see what we can do fer the girl . . ."

He doubted there would be anything he could do. He'd arrived at the train too late.

Still, he had to investigate. There was a chance she might still be alive.

He stumbled down off the passenger coach, past the two stock cars in which he could hear the horses shuffling nervously, and shambled up to the first of the fancily appointed cars in the senator's combination. He stopped suddenly, his half-frozen and swollen face shaping a grimace.

"Well, hello there, Rawdney," he muttered. "We meet again."

The fancy Dan had been stripped naked and hung by his bent legs upside down from the vestibule's brass rail, facing outward. He was a bloody mess. Prophet wasn't sure how much of that mess was the result of his work and how much was the result of the Cut-Heads' work, but Rawdney was a mess, all right. The senator's dead son stared up at Prophet in silent pleading.

Something had been stuffed into his mouth. Prophet

didn't look too closely. He didn't need to. He knew what the Cut-Heads had stuffed into Rawdney's mouth.

Prophet jerked his head up when he heard voices from inside the coach. Voices and shuffling sounds. Someone was still alive in there, moving around.

Prophet clambered up onto the vestibule. The door was closed. He crouched to gaze through the glass pane in the upper panel. Anger flared in him as he stared through the glass. Several braves remained in the car. They were lounging around, smoking fat cigars and drinking expensive firewater straight out of cut glass decanters.

One of them had Tatiana on the floor in the middle of the car while the others watched, laughing and yelling encouragement.

Prophet stepped back. He rammed a live round into the Winchester's action. He pushed the door open and rushed into the car, roaring, "*She had nothin' to do with Little Fawn's killin', you gutless savages!*"

He went to work with the Winchester.

For nearly a minute, the inside of the fancy coach car sounded like a pitched battle. But only one man was shooting.

By the time the Winchester's trigger pinged benignly against the firing pin, all nine rounds having found the flesh of the drunken Cut-Head braves, five rapists lay strewn about the car, dead, while two more staggered out the front door, each dropping to an opposite side of the car to run, stumbling and bleeding and screaming, before they dropped to the ground and bled out their lives in the snow beside the train.

Prophet tossed the empty Winchester onto a fainting couch and fell to a knee beside the poor battered girl. She groaned, shook her head, opened her eyes.

Recognition showed in those chocolate orbs.

"Lou . . . ?"

Prophet picked her up, held her taut against him. "I'm here, darlin'. I'm here. Ole Lou's here. You're safe now, honey."

"Oh, Lou!" the countess sobbed into his chest.

Footsteps sounded at the far end of the car.

Prophet jerked his head up with a start, dropping his right hand to his coat pocket, wrapping his fingers around the handle of his Colt.

"Easy, easy," said the man moving through the front door.

He was a stocky, heavy-shouldered white man in heavy, cold-weather gear and sporting an enormous, handlebar mustache. Frost bathed his face. A leather-billed watch cap was tied to his head with a thick, cream muffler.

"I'm Will Decker, the engineer." He stepped to one side to indicate the slightly shorter man moving into the car behind him. "This is Bart Stonecraft, my fireman."

The men looked around the blood-drenched car, wide-eyed. Twice as many Russians as Indians lay strewn about the car. The senator was here, as well, draped across a card table to Prophet's left. What was left of him, that was.

The old count sat in a chair against the window to Prophet's right. He'd been shot so many times he probably weighed more in lead than in gristle and bone. Leo lay at his feet in much the same condition.

Lou returned his gaze to the shocked faces of the engineer and the fireman.

"We was holed up in the tender car . . . hidin'," said the fireman, Stonecraft.

"We only had a single pistol between the two of us," Decker said a little defensively.

"Besides . . . there was so many of 'em," added Stonecraft. "Twenty, at least."

Prophet removed his hand from his coat pocket and wrapped that arm around the countess, sobbing against his chest. "Are there any other survivors?"

Decker shook his head. "We been through the whole train. The senator's whole party . . ." He shook his head again slowly, darkly. "Dead."

"That was Leaps High's bunch," Stonecraft said. "They lit a shuck."

"Yeah, well, they had every right to be piss-burned," Prophet said, rocking the countess gently. "But they done went a little too kill-crazy. This poor girl had nothin' to do with Little Fawn's death."

"Poor Little Fawn," Stonecraft said. "He was a good kid."

"How'd the train stall?" Prophet asked.

"Snowdrift broke away from the top of the butte," Decker said. "Covered the tracks. Not a whole lot but enough to get us stuck."

Stonecraft said, "We'll get 'er shoveled out in an hour."

"We'll pull out then," Decker said, looking at the countess in Prophet's arms. "Get that girl to a warm bed in Sundown. They got 'em a good hotel there."

"Yeah, it'll be safe there in Sundown," Stonecraft said. "It's always quiet in Sundown."

The two trainmen left the coach and got to work clearing the tracks.

Chapter 39

Louisa stared down in shock at the man lying in the street before her. "You're . . ."

"N-Name's R-Ram-Ramsay Willis!" The man was shivering so violently that he could barely spit the words out. "I r-ro . . . r-rode . . . all night . . . t-t-t-town. Had . . . had to warn . . . 'bout . . . Clay . . . Clay—"

"Clayton?"

"He's . . . he's *c-razy!*" Willis jerked his head and shoulder up slightly. The blanket fell away from his left arm. Or where that arm had been. As it was, all that Willis sported on that side was a badly shredded shirtsleeve caked with frozen blood. "He-he did this . . . thought . . . thought me an' Rose . . . was . . . was . . . c-carryin' . . . on!"

Willis shook his head. He wrapped his right hand around Louisa's right forearm and gazed up at her sharply. "He's . . . he's . . . k-k-killin' ever'body. He killed R-Rose. T-t-tried to kill me . . . lef . . . lef . . . lef me f-for *dead!* I . . . I r-rode . . . fast as I could t-t . . . to w-war . . . warn Sundown!"

"Oh my God," Louisa said under her breath, staring down in hang-jawed shock at the mangled man.

Willis squeezed Louisa's forearm harder. "H-He's . . . g-g-got the . . . the *w-winter fever*!"

Louisa remembered Morris Tutwiler pointing toward her as he'd staggered into the saloon with the ax embedded in his back. Only, the barman hadn't been pointing at her. He'd been pointing at Edgar Clayton entering the saloon by the front door behind her. Clayton had sported the bruise on his forehead that Tutwiler must have given him when trying to fight the crazy Clayton off, when the barman had gone out for more firewood and Clayton had buried the hatchet in his back for his trouble.

Clayton must have stolen out of the saloon last night to kill Cully at the depot.

He'd been biding his time, killing the entire town slowly. He'd started with the banker, an obvious choice probably to most men. He continued from Emory in a feverish frenzy, one person at a time before focusing his malevolent energy on . . .

A scream sounded from inside the Territorial Hotel.

A rifle thundered.

More screams.

The rifle thundered again and again, evoking more screams.

"*Nooo!*" a man bellowed.

Louisa heaved herself to her feet and ran south along the main street of Sundown, leaping drifts. As she ran, she fed fresh cartridges into her Winchester's breech. It was a fumbling effort. Her fingers were so cold and numb that she lost as many bullets as she fed to the rifle.

She racked a fresh round into the Winchester's action and glanced at the ground. Clayton's tracks led down the middle of the street, angling to the Sundown.

"No, you crazy devil!" a man inside the Territorial wailed as more rifle fire exploded inside the hotel, accompanied by the screeching laughter of what could only be a lunatic.

Louisa mounted the stoop and pushed through the front door. Her eyes had been compromised by the bright sunlight. She couldn't see much in the dingy shadows, but she saw the flames of a rifle lapping toward her from the room's bowels. As she flung herself left, a bullet punched into the door's glass pane. Louisa hit the floor and rolled, losing the Winchester when she inadvertently slammed it against a chair.

Another bullet thumped into the floor a few inches from her scrambling, moccasin-clad feet. She peered through the legs of the table she'd found herself behind, left of the front door, to see both Mose and Nasty Ralph lying dead on the floor before her. To their left, Mrs. Emory sprawled on her back, limbs akimbo.

More men—likely the drummers—were wailing as the rifle continued barking and Clayton continued venting his howling, high-pitched, witchlike laughter.

The shooting stopped. A heavy, pulselike silence descended on the room.

Louisa reached under the chair for her Winchester. Taking the rifle in both hands, she edged a look over the table before her.

Her eyes adjusted to the murky shadows near the bar. Smoke hung heavily over the room, smelling like rotten eggs. A man's vague shadow moved to the left of the bar, near the bottom of the stairs.

"Oh God—I'm dyin'," announced a man's thin, dull voice.

The man-shaped shadow swung sharply to his left and triggered a pistol toward the floor. A gurgling sounded as one of the last surviving drummers died.

Edgar Clayton swung around to face the bar, striding toward it, clicking back the hammer of the Remington revolver in his right hand.

"Please, Mr. Clayton," Toni's quavering voice sounded from where she must have been cowering behind the bar. "Don't kill me!"

Clayton opened his mouth and loosed another round of cackling laughter. As he approached the bar, he aimed his cocked pistol over the top, toward the floor on the other side.

"Hold it, Clayton!"

Clayton froze. Slowly, he turned his head toward Louisa standing near where Mose and Nasty Ralph lay dead. The Vengeance Queen aimed her cocked Winchester from her right shoulder. She narrowed one hazel eye down along the rifle she held rock steady in her half-frozen hands.

The bright sunlight, angling through the windows and the open door behind her, glittered in Clayton's eyes. It fairly glowed in them—the eyes of a specter who'd stolen out of hell on a mission of madness and blood.

Clayton loosed another round of howling laughter, ending with, "I got her dead to rights, Miss Bonnyventure!"

He swung his head back toward Toni cowering behind the bar.

He didn't get off a single shot before Louisa's Winchester roared. She punched two bullets into the crazy man's belly, sending him stumbling back along the bar. Walking slowly toward him, she continued working the cocking lever and firing, empty shell casings pinging onto the floor behind her.

Wailing shrilly, Clayton dropped his gun and then followed it to the floor, piling up at the far end of the bar, near the stairs, at the same spot Del Rainy and Morris Tutwiler had breathed their last.

Louisa cocked the Winchester once more and punched one more round into Clayton's chest. He grunted, gurgled. His crazy eyes rolled up in their sockets, dimming.

Louisa lowered the smoking Winchester.

Powder smoke hung heavy in the air before her.

Into the heavy silence following the din of the fusillade, she said, "It's Bonaventure, you cork-headed fool. If you listened closely, you wouldn't hear a *y* in it."

A face slid slowly into view from behind the bar.

Louisa turned to see the redhead regarding her dubiously.

Several hours later, in the winter's early darkness, Prophet stepped down off the vestibule of the countess's coach onto the cold, windy brick platform. He held the countess herself in his arms. The girl, half-asleep and swathed in several heavy quilts, clung to him desperately, her arms wrapped tightly around his thick neck.

Prophet's eyes probed the murk around the Sundown depot. A slender, silhouetted, female figure in a man's hat and a heavy coat stepped out of the shadows beneath the station roof's overhang. Louisa limped slightly on her right leg.

The ends of her red muffler blew around her head in the wind. Her blond hair blew around, as well. Holding her Winchester on her shoulder, she stopped before Prophet, looked him over, wincing a little when she saw the ground beef of his face and his swollen eyes.

She glanced at the girl in his arms.

"You're late," she said, returning her gaze to his.

"Yeah, well." Prophet shrugged and sighed.

Louisa glanced along the train. No one else was getting off. She returned her gaze to Prophet and said, "How did it go?"

"I lost a thousand dollars." Lou looked at the red neckerchief knotted around her right thigh, just beneath the hem of her coat. "How'd it go for you?"

Louisa nodded. "Me, too."

"Yeah, but you don't care about the money. It grieves me to think how much fun that extra thousand could have bought me down in Mexico."

Louisa half turned, jerked her chin toward town. "Come on. Your friend looks like she could use a warm bed. I'll buy you a drink."

"I could stand a drink. Stiffer, the better."

Louisa began walking in the direction of Sundown, favoring her right leg. "I'll buy you one. A stiff one. Might even buy myself one."

"Oh Lordy—heaven help us all!" Limping along beside the Vengeance Queen, Prophet arched a plaintive brow at her. "Could you buy me two?"

"Okay," Louisa said. "I'll buy you two." She glanced up at him, a wry half smile dimpling her cheek. "But only two."

Keep reading for a special excerpt of

STAGECOACH TO PURGATORY
The Violent Days of Lou Prophet, Bounty Hunter
by Peter Brandvold

When it comes to gun-blazing, bone-crushing action,
no one tells a tale like acclaimed
Western writer Peter Brandvold.
These are the violent days (and reckless nights)
of Lou Prophet, as told to his ink-stained confessor.
Most of these recollections are brutal.
Others are bloody. Some might even be true . . .

LAST STAGE TO HELL
What do you get when you take one stagecoach out
of Denver, add a thousand-or-so bullets whizzing past
your head, while sitting next to two headless corpses
caught in the crossfire? If your name is Lou Prophet,
you get revenge. Raucous, rowdy, ruthless revenge.
Next question?

DEVIL BY THE TAIL
How do you catch a fork-tongued demon who's
busted out of prison to wreak all sorts of unholy hell
on a small Texas town? If you're Lou Prophet, you
team up with red-hot Louisa Bonaventure, aka "The
Vengeance Queen," and cut a swath of merciless
Prophet mayhem in return.

Due process be damned . . .

On sale now, wherever books are sold.

From *The Life and Times of Lou Prophet, Bounty Hunter*
by HEYWOOD WILDEN SCOTT

I'd been a tough-nosed newsman for nearly sixty
years, yet it was with more trepidation than I like to
admit that I knocked on the big, old rebel's door.

I'd heard the stories about him. Hell, I'd printed
many of those yarns in the various newspapers I'd
written and edited in that grand old time of the Old
West gunfighters, larger-than-life lawmen, and the
much-maligned, death-dealing bounty hunters, of
which he'd been one.

Yes, I'd heard the tales. I'd printed the tales. With
feigned reluctance (I was a journalist, after all—not a
reader or writer of dime novels!) but with unabashed
delight, if the truth be known. With admiration and
even envy. Imagine such a man living such a life at
such a time, hoorawing badmen of every stripe, risking
life and limb with every adventure while the rest of us
suffered little more than festering galls to our posteri-
ors while scribbling ink by the barrel onto endless rolls
of foolscap in dingy, smoky, rat-infested offices off
backstreet alleys, the big presses making the whole
building rock.

I'd never met him.

I'd heard from those who had crossed his trail that he
was a formidable, mercurial cuss, by turns kindhearted
and generous and foulmouthed and dangerous, and

he'd grown more and more formidable, unpredictable,
and recalcitrant with age. The years had not been kind
to him. But, then, what would you expect of a man
who had lived such a life and who, it was said, had sold
his soul to the devil, exchanging an eternity of coal-
shoveling in hell's bowels for a few good years after the
War Between the States "on this side of the sod, stomping with his tail up," as he was known to call what he
did between his bounty hunting adventures?

In fact, I once heard that he'd hunted only men
with prices on their heads in order to pay for his notorious appetite for whiskey, women, and poker.

He'd seen so much killing during the war, out of
which he'd emerged something of a hero of the Confederacy, that he really wanted only to dance and make
love and swill the Taos Lightning to his heart's delight.
But he was not an independently wealthy man, so it
was only with great reluctance, I'm told, that after such
bouts of manly indiscretions he took up his Colt .45,
his Winchester '73 rifle, his double-bore, sawed-off,
twelve-gauge Richards coach gun, and his razor-edged
bowie knife, and stepped into the saddle of his
beloved but appropriately named horse, Mean and
Ugly, and fogged the sage in pursuit of death-dealing
curly wolves prowling the long coulees of the wild and
woolly western frontier.

He usually had a fresh wanted circular or two stuffed
into his saddlebag pouches, carelessly ripped from
post office or Wells Fargo bulletin boards.

Now, as I rolled my chair up to his room, I'd recently seen for myself that he was every bit the colorful
albeit formidable old codger I'd heard he was. It had
been only within a week or so of this recounting that
the old warrior had shown up at the same Odd Fellows

House of Christian Charity in Pasadena, California, that I, too, after several grave illnesses had broken me both financially and spiritually, had found myself shut away in, whiling away the long, droll hours until my own annihilation.

He'd been working as a consultant in the silent western flickers, I'd heard, until a grievous accident involving a Chrysler Model B-70, a couple of pretty starlets, and several jugs of corn liquor caromed off a perilous mountain road in the hills above Malibu. Now he prowled the halls on crutches—a big, one-legged man with a face like the siding of a ruined barn, at times grunting and bellowing blue curses (especially when one of the attendants confiscated his proscribed cigarettes and whiskey) or howling songs of the old Confederacy out on the narrow balcony off his second-story room, his raspy voice ratcheting up out of his tar-shrunken lungs like the engines of the horseless carriages sputtering past on Pacific Avenue.

As I was saying, I knocked on his door.

I shrank back in my chair when the door was flung open and the big bear of the one-legged man, broad as a coal dray and balancing precariously on one crutch, peered out from the roiling smoke fog inundating his tiny, sparsely furnished room.

"What?" he said.

At least, that's how I'm translating it. It actually sounded more like the indignant grunt of a peevish grizzly bear prodded from a long winter's slumber.

Out of that ruin of a face, two pale blue eyes burned like the last stars at the end of the night. At once keen and bold, flickering and desperate.

Wedged between my left thigh and the arm of my wheelchair was a bottle of rye whiskey. On my right leg were a fresh notepad, a pen, and a bottle of ink. I hoisted the bottle high, grinned up at the old roarer scowling down at me, a loosely rolled cigarette drooping from a corner of his broad mouth, and said, "Tell me a story, Lou!"

Chapter 1

Something or someone peeled Lou Prophet's right eyelid open.

A female voice, soft as tiny wooden wind chimes stirred by an April breeze, said as though from far away, "You've ruined me!"

The bounty hunter's rye-logged brain was only half registering what his optic nerve was showing it, what his ears were telling it.

A face hovered over him, down close to his own, in fact, but the features of that face were a blur. He could better make out what he was not looking at directly. The head that the face belonged to owned a pretty, thick, long mess of light red tresses curling down onto slender shoulders as white as new-fallen snow on Christmas Day in the north Georgia mountains of Lou Prophet's original and long-ago home.

The girl released Prophet's lid, and she disappeared behind a veil of darkness. The accusatory words had stirred him somewhat, despite that his brain was a sponge still soaked in last night's tornado

juice. He had no idea what had been meant by the
accusation, and, while vaguely curious, slumber tugged
at the ex-rebel bounty hunter like a heavy wind, albeit
a wind that owned the inviting aroma of lilac water
and natural, bed-fermented female musk.

Down, down, Prophet fell . . . until his other lid was
tugged open, and the face appeared again, even closer
to his own this time, so that he could see a gunmetal
blue eye staring into his own left one. "Did you hear
me? You've utterly and completely ruined me! *Ohh!*"

That nudged Prophet closer to full wakefulness.
What in the hell was this girl, whoever in hell she was,
talking about?

Ruined?

While Prophet had a somewhat wide-ranging reputation as a hard-nosed man hunter, he'd never been
anything but gentle with women. Unless said women
were running on the wrong side of the law and had
tried to kill him, of course. (One of the first things
he'd learned when he'd first turned to bounty hunting
after venturing west after his beloved South had been
whipped during the War of Northern Aggression was
that not all hardened outlaws were men.) But those
women were the exception rather than the rule, and he
doubted that any of them would say he'd "ruined" them.

Prophet tried to say the word but, just as his brain
was not yet hooked up to his eyes, it was not attached
to his mouth, either, so that what he heard his own lips
say as they moved stiffly against each other was: "Roo-
hoom . . . d . . . ?"

"Ruined!" the girl said, louder, heartbroken. "Purely
ruined!"

The half squeal, half moan was a cold hand reaching down into the warm water of the bounty hunter's

slumber and plucking him into full wakefulness. He bolted upright in bed, blinking, heart thudding, wondering if he'd done something untoward during his inebriation.

Untoward, that was, beyond the usual transgressions of gambling himself into mind-numbing debt, drinking himself (as he'd obviously done last night) into a coma, frolicking with fallen women, brawling, fighting with knives, pistol-shooting shot glasses off neat pyramids arranged on bar tops, howling at the moon, swinging from the rafters, herding chickens, stealing bells from courthouse cupolas, singing to his horse, getting beaten up or thrown in jail or both, and, as per one occasion, asking a fallen woman to be his bride and actually going through with the ceremony. (Fortunately, the union had been rendered null and void when it was revealed that the minister had been defrocked due to his having had carnal knowledge of his organist.)

Prophet turned to the girl sitting naked beside him, not having any recollection of who she was or where he had met her but vaguely amazed at her sparkling, Christmas-morning beauty, and wrapped his left arm around her. "Oh, honey, I'm sooo sorry if I did *anything* last night that . . . that—"

"Oh, Lou—you've ruined me for all men hereafter. Last night was . . . well, it was absolutely *magical.* I've never been treated that way before . . ."

"Honey, who is your pa, anyway? Apparently, he knows me . . . ?"

"Oh, Lou," she said, rubbing against him and purring like a kitten, "stop fooling around, would you? You know very well my father is Richard Teagarden, governor of Colorado."

Prophet's heart hiccupped. He jerked his head up as a rush of disconnected images from last night battered his tender, sodden brain. As disjointed as the images were, they told the story of Prophet recently riding into Denver with the body of Lancaster Smudge draped over the saddle of the horse Prophet had trailed behind his own hammerheaded dun, Mean and Ugly.

Over the past year and a half, Lancaster Smudge and his gang of five other owlhoots had become the bane of the territory not to mention of the Denver & Santa Fe Railroad, whose trains they'd preyed on without mercy, threatening to run the company into the ground and leave Colorado where it had been ten years before—relying on stagecoach services and mule trains for transport and commerce.

Many lawmen had been sicced on the gang, and a goodly portion of those few lawmen who'd gotten close to their quarry had ended up turned toe-down and snuggling with the diamondbacks in a Rocky Mountain canyon. The Smudge Bunch, as the papers had cheekily called Smudge's gang, were as elusive as Arizona sidewinders.

Prophet, however, working in cahoots with his sometime partner, Louisa Bonaventure, had proven the equals of the Smudge Bunch, and taken them down in their hideout up near the little mining town of Frisco, when the boys had let their hair as well as their pants down to enjoy a romp in Mrs. Beauchamp's House of the Seven Enchantments.

After Prophet had turned Smudge into the federals for the two-thousand-dollar reward, the jubilant governor had insisted on inviting the bounty hunter out to the Larimer Hotel for a meal on the state's tab. There, Prophet had met the stately, smiling but distracted-seeming Mrs. Teagarden as well as the governor's pretty, precocious daughter, Clovis.

Clovis! Her name was Clovis Teagarden! Whew!

Prophet had never been given such grand treatment before. Bounty hunters were more or less considered vermin on the frontier, not all that higher on the human ladder than the men they hunted for the bounties on their heads. So Prophet was more accustomed to being treated like dog dung on a grub line rider's boots when he wasn't being ignored altogether by those of a more prestigious link in society's chain.

He certainly had never been invited out to dinner by anyone as important as a governor.

However, it had turned out that Governor Teagarden, being of a romantic turn of mind as well as a frequent reader of dime novels and the *Police Gazette*, was a secret fan of both Prophet and Louisa Bonaventure, whom the pulp rags had dubbed "the Vengeance Queen." Teagarden had apparently followed the duo's bounty hunting careers in the western newspapers, including Denver's own *Rocky Mountain News*.

Prophet suspected that the dapper little gray-haired man, who wore a gold ring on his arthritic little right finger and a giant, gray, walrus mustache on his lean, pasty face, had wanted to meet the comely blond Louisa far more than he'd wanted to dine with the scruffy Prophet. When Lou had informed the man that Louisa would not be joining them, as she'd decided to light out after a trio of outlaws they'd learned about near Leadville rather than accompany her partner back to Denver with a dead man, Teagarden had acquired a fleeting but poignant expression of deep disenchantment.

His sprightly and precocious daughter, Clovis, however, had kept her eyes on Prophet all through dinner, till he thought her smoldering gaze would burn a hole right through him. Still, the bounty man had been more than mildly taken aback when she'd slipped him a room key as he'd shaken her hand after dinner. It turned out the girl often spent nights in her father's private suite in the Larimer Hotel—under the strict supervision of a female chaperone, of course—because she attended a finishing school only two blocks from the hotel.

It also turned out, to Prophet's incredulity, that the girl's chaperone, Mrs. Borghild Rasmussen, who supposedly resided in the hotel, did not, in fact, exist, and that the bank drafts the governor wrote her were, in fact, never cashed. The governor's private secretary, a male no doubt under the mesmerizing influence of the carnal Clovis, kept it all a secret from the doddering fool.

So Clovis was pretty much running off her leash in the burgeoning and colorful cow town of Denver, inviting bounty hunters—well, one, at least—to her room.

Prophet rubbed the heels of his hands against his temples. "Clovis, I, uh . . . don't know what to say."

"You did remember my name!" the girl said.

"How could I forget a girl like you? It was a wonderful night, Clovis, but I tell you, honey, I never realized you were only sixteen. Hell, I thought you were at least twenty-one pushin' forty-five!"

Prophet scuttled over to the side of the bed that

was, he saw now, enormous. It was easily the largest bed he'd ever seen let alone slept in.

"Oh, Lou—where are you going? You can't go yet! The day is just getting started!"

Prophet scowled over his shoulder at her, trying to ignore the fact that she was naked, not an easy task even in his whiskey-logged state. "You best get ready for school, little girl."

"Oh, phooey," Clovis said, leaning back on her elbows, pooching her pink lips out in a pout. "I'm going to skip school today. I often do. Father doesn't care. Neither does Mother. She'll be busy with her tea parties and such. Father's so busy with affairs of state he doesn't think about much of anything but work, work, work . . . and getting reelected, of course."

She rolled her eyes then beamed at Prophet. "That's why we can spend the whole day together, Lou."

"Doesn't your father ever check up on you?"

She only tittered an ironic laugh and wrapped her hands around her ankles, pulling her feet back toward her shoulders, giving him a haunting but unwanted eyeful.

Between love bouts the previous night, she'd told him a lot about herself, but he'd drunk so much whiskey, having gone without any skull pop for the past month he'd been hunting owlhoots in the mountains with the teetotaling Vengeance Queen, that he could remember only bits and pieces.

Clovis was a talker, though—he remembered that.

He'd made a mistake when he'd tramped up the Larimer's broad, carpeted stairs to find the lock that fit the key Clovis had given him.

Having entered a celebratory frame of mind the second he'd hit town, he'd gotten drunk before he'd dined with the governor's family, so his judgment had been off. And, if the truth be told, Prophet was far too weak a man to be able to ignore the fact of a pretty young woman handing him her room key with a co-quettish dip of her chin and alluring glint in her eye.

In such a situation he was not now nor ever had been the type of jake who could shake his head and say, "Sorry, ma'am, but I'm not that sort of fella," and walk away. Just as he was having trouble averting his atten-tion to what she was teasing him with now . . .

And some day he'd likely be fed a couple loads of buckshot for just that failing . . .

Or . . . maybe that day was here now, he amended the unspoken warning to himself as someone ham-mered on the room's door and a man's angry voice said, "Clovis? Clovis, are you in there?"

Connect with

Us

Visit us online at
KensingtonBooks.com
to read more from your favorite authors, see books
by series, view reading group guides, and more.

Join us on social media

for sneak peeks, chances to win books and prize packs,
and to share your thoughts with other readers.

facebook.com/kensingtonpublishing
twitter.com/kensingtonbooks

Tell us what you think!

To share your thoughts, submit a review,
or sign up for our eNewsletters, please visit:
KensingtonBooks.com/TellUs.